"Leonardo, meet Albert Einstein."

• • •

Thus begins a journey through Realms of Myth and Magic such as is given few of Mortal Birth. Learn the True History of the Aryan Race (You have nothing much to lose), Pierce the Heart of Publishing (and watch a mythic pirate pale before its pulsations)... Experience the True Nature of False Courage (Must we *spell* it out?)... Join Elves against Aliens in War to the Knife (and Knife to the Hilt)... form an Unholy Pact (with a Usually Reliable Demon)... visit Other Worlds (through sheer force of personality) ... Discover the Meaning and the Joy of Fantasy in the Age of Science.

Through the magic of Poul Anderson (whose spells never miss) all this can be yours, Mortal. So come, enter the world of ...

FANTASY

D1559232

POUL ANDERSON
Fantasy

With an Afterword
by Sandra Miesel

A TOM DOHERTY
ASSOCIATES BOOK

Distributed by Pinnacle Books, New York

FANTASY

Copyright © 1981, by Poul Anderson

A TOR Book.

First printing: September, 1981

ISBN: 48-51518

Printed in the United States of America

PINNACLE BOOKS, INC.
1430 Broadway
New York, N.Y. 10018

ACKNOWLEDGEMENTS

The stories and articles in this volume were first published and are copyright as follows:

"House Rule," *Homebrew* (NESFA Press), © 1976 by Poul Anderson

"The Tale of Hauk," *Swords Against Darkness I,* © 1977 by Andrew J. Offutt

"Of Pigs and Men," *Swords Against Darkness IV,* © 1979 by Andrew J. Offutt

"Logical Conclusion," *Fantastic Universe,* © 1960 by Ultimate Publications

"The Valor of Cappen Varra," *Fantastic Universe,* © 1957 by King-Size Publications

"The Gate of the Flying Knives," *Thieves World,* © 1979 by Poul Anderson

"The Barbarian," *The Magazine of Fantasy and Science Fiction,* © 1956 by Fantasy House, Inc.

"On Thud and Blunder," *Swords Against Darkness III,* © 1978 by Andrew J. Offutt

"Interloper," *The Magazine of Fantasy and Science Fiction,* © 1959 by Mercury Publications, Inc.

"Pact" *The Magazine of Fantasy and Science Fiction,* © 1951 by Mercury Publications, Inc.

"Superstition," *The Magazine of Fantasy and Science Fiction,* © 1952 by Mercury Publications, Inc.

"Fantasy in the Age of Science" is original to this edition, and is copyright © 1981 by Poul Anderson.

"The Visitor," *The Magazine of Fantasy and Science Fiction,* © 1974 by Mercury Press, Inc.

"Bullwinch's Mythology," *Galaxy Magazine,* originally published as "Poulfinch's Mythology," © 1967 by Galaxy Publications, Inc.

"An Invitation to Elfland" is original to this edition, and is copyright © 1981 by Sandra Miesel.

TABLE OF CONTENTS

HISTORICAL

A-HISTORICAL

IT COULD HAPPEN TO YOU

HOUSE RULE

Look for it anywhere, anytime, by day, by dusk, by night, up an ancient alley or out on an empty heath or in a forest where hunters whose eyes no spoor can escape nonetheless pass it by unseeing. Myself, I found its doorhandle under my fingers and its signboard creaking over my head when I was about to enter the saloon of a ship far at sea. You cannot really seek this house; it will seek you. But you must be alert for its fleeting presence, bright or curious or adventurous or desperate enough to enter, the first time. Thereafter, if you do not abuse its hospitality, you will be allowed to come back every once in a while.

The odds are all against you, of course. Few ever get this chance. Yet, since nobody knows what basis the landlord has for admitting his guests, and when asked he says merely that they are those who have good stories wherewith to pay him, you too may someday be favored. So keep yourself open to everything, and perhaps, just perhaps, you will have the great luck of joining us in that tavern called the Old Phoenix.

I'm not quite sure why the innkeeper and his wife the barmaid think I deserve it. There are countless others more worthy, throughout the countless dimensional sheaves, whom I have never met. When I suggest such a person, mine host shrugs, smiles, and amiably evades the question, a

9

tactic in which he is skilled. Doubtless I've simply not happened on some of them. After all, a guest may only stay till the following dawn. Then the house won't reappear to him for a stretch which in my case has always been at least a month. Furthermore, I suspect that besides being at a nexus of universes, the hostel exists on several different space-time levels of its own.

Well, let's not speculate about the unanswerable. I want to tell of an incident I can't get out of my mind.

That evening would have been spectacular aplenty had nothing else gone on than my conversation with Leonardo da Vinci. I recognized that tall, golden-bearded man the instant he stepped into the taproom and shook raindrops off his cloak, and ventured to introduce myself. By and large, we're a friendly, informal bunch at the Old Phoenix. We come mainly to meet people. Besides, of the few who were already present, nobody but landlord, barmaid, and I knew Italian. Oh, Leonardo could have used Latin or French with the nun who sat offside and quietly listened to us. However, their accents would have made talk a struggle.

The goodwife was busy, pumping out beer for Erik the Red, Sancho Panza, and Nicholas van Rijn, interpreting and chattering away in early Norse, a peasant dialect of Spanish, and the argot of a spacefaring future, while now and then she helped herself to a tankardful. Mine host, among whose multiple names I generally choose Taverner, was off in a dim corner with beings I couldn't see very well, except that they were shadowy and full of small starlike sparkles. His round face was more solemn than usual, he often ran a hand across his bald pate, and the sounds that came from his mouth, answering those guests, were a ripple of trills and purrs.

Thus Leonardo and I were alone, until the nun entered and shyly settled down at our table. I include medieval varieties of French in my languages; being an habitue of the Old Phoenix mightily encourages such studies. But by then we two were so excited that, while we greeted her as courteously as Taverner expects, neither of us caught her name, and I barely noticed that within its coif her face was quite lovely. I did gather that she was from a convent at Argenteuil in the twelfth century. But she was content to sit and try to follow our discourse. Renaissance Florentinian was not hopelessly alien to her mother tongue.

The talk was mainly Leonardo's. Given a couple of goblets of wine to relax him, his mind soared and ranged like an eagle in a high wind. Tonight was his second time, and the first had naturally been such a stunning experience that he was still assimilating it. But the drink at our inn, like the food, is unearthly superb. (It should be; Taverner can ransack all the worlds, all the ages of a hypercosmos which, perhaps, is infinitely branched in its possibility-lines.) Leonardo soon felt at ease. In answer to a question, he told me that he was living in Milan in the year 1493 and was forty-one years old. This squared with what I recollected; so quite likely he was the same Leonardo as existed in my continuum. Certainly, from what he said, he was at the height of his fame, brilliance, powers, and longings.

"But why, Messer, why may you not say more?" he asked. His voice was deep and musical.

"Maybe I could," I replied. "None has ever given me a hard and fast catalogue of commandments. I imagine they judge each case singly. But . . . would *you* risk being forever barred from this place?"

His big body, richly clad though in hues that my era of synthetic dyes would have found subdued, twisted around in his chair. As his glance traveled over the taproom, I caught the nun admiring his profile—the least bit wistfully? She was indeed beautiful, I admitted to myself. A shapeless dark habit of rather smelly, surely heavy and scratchy wool could not altogether hide a slim young figure; her countenance was pale, delicately sculptured, huge-eyed. I wondered why, even in her milieu, she had taken vows.

The room enclosed us in cheer, long, wide, wainscotted in carven oak, ceiling massively beamed. A handsome stone fireplace held a blaze of well-scented logs, whose leap and crackle gave more warmth than you'd expect, just as the sconced candles gave more light. That light fell on straight chairs around small tables, armchairs by themselves, benches flanking the great central board, laid out ideally for fellowship. Along the walls, it touched books, pictures, and souvenirs from afar. At one end, after glowing across the bar where my lady hostess stood between the beer pumps and the racked bottles and vessels, it lost itself beyond an open doorway; but I made out a stair going up to clean, unpretentious chambers where you can sleep if you like. (People seldom do. The company is too good, the hours too precious.) Windows are always shuttered, I suppose because they would not look out over any of the worlds on which the front door opens, but onto something quite peculiar. That thought makes the inside feel still more snug.

"No," Leonardo sighed, "I daresay I too will grow careful. And yet . . . 'tis hard to understand . . . if we are mainly here for colloquy, that Messer Albergatore may enjoy the spectacle and the tales, why does he set bounds on our speech? I assure you, for instance, I do not fear your telling me the date and manner of my death, if you know them. God will call me when He chooses."

"You utter a deep truth there," I said. "For I am not necessarily from your future. For all we can tell, I may be from the future of another Leonardo da Vinci, whose destiny is, or was, not yours. Hence 'twould be a pointless unpleasantness to discuss certain matters."

"But what of the rest?" he protested. "You bespeak flying machines, automatons, elixirs injected into the flesh which prevent illness—oh, endless wonders—Why must you merely hint?"

I said into his intensity: "Messer, you have the intellect to see the reason. If I gave you over-much knowledge or foresight, what might ensue? We lack wisdom and restraint, we mortals. Taverner has a—a license?—to entertain certain among us. But it must strictly be entertainment. Nothing decisive may happen here. We meet and part as in dreams, we at the Old Phoenix."

"What then can we do?" he demanded.

"Why, there are all the arts, there are stories real and imaginary, there are the eternal riddles of our nature and purpose and meaning, there are songs and games and jests and simply being together—But it is wrong that I act pompous toward you. I feel most honored and humble, and would like naught better than to hear whatever you wish to say."

Humanly pleased, he answered, "Well, if you'll not tell me how the flying machine works—and, indeed, I can understand that if you did, 'twould avail me little, who lack the hoarded lore and instrumentalities of four or five hundred years— pray continue as you were when I interrupted. Finish relating your adventure."

I reminisced about a flight which had been forced down above the Arctic Circle, and how some Eskimos had helped us. His inquiries concerning them were keen, and led him on to experiences of his own, and to remarks about the variety and strangeness of man—As I said, had nothing else happened, this would still have been among the memorable evenings of my life.

The door opened and closed. We heard a footfall, caught a whiff of city streets which also served as garbage dumps and sewers, glimpsed crowded wooden houses on a cloudy day. The man who had appeared was rather short by my standards or against Leonardo, and middle-aged to gauge by features deeply lined though still sharply cut. Grizzled brown hair fell past his ears from under a flat velvet cap. He wore a monastic robe, with rosary and crucifix, but shoes and hose rather than sandals. His form was slender and straight, his gaze extraordinarily vivid.

Taverner excused himself from his conversation and hurried across the floor to give greeting. "Ah, welcome, welcome anew," he said in Old French— *langue d'oïl*, to be exact. "At yonder table sit two gentlemen whose companionship will surely pleasure you." He took the monk's arm. "Come, let me introduce you, my learned Master Abélard—"

The nun's voice cut through his. She surged to her feet; the chair clattered behind her. "Pier!" she cried. "O Jésu, O Maria, Pier!"

And he stood where he was for an instant as if a sword in his guts had stopped him. Then: "Héloise," cracked out his throat. "But thou art dead." He crossed himself, over and over. "Hast thou, thou, thou come back to comfort me, Héloise?"

Taverner looked disconcerted. He must have forgotten her presence. The noise and dice-casting at the bar died away. The starry gray ones became still. Alone the hearthfire spoke.

"No, what art thou saying, I, I am alive, Pier," the nun stammered. "But thou, my poor hurt darling—" She stumbled toward him. I saw how he half flinched, before he gathered courage and held out his arms.

They met, and embraced, and stood like that: until our plump, motherly barmaid suddenly shouted, "Well, good for you, dears!" They didn't notice, they had nobody but each other.

The rest of us eased a trifle. Evidently this wasn't a bad event. Erik lifted his drinking horn, Sancho guffawed at such behavior of ecclesiastics, van Rijn held out his mug for a refill, the strangers in the corner rustled and twinkled, Taverner wryly shrugged.

Leonardo leaned across the table and whispered to me, "Did I hear aright? Are those in truth Héloïse and Abélard?"

"They must be," I answered, and knew not what to feel. "Belike not from your history or mine, however."

He had grasped the idea of universes parallel in multi-dimensional reality, in some of which magic worked, in some of which it did not, in some of which King Arthur or Orlando Furioso had actually lived, in some of which he himself had not. Now he murmured, "Well, quickly, lest we say unwitting a harmful thing, let's compare what our chronicles tell about them."

"Peter Abélard was the greatest Scholastic of his century," ran from me, while I tried to take my eyes off the weeping pair and could not. "He was in his forties when he met Héloïse, a girl in her twenties. She was the niece and ward of a powerful, high-born canon. They fell in love, had a child, couldn't marry because of his career in the Church but—Anyway, her uncle found out and was enraged. He hired a gang of bullies to waylay Abélard and castrate him. After that, Héloïse entered a convent—against her uncle's wish, I believe—and never saw her lover again. But the bond that held them was unchanged—the world will always remember the letters that passed between them—and in my day they lie buried together."

Leonardo nodded. "Yes, that sounds like what I read. I seem to recall that they did marry, albeit secretly."

"Perhaps my memory is at fault."

"Or mine. It was long ago. For us. God in Heaven, though, they two yonder—!"

Maybe they consciously recalled this was the single place they could meet; or maybe they, like most people in their age, had scant notion of privacy; or maybe they didn't give a damn. I heard what they blurted forth through their tears.

They were from separate time-lines. She might belong to Leonardo's and mine, if ours were the same; her story was familiar to us both. But he, he was still a whole man. For him, three years before, she had died in childbirth.

Meanwhile Taverner led them to an offside couch; and the barmaid fetched refreshments, which they didn't see; and host and hostess breathed to them what no one else could hear. Not that anybody wanted to. As if half ashamed, they at the bar returned to their boozing, Leonardo and I to our talk; they in the corner waited silent.

My companion soon lost his embarrassment. Tender-heartedness is not notably a Renaissance trait. Since we knew equally little about the branchings of existence, we were free to wonder aloud about them. He got onto constructing such a world-of-if (suppose Antony had triumphed at Actium, because the library at Alexandria had not caught fire when Julius Caesar laid siege, and in it were Heron's plans for a submersible warcraft . . . well, conceivably, somewhere among the dimensions it *did* happen) that I too, chiming in here and there, well-nigh lost awareness of the nun and her Schoolman.

Again the door interrupted us—half an hour later, an hour, I'm not sure. This time I spied a lawn, trees, ivy-covered red brick buildings, before it shut. The man who had arrived was old but stood tall, and much robustness remained to him. He wore an open-necked shirt, fuzzy sweater, faded slacks, battered sneakers. A glory of white hair framed the kind of plain, gentle, but thoughtful and characterful Jewish face that Rembrandt liked to portray.

He saw Héloïse and Abélard together, and smiled uncertainly. *"Guten Abend,"* he ventured; and in English: "Good evening. Maybe I had better not—"

"Ah, do stay!" exclaimed Taverner, hurrying toward him, while the eyes popped in van Rijn's piratical visage and my pulse ran wild.

Taverner took the newcomer by the elbow and steered him toward us. "By all means, do," he urged. "True, we've had a scene, but harmless, yes, I'd say benign. And here's a gentleman I know you've been wanting to meet." He reached our table and made a grand flourish. "Messer Leonardo da Vinci ... Herr Doktor Albert Einstein . . . ." I suppose he included me.

Of course, the Italian had not heard of the Jew, but he sensed what was afoot and bowed deeply. Einstein, more diffident, nevertheless responded with similar grace and sat down amidst polite noises all around. "Do you mind if I smoke?" he asked. We didn't, so he kindled a pipe while the barmaid brought new drinks. Neither of my tablemates did more than sip, however, and I wasn't about to spoil this for myself by getting drunk the way they were doing over at the bar.

Besides, I must be interpreter. Einstein's Italian was limited, and of a date centuries later than Leonardo's, who had neither German nor English.

I interpreted. Do you see why I will never risk my standing at the Old Phoenix?

They needed a while to warm up. Einstein was eager to learn what this or that cryptic notation of Leonardo's referred to. But Leonardo must have Einstein's biography related to him.

When he realized what that signified, his blue eyes became blowtorches, and I had trouble following every word that torrented from him. We thus got some pauses. Furthermore, occasionally even those chain lightning minds must halt and search before going on. Hence, unavoidably, I noticed Héloise and Abélard anew.

They sat kissing, whispering, trembling. This was the sole night they could have, she alive, he his entire self—the odds against their ever chancing to meet here were unmeasurably huge—and what was allowed them, by the law of their hostel and the law of their holy orders? Tick, said a grandfather clock by the wall, tick, tick; here too, a night is twelve hours long.

Taverner scuttled around in the unobtrusive way he can don when he wants to. They started trading songs at the bar. The taproom is big enough that that doesn't annoy anyone who hasn't a very good ear; and Einstein and Leonardo, who did, were too engaged with each other.

What does the smile mean upon Mona Lisa and your several Madonnas?

Will you give to me again that melody of Bach's?

How did you fare under Sforza, how under Borgia, how under King Francis?

How did you fare in Switzerland, how against Hitler, how with Roosevelt?

What physical considerations led you to think men might build wings?

What evidence proves that the earth goes around the sun, that light has a finite speed, that the stars are also suns?

What makes you doubt the finiteness of the universe?

Well, sir, why have you not analyzed your concept of space-time as follows?

Taverner and the barmaid spoke low behind their hands. Finally she went to Héloise and Abélard. "Go on upstairs," she said through tears of her own. "You've only this while, and it's wearing away."

He looked up like a blind man. "We took vows," came from his lips.

Héloise closed them with hers. "Thou didst break thine before," she told him, "and we praised the goodness of God."

"Go, go," said the barmaid. Almost by herself, she raised them to their feet. I saw them leave, I heard them on the stairs.

And then Leonardo: "Doctor Alberto, you waste your efforts." He grimaced; the hands knotted around his goblet. "I cannot follow your mathematics, your logic. I have not the knowledge—"

But Einstein leaned forward, and his voice too was less than steady. "You have the brain. And, yes, a fresh view, an insight not blinkered by four centuries of progress point by point . . . down a single road, when we know in this room there are many, many . . . ."

"You cannot explain to me in a few hours—"

"No, but you can get a general idea of what I mean, and I think you, out of everybody who ever lived, can see where . . . where I am astray—and from me, you can carry back home—"

Leonardo flamed.

"No."

That was Taverner. He had come up on the empty side of our table; and he no longer seemed stumpy or jolly.

"No, gentlemen," he said in language after language. His tone was not stern, it was regretful.

but it never wavered. "I fear I must ask you to change the subject. You would learn more than should be. Both of you."

We stared at him, and the silence around us turned off the singing. Leonardo's countenance froze. Finally Einstein smiled lopsidedly, scraped back his chair, stood, knocked the dottle from his pipe. Its odor was bittersweet. "My apologies, Herr Gastwirt," he said in his soft fashion. "You are right. I forgot." He bowed. "This evening has been an honor and a delight. Thank you."

Turning, his stooped form departed.

When the door had shut on him, Leonardo sat unmoving for another while. Taverner threw me a rueful grin and went back to his visiting mysteries. The men at the bar, who had sensed a problem and quieted down, now cheered up and grew rowdier yet. When Mrs. Hauksbee walked in, they cheered.

Leonardo cast his goblet on the floor. Glass flew outward, wine fountained red. "Héloise and Abélard!" he roared. "*They* will have had their night!"

THE TALE OF HAUK

A man called Geirolf dwelt on the Great Fjord in Raumsdal. His father was Bui Hardhand, who owned a farm inland near the Dofra Fell. One year Bui went in viking to Finnmark and brought back a woman he dubbed Gydha. She became the mother of Geirolf. But because Bui already had children by his wife, there would be small inheritance for this by-blow.

Folk said uncanny things about Gydha. She was fair to see, but spoke little, did no more work than she must, dwelt by herself in a shack out of sight of the garth, and often went for long stridings alone on the upland heaths, heedless of cold, rain, and rovers. Bui did not visit her often. Her son Geirolf did. He too was a moody sort, not much given to playing with others, quick and harsh of temper. Big and strong, he went abroad with his father when he was twelve, and in the next few years won the name of a mighty though ruthless fighter.

Then Gydha died. They buried her near her shack, and it was whispered that she spooked around it of nights. Soon after, walking home with some men by moonlight from a feast at a neighbor's, Bui clutched his breast and fell dead. They wondered if Gydha had called him, maybe to accompany her home to Finmark, for there was no more sight of her.

Geirolf bargained with his kin and got the price of a ship for himself. Thereafter he gathered a crew, mostly younger sons and a wild lot, and fared west. For a long while he harried Scotland, Ireland, and the coasts south of the Channel, and won much booty. With some of this he bought his farm on the Great Fjord. Meanwhile he courted Thyra, a daughter of the yeoman Sigtryg Einarsson, and got her.

They had one son early on, Hauk, a bright and lively lad. But thereafter five years went by until they had a daughter who lived, Unn, and two years later a boy they called Einar. Geirolf was in viking every summer, and sometimes wintered over in the Westlands. Yet he was a kindly father, whose children were always glad to see him come roaring home. Very tall and broad in the shoulders, he had long red-brown hair and a full beard around a broad blunt-nosed face whose eyes were ice-blue and slanted. He liked fine clothes and heavy gold rings, which he also lavished on Thyra.

Then the time came when Geirolf said he felt poorly and would not fare elsewhere that season. Hauk was fourteen years old and had been wild to go. "I'll keep my promise to you as well as may be," Geirolf said, and sent men asking around. The best he could do was get his son a bench on a ship belonging to Ottar the Wide-Faring from Haalogaland in the north, who was trading along the coast and meant to do likewise overseas.

Hauk and Ottar took well to each other. In England, the man got the boy prime-signed so he could deal with Christians. Though neither was baptized, what he heard while they wintered there made Hauk thoughtful. Next spring they fared south to trade among the Moors, and did not come home until late fall.

Ottar was Geirolf's guest for a while, though he scowled to himself when his host broke into fits of deep coughing. He offered to take Hauk along on his voyages from now on and start the youth toward a good livelihood.

"You a chapman—the son of a viking?" Geirolf sneered. He had grown surly of late.

Hauk flushed. "You've heard what we did to those vikings who set on *us*," he answered.

"Give our son his head," was Thyra's smiling rede, "or he'll take the bit between his teeth."

The upshot was that Geirolf grumbled agreement, and Hauk fared off. He did not come back for five years.

Long were the journeys he took with Ottar. By ship and horse, they made their way to Uppsala in Svithjodh, thence into the wilderness of the Keel after pelts; amber they got on the windy strands of Jutland, salt herring along the Sound; seeking beeswax, honey, and tallow, they pushed beyond Holmgard to the fair at Kiev; walrus ivory lured them past North Cape, through bergs and floes to the land of the fur-clad Biarmians; and they bore many goods west. They did not hide that the wish to see what was new to them drove them as hard as any hope of gain.

In those days King Harald Fairhair went widely about in Norway, bringing all the land under himself. Lesser kings and chieftains must either plight faith to him or meet his wrath; it crushed whomever would stand fast. When he entered Raumsdal, he sent men from garth to garth as was his wont, to say he wanted oaths and warriors.

"My older son is abroad," Geirolf told these, "and my younger still a stripling. As for myself—" He coughed, and blood flecked his beard. The king's men did not press the matter.

But now Geirolf's moods grew ever worse. He snarled at everybody, cuffed his children and housefolk, once drew a dagger and stabbed to death a thrall who chanced to spill some soup on him. When Thyra reproahed him for this, he said only, "Let them know I am not altogether hollowed out. I can still wield blade." And he looked at her so threateningly from beneath his shaggy brows that she, no coward, withdrew in silence.

A year later, Hauk Geirolfsson returned to visit his parents.

That was on a chill fall noontide. Whitecaps chopped beneath a whistling wind and cast spindrift salty onto lips. Clifftops on either side of the fjord were lost in mist. Above blew cloud wrack like smoke. Hauk's ship, a wide-beamed knorr, rolled, pitched, and creaked as it beat its way under sail. The owner stood in the bows, wrapped in a flame-red cloak, an uncommonly big young man, yellow hair tossing around a face akin to his father's, weatherbeaten though still scant of beard. When he saw the arm of the fjord that he wanted to enter, he pointed with a spear at whose head he had bound a silk pennon. When he saw Disafoss pouring in a white stream down the blue-gray stone wall to larboard, and beyond the waterfall at the end of that arm lay his old home, he shouted for happiness.

Geirolf had rich holdings. The hall bulked over all else, heavy-timbered, brightly painted, dragon heads arching from rafters and gables. Elsewhere around the yard were cookhouse, smokehouse, bathhouse, storehouses, workshop, stables, barns, women's bower. Several cabins for hirelings and their families were strewn beyond. Fishing boats lay on the strand near a shed which held the master's dragonship. Behind the steading, land sloped sharply upward through a narrow dale, where fields were walled with stones grubbed out of them and now stubbled after harvest. A bronze-leaved oakenshaw stood untouched not far from the buildings; and a mile inland, where hills humped themselves toward the mountains, rose a darkling wall of pinewood.

Spearheads and helmets glimmered ashore. But men saw it was a single craft bound their way, white shield on the mast. As the hull slipped alongside the little wharf, they lowered their weapons. Hauk sprang from bow to dock in a single leap and whooped.

Geirolf trod forth. "Is that you, my son?" he called. His voice was hoarse from coughing; he had grown gaunt and sunken-eyed; the ax that he bore shivered in his hand.

"Yes, father, yes, home again," Hauk stammered. He could not hide his shock.

Maybe this drove Geirolf to anger. Nobody knew; he had become impossible to get along with. "I could well-nigh have hoped otherwise," he rasped. "An unfriend would give me something better than straw-death."

The rest of the men, housecarls and thralls alike, flocked about Hauk to bid him welcome. Among them was a burly, grizzled yeoman whom he knew from aforetime, Leif Egilsson, a neighbor come to dicker for a horse. When he was small, Hauk had often wended his way over a woodland trail to Leif's garth to play with the children there.

He called his crew to him. They were not just Norse, but had among them Danes, Swedes, and English, gathered together over the years as he found them trustworthy. "You brought a mickle for me to feed," Geirolf said. Luckily, the wind bore his words from all but Hauk. "Where's your master Ottar?"

The young man stiffened. "He's my friend, never my master," he answered. "This is my own ship, bought with my own earnings. Ottar abides in England this year. The West Saxons have a new king, one Alfred, whom he wants to get to know."

"Time was when it was enough to know how to

get sword past a Westman's shield," Geirolf
grumbled.

Seeing peace down by the water, women and
children hastened from the hall to meet the newcomers. At their head went Thyra. She was tall
and deep-bosomed; her gown blew around a form
still straight and freely striding. But as she
neared, Hauk saw that the gold of her braids was
dimmed and sorrow had furrowed her face. Nonetheless she kindled when she knew him. "Oh,
thrice welcome, Hauk!" she said low. "How long
can you bide with us?"

After his father's greeting, it had been in his
mind to say he must soon be off. But when he
spied who walked behind his mother, he said, "We
thought we might be guests here the winter
through, if that's not too much of a burden."

"Never—" began Thyra. Then she saw where his
gaze had gone, and suddenly she smiled.

Alfhild Leifsdottir had joined her widowed
father on this visit. She was two years younger
than Hauk, but they had been glad of each other as
playmates. Today she stood a maiden grown,
lissome in a blue wadmal gown, heavily crowned
with red locks above great green eyes, straight
nose, and gently curved mouth. Though he had
known many a woman, none struck him as being
so fair.

He grinned at her and let his cloak flap open to
show his finery of broidered, fur-lined tunic, linen
shirt and breeks, chased leather boots, gold on
arms and neck and sword-hilt. She paid them less
heed than she did him when they spoke.

Thus Hauk and his men moved to Geirolf's hall.
He brought plentiful gifts, there was ample food
and drink, and their tales of strange lands—
their songs, dances, games, jests, manners—made
them good housefellows in these lengthening
nights.

Already on the next morning, he walked out with Alfhild. Rain had cleared the air, heaven and fjord sparkled, wavelets chuckled beneath a cool breeze from the woods. Nobody else was on the strand where they went.

"So you grow mighty as a chapman, Hauk," Alfhild teased. "Have you never gone in viking . . . only once, only to please you father?"

"No," he answered gravely. "I fail to see what manliness lies in falling on those too weak to defend themselves. We traders must be stronger and more war-skilled than any who may seek to plunder us." A thick branch of driftwood, bleached and hardened, lay nearby. Hauk picked it up and snapped it between his hands. Two other men would have had trouble doing that. It gladdened him to see Alfhild glow at the sight. "Nobody has tried us twice," he said.

They passed the shed where Geirolf's dragon lay on rollers. Hauk opened the door for a peek at the remembered slim shape. A sharp whiff from the gloom within brought his nose wrinkling. "Whew!" he snorted. "Dry rot."

"Poor *Fireworm* has long lain idle," Alfhild sighed. "In later years, your father's illness has gnawed him till he doesn't even see to the care of his ship. He knows he will never take it a-roving again."

"I feared that," Hauk murmured.

"We grieve for him on our own garth too," she said. "In former days, he was a staunch friend to us. Now we bear with his ways, yes, insults that would make my father draw blade on anybody else."

"That is dear of you," Hauk said, staring straight before him. "I'm very thankful."

"You have not much cause for that, have you?" she asked. "I mean, you've been away so long . . . Of course, you have your mother. She's borne the

brunt, stood like a shield before your siblings—"
She touched her lips. "I talk too much."

"You talk as a friend," he blurted. "May we
always be friends."

They wandered on, along a path from shore to
fields. It went by the shaw. Through boles and
boughs and falling leaves, they saw Thor's image
and altar among the trees. "I'll make offering here
for my father's health," Hauk said, "though truth
to tell, I've more faith in my own strength than in
any gods."

"You have seen lands where strange gods rule,"
she nodded.

"Yes, and there too, they do not steer things
well," he said. "It was in a Christian realm that a
huge wolf came raiding flocks, on which no iron
would bite. When it took a baby from a hamlet
near our camp, I thought I'd be less than a man did
I not put an end to it."

"What happened?" she asked breathlessly, and
caught his arm.

"I wrestled it barehanded—no foe of mine was
ever more fell—and at last broke its neck." He
pulled back a sleeve to show scars of terrible
bites. "Dead, it changed into a man they had outlawed that year for his evil deeds. We burned the
lich to make sure it would not walk again, and
thereafter the folk had peace. And . . . we had
friends, in a country otherwise wary of us."

She looked on him in the wonder he had hoped
for.

Erelong she must return with her father. But
the way between the garths was just a few miles,
and Hauk often rode or skied through the woods.
At home, he and his men helped do what work
there was, and gave merriment where it had long
been little known.

Thyra owned this to her son, on a snowy day
when they were by themselves. They were in the

women's bower, whither they had gone to see a tapestry she was weaving. She wanted to know how it showed against those of the Westlands; he had brought one such, which hung above the benches in the hall. Here, in the wide quiet room, was dusk, for the day outside had become a tumbling whiteness. Breath steamed from lips as the two of them spoke. It smelled sweet; both had drunk mead until they could talk freely.

"You did better than you knew when you came back," Thyra said. "You blew like spring into this winter of ours. Einar and Unn were withering; they blossom again in your nearness."

"Strangely has our father changed," Hauk answered sadly. "I remember once when I was small, how he took me by the hand on a frost-clear night, led me forth under the stars, and named for me the pictures in them, Thor's Wain, Freyja's Spindle—how wonderful he made them, how his deep slow laughterful voice filled the dark."

"A wasting illness draws the soul inward," his mother said. "He . . . has no more manhood . . . and it tears him like fangs that he will die helpless in bed. He must strike out at someone, and here we are."

She was silent a while before she added: "He will not live out the year. Then you must take over."

"I must be gone when weather allows," Hauk warned. "I promised Ottar."

"Return as soon as may be," Thyra said. "We have need of a strong man, the more so now when yonder King Harald would reave their freehold rights from yeomen."

"It would be well to have a hearth of my own." Hauk stared past her, toward the unseen woods. Her worn face creased in a smile.

Suddenly they heard yells from the yard below. Hauk ran out onto the gallery and looked down.

Geirolf was shambling after an aged carl named Atli. He had a whip in his hand and was lashing it across the white locks and wrinkled cheeks of the man, who could not run fast either and who sobbed.

"What is this?" broke from Hauk. He swung himself over the rail, hung, and let go. The drop would at least have jarred the wind out of most. He, though, bounced from where he landed, ran behind his father, caught hold of the whip and wrenched it from Geirolf's grasp. "What are you doing?"

Geirolf howled and struck his son with a doubled fist. Blood trickled from Hauk's mouth. He stood fast. Atli sank to hands and knees and fought not to weep.

"Are you also a heelbiter of mine?" Geirolf bawled.

"I'd save you from your madness, father," Hauk said in pain. "Atli followed you to battle ere I was born—he dandled me on his knee—and he's a free man. What has he done, that you'd bring down on us the anger of his kinfolk?"

"Harm not the skipper, young man," Atli begged. "I fled because I'd sooner die than lift hand against my skipper."

"Hell swallow you both!" Geirolf would have cursed further, but the coughing came on him. Blood drops flew through the snowflakes, down onto the white earth, where they mingled with the drip from the heads of Hauk and Atli. Doubled over, Geirolf let them half lead, half carry him to his shut-bed. There he closed the panel and lay alone in darkness.

"What happened between you and him?" Hauk asked.

"I was fixing to shoe a horse," Atli said into a ring of gaping onlookers. "He came in and wanted to know why I'd not asked his leave. I told him 'twas plain Kolfaxi needed new shoes. Then he hollered, "I'll show you I'm no log in the woodpile!" and snatched yon whip off the wall and took after me." The old man squared his shoulders. "We'll speak no more of this, you hear?" he ordered the household.

Nor did Geirolf, when next day he let them bring him some broth.

For more reasons than this, Hauk came to spend much of his time at Leif's garth. He would return in such a glow that even the reproachful looks of his young sister and brother, even the sullen or the weary greeting of his father, could not dampen it.

At last, when lengthening days and quickening blood bespoke seafarings soon to come, that happened which surprised nobody. Hauk told them in the hall that he wanted to marry Alfhild Leifsdottir, and prayed Geirolf press the suit for him. "What must be, will be," said his father, a better grace than awaited. Union of the families was clearly good for both.

Leif Egilsson agreed, and Alfhild had nothing but aye to say. The betrothal feast crowded the whole neighborhood together in cheer. Thyra hid the trouble within her, and Geirolf himself was calm if not blithe.

Right after, Hauk and his men were busking themselves to fare. Regardless of his doubts about gods, he led in offering for a safe voyage to Thor, Aegir, and St. Michael. But Alfhild found herself a quiet place alone, to cut runes on an ash tree in the name of Freyja.

When all was ready, she was there with the folk of Geirolf's stead to see the sailors off. That morning was keen, wind roared in trees and skirled between cliffs, waves ran green and white beneath small flying clouds. Unn could not but hug her brother who was going, while Einar gave him a handclasp that shook. Thyra said, "Come home hale and early, my son." Alfhild mostly stored away the sight of Hauk. Atli and others of the household mumbled this and that.

Geirolf shuffled forward. The cane on which he leaned rattled among the stones of the beach. He was hunched in a hairy cloak against the sharp air. His locks fell tangled almost to the coal-smoldering eyes. "Father, farewell," Hauk said, taking his free hand.

"You mean 'fare far,' don't you?" Geirolf grated. " 'Fare far and never come back.' You'd like that, wouldn't you? But we will meet again. Oh, yes, we will meet again."

Hauk dropped the hand. Geirolf turned and sought the house. The rest behaved as if they had not heard, speaking loudly, amidst yelps of laughter, to overcome those words of foreboding. Soon Hauk called his orders to begone.

Men scrambled aboard the laden ship. Its sail slatted aloft and filled, the mooring lines were cast loose, the hull stood out to sea. Alfhild waved until it was gone from sight behind the bend where Disafoss fell.

The summer passed—plowing, sowing, lambing, calving, farrowing, hoeing, reaping, flailing, butchering—rain, hail, sun, stars, loves, quarrels, births, deaths—and the season wore toward fall. Alfhild was seldom at Geirolf's garth, nor was Leif; for Hauk's father grew steadily worse. After midsummer he could no longer leave his bed. But often he whispered, between lung-tearing coughs, to those who tended him, "I would kill you if I could."

On a dark day late in the season, when rain roared about the hall and folk and hounds huddled close to fires that hardly lit the gloom around, Geirolf awoke from a heavy sleep. Thyra marked it and came to him. Cold and dankness gnawed their way through her clothes. The fever was in him like a brand. He plucked restlessly at his blanket, where he half sat in his short shut-bed. Though flesh had wasted from the great bones, his fingers still had strength to tear the wool. The mattress rustled under him. "Straw-death, straw-death," he muttered.

Thyra laid a palm on his brow. "Be at ease," she said.

It dragged from him: "You'll not be rid . . . of me . . . so fast . . . by straw-death." An icy sweat broke forth and the last struggle began.

Long it was, Geirolf's gasps and the sputtering flames the only noises within that room, while rain and wind ramped outside and night drew in. Thyra stood by the bedside to wipe the sweat off her man, blood and spittle from his beard. A while after sunset, he rolled his eyes back and died.

Thyra called for water and lamps. She cleansed him, clad him in his best, and laid him out. A drawn sword was on his breast.

In the morning, thralls and carls alike went forth under her orders. A hillock stood in the fields about half a mile inland from the house. They dug a grave chamber in the top of this, lining it well with timber. "Won't you bury him in his ship?" asked Atli.

"It is rotten, unworthy of him," Thyra said. Yet she made them haul it to the barrow, around which she had stones to outline a hull. Meanwhile folk readied a grave-ale, and messengers bade neighbors come.

When all were there, men of Geirolf's carried him on a litter to his resting place and put him in, together with weapons and a jar of Southland coins. After beams had roofed the chamber, his friends from aforetime took shovels and covered it well. They replaced the turfs of sere grass, leaving the hillock as it had been save that it was now bigger. Einar Thorolfsson kindled his father's

ship. It burned till dusk, when the horns of the
new moon stood over the fjord. Meanwhile folk
had gone back down to the garth to feast and
drink. Riding home next day, well gifted by Thyra,
they told each other that this had been an honor-
able burial.

The moon waxed. On the first night that it rose
full, Geirolf came again.

A thrall named Kark had been late in the woods,
seeking a strayed sheep. Coming home, he passed
near the howe. The moon was barely above the
pines; long shivery beams of light ran on the
water, lost themselves in shadows ashore, glinted
wanly anew where a bedewed stone wall snaked
along a stubblefield. Stars were few. A great stillness lay on the land, not even an owl hooted, until
all at once dogs down in the garth began howling.
It was not the way they howled at the moon;
across the mile between, it sounded ragged and
terrified. Kark felt the chill close in around him,
and hastened toward home.

Something heavy trod the earth. He looked
around and saw the bulk of a huge man coming
across the field from the barrow. "Who's that?" he
called uneasily. No voice replied, but the weight of
those footfalls shivered through the ground into
his bones. Kark swallowed, gripped his staff, and
stood where he was. But then the shape came so
near that moonlight picked out the head of
Geirolf. Kark screamed, dropped his weapon, and
ran.

Geirolf followed slowly, clumsily behind.

Down in the garth, light glimmered red as doors
opened. Folk saw Kark running, gasping for
breath. Atli and Einar led the way out, each with a
torch in one hand, a sword in the other. Little
could they see beyond the wild flame-gleam. Kark
reached them, fell, writhed on the hard-beaten
clay of the yard, and wailed.

"What is it, you lackwit?" Atli snapped, and kicked him. Then Einar pointed his blade.

"A stranger—" Atli began.

Geirolf rocked into sight. The mould of the grave clung to him. His eyes stared unblinking, unmoving, blank in the moonlight, out of a gray face whereon the skin crawled. The teeth in his tangled beard were dry. No breath smoked from his nostrils. He held out his arms, crook-fingered.

"Father!" Einar cried. The torch hissed from his grip, flickered weakly at his feet, and went out. The men at his back jammed the doorway of the hall as they sought its shelter.

"The skipper's come again," Atli quavered. He sheathed his sword, though that was hard when his hand shook, and made himself step forward. "Skipper, d'you know your old shipmate Atli?"

The dead man grabbed him, lifted him, and dashed him to earth. Einar heard bones break. Atli jerked once and lay still. Geirolf trod him and Kark underfoot. There was a sound of cracking and rending. Blood spurted forth.

Blindly, Einar swung blade. The edge smote but would not bite. A wave of grave-chill passed over him. He whirled and bounded back inside.

Thyra had seen. "Bar the door," she bade. The windows were already shuttered against frost. "Men, stand fast. Women, stoke up the fires."

They heard the lich groping about the yard. Walls creaked where Geirolf blundered into them. Thyra called through the door, "Why do you wish us ill, your own household?" But only those noises gave answer. The hounds cringed and whined.

"Lay iron at the doors and under every window," Thyra commanded. "If it will not cut him, it may keep him out."

All that night, then, folk huddled in the hall. Geirolf climbed onto the roof and rode the ridge-pole, drumming his heels on the shakes till the whole building boomed. A little before sunrise, it stopped. Peering out by the first dull dawnlight, Thyra saw no mark of her husband but his deep-sunken footprints and the wrecked bodies he had left.

"He grew so horrible before he died," Unn wept. "Now he can't rest, can he?"

"We'll make him an offering," Thyra said through her weariness. "It may be we did not give him enough when we buried him."

Few would follow her to the howe. Those who dared, brought along the best horse on the farm. Einar, as the son of the house when Hauk was gone, himself cut its throat after a sturdy man had given the hammer-blow. Carls and wenches butchered the carcass, which Thyra and Unn cooked over a fire in whose wood was blent the charred rest of the dragonship. Nobody cared to eat much of the flesh or broth. Thyra poured what was left over the bones, upon the grave.

Two ravens circled in sight, waiting for folk to go so they could take the food. "Is that a good sign?" Thyra sighed. "Will Odin fetch Geirolf home?"

That night everybody who had not fled to neighboring steads gathered in the hall. Soon after the moon rose, they heard the footfalls come nearer and nearer. They heard Geirolf break into the storehouse and worry the laid-out bodies of Atli and Kark. They heard him kill cows in the barn. Again he rode the roof.

In the morning Leif Egilsson arrived, having gotten the news. He found Thyra too tired and shaken to do anything further. "The ghost did not take your offering," he said, "but maybe the gods will."

In the oakenshaw, he led the giving of more beasts. There was talk of a thrall for Odin, but he said that would not help if this did not. Instead, he saw to the proper burial of the slain, and of those kine which nobody would dare eat. That night he abode on the farm.

And Geirolf came back. Throughout the darkness, he tormented the home which had been his.

"I will bide here one more day," Leif said next sunrise. "We all need rest—though ill is it that we must sleep during daylight when we've so much readying for winter to do."

By that time, some other neighborhood men were also on hand. They spoke loudly of how they would hew the lich asunder.

"You know not what you boast of," said aged Grim the Wise. "Einar smote, and he strikes well for a lad, but the iron would not bite. It never will. Ghost-strength is in Geirolf, and all the wrath he could not set free during his life."

That night folk waited breathless for moonrise. But when the gnawed shield climbed over the pines, nothing stirred. The dogs, too, no longer seemed cowed. About midnight, Grim murmured into the shadows, "Yes, I thought so. Geirolf walks only when the moon is full."

"Then tomorrow we'll dig him up and burn him!" Leif said.

"No," Grim told them. "That would spell the worst of luck for everybody here. Don't you see, the anger and unpeace which will not let him rest, those would be forever unslaked? They could not but bring doom on the burners."

"What then can we do?" Thyra asked dully.

"Leave this stead," Grim counselled, "at least when the moon is full."

"Hard will that be," Einar sighed. "Would that my brother Hauk were here."

"He should have returned erenow," Thyra said. "May we in our woe never know that he has come to grief himself."

In truth, Hauk had not. His wares proved welcome in Flanders, where he bartered for cloth that he took across to England. There Ottar greeted him, and he met the young King Alfred. At that time there was no war going on with the Danes, who were settling into the Danelaw and thus in need of household goods. Hauk and Ottar did a thriving business among them. This led them to think they might do as well in Iceland, whither Norse folk were moving who liked not King Harald Fairhair. They made a voyage to see. Foul winds hampered them on the way home. Hence fall was well along when Hauk's ship returned.

The day was still and cold. Low overcast turned sky and water the hue of iron. A few gulls cruised and mewed, while under them sounded creak and splash of oars, swearing of men, as the knorr was rowed. At the end of the fjord-branch, garth and leaves were tiny splashes of color, lost against rearing cliffs, brown fields, murky wildwood. Straining ahead from afar, Hauk saw that a bare handful of men came down to the shore, moving listlessly more than watchfully. When his craft was unmistakable, though, a few women—no youngsters —sped from the hall as if they could not wait. Their cries came to him more thin than the gulls'.

Hauk lay alongside the dock. Springing forth, he called merrily, "Where is everybody? How fares Alfhild?" His words lost themselves in silence. Fear touched him. "What's wrong?"

Thyra trod forth. Years might have gone by during his summer abroad, so changed was she. "You are barely in time," she said in an unsteady tone. Taking his hands, she told him how things stood.

Hauk stared long into emptiness. At last, "Oh, no," he whispered. "What's to be done?"

"We hoped you might know that, my son," Thyra answered. "The moon will be full tomorrow night."

His voice stumbled. "I am no wizard. If the gods

themselves would not lay this ghost, what can I do?"

Einar spoke, in the brashness of youth: "We thought you might deal with him as you did with the werewolf."

"But that was—No, I cannot!" Hauk croaked. "Never ask me."

"Then I fear we must leave," Thyra said. "For aye. You see how many have already fled, thrall and free alike, though nobody else has a place for them. We've not enough left to farm these acres. And who would buy them of us? Poor must we go, helpless as the poor ever are."

"Iceland—" Hauk wet his lips. "Well, you shall not want while I live." Yet he had counted on this homestead, whether to dwell on or sell.

"Tomorrow we move over to Leif's garth, for the next three days and nights," Thyra said.

Unn shuddered. "I know not if I can come back," she said. "This whole past month here, I could hardly ever sleep." Dulled skin and sunken eyes bore her out.

"What else would you do?" Hauk asked.

"Whatever I can," she stammered, and broke into tears. He knew: wedding herself too young to whoever would have her dowryless, poor though the match would be—or making her way to some town to turn whore, his little sister.

"Let me think on this," Hauk begged. "Maybe I can hit on something."

His crew were also daunted when they heard. At eventide they sat in the hall and gave only a few curt words about what they had done in foreign parts. Everyone lay down early on bed, bench, or floor, but none slept well.

Before sunset, Hauk had walked forth alone. First he sought the grave of Atli. "I'm sorry, dear old friend," he said. Afterward he went to Geirolf's howe. It loomed yellow-gray with withered grass wherein grinned the skull of the slaughtered horse. At its foot were strewn the charred bits of the ship, inside stones which outlined a greater but unreal hull. Around reached stubblefields and walls, hemmed in by woods on one side and water on the other, rock lifting sheer beyond. The chill and the quiet had deepened.

Hauk climbed to the top of the barrow and stood there a while, head bent downward. "Oh, father," he said, "I learned doubt in Christian lands. What's right for me to do?" There was no answer. He made a slow way back to the dwelling.

All were up betimes next day. It went slowly over the woodland path to Leif's, for animals must be herded along. The swine gave more trouble than most. Hauk chuckled once, not very merrily, and remarked that at least this took folk's minds off their sorrows. He raised no mirth.

But he had Alfhild ahead of him. At the end of the way, he sprinted shouting into the yard. Leif owned less land than Geirolf, his buildings were smaller and fewer, most of his guests must house outdoors in sleeping bags. Hauk paid no heed. "Alfhild!" he called. "I'm here!"

She left the dough she was kneading and sped to him. They hugged each other hard and long, in sight of the whole world. None thought that shame, as things were. At last she said, striving not to weep, "How we've longed for you! Now the nightmare can end."

He stepped back. "What mean you?" he uttered slowly, knowing full well.

"Why—" She was bewildered. "Won't you give him his second death?"

Hauk gazed past her for some heartbeats before he said: "Come aside with me."

Hand in hand, they wandered off. A meadow lay hidden from the garth by a stand of aspen. Elsewhere around, pines speared into a sky that today

was bright. Clouds drifted on a nipping breeze.
Far off, a stag bugled.

Hauk spread feet apart, hooked thumbs in belt,
and made himself meet her eyes. "You think over-
highly of my strength," he said.

"Who has more?" she asked. "We kept ourselves
going by saying you would come home and make
things good again."

"What if the drow is too much for me?" His
words sounded raw through the hush. Leaves
dropped yellow from their boughs.

She flushed. "Then your name will live."

"Yes—" Softly he spoke the words of the High
One:

Kine die, kinfolk die,
and so at last oneself.
This I know that never dies:
how dead men's deeds are deemed."

"You will do it!" she cried gladly.

His head shook before it drooped. "No. I will
not. I dare not."

She stood as if he had clubbed her.

"Won't you understand?" he began.

The wound he had dealt her hopes went too
deep. "So you show yourself a nithing!"

"Hear me," he said, shaken. "Were the lich anybody else's—"

Overwrought beyond reason, she slapped him
and choked, "The gods bear witness, I give them
my holiest oath, never will I wed you unless you
do this thing. See, by my blood I swear." She
whipped out her dagger and gashed her wrist. Red
rills coursed out and fell in drops on the fallen
leaves.

He was aghast. "You know not what you say.
You're too young, you've been too sheltered.
Listen."

She would have fled from him, but he gripped
her shoulders and made her stand. "Listen," went

between his teeth. "Geirolf is still my father—my father who begot me, reared me, named the stars for me, weaponed me to make my way in the world. How can I fight him? Did I slay him, what horror would come upon me and mine?"

"O-o-oh," broke from Alfhild. She sank to the ground and wept as if to tear loose her ribs.

He knelt, held her, gave what soothing he could. "Now I know," she mourned. "Too late."

"Never," he murmured. "We'll fare abroad if we must, take new land, make new lives together."

"No," she gasped. "Did I not swear? What doom awaits an oathbreaker?"

Then he was long still. Heedlessly though she had spoken, her blood lay in the earth, which would remember.

He too was young. He straightened. "I will fight," he said.

Now she clung to him and pleaded that he must not. But an iron calm had come over him. "Maybe I will not be cursed," he said. "Or maybe the curse will be no more than I can bear."

"It will be mine too, I who brought it on you," she plighted herself.

Hand in hand again, they went back to the garth. Leif spied the haggard look on them and half guessed what had happened. "Will you fare to meet the drow, Hauk?" he asked. "Wait till I can have Grim the Wise brought here. His knowledge may help you."

"No," said Hauk. "Waiting would weaken me. I go this night."

Wide eyes stared at him—all but Thyra's; she was too torn.

Toward evening he busked himself. He took no helm, shield, or byrnie, for the dead man bore no weapons. Some said they would come along, armored themselves well, and offered to be at his side. He told them to follow him, but no farther than to watch what happened. Their iron would be of no help, and he thought they would only get in each other's way, and his, when he met the over-human might of the drow. He kissed Alfhild, his mother, and his sister, and clasped hands with his brother, bidding them stay behind if they loved him.

Long did the few miles of path seem, and gloomy under the pines. The sun was on the world's rim when men came out in the open. They looked past fields and barrow down to the empty garth, the fjordside cliffs, the water where the sun lay as half an ember behind a trail of blood. Clouds hurried on a wailing wind through a greenish sky. Cold struck deep. A wolf howled.

"Wait here," Hauk said.

"The gods be with you," Leif breathed.

"I've naught tonight but my own strength," Hauk said. "Belike none of us ever had more."

His tall form, clad in leather and wadmal, showed black athwart the sunset as he walked from the edge of the woods, out across plowland toward the crouching howe. The wind fluttered his locks, a last brightness until the sun went below. Then for a while the evenstar alone had light.

Hauk reached the mound. He drew sword and leaned on it, waiting. Dusk deepened. Star after star came forth, small and strange. Clouds blowing across them picked up a glow from the still unseen moon.

It rose at last above the treetops. Its ashen sheen stretched gashes of shadow across earth. The wind loudened.

The grave groaned. Turves, stones, timbers swung aside. Geirolf shambled out beneath the sky. Hauk felt the ground shudder under his weight. There came a carrion stench, though the only sign of rotting was on the dead man's clothes.

His eyes peered dim, his teeth gnashed dry in a face at once well remembered and hideously changed. When he saw the living one who waited, he veered and lumbered thitherward.

"Father," Hauk called. "It's I, your eldest son." The drow drew nearer.

"Halt, I beg you," Hauk said unsteadily. "What can I do to bring you peace?"

A cloud passed over the moon. It seemed to be hurtling through heaven. Geirolf reached for his son with fingers that were ready to clutch and tear. "Hold," Hauk shrilled. "No step farther."

He could not see if the gaping mouth grinned. In another stride, the great shape came well-nigh upon him. He lifted his sword and brought it singing down. The edge struck truly, but slid aside. Geirolf's skin heaved, as if to push the blade away. In one more step, he laid grave-cold hands around Hauk's neck.

Before that grip could close, Hauk dropped his useless weapon, brought his wrists up between Geirolf's, and mightily snapped them apart. Nails left furrows, but he was free. He sprang back, into a wrestler's stance.

Geirolf moved in, reaching. Hauk hunched under those arms and himself grabbed waist and thigh. He threw his shoulder against a belly like rock. Any live man would have gone over, but the lich was too heavy.

Geirolf smote Hauk on the side. The blows drove him to his knees and thundered on his back. A foot lifted to crush him. He rolled off and found his own feet again. Geirolf lurched after him. The hastening moon linked their shadows. The wolf howled anew, but in fear. Watching men gripped spearshafts till their knuckles stood bloodless.

Hauk braced his legs and snatched for the first hold, around both of Geirolf's wrists. The drow strained to break loose and could not; but neither could Hauk bring him down. Sweat ran moon-bright over the son's cheeks and darkened his shirt. The reek of it was at least a living smell in his nostrils. Breath tore at his gullet. Suddenly Geirolf wrenched so hard that his right arm tore from between his foe's fingers. He brought that hand against Hauk's throat. Hauk let go and slammed himself backward before he was throttled.

Gierolf stalked after him. The drow did not move fast. Hauk sped behind and pounded on the broad back. He seized an arm of Geirolf's and twisted it around. But the dead cannot feel pain. Geirolf stood fast. His other hand groped about, got Hauk by the hair, and yanked. Live men can hurt. Hauk stumbled away. Blood ran from his scalp into his eyes and mouth, hot and salt.

Geirolf turned and followed. He would not tire. Hauk had no long while before strength ebbed. Almost, he fled. Then the moon broke through to shine full on his father. "You . . . shall not . . . go on . . . like that," Hauk mumbled while he snapped after air.

The drow reached him. They closed, grappled, swayed, stamped to and fro, in wind and flickery moonlight. Then Hauk hooked an ankle behind Geirolf's and pushed. With a huge thud, the drow crashed to earth. He dragged Hauk along.

Hauk's bones felt how terrible was the grip upon him. He let go his own hold. Instead, he arched his back and pushed himself away. His clothes ripped. But he burst free and reeled to his feet.

Geirolf turned over and began to crawl up. His back was once more to Hauk. The young man sprang. He got a knee hard in between the shoulderblades, while both his arms closed on the frosty head before him.

He hauled. With the last and greatest might that

was in him, he hauled. Blackness went in tatters before his eyes.

There came a loud snapping sound. Geirolf ceased pawing behind him. He sprawled limp. His neck was broken, his jawbone wrenched from the skull. Hauk climbed slowly off him, shuddering. Geirolf stirred, rolled, half rose. He lifted a hand toward Hauk. It traced a line through the air and a line growing from beneath that. Then he slumped and lay still.

Hauk crumpled too.

"Follow me who dare!" Leif roared, and went forth across the field. One by one, as they saw nothing move ahead of them, the men came after. At last they stood hushed around Geirolf—who was only a harmless dead man now, though the moon shone bright in his eyes—and on Hauk, who had begun to stir.

"Bear him carefully down to the hall," Leif said. "Start a fire and tend it well. Most of you, take from the woodpile and come back here. I'll stand guard meanwhile . . . though I think there is no need."

And so they burned Geirolf there in the field. He walked no more.

In the morning, they brought Hauk back to Leif's garth. He moved as if in dreams. The others were too awestruck to speak much. Even when Alfhild ran to meet him, he could only say, "Hold clear of me. I may be under a doom."

"Did the drow lay a weird on you?" she asked, spear-stricken.

"I know not," he answered. "I think I fell into the dark before he was wholly dead."

"What?" Leif well-nigh shouted. "You did not see the sign he drew?"

"Why, no," Hauk said. "How did it go?"

"Thus. Even afar and by moonlight, I knew." Leif drew it.

"That is no ill-wishing!" Grim cried. "That's

naught but the Hammer."

Life rushed back into Hauk. "Do you mean what I hope?"

"He blessed you," Grim said. "You freed him from what he had most dreaded and hated—his straw-death. The madness in him is gone, and he has wended hence to the world beyond."

Then Hauk was glad again. He led them all in heaping earth over the ashes of his father, and in setting things right on the farm. That winter, at the feast of Thor, he and Alfhild were wedded. Afterward he became well thought of by King Harald, and rose to great wealth. From him and Alfhild stem many men whose names are still remembered. Here ends the tale of Hauk the Ghost Slayer.

OF PIGS AND MEN

The following was written to see if I could handle the rhetorical and logical style of today's most prominent sociopolitical thinkers. After trying it, I'm afraid my preferences remain with men like Jefferson or Burke, hopelessly outmoded though these be.

Amidst the current furore over persecuted minorities and how society has got to make up to them for the troubles their ancestors endured, nobody seems to remember the one which took the worst beating of the lot. So cruelly has it been discriminated against that there isn't even a proper name for it.

Oh, its members are often called WASPS. But that isn't simply dehumanizing, it's inaccurate, doubtless deliberately so in implementation of a calculated policy of dividing them against each other. The fact is, only a part of them are Anglo-Saxons, they were not always Protestants, and many of them still aren't. They have sometimes been called Nordics, but this again is correct for a mere fraction. I'm convinced that that term is misapplied in order to saddle them all with the racial stereotype. You know: a funny-looking person, tall, lanky, long-skulled, with a big nose and straight yellow hair and deepset washed-out eyes and easily sunburned skin and would you want your daughter to marry one? In actuality, more of them are black-haired, brown-eyed, and stocky than not. They consist of those who inhabit a certain part of the world, or whose forebears did.

That homeland covers the British Isles, the Low Countries, the Scandinavian peninsula including most of Finland, Denmark, the Baltic and North Sea littorals, and a large piece of central Europe. It's not very good country—apt to be wet and cold, with boggy or stony or heath-grown soil, gloomy forests, interminable winter nights, few mineral resources except a bit of iron and coal. That is the reason the inhabitants long remained under-developed and thus became easy victims of exploitation by southerners whose own good fortune ought to have made them kind and loving but didn't. In order to give this minority a name free of pejorative associations, let us form a neologism from the core area and call them People Inhabiting Germanic Settlements, or PIGS for short. I want to emphasize that this is also a loose phrase, since many Celts, Slavs, Balts, Finns, Jews, etc. are included. However, the principal languages belong to the Germanic family.

The original PIGS were peaceful reindeer hunters, drifting north when the glaciers receded if they were not refugees from warlike invaders. Once settled down, some of them took to the sea while others farmed their poor little plots of cleared land as best they might. When the Iron Age reached them the Celts were dominant throughout their territory. But the vicious aggression of Mediterranean armies, especially the Roman, reduced this brilliant culture to a set of starveling enclaves. Perforce the Teutons took over the burden of defending northern Europe.

From time immemorial, PIGS have been subject to the most callous racism. Aristotle described their children as having hair "like old men," as if its flaxen hue were a deformity. Pliny counselled against buying German slaves, declaring that they were innately too stupid to learn anything useful. While Tacitus did call them noble savages, his patronizing fantasies never touched the slave raiders or the greedy and unscrupulous merchants who dealt with those innocent tribesmen.

The first major clash occurred about 100 B.C., when Cimbrian and Teutonic immigrants, seeking a haven from famine, were brutally attacked by the Romans. Those who survived were sold into slavery. Given this kind of provocation, it is not to be wondered at that PIGS retaliated with border raids. Finally, at Teutoburger Wald, the heroic people's leader Arminius secured their frontiers against further imperialism. The utter corruption of the fascist Roman society was demonstrated when the western Empire collapsed a bare 400 years later.

At that time, with their usual charity, several organizations of PIGS did their best to help those who had so greatly abused them. Vandals went down to North Africa, Visigoths to Iberia, Ostrogoths to Italy itself, bringing honest government and folk culture. But the Mediterranean Ethnic Neighbors (MEN) would have none of it. Instead, they forced the Latin language on the newcomers; they persecuted the Arian religion; at last Byzantines from the east and Moslems from the south came in armed hordes to crush the liberation movement.

Events developed a little more happily in the north, where the reborn imperialism was weaker. At the request of the Romano-British king Vortigern, the Jutes Hengist and Horsa brought gallant soldiers to assist him in restoring order. When he treacherously turned on them, killing Horsa, Hengist had no choice but to send for reinforcements and give peace to the country. Later English arrivals were welcomed with such joyous admiration—except by a handful of reactionaries in Wales and the Scottish highlands—that no trace of Romano-British culture remains. Similarly, the Gauls renamed their country for the Franks who had set them free.

However, the fascist MEN never stopped their plots to seize back power from the people. They began by sending glib missionaries who converted the Franks and other tribes, not to a pure Arian Christianity, but to a Catholicism directed by Rome. Next—after the Franks had saved them from the Moors—the MEN installed a puppet ruler, Charlemagne, who swept through Saxony with fire and sword, enslaving the dwellers and demolishing their sacred groves. With that example before them, what could the remaining free PIGS do except try to save their oppressed brethren? Tragically, this selfless effort of the Vikings failed, both because of missionary subversion and because a Papal stalking horse named William (a real bastard) usurped the crown of pivotal England.

The next several centuries were an age of unrelieved misery; of paupers groaning beneath the heel of Rome, their Emperor himself having to walk barefoot through the snow; of fighting wars for the benefit of Italian shipping interests, the so-called Crusades; of struggle to keep native languages alive in the face of the Latin which had already extinguished Frankish and Gothic. In this last connection, the prejudice against PIGS is vividly illustrated by the fact that, when a new style of church architecture evolved, its detractors sneeringly labeled it "Gothic." (And we might note that in later times the same adjective was applied to forms of literature that were looked down upon.)

When the Renaissance blessed the MEN with unprecedented opulence, did they send aid to the impoverished PIGS? No. They did nothing of the sort. The Flemings, Prussians, and other wretched of the earth were left gnawing their stockfish and coughing over their peat fires. Not content with hoarding the immense profits of capitalism, the MEN brazenly tried to sell them indulgences.

But then the spirit of Freedom Now broke forth. The Protestant Reformation cast off rusty medieval shackles. This did not happen easily or at once. Think only how the Spaniards ravaged the Netherlands and sent an armada against England, consider the atrocities of Wallenstein and the martyrdom of the Huguenots, the latter not even being PIGS although expressing solidarity with them. Nevertheless, the indomitable resistance movement prevailed.

With a degree of national liberation achieved, the PIGS naturally looked for their rightful share in the affluence that the rest of Europe was enjoying. Again they found themselves barred from opportunity. The Spanish, the Portuguese, the French denied them real estate in America and the Orient. A pitiful few PIGS managed to obtain footholds in such slum areas as New England and Virginia. They were promptly set on by ravening, murdering, scalping lynch mobs of a different race, on the transparent excuse that the latter were there first—which is to say that property rights were considered above human rights. Incredible though it seems, when the PIGS attempted penal reform in Georgia and Botany Bay, this likewise met with violence.

Of course, we must be realistic. PIGS are mortal too, and therefore prone to error. When African chiefs offered slaves for sale, PIGS were occasionally known to buy. And they fell for numerous other capitalist tricks, e.g., they purchased Manhattan Island for $24 and a case of whiskey from some Indians who, it later turned out, had no title to it.

Meanwhile the influence of the MEN was as persistent as it was pernicious. For centuries French literature, Italian art and manners, were emulated in the north to the detriment of a true expression. Spanish courage and Arabic lovemaking (the notorious Sheikh image) are still held up to women as emblems of masculinity, regardless of the castrating effect this may have on male PIGS. When, in the eighteenth and nineteenth centuries, northern poets sought to re-create a northern culture, they were compelled to use half-Latinized tongues and, indeed, to call their efforts by the name Romanticism!

Not having been enlightened about the true meaning of their situation, the PIGS were repeatedly duped into fighting wars that could benefit none but the MEN. In Asia, Africa, Oceania, America they put down one non-Catholic nation after another; as viceroys and garrison troops they endured patiently the humiliation of being excluded from local fraternal groups; and what have they left now for all their toil and bloodshed? Scarcely an acre. In Europe itself, PIGS served as MEN's cat's-paws: for instance, remember Napoleon's German grenadiers, or the Gaulish Bernadotte family which to this day tyrannizes over Sweden. Sometimes they were maneuvered into battling each other to keep them weak, notably in the World Wars. (Nazism is obviously a Mediterranean invention. I have already described the ravings of those mad dogs Aristotle and Pliny; now I remind you of the Graeco-Syrian anti-Semitism commemorated in *Maccabees* and the destruction of the Temple by Romans.)

Throughout history, PIGS have been the butt of scorn. Think of the Chinese phrase "foreign devil," the Japanese "Yankee monkey," the Mexican "gringo," and imagine how you would feel if you were similarly labelled. Does anyone ever say "Blond is beautiful"? No, blondes are automatically assumed to be intellectually deficient and, except for an animal sexuality, emotionally shallow.

I could go on, but this sketch is enough. And enough is enough. I say to you, we have had it up to here. The time has come for action.

Let those of us who were born with light complexions, who speak English with a special accent, who have distinctive patterns of thought, religion, politics, professions, family structure, and taste—let us no longer cringe, let us no longer sycophantically attempt to be what we are not—no, let us stand up and be ourselves, proudly assert that we are just as human and have just as many rights as anybody else, and demand proper compensation for the countless wrongs we have suffered.

PIGS OF THE WORLD, UNITE! YOU HAVE NOTHING TO LOSE BUT YOUR BRAINS!

A LOGICAL CONCLUSION

"No," said the little man, "that's one thing I never did find out. Perhaps I could have asked Her, but at those times—in that presence—and with so much else to think about, you know, so much strangeness . . . ." He stared at his empty glass. I remembered it was my turn to buy and signalled the waiter. The bar was dimly lit, but not very busy at this hour, so he came over at once.

"Two more," I said.

"Gosh!" My companion started. He'd not been hinting at all, had merely lost himself in reverie. (Unless he was a consummate actor. But that didn't square with his bespectacled, gray-suited ordinariness.) "I'd better not. My wife'll be meeting me here. I told you that, didn't I? She's shopping today. That's why I didn't go straight home when it turned out I could quit early. Came in here to wait, and—I really shouldn't. I don't have the capacity I once did."

"Oh, another won't hurt you, Mr. Greenough," I urged. Of course I didn't believe his fantasy, but I wanted to hear it out. In a long succession of garrulous tavern acquaintances, encountered once and never again, he was unique. He gave in without a struggle.

"You were saying," I reminded him, "you don't know where this other world lies."

"*When* might be a better word," he answered.

"I'm positive it wasn't simply another planet. The moon and stars were the same as here . . . people . . . most of the animals, if not all. To be sure, the laws of nature appeared somewhat different. Magic did work, within limits. But then, perhaps the Warlocks had discovered principles—action at a distance, similarity, or something—real laws that our physicists haven't come across."

"You mean this might have been our own world, but far in the future?"

"Or the past. I don't suppose archeologists know every civilization which has risen and died in a hundred thousand years. . . . And yet, in a long time, wouldn't the constellations change? They hadn't. I've stood in the prow of the *Dragon*, with the rigging creaking behind me and a kraken rising far out across moonlit waves, and seen the same Great Bear turning around the Pole Star that I've watched from my own suburban back yard."

He took out a cigarette. I lit it for him. "I suppose one of those parallel-universes concepts fits best," he decided. "But I'm not certain. Neither Carl Greenough nor Kendrith of Narr were ever much good at mathematics."

"Then you never knew what the Goddess was, either?"

"Oh, heavens, no. I don't want to. Still don't. She was the Goddess, that's all. If you'd like to speculate about some lonely and beautiful and ultimately evolved being, come from elsewhere to live in that blue cave and give our race as much of Her wisdom as we could stand to have . . . go ahead. You'd need to be in the presence itself before you could really see what a meaningless noise any such 'explanation' is."

He didn't have the air of a religious crank, though love was in his tones. Therefore I ventured to suggest that She treated humans rather cavalierly. Not just interchanging two men's minds, across time or space or might-have-been, though that was bad enough. But making poor Greenough, trapped in a pirate's body, fight and suffer and come close to death, again and again, for a cause which was not his own.

He didn't see it that way. "The cause was Hers," he said.

The waiter brought our drinks. I raised my glass. "Here's to you," I said. "Uh, let's leave off theorizing and get back to the story. For two years, you say, Kendrith's pirates fought along with Emperor Oterron, because Kendrith said to and they didn't know another mind was using their chief's body. But what was Kendrith himself, in Greenough's body, here in this world, what was he doing all the while?"

He shrugged. "Being Carl Greenough. Remember, the mind . . . ego . . . whatever you call it . . . isn't separate from the physical nerves and flesh. It's a function of them. What the Goddess replaced was something very subtle. Each of us had full command of the other's language, reflexes, habits, skills. Actual memories of the other's past were blurred and incomplete, but as time went on they improved. Even initially, we could pass muster, claiming a blow on the head had addled our wits a trifle." He grinned. "And being an up-and-coming New York publisher does call for much the same temperament as being a buccaneer from Narr."

"Toughest on Kendrith, in a way," I said. "He could only wait. If Oterron's war was won, and the pirate boss hadn't gotten killed in the process, the Goddess would put the two minds back in their rightful places. Otherwise—" I stopped. After all, I thought, Kendrith would be alive, though captive in this world. And from Greenough's account, he was a roughneck without close emotional ties.

How must it have been for Greenough himself,

knowing his wife was living with his body
unaware his soul was not therein?

Whoa! At this rate I'd soon believe the yarn!

"Go on," I said hastily. "After two years, you've
related, the usurper and his remaining men were
beaten back to a single island. What then?"

"It was vital to capture that stronghold," he
replied. "As long as Roches held fast, the revolt
might break out all over again, for numerous
barons in the Empire were still Muntarists. Or his
distant relative, the Khan of Barjad, might come
riding in from beyond the mountains to help. We
knew Roches had one first-class Warlock in his
employ, old Yamaz, who could turn air into food
and fuel and ammunition. Thus we had no hope of
starving them into surrender. Yamaz could also
turn himself into a condor and fly out across the
Empire, stirring up trouble. We had no comparable adept on our side. (Should I say 'we'?
Well, I guess I've been doing it along. May as well
continue. The Kendrith body was on Oterron's
side, and I naturally tend to think—Anyhow.) You
see, then, in spite of the fact that by now Oterron's
followers much outnumbered those of Roches, the
contest still looked fairly equal. Every day,
Roches' daughter Fiamma used to walk on the
castle walls and taunt us. Her hair blew like fire in
the wind. God, she was beautiful! I think
thousands of the Portula and Sontundar men who
first supported Roches, when he overthrew
Oterron and seized the crown, I think they did
it—against all their own best interests—because
Fiamma had smiled on them. But us she
mocked . . . ."

Greenough climbed to the crow's nest to watch
the attack. From there, atop the *Dragon's* main-
mast, he could look far across the blue waters.
They glittered and danced under the westering

sun; warm airs ruffled the long yellow hair in
which Kendrith of Narr had taken such pride. But
sharply before him stood the image of a northern
ocean, green and unrestful, beneath a pine-topped
cliff down which the River Oush hurled itself in a
thousand-foot leap.

Now cut that out! he told himself. *You never saw
Narr. Kendrith did. It's his homeland, and his
memories making you homesick, because his body
has been so many years down here along the
Chabarro coast. If you must get maudlin, then
wonder how Ellen's rosebushes are doing in Westchester County.*

He tried to summon his wife's face, for comfort,
but found himself too preoccupied. He remembered her eyes and hair were brown, but he couldn't
really see them. Perversely, the full-blown recollection of Unia popped into his consciousness and
wouldn't go away. She was no one—the latest of
many giggling tavern wenches, meek slave girls,
tattooed barbarian lasses, for Carl Greenough had
not long remained able to deny the needs of Kendrith's vigorous flesh—but his mind insisted on re-
calling her in plump and playful detail. Maybe
only as a defense against the disturbing lean
loveliness of Fiamma.

Trumpets jolted him back to immediacy. There
followed a great snapping of catapults, and the
gliders lifted.

Their information was good. In the course of the
past two years, a skilled corps of pilots and paratroopers had developed from Greenough-
Kendrith's original suggestion, and had done
heroic service. But if they could take this island of
Tabirra, all else they had accomplished would
seem as nothing.

Certainly the amphibious tactics which
Greenough had also supplied from his foreign
background, and which had enabled the rightful

Emperor to recapture the Duchy of Portula . . .
certainly they wouldn't work here. Nor would
methods more traditional in this world. Greenough focused his telescope with sweating hands.

Like skeletal birds, the gliders soared up. Ships
and ships and ships lay below them, the besieging
fleet at anchor, sailors of the Empire come to
avenge the years of Roche's misrule, volunteers
from a dozen lesser nations come to avenge his
slaving raids upon them. Not only square-riggers
like the gold-trimmed four-master of Oterron himself, or the oar-powered "aircraft carriers" built
to Greenough's order, or the double-ended
schooners of the Northland pirates who followed
Kendrith were there. Galleons, dhows, feluccas,
caravels, catamarans raked the sky with their
masts. The low sun burned off cannon gaping from
gun ports and off pikes crowding the decks, off
banners and armor and eyes. The gliders swirled
high and lined out toward the island.

"Get 'em!" Greenough heard himself mutter, be-
tween teeth clenched so tight that his jaws hurt.
"Go get 'em, lads! Cast 'em down into
Ginnungagap!"

Was it the waiting that chilled him? Those were
his men—some of them pirates, some Imperials,
some allies, but all of them trained and sworn at
and fought beside, for two wild years—Kendrith's
flying tigers, by the Goddess! If something
happened to them, while he must sit here with
sword in sheath . . . He remembered how young
Iro had talked, on nights when the sea was phos-
phorescent and the ship walked through cool wet
fire. After the war, Iro said, he was going to outfit
a squadron and sail due west across the ocean. For
if the world was round, as all modern
philosophers agreed, then new lands and limitless
adventure must lie on the farther shore. Why
wouldn't Kendrith come too, as admiral? Iro wor-

shipped the big Northling more ardently than he did the Goddess Herself . . . . But Iro hunched in a shell of cloth and bamboo, nearing Tabirra's sharp towers, while Kendrith must wait.

No, his shiver was more than excitement. The air was turning cold, darkening, as the wind rose. A haze in the east thickened unnaturally fast to blue-black cloud masses, where lightning crawled. An aurora shimmered green about the castle.

"Yamaz," he said: a curse.

But Lady, Lady, who could have known the Warlock also had power over storm? He had saved it for his final test, and now—"Come back, you idiots!" Greenough roared futilely at his gliders. "Get back down! You can't make it!"

A few managed a return to the nearest flattop. Most ditched in the sea, where the waves chopped them up but the men swam around until boats could rescue them. Some, Greenough saw dashed to flinders against the island cliffs; and some fell into the surf below, where no man could live. Two landed crippled within the castle walls. It was not good to think of what Roches' garrison did to their crews.

Carl Greenough's eyes stung and blurred. But Kendrith was more used to death, and Kendrith's nerves and glands powered this body's emotions. Even before the aerial disaster was complete, the pirate chief swarmed down the shrouds to the deck.

Gray-bearded, peg-legged Wolden, who was still the toughest man with a battle ax in all this fleet, stumped over to him. Both were simply clad, wearing little more than their weapons and kilts. There would be time enough to don ringmail and conical helmet when fighting broke out. The mate flung a mantle across his captain's shoulders, for the wind was now cold on the skin, loud in the rigging. The sun was not yet down, but already night came boiling from the east.

"What next, skipper?" asked Wolden through the noise.

Greenough rubbed his jaw. Kendrith had adopted the Southland custom of shaving: an exotic ornamentation, like the golden wristlets and silken robes looted from Chabarroan ports, in the years before he had suddenly decreed the pirates would make alliance with exiled Emperor Oterron. The first anger and despair were leaving him and a scheme which he had regarded as a desperation measure began to appear more attractive. Greenough was horrified at its recklessness, or should have been, but Kendrith's slam-bang habits were too strong. He found himself looking forward to the attempt. If they carried it off—what a gorgeous exploit! The balladeers would be singing of it a thousand years hence.

"We'll have a go at the gate, the way we once talked about," he said.

"Huh? You serious?" Wolden's battered face, his whole shaggy body, registered dismay. "It's madness, skipper. Plain, scuppered madness. I got a responsibility—my family's been attending yours since the gods first moved north—I can't let you do any such thing till you beget a proper heir. No, sir, I can't."

"You damn well can. Now go find me some volunteers. Don't tell 'em anything except that it's dangerous and they'll need to be uncommon good swimmers. The Goddess only knows what that old bastard Yamaz can do in the way of eavesdropping."

"Oh, I'll get the men, all right," said Wolden. "About forty, d' you think? But you're not going. Bad enough to risk your neck hellraising halfway across the world, but this—! No, sir, you stay here, same as when the gliders went up."

"That was different," said Greenough. "That was only to be part of an operation. The rest of the fleet would've moved in and attacked the gate while the paratroopers kept the garrison busy, and then I'd have been useful. But under the new plan, the swimmers will *be* the operation, damn near. I'm not going to let my men be chopped into fishbait while I sit here swilling ale."

Or did Greenough speak? Quixotry was more natural to Kendrith's people than to twentieth-century Americans. It felt resoundingly good, too: to Kendrith!

"If you only had an heir," pleaded Wolden. "I don't mean your ordinary by-blow, you must have hundreds but none could rule Bua after you. The yeomen wouldn't accept a base-born's judgments. They want a son by a properly wedded wife, of high enough standing to do the Bua men honor."

"Shut up!" Greenough dismissed the mate with a chopping gesture. At first he had been astonished to see husky warriors jump to his command, the moment he barked at them. Now it seemed only normal. Wolden sighed and went off, among coils and bollards and grimly silent crewmen.

Greenough braced his feet against the roll of the deck. A gust of rain stung his cheeks. *I shouldn't have yelled at him that way,* he thought. *He means well. He's served me and fought for me and given me his blanket in winter lairs and taught me half of what I know. Ever since I was a boy at Bua.*

Almost, he was there again, under the birches that grew along the swift Oush. A meadow starred with daisies rippled in the wind, where horses and the tame unicorn which was the Luck of Bua cropped. On a hillcrest overlooking the sea, the rough-hewn buildings of the thorp blew smoke skyward. In other directions stretched forest and mountain, for this was one of the greatest estates in all Narr. But he had spent most of his time at the dock and in the boathouses, listening as Wolden yarned of journeys across the sea.

No! That was Kendrith! I, Carl Greenough, was born among sober brick walls in Baltimore. I attended a good school, watched many movies, and camped out with the Boy Scouts. Why do I envy Kendrith his childhood?

The broadsword at his hip was a welcome anchor to present reality. He squinted through the rain at the island.

It was not large, but rose sheer on every side, two hundred feet of basalt precipice with murderous white surf below. The fortress walls were built to the very edge, further increasing that height. Above them loomed roofs and spires, gaunt against the lightning. Only at one point was there entrance. The narrow mouth of a lagoon made a gap in the cliff, protected by two skerries that formed a natural breakwater. Roches still kept numerous ships moored inside, against the day when lack of supplies must force his enemy to retreat. Though cannon were placed within the harbor to cover the mouth, it would not have been impossible for armored galleys such as Oterron possessed to force an entrance.

Except . . . a gate of thick bronze bars was set in the stone. No ship could batter that down before the cannon, firing between the bars, sank it. Erenow many had tried, and been knocked to pieces. Tabirra was as impregnable as—

Greenough continued the train of thought, grinning. Sometimes he was brought up short by a recognition of how far he had adopted Kendrith's earthy sense of humor. But mostly, these days, he took it for granted. He wondered how he could re-adapt to the relative decorum of a publisher's life.

Well, he'd be back in a body whose reflexes were conditioned otherwise than this one's. The first several weeks he'd doubtless have to watch himself. Thereafter, this whole world would seem as remote and dreamlike as . . . as his proper world now did.

If Kendrith, in that other body, hadn't loused everything up.

Greenough bit his lip. Ellen. How long since he'd thought about her side of this affair? Not that she knew the truth, but—

Had his final, fleeting appeal to Kendrith registered?

He harked back, trying to recall that instant in the time beyond time and the space beyond space where the Goddess worked. Blurred, unreal, the experience had not been anything men were ever designed to endure, or to remember. First a dreadfulness, when he slumped in his office, thinking he must have had a stroke, when his soul left his body. And then Her presence.

He could certainly remember, in essence, what She told him. (If "told" was the right word.) Infinitely pitying and infinitely ruthless, that flame of a Self ordered Carl Greenough to aid Her worshipper Oterron. She could not destroy Roches and Yamaz and their gang Herself, Her power was not physical and She must work through human tools. After the final victory, if he was still alive, Greenough should return Kendrith's body to the cave, and She would put the two men back into their rightful flesh.

That much he remembered. He had rehearsed it a thousand times since. And he remembered the moment he opened Kendrith's blue eyes, which needed no glasses, and raised Kendrith's muscular frame off the cave floor. Even then he knew the pirate chief had visited this oracular grotto on an impulse which must have originated with its Dweller.

The white-robed priestess led forth outlawed

Oterron, the true Emperor, to meet him . . .

Oh, yes, thought Carl Greenough on the *Dragon's* pitching deck. That much was perfectly clear. But Kendrith's poor little ego had been there too, as overwhelmed as the other man's, so insignificant compared to Her that he had paid it scant heed. *You yourself will not do, Kendrith of Narr,* She had said. *Once out of this place, you would again be beyond My power. You would not join this war from simple love of justice; when ever did the wolf protect the lamb? Nor do you have the alien knowledge and the outworld way of thinking, which may turn the course of battle. So your part is to wait and wear the mask you are given, in that other world. I warn you, it is not like this. Your violent ways would there bring you nothing but punishment, belike death. Therefore curb yourself, wait, and hope.*

Something like that. And—*Be kind to Ellen!* Greenough had cried, as the two souls were flung past each other. He didn't know if it was heard, or had made any difference.

Since then, he'd been too busy to think much about home.

Still was, as a matter of fact.

He dismissed all feelings except an animal pleasure at the thought of combat. And of getting close to Princess Fiamma, if he lived!

Slowly the squall eased off, but the sky remained overcast and the sun went down invisible. A gig from Oterron's flagship drew alongside the *Dragon* and young Count Alunar, gorgeous in red satin and plumed helmet, came aboard. He picked his way through deepening twilight, among hairy half-naked corsairs who squatted on the deck gnawing their hardtack and polishing their weapons with no regard for his rank.

"I say, old chap, a bit of a reverse, what?" he

exclaimed.

"Tell me more," snorted Greenough.

Alunar stroked his shoulder-length curls with a bediamonded hand. "But what are we to do now, eh?" he asked. "I mean to say, we've got to do something. Can't lie here forever. Apart from supplies, why, that Warlock may whistle up a storm that'll jolly well sink us all. What, what, what?"

"Does his majesty have any ideas?"

"No. He sent me here to—that is to say, no, he doesn't. Unless to try building that underwater boat you talked of."

"Useless in this situation," said Greenough. "But I'm glad you're here. Saves me the trouble of sending a man to the Emperor. Because I do have a plan."

"Eh?" Alunar adjusted his monocle. "A plan? Capital! What, may I ask?"

"Stick around. I'm about to inform my men."

Wolden rolled up with a hardbitten two score. Greenough took them into the forepeak, where no magician in bird shape was apt to be hidden. They sat on the deck, on waterbutts and powderkegs, with swords and axes to hand, pantherishly at ease. A single swinging lantern threw yellow light across a scarred brow, a bent nose, a heavy-thewed arm, then a big misshapen shadow gulped down the sight. The timbers groaned and the sea beat loudly just beyond.

"We should have better weather toward morning," said Greenough. "The waves'll be down, too. But plenty dark. We'll edge within a few hundred yards of the gate and go over the side. The ship'll proceed, so the harbor gunners won't suspect anything."

"Till they see our boats come rowing, and give us a blast o' grapeshot," said Hallfrey the Red.

"They won't see us at all," said Greenough.

"We're swimming."

In the silence that followed, the night noises leaped forth. "I think we can seize the guns and stand off the castle garrison, long enough to unchain the gate." Greenough continued after a while. "To be sure, we won't have any armor. Our casualties may be high. They'll be total if everything doesn't work out exactly right. So if any of you want to resign, do so right now. There'll be no hard feelings."

None stirred. "Holy Tree," breathed Vandring the Smith, "what a stunt!"

Wolden had chosen his men well.

Greenough glanced at Alunar's astounded face. "We'll need a brace of galleys standing close in, but out of sight until the gates have been captured," he said. "They should be able to tell that from the noise of fighting! Then they're to row like slaves, to help open the place up and reinforce us. Once we've secured the entrance, we can admit the rest of the fleet, land our men, and fight our way up into the castle conventionally."

Alunar's monocle dropped from his eye and bobbled at the end of its string. "My dear fellow! My dear old chap! You must be crazy."

"I've known that for years," grumbled Wolden.

Hallfrey grinned. "All good Northlings are," he said.

Alunar fiddled with his rapier. "I really don't know if I should approve this."

"You have a better notion?" said Greenough. "Failure can't cost us much more than a few hundred men and a couple of galleys."

"True. True. When did you plan to, ah, embark?"

"Disembark, you damned landlubber. One hour before dawn."

"Good. Capital." Alunar's hesitation ended. "We'll have the fleet alerted and all that sort of rot, well in advance. I'll even have time for a bit of tea and a nap before coming back.''

"You?" Greenough was startled.

"Well, I mean to say, dash it all," said Alunar, "we Imperials can't let you chaps hog all the glory, can we? I do hold a few swimming trophies myself, don't you know."

Remembering how the count had led the cavalry charge which turned the battle of Donda, Greenough gulped and nodded.

After that he must wait. And wait. War was mostly waiting. Pfc. Carl B. Greenough, US 57460280, had found it even more miserable to wait around in Korea than in Fort Bragg. Captain Kendrith, though, sent for a bottle of beer, relaxed on his bunk, swapped a few bawdy reminiscences with Wolden, and fell quickly asleep.

He was awakened shortly before the hour, and went forth into darkness. One hooded lantern picked out the men clustered at the schooner's rail. Like himself, they were naked except for helmets, knives belted at their waists, swords or axes slung across their backs under the shields. The air had turned mild again, but the sea still ran heavily.

Alunar wet his lips. He resembled a pure-bred warhorse, close to the breaking point until he could find release in action. Greenough felt glad that Kendrith's body was of more stolid temperament. If he bought it in this encounter, he bought it, and so what? That was the aristocratic warrior training which spoke: most useful in a world where warriors ruled. He clapped the young man's shoulder. "Have a drink," he advised.

"I d-d-did. On the flagship. A prime Catarunian vintage." The slender form relaxed a trifle. "Just like home, before Roches came to power. Why don't you come home with me after the war, when

we've restored the good old days? To my estate.
I'll show you how a gentleman deserves to live.
Hunting, tourneys, actors and balladeers, feasts,
boozings. And the ladies, well, the whole world
knows what Catarunian ladies are like, and you'll
be *the* social lion." Alunar blew a kiss at heaven.
"What say, Kendrith?"

*And afterward sail off with Iro to discover a new
hemisphere? And eventually, rich in gold, richer in
contentment, settle down to be the squire of Bua?*

*No! That's for Kendrith! I'm to go back and com-
mute every day between Manhattan and
Westchester, remember? My proper job is to woo
authors, and ride herd on editors, and goose the
sales department, and out-argue the tax collector.
Occasionally I'll let myself publish a book I know
is going to lose money, because it's good, and that
will feel very adventurous.*

Greenough spat over the side. "Let's go," he
said.

He led the way down a Jacob's ladder. The
water closed about him, chill and sensuous. He
needed all his muscles to keep direction in the
waves, which broke over his head with a roar the
helmet magnified. But Kendrith's body was a
superb engine.

The schooner slid past and was lost in the dark.
Ahead, a deeper blackness against the sky, rose
Tabirra. He heard the surf boom on its reefs.
There were no stars, but a cold blue light burned
high in the air at the topmost pinnacle of the
castle. Did Yamaz hunch over his books? Or
Roches scowl and twist the rings on his big
fingers? Or Fiamma stand at a mirror, combing
her fire-colored hair before she dressed herself to
walk the parapets and mock the Emperor?
Greenough struck out more vigorously.

Close up, he saw white blurs defining a channel,
where the sea exploded on the guardian rocks. It

was calm in between. He eased his pace, gliding with enormous caution, up to the mast-high bars across the lagoon mouth. There he stopped, hanging onto a crosspiece while he caught his breath.

The metal was cold and hard in his grasp. Salt water ran down his helmet and down his face; the cap and hair beneath were sodden. A wan light flickered from either side of the entrance, touching with red the cannon that jutted out on concrete emplacements. Beyond gleamed the broad sheet of the lagoon, where ships were scattered like blocks. The cliffs rose on all sides, the castle behind the harbor.

He looked to right and left. The others had joined him. They clung to green bronze: a glimpsed shield, a shadow in the water, a mumbled oath. Despite all contempt for danger, Greenough's heart thumped.

This is it. Here goes!

He imitated a gull's mew and slipped between the bars. At the signal, his men followed. On the other side, ledges had been built along the cliff walls. They were deserted. Greenough reached up, chinned himself high, got a knee over the edge and sprang to his feet. Swiftly he slipped the shield from his back and onto his left arm, big and round and comforting to his bareness. He drew the sword at his shoulder and padded forward.

Immediately beyond the angle of the deep gateway, shielded from the sea breezes, a small fire on a hearthstone warmed Roches' gunners. They were half a dozen, seated next to a stack of cannonballs and a powder shed. Their boots and hose, curiasses and kettle helmets, were similar to Imperial uniform. One stood up, leaning on a pike. *City scum!* thought Greenough. *They wouldn't have heard me if I'd ridden a buffalo.*

He rushed.

The pikeman saw him and yelled. Firelight glistened off eyeballs beneath the headpiece. Greenough raised his shield. The point glided off its brass facing. Before the man could club his shaft, Greenough was in under his guard. The sword rose and fell. There came the heavy sensation of metal biting flesh. Wounded in the thigh, the pikeman went to his knees.

"To arms! Attack! Attack at the portal!" A trumpet brayed. Hallfrey charged and beheaded the trumpeter with one swing of blade. But the harm was done.

Another sentry stood beyond the fallen pikeman. Through the gloom, Greenough saw him raise an ax. He dropped to one knee himself, holding the shield up so he could take the blow with all his shoulder. Even so, the shock numbed his arm. He heard the wooden framework crack somewhere. His broadsword chopped at the axman's nearer wrist. It wasn't there, quite. This fellow was good! Greenough bounced back to his feet and cut again. His blow was parried by the ax handle. As he crouched, looking for an opening, the wounded pikeman seized him around the legs.

He toppled. The pikeman fell on top of him and slashed at his throat with a dagger. "Nothing doing!" Greenough snarled. He pushed the boss of his shield into the man's teeth. Rolling free, he saw the ax descend where he had been. The pikeman got in its way. Kendrith's laughter barked forth. He fell on the axman anew, wounded him also, but continued to have a fight on his hands. Sparks showered where steel met steel. They circled about, smiting. Greenough took several cuts on his bare skin, and several of his own blows were turned by the opponent's breastplate.

The cannon bulked beside him. Hardly stopping to think, he ducked around the barrel and vaulted to the top. The axman blundered past, hunting for him in the dull shadow-choked light. Greenough sprang from above, landed with both feet on the man's shoulders. He crashed to the dock. Greenough killed him.

Panting, he looked about. The fight was over, as the outnumbered gunners were cut down. One pirate was dead. On the steps which led down from the heights to the rear of the harbor, lanterns bobbed. He heard voices calling up there, trumpets, drums, a metal clangor. The garrison would arrive in moments.

"Get going!" he rapped.

Wolden and Vandring hefted their tools and disappeared into the night. Opening yonder gate would be no simple job, even with help from a galley when one arrived. It was fastened with chains heavy enough to anchor a ship, whose locks must be broken. Meanwhile the workers required protection.

"All clear over here, old chap," called Alunar merrily through the night, from the other side of the channel. "But the ruddy cannon can't be swung around to cover the shoreward approach."

"I knew that," answered Greenough. "So mine the approach." He fumbled his way into the shed, picked up a bag, and ran out again. His men labored with him. They piled the stuff some distance from the gun and returned, laying a powder train. Someone handed Greenough a brand from the fire.

"Take shelter, or lie down flat," instructed the captain. "All hell is about to let out for noon." Several men chuckled. He'd gotten quite a reputation as a wit in the last couple of years, merely by translating the cliches of his own world. He wondered, briefly and irrelevantly, if Kendrith had done likewise.

The garrison swarmed down onto the docks and hurried toward the portal. A few primitive hand guns barked. More to be feared were the cross-bows, whose quarrels buzzed nastily past Greenough's ears. Now he could see the faint sheen of armor, as the leading squad climbed his barricade . . . . He touched the brand to the powder.

Fire spurted. A wave of it rose to the sky. Some bags flared up, others exploded. Sparks and bolts and meteors fountained from end to end of the harbor. The ground jumped beneath Greenough's belly. Thunder banged in his head. Darkness followed, full of echoes and hot afterimages.

For a space only the injured screamed. Then orders were shouted, whistles blown, a trumpet winded. The rebels reformed and advanced. They had guts, for sure! Unless it was only that they knew how little merciful the people they had squeezed and tormented would be to them.

"For the Goddess' sake," bawled Greenough, "aren't you ever going to get that obscenity lock busted?"

A ragged line of soldiers came into view. Behind them, some of the ships which had been ignited by flying fire started to burn more brightly. They limned the walls and stark towers of the castle against night.

"Fall in," snapped Greenough. His score stood shield to shield, next the cannon, barring the way to the gate. Thus they would stand till relieved, or slain.

A big, bearded cuirassier darted at him, sword aloft. He interposed his shield. The blow rebounded, grazing the nosepiece of his helmet. He cut at the neck. The cuirassier parried. Their blades locked. For a moment, black under a lifting yellow curtain of fire, they strained muscle against muscle. Kendrith's body was stronger. The soldier's blade was forced back to his chest. Greenough made a sudden, sharp thrust. His point entered below the chin. The cuirassier gurgled blood.

As he sank, Greenough struck at the man behind him. An ax thundered on the Northling helmet. Greenough staggered, regained his feet, scythed at the ankles of someone else. Then it was strike and ward and strike again, grunting, sweating, gasping for breath, slipping in blood, and one by one seeing his comrades die.

His shield was beaten to a rag. He threw it into a man's face and defended himself with sword alone. A blade furrowed his calf. He chopped down and struck the arms which had wielded it, but his edge was so blunted that he didn't cut deeply. Bones broke, though. Hallfrey went down at his side, a spear in his guts. The buccaneer line dissolved into a few survivors, each surrounded by a pack of enemies. A halberd smote Greenough's sword so fiercely that it was torn from his grasp.

He knocked a man down with his fist, snatched a cannonball from the pile, and threw it at a tall person in a visored helmet. The helmet crumpled. The skull beneath went too. Greenough backed up to the great gun. At least they wouldn't kill him from behind.

A fresh racket broke loose. Through the brightening firelight, the haze of smoke and clamor of destruction, he saw Oterron's men. The gate was open and the galleys had entered. The enemy pulled away.

He sat down and wheezed.

"Here, skipper. I got this from the boat."

Greenough snatched the wine crock and drained half of it. Wolden chuckled in his gray whiskers. The mate's blacksmith hammer was splashed red. Evidently he'd waded into battle the moment the gate was unlocked. Strength flowed back through Greenough. He climbed up on the gun and peered through the murk. Another Imperial ship warped into the harbor and began disgorging men. But it would take time to land the whole army, or even enough to outnumber the rebels. Meanwhile they were retreating in good order.

"If they reach the castle, they'll still have a chance of standing us off," Greenough said. "We've got to forestall that. Gather a bunch of troopers, Wolden."

He searched among the fallen around him until he found a shield to his liking. No sword looked worthwhile, but that axman who gave him so much trouble at first had wielded a lovely weapon . . . ah, here. Impulsively, Greenough closed the staring eyes. That had been a brave lad. "Thanks," he said, and went to rejoin Wolden.

The mate had assembled some thirty armored Imperials, who gaped at their leaders' unconventional costume. "We want to cut the enemy off from the castle," Greenough told them. "We might also bag good King Roches."

"Didn't you know, skipper?" said Wolden. "That's been done."

"What?"

"That big man over there, who got his noodle bashed in with a cannonball somebody pitched. I noticed royal insignia on his breastplate, and opened the visor to make sure. I've seen him myself a few times before the war, when I came trading."

"Why . . . in that case—No. I suppose we're in as much danger while Yamaz is alive."

"And Fiamma," said a man-at-arms harshly.

"Well—uh—a woman can't succeed to the throne, so if she was safely married off, to somebody without Muntarist pretensions—" Greenough felt his countenance go hot. The fire in the harbor wasn't entirely responsible. "Come on, you sons," he growled.

They hastened over the piers, avoiding combat. The principal fight on this side was taking place near the cliff, where the rebels had rallied into formation and were beating off the Imperial attacks as they moved slowly toward the stairs. On Greenough's right, the lagoon was a cauldron, bellowing and reeking, its flames as high as the castle walls. Heat gusted around him. Still another ship negotiated the gateway and started landing men.

Greenough put foot on rock-hewn treads. Smoke stung his eyes. Halfway up, it was so thick he must grope through red-shot murk. But the air at the clifftop was clear. He looked across a sea gleaming like mercury in the first false dawnlight. Had the battle lasted that long? Or, rather, only that long?

The iron door at the head of the staircase was open. A squad of sentries challenged the approaching men. "For the House of Muntar," Greenough yelled back. Not the rebel password, surely, but their slogan—and what with the similarity of equipment, and the general confusion—The door was not closed in his face. He fell upon the squad with his troop and cut them to pieces.

Beyond, a wide, paved court reached to the far side of the island. Part of it was covered by gardens, part by lesser buildings. Mountainous in the center rose the donjon keep. Smoke and fog streamers drifted across emptiness, under the graying sky. "Stay here," Greenough commanded. "Shut the gate against the enemy. They won't have a chance to ram it down, with our forces at their backs. I'm going to the entrance on the other side."

The flagstones were cool and wet with dew under his feet. The threshing of battle seemed very distant. Until he rounded a buttress and saw the twin gate, where men struck each other. So someone else had had the same idea! Greenough ran to help.

A clear, happy voice soared above the cursing and clashing. Alunar. Good to know he was alive. As Greenough approached, the count broke through the defending line and crossed swords with a guard.

A blackness glided down above them. For one second, Greenough thought wildly about clouds . . . nothing else could be so huge. . . . He saw wings and beak and talons. The condor snatched at Alunar's head.

Greenough hurled his ax.

The bird shrieked as it fell. The enemy guardsman stared, threw down his sword, and ran. Alunar sprang to skewer the condor. A wing knocked him rolling. Then the black bird shuddered, once, and became an old dead man.

Greenough helped Alunar rise. "Whoof!" said the noble. "A rum go, what? Blasted thing would've had my eyes in another tick. Much thanks, old chap."

"Yamaz?" asked Greenough.

Alunar nodded. "Quite. Nice work."

"And Roches is dead. I think we've won."

"True. Take an hour or so yet to convince the jolly old opposition." Alunar withdrew his rapier from the carcass, but its point was corroded off. He flung the weapon aside. There was no need for it anyway. Shaken, the sentries had fled down the stairs. His own men warded the door.

"Any other holdouts up here?" wondered Greenough.

"Doesn't seem so." Alunar swept the utter stillness of the castle with a monocled glance.

"Let's check. The boys won't need our help to maintain these gates."

As he swung across the courtyard with his friend, Greenough felt his heartbeat accelerate. By the time he had entered the high main archway of the keep, his blood was brawling.

Victory! A whole empire ready to embrace and reward the Northling who had liberated her. Afterward, a world to wander, and the dear green hills of Bua, and—

No, what was he thinking? He could go home to Ellen now. That was all he was thinking. Nothing more. The grotto of the Goddess lay a few days' sail from here. He could be himself, Carl Greenough, in his own proper body and his own proper house, within the week.

The castle chambers were magnificent with tapestry and beaten gold. What a place to loot! Slaves bent low to conquerors bloodstained, bristle-chinned, clad in helmets and smoke smudges. "Where's Princess Fiamma?" Alunar inquired. "We'd best make sure of her, don't you know. Potential troublemaker, yes, rather."

"Especially with her father to avenge," nodded Greenough. His quick, irrational sadness jumped over to joy when Alunar replied:

"Oh, that doesn't matter. It's been notorious for years, she couldn't stand him. He murdered her mother, you see, in one of his drunken rages. But because of pride and all that sort of rot, she stayed by him as Princess of the Empire. Even now, I

wager, she won't swear fealty to Oterron; or she'll
break whatever oath she does give at the first
opportunity. There are still plenty of Muntarists
around. If she married one of 'em—'' Alunar
sighed. ''At the same time, one rather hates to
decapitate her. Ungallant, what?''

A shaking eunuch conducted them to the
gynaeceum. Its door was locked. Greenough
rapped with his ax. ''Open up in there!'' he called.

''Open to a barbarian?'' answered a voice which
was ice and music. ''I'll see you in Ginnungagap
first!''

With Kendrith's blunt practicality, Greenough
struck the lock a few shrewd ax blows. It burst. He
entered.

A vase whizzed through the air and shattered on
his helmet. Her maidservants screamed and fled
through the dawnlit rooms beyond, but Fiamma
sprang at Greenough with a knife.

He barely ducked the blow. She hissed and tried
again. He caught her arm and yanked the dagger
free. As it tinkled to the floor, she cursed him and
tried to claw his eyes. He closed one big hand
around both her wrists, clasping them firmly
behind her back. Her thin robe got torn in the
process, but he didn't mind. With his other arm he
pulled her close.

Never had he imagined so much beauty.

It was as if someone else spoke with his voice,
arrogant and desirous: ''Your cause is finished. I,
Kendrith, broke you. Now I've come for my
booty.''

''You filthy savage!'' She bit him. He cuffed her.

Laughing, he picked her up. She struggled like a
lynx, but he was so much stronger that he merely
enjoyed it. ''Let's talk this over in private,'' he said,
and carried her into the next room.

Alunar raised his brows, clicked his tongue, and
settled down to wait.

Much later, when Oterron's men swarmed triumphant through the castle, Greenough emerged. Fiamma walked beside him, leaning on his arm. Now and then she rubbed her tousled red head against his shoulder, or nuzzled his cheek. "Tell me more about Narr," she purred. "I can't wait to get there."

"I can," he said. "We'll take the *Dragon* and cruise along the Chabarro, visit Alunar, take a long vacation. How I need one!"

Her lashes fluttered downward. "As my lord wishes. What do you plan beyond that . . . for us?"

He didn't answer.

But surely the Goddess wouldn't mind if he took a month with Fiamma. Only one little month.

He stood in too much awe of Her not to return them. But his unaided sense of duty would never have drawn him back.

Back to being Carl Greenough.

The little man finished his drink and looked at his watch. "Where can Ellen have got to?" he fussed. "She was supposed to have been here half an hour ago."

"You know what women are like," I smiled.

"Not in that other world," he said with a touch of wistfulness.

"You've certainly made the place sound like an adolescent's paradise."

"Really? I didn't mean to. In talking about it, naturally I dwelt on the more colorful aspects. There was also the usual quota of everyday problems and everyday frustrations. Of course."

"Then why didn't you want to return home?"

"I'd been another man for so long. Can't you see? I told you several times, the body and the mind are indivisible. I'd thought with his brains, wrestled with his problems, played with his friends, wondered what lay beyond his horizons, for two years. I'd become him. Far more, toward the end, than I remained my old self."

He gazed into his empty glass. "It makes me wonder what the self is," he mused. "What's the basic thing we call 'I'? Not a bundle of personality traits. You're nothing like the person you were twenty years ago; yet both have been you. Isn't your ego, your inmost identity, isn't it precisely the continuity of experience? The evolution itself, from phase to phase of life?"

I wasn't interested in half-baked philosophy, and told him so. "Once you'd made the transition," I said, "you'd soon grow to prefer your original body again. Wouldn't you?"

"Well, no." He frowned in somewhat alcoholic thought. "I don't believe so. I'd always miss what I'd had in those two years—a freshness, a glamor, a sense of accomplishing something important and meaningful instead of playing with uninteresting toys. And my wife, the new one I'd gained. I loved her, you can't imagine how I loved her. When I felt the Goddess wrench my mind free, it was worse than dying. May I never have such a moment again."

His distress was so plain that I wondered with a chill along my spine, if he really had been telling me a fable for our mutual amusement. Perhaps he believed it! Though he didn't act like a man with delusions.

"How I cursed Greenough and his damned sense of duty," he muttered. "I did so in Her very presence. When our egos met, and merged, and scanned each other's memories of the last two years, I told him what a dreary fool he was."

"At least you—Hey! Greenough, did you say?" I gaped across the table.

He looked surprised too, then recovered his poise. "Why, sure," he said. "I didn't mean to admit it, but there's no reason why I shouldn't. If you think back, you'll note I never claimed otherwise. Who do you suppose I'd be?

"Look, for two years I'd been here, among towers as high as mountains, served by machines more powerful than magic, the most fabulous parts of the world no further away than a few days' flying. Flying!" His eyes glittered behind their lenses. "No famines, no pestilences, no smoky chimneys, no plodding sailships and springless wagons, no surly slaves, no ignorant barbarians, no unwashed hussies or damned would-be queens, half cat—the sweetest, loyallest women ever created, all to myself! And I could relax, didn't have to take a spear along everytime I went out for a breath of air. And my IQ must have been thirty points higher, with all that that means in the way of awareness. And I'd applied some notions of my own world to the publishing business and had just really got them going good. In another five years I'd be running rings around my competitors. Judas priest!" he burst out. "Did you think *I* wanted to return?"

I sat still for a while. The bar clattered around us, filling up with the cocktail hour crowd. "So you didn't?" I asked gently.

He smiled. "No. The Goddess laughed and put us both where we desired. I'll always remember Her laughter."

He twisted around in his seat. An ordinary-looking woman had come through the door, her arms full of packages. "Ah, there's Ellen," he said, rising. "Will you join us for a drink?"

I got up also. Plain to see, his invitation was from politeness only. He was starting to regret his lubricated tongue. In any case, he had eyes for none but the woman.

"No, thanks," I said. "I've had enough."

THE VALOR OF
CAPPEN VARRA

The wind came from the north with sleet on its back. Raw shuddering gusts whipped the sea till the ship lurched and men felt driven spindrift stinging their faces. Beyond the rail there was winter night, a moving blackness where the waves rushed and clamored; straining into the great dark, men sensed only the bitter salt of sea-scud, the nettle of sleet and the lash of wind.

Cappen lost his footing as the ship heaved beneath him, his hands were yanked from the icy rail and he went stumbling to the deck. The bilge water was new coldness on his drenched clothes. He struggled back to his feet, leaning on a rower's bench and wishing miserably that his quaking stomach had more to lose. But he had already chucked his share of stockfish and hardtack, to the laughter of Svearek's men, when the gale started.

Numb fingers groped anxiously for the harp on his back. It still seemed intact in its leather case. He didn't care about the sodden wadmal breeks and tunic that hung around his skin. The sooner they rotted off him, the better. The thought of the silks and linens of Croy was a sigh in him.

Why had he come to Norren?

A gigantic form, vague in the whistling dark, loomed beside him and gave him a steadying hand. He could barely hear the blond giant's bull tones:

"Ha, easy there, lad. Methinks the sea horse road is overly rough for yer feet."

"Ulp," said Cappen. His slim body huddled on the bench, too miserable to care. The sleet pattered against his shoulders and the spray congealed in his red hair.

Torbek of Norren squinted into the night. It made his leathery face a mesh of wrinkles. "A bitter feast of Yolner we hold," he said. " 'Twas a madness of the king's, that he would guest with his brother across the water. Now the other ships are blown from us and the fire is drenched out and we lie alone in the Wolf's Throat."

Wind piped shrill in the rigging. Cappen could just see the longboat's single mast reeling against the sky. The ice on the shrouds made it a pale pyramid. Ice everywhere, thick on the rails and benches, sheathing the dragon head and the carved stern-post, the ship rolling and staggering under the great march of waves, men bailing and bailing in the half-frozen bilge to keep her afloat, and too much wind for sail or oars. Yes—a cold feast!

"But then, Svearek has been strange since the troll took his daughter, three years ago," went on Torbek. He shivered in a way the winter had not caused. "Never does he smile, and his once open hand grasps tight about the silver and his men have poor reward and no thanks. Yes, strange—" His small frost-blue eyes shifted to Cappen Varra, and the unspoken thought ran on beneath them: Strange, even that he likes you, the wandering bard from the south. Strange, that he will have you in his hall when you cannot sing as his men would like.

Cappen did not care to defend himself. He had drifted up toward the northern barbarians with the idea that they would well reward a minstrel who could offer them something more than their

own crude chants. It had been a mistake; they
didn't care for roundels or sestinas, they yawned
at the thought of roses white and red under the
moon of Caronne, a moon less fair than my lady's
eyes. Nor did a man of Croy have the size and
strength to compel their respect; Cappen's light
blade flickered swiftly enough so that no one
cared to fight him, but he lacked the power of
sheer bulk. Svearek alone had enjoyed hearing
him sing, but he was niggardly and his brawling
thorp was an endless boredom to a man used to
the courts of southern princes.

If he had but had the manhood to leave— But he
had delayed, because of a hope that Svearek's
coffers would open wider; and now he was
dragged along over the Wolf's Throat to a mid-
winter feast which would have to be celebrated on
the sea.

"Had we but fire—" Torbek thrust his hands
inside his cloak, trying to warm them a little. The
ship rolled till she was almost on her beam ends;
Torbek braced himself with practiced feet, but
Cappen went into the bilge again.

He sprawled there for a while, his bruised body
refusing movement. A weary sailor with a bucket
glared at him through dripping hair. His shout
was dim under the hoot and skirl of wind: "If ye
like it so well down here, then help us bail!"

" 'Tis not yet my turn," groaned Cappen, and got
slowly up.

The wave which had nearly swamped them had
put out the ship's fire and drenched the wood
beyond hope of lighting a new one. It was cold fish
and sea-sodden hardtack till they saw land again
—if they ever did.

As Cappen raised himself on the leeward side,
he thought he saw something gleam, far out across
the wrathful night. A wavering red spark— He
brushed a stiffened hand across his eyes, wonder-

ing if the madness of wind and water had struck through into his own skull. A gust of sleet hid it again. But—

He fumbled his way aft between the benches. Huddled figures cursed him wearily as he stepped on them. The ship shook herself, rolled along the edge of a boiling black trough, and slid down into it; for an instant, the white teeth of combers grinned above her rail, and Cappen waited for an end to all things. Then she mounted them again, somehow, and wallowed toward another valley.

King Svearek had the steering oar and was trying to hold the longboat into the wind. He had stood there since sundown, huge and untiring, legs braced and the bucking wood cradled in his arms. More than human he seemed, there under the icicle loom of the stern-post, his gray hair and beard rigid with ice. Beneath the horned helmet, the strong moody face turned right and left, peering into the darkness. Cappen felt smaller than usual when he approached the steersman.

He leaned close to the king, shouting against the blast of winter: "My lord, did I not see firelight?"

"Aye. I spied it an hour ago," grunted the king. "Been trying to steer us a little closer to it."

Cappen nodded, too sick and weary to feel reproved. "What is it?"

"Some island—there are many in this stretch of water—now shut up!"

Cappen crouched under the rail and waited.

The lonely red gleam seemed nearer when he looked again. Svearek's tones were lifting in a roar that hammered through the gale from end to end of the ship: "Hither! Come hither to me, all men not working!"

Slowly, they groped to him, great shadowy forms in wool and leather, bulking over Cappen like storm-gods. Svearek nodded toward the flickering glow. "One of the islands, somebody must be living there. I cannot bring the ship closer for fear of surf, but one of ye should be able to take the boat thither and fetch us fire and dry wood. Who will go?''

They peered overside, and the uneasy movement that ran among them came from more than the roll and pitch of the deck underfoot.

Beorna the Bold spoke at last, it was hardly to be heard in the noisy dark: ''I never knew of men living hereabouts. It must be a lair of trolls.''

''Aye, so . . . aye, they'd but eat the man we sent . . . out oars, let's away from here though it cost our lives . . . '' The frightened mumble was low under the jeering wind.

Svearek's face drew into a snarl. ''Are ye men or puling babes? Hack yer way through them, if they be trolls, but bring me fire!''

''Even a she-troll is stronger than fifty men, my king,'' cried Torbek. ''Well ye know that, when the monster woman broke through our guards three years ago and bore off Hildigund.''

''Enough!'' It was a scream in Svearek's throat. ''I'll have yer craven heads for this, all of ye, if ye gang not to the isle!''

They looked at each other, the big men of Norren, and their shoulders hunched bearlike. It was Beorna who spoke it for them: ''No, that ye will not. We are free housecarls, who will fight for a leader—but not for a madman.''

Cappen drew back against the rail, trying to make himself small.

''All gods turn their faces from ye!'' It was more than weariness and despair which glared in Svearek's eyes, there was something of death in them. ''I'll go myself, then!''

''No, my king. That we will not find ourselves in.''

''I am the king.''

''And we are yer housecarls, sworn to defend ye —even from yerself. Ye shall not go.''

The ship rolled again, so violently that they were

all thrown to starboard. Cappen landed on
Torbek, who reached up to shove him aside and
then closed one huge fist on his tunic.

"Here's our man!"

"Hi!" yelled Cappen.

Torbek hauled him roughly back to his feet. "Ye
cannot row or bail yer fair share," he growled,
"nor do ye know the rigging or any skill of a sailor
—'tis time ye made yerself useful!"

"Aye, aye—let little Cappen go—mayhap he can
sing the trolls to sleep—" The laughter was hard
and barking, edged with fear, and they all hemmed
him in.

"My lord!" bleated the minstrel. "I am your
guest—"

Svearek laughed unpleasantly, half crazily.
"Sing them a song," he howled. "Make a fine roun
—whatever ye call it—to the troll-wife's beauty.
And bring us some fire, little man, bring us a flame
less hot than the love in yer breast for yer lady!"

Teeth grinned through matted beards. Someone
hauled on the rope from which the ship's small
boat trailed, dragging it close. "Go, ye scut!" A
horny hand sent Cappen stumbling to the rail.

He cried out once again. An ax lifted above his
head. Someone handed him his own slim sword,
and for a wild moment he thought of fighting. Useless—too many of them. He buckled on the sword
and spat at the men. The wind tossed it back in his
face, and they raved with laughter.

Over the side! The boat rose to meet him, he
landed in a heap on drenched planks and looked
up into the shadowy faces of the northmen. There
was a sob in his throat as he found the seat and
took out the oars.

An awkward pull sent him spinning from the
ship, and then the night had swallowed it and he
was alone. Numbly, he bent to the task. Unless he

wanted to drown, there was no place to go but the island.

He was too weary and ill to be much afraid, and such fear as he had was all of the sea. It could rise over him, gulp him down, the gray horses would gallop over him and the long weeds would wrap him when he rolled dead against some skerry. The soft vales of Caronne and the roses in Croy's gardens seemed like a dream. There was only the roar and boom of the northern sea, hiss of sleet and spindrift, crazed scream of wind, he was alone as man had ever been and he would go down to the sharks alone.

The boat wallowed, but rode the waves better than the longship. He grew dully aware that the storm was pushing him toward the island. It was becoming visible, a deeper blackness harsh against the night.

He could not row much in the restless water; he shipped the oars and waited for the gale to capsize him and fill his mouth with the sea. And when it gurgled in his throat, what would his last thought be? Should he dwell on the lovely image of Ydris in Seilles, she of the long bright hair and the singing voice? But then there had been the tomboy laughter of dark Falkny, he could not neglect her. And there were memories of Elvanna in her castle by the lake, and Sirann of the Hundred Rings, and beauteous Vardry, and hawk-proud Lona, and— No, he could not do justice to any of them in the little time that remained. What a pity it was!

No, wait, that unforgettable night in Nienne, the beauty which had whispered in his ear and drawn him close, the hair which had fallen like a silken tent about his cheeks . . . ah, that had been the summit of his life, he would go down into darkness with her name on his lips . . . But hell! What *had* her name been, now?

Cappen Varra, minstrel of Croy, clung to the bench and sighed.

The great hollow voice of surf lifted about him, waves sheeted across the gunwale and the boat danced in madness. Cappen groaned, huddling into the circle of his own arms and shaking with cold. Swiftly, now, the end of all sunlight and laughter, the dark and lonely road which all men must tread. *O Ilwarra of Syr, Aedra in Tholis, could I but kiss you once more—*

Stones grated under the keel. It was a shock like a sword going through him. Cappen looked unbelievingly up. The boat had drifted to land—he was alive!

It kindled the sun in his breast. Weariness fell from him, and he leaped overside, not feeling the chill of the shallows. With a grunt, he heaved the boat up on the narrow strand and knotted the painter to a fang-like jut of reef.

Then he looked about him. The island was small, utterly bare, a savage loom of rock rising out of the sea that growled at its feet and streamed off its shoulders. He had come into a little cliff-walled bay, somewhat sheltered from the wind. He was here!

For a moment he stood, running through all he had learned about the trolls which infested these northlands. Hideous and soulless dwellers underground, they knew not old age; a sword could hew them asunder, but before it reached their deep-seated life, their unhuman strength had plucked a man apart. Then they ate him—

Small wonder the northmen feared them. Cappen threw back his head and laughed. He had once done a service for a mighty wizard in the south, and his reward hung about his neck, a small silver amulet. The wizard had told him that no supernatural being could harm anyone who carried a piece of silver.

The Northmen said that a troll was powerless against a man who was not afraid; but, of course, only to see one was to feel the heart turn to ice. They did not know the value of silver, it seemed—odd that they shouldn't, but they did not. Because Cappen Varra did, he had no reason to be afraid; therefore he was doubly safe, and it was but a matter of talking the troll into giving him some fire. If indeed there was a troll here, and not some harmless fisherman.

He whistled gaily, wrung part of the water from his cloak and ruddy hair, and started along the beach. In the sleety gloom, he could just see a hewn-out path winding up one of the cliffs and he set his feet on it.

At the top of the path, the wind ripped his whistling from his lips. He hunched his back against it and walked faster, swearing as he stumbled on hidden rocks. The ice-sheathed ground was slippery underfoot, and the cold bit like a knife.

Rounding a crag, he saw redness glow in the face of a steep bluff. A cave mouth, a fire within—he hastened his steps, hungering for warmth, until he stood in the entrance.

"Who comes?"

It was a hoarse bass cry that rang and boomed between walls of rock; ice and horror were in it, and for a moment Cappen's heart stumbled. Then he remembered the amulet and strode boldly inside.

"Good evening, mother," he said cheerily.

The cave widened out into a stony hugeness that gaped with tunnels leading further underground. The rough, soot-blackened walls were hung with plundered silks and cloth-of-gold, gone ragged through age and damp; the floor was strewn with stinking rushes, and gnawed bones were heaped in disorder. Cappen saw the skulls of men among them. In the center of the room, a great fire leaped and blazed, throwing billows of heat against him; some of its smoke went up a hole in the roof, the rest stung his eyes to watering and he sneezed.

The troll-wife crouched on the floor, snarling at him. She was quite the most hideous thing Cappen had ever seen: nearly as tall as he, she was twice as broad and thick, and the knotted arms hung down past bowed knees till their clawed fingers brushed the ground. Her head was beast-like, almost split in half by the tusked mouth, the eyes wells of darkness, the nose an ell long; her hairless skin was green and cold, moving on her bones. A tattered shift covered some of her monstrousness, but she was still a nightmare.

"Ho-ho, ho-ho!" Her laughter roared out, hungry and hollow as the surf around the island. Slowly, she shuffled closer. "So my dinner comes walking in to greet me, ho, ho, ho! Welcome, sweet flesh, welcome, good marrow-filled bones, come in and be warmed."

"Why, thank you, good mother." Cappen shucked his cloak and grinned at her through the smoke. He felt his clothes steaming already. "I love you too."

Over her shoulder, he suddenly saw the girl. She was huddled in a corner, wrapped in fear, but the eyes that watched him were as blue as the skies over Caronne. The ragged dress did not hide the gentle curves of her body, nor did the tear-streaked grime spoil the lilt of her face. "Why, 'tis springtime in here," cried Cappen, "and Prima-vera herself is strewing flowers of love."

"What are you talking about, crazy man?" rumbled the troll-wife. She turned to the girl. "Heap the fire, Hildigund, and set up the roasting spit. Tonight I feast!"

"Truly I see heaven in female form before me," said Cappen.

The troll scratched her misshapen head.

"You must surely be from far away, moonstruck man," she said.

"Aye, from golden Croy am I wandered, drawn over dolorous seas and empty wild lands by the fame of loveliness waiting here; and now that I have seen you, my life is full." Cappen was looking at the girl as he spoke, but he hoped the troll might take it as aimed her way.

"It will be fuller," grinned the monster. "Stuffed with hot coals while yet you live." She glanced back at the girl. "What, are you not working yet, you lazy tub of lard? Set up the spit, I said!"

The girl shuddered back against a heap of wood. "No," she whispered. "I cannot—not . . . not for a man."

"Can and will, my girl," said the troll, picking up a bone to throw at her. The girl shrieked a little.

"No, no, sweet mother. I would not be so ungallant as to have beauty toil for me." Cappen plucked at the troll's filthy dress. "It is not meet—in two senses. I only came to beg a little fire; yet will I bear away a greater fire within my heart."

"Fire in your guts, you mean! No man ever left me save as picked bones."

Cappen thought he heard a worried note in the animal growl. "Shall we have music for the feast?" he asked mildly. He unslung the case of his harp and took it out.

The troll-wife waved her fists in the air and danced with rage. "Are you mad? I tell you, you are going to be eaten!"

The minstrel plucked a string on his harp. "This wet air has played the devil with her tone," he murmured sadly.

The troll-wife roared wordlessly and lunged at him. Hildigund covered her eyes. Cappen tuned his harp. A foot from his throat, the claws stopped.

"Pray do not excite yourself, mother," said the

bard. "I carry silver, you know."

"What is that to me? If you think you have a charm which will turn me, know that there is none. I've no fear of your metal!"

Cappen threw back his head and sang:

"A lovely lady full oft lies.
The light that lies within her eyes
and lies and lies, is no surprise.
All her unkindness can devise
to trouble hearts that seek the prize
which is herself, are angel lies—"

"Aaaarrgh!" It was like thunder drowning him out. The troll-wife turned and went on all fours and poked up the fire with her nose.

Cappen stepped softly around her and touched the girl. She looked up with a little whimper.

"You are Svearek's only daughter, are you not?" he whispered.

"Aye—" She bowed her head, a strengthless despair weighing it down. "The troll stole me away three winters agone. It has tickled her to have a princess for slave—but soon I shall roast on her spit, even as ye, brave man—"

"Ridiculous. So fair a lady is meant for another kind of, um, never mind! Has she treated you very ill?"

"She beats me now and again—and I have been so lonely, naught here at all save the troll-wife and I—" The small work-roughened hands clutched desperately at his waist, and she buried her face against his breast.

"Can ye save us?" she gasped. "I fear 'tis for naught ye ventured yer life, bravest of men. I fear we'll soon both sputter on the coals."

Cappen said nothing. If she wanted to think he had come especially to rescue her, he would not be so ungallant to tell her otherwise.

The troll-wife's mouth gashed in a grin as she walked through the fire to him. "There is a price," she said. "If you cannot tell me three things about myself which are true beyond disproving, not courage nor amulet nor the gods themselves may avail to keep that head on your shoulders."

Cappen clapped a hand to his sword. "Why, gladly," he said; this was a rule of magic he had learned long ago, that three truths were the needful armor to make any guardian charm work. "Imprimis, yours is the ugliest nose I ever saw poking up a fire. Secundus, I was never in a house I cared less to guest at. Tertius, even among trolls you are little liked, being one of the worst."

Hildigund moaned with terror as the monster swelled in rage. But there was no movement. Only the leaping flames and the eddying smoke stirred.

Cappen's voice rang out, coldly: "Now the king lies on the sea, frozen and wet, and I am come to fetch a brand for his fire. And I had best also see his daughter home."

The troll shook her head, suddenly chuckling. "No. The brand you may have, just to get you out of this cave, foulness; but the woman is in my thrall until a man sleeps with her—here—for a night. And if he does, I may have him to break my fast in the morning!"

Cappen yawned mightily. "Thank you, mother. Your offer of a bed is most welcome to these tired bones, and I accept gratefully."

"You will die tomorrow!" she raved. The ground shook under the huge weight of her as she stamped. "Because of the three truths, I must let you go tonight; but tomorrow I may do what I will!"

"Forget not my little friend, mother," said Cappen, and touched the cord of the amulet.

"I tell you, silver has no use against me—"

Cappen sprawled on the floor and rippled fingers across his harp. *"A lovely lady full oft lies—"*

The troll-wife turned from him in a rage. Hildigund ladled up some broth, saying nothing, and Cappen ate it with pleasure, though it could have used more seasoning.

After that he indited a sonnet to the princess, who regarded him wide-eyed. The troll came back from a tunnel after he finished, and said curtly: "This way." Cappen took the girl's hand and followed her into a pitchy, reeking dark.

She plucked an arras aside to show a room which surprised him by being hung with tapestries, lit with candles, and furnished with a fine broad featherbed. "Sleep here tonight, if you dare," she growled. "And tomorrow I shall eat you —and you, worthless lazy she-trash, will have the hide flayed off your back!" She barked a laugh and left them.

Hildigund fell weeping on the mattress. Cappen let her cry herself out while he undressed and got between the blankets. Drawing his sword, he laid it carefully in the middle of the bed.

The girl looked at him through jumbled fair locks. "How can ye dare?" she whispered. "One breath of fear, one moment's doubt, and the troll is free to rend ye."

"Exactly." Cappen yawned. "Doubtless she hopes that will come to me lying wakeful in the night. Wherefore 'tis but a question of going gently to sleep. O Svearek, Torbek, and Beorna, could you but see how I am resting now!"

"But . . . the three truths ye gave her . . . how knew ye . . . ?"

"Oh, those. Well, see you, sweet lady, Primus and Secundus were my own thoughts, and who is to disprove them? Tertius was also clear, since you said there had been no company here in three years—yet are there many trolls in these lands, ergo even they cannot stomach our gentle hostess." Cappen watched her through heavy-lidded eyes.

She flushed deeply, blew out the candles, and he heard her slip off her garment and get in with him. There was a long silence.

Then: "Are ye not—"

"Yes, fair one?" he muttered through his drowsiness.

"Are ye not . . . well, I am here and ye are here and—"

"Fear not," he said. "I laid my sword between us. Sleep in peace."

"I . . . would be glad—ye have come to deliver—"

"No, fair lady. No man of gentle breeding could so abuse his power. Goodnight." He leaned over, brushing his lips gently across hers, and lay down again.

"Ye are . . . I never thought man could be so noble," she whispered.

Cappen mumbled something. As his soul spun into sleep, he chuckled. Those unresting days and nights on the sea had not left him fit for that kind of exercise. But, of course, if she wanted to think he was being magnanimous, it could be useful later—

He woke with a start and looked into the sputtering glare of a torch. Its light wove across the crags and gullies of the troll-wife's face and shimmered wetly off the great tusks in her mouth.

"Good morning, mother," said Cappen politely.

Hildigund thrust back a scream.

"Come and be eaten," said the troll-wife.

"No, thank you," said Cappen, regretfully but firmly. "'Twould be ill for my health. No, I will but trouble you for a firebrand and then the princess and I will be off."

"If you think that stupid bit of silver will protect you, think again," she snapped. "Your three sentences were all that saved you last night. Now I hunger."

"Silver," said Cappen didactically, "is a certain shield against all black magics. So the wizard told me, and he was such a nice white-bearded old man I am sure even his attendant devils never lied. Now please depart, mother, for modesty forbids me to dress before your eyes."

The hideous face thrust close to his. He smiled dreamily and tweaked her nose—hard.

She howled and flung the torch at him. Cappen caught it and stuffed it into her mouth. She choked and ran from the room.

"A new sport—trollbaiting," said the bard gaily into the sudden darkness. "Come, shall we not venture out?"

The girl trembled too much to move. He comforted her, absentmindedly, and dressed in the dark, swearing at the clumsy leggings. When he left, Hildigund put on her clothes and hurried after him.

The troll-wife squatted by the fire and glared at them as they went by. Cappen hefted his sword and looked at her. "I do not love you," he said mildly, and hewed out.

She backed away, shrieking as he slashed at her. In the end, she crouched at the mouth of a tunnel, raging futilely. Cappen pricked her with his blade.

"It is not worth my time to follow you down underground," he said, "but if ever you trouble men again, I will hear of it and come and feed you to my dogs. A piece at a time—a very small piece—do you understand?"

She snarled at him.

"An *extremely* small piece," said Cappen amiably. "Have you heard me?"

Something broke in her. "Yes," she whimpered.

He let her go, and she scuttled from him like a rat.

He remembered the firewood and took an armful; on the way, he thoughtfully picked up a few jeweled rings which he didn't think she would be needing and stuck them in his pouch. Then he led the girl outside.

The wind had laid itself, a clear frosty morning glittered on the sea and the longship was a distant sliver against white-capped blueness. The minstrel groaned. "What a distance to row! Oh, well—"

They were at sea before Hildigund spoke. Awe was in the eyes that watched him. "No man could be so brave," she murmured. "Are ye a god?"

"Not quite," said Cappen. "No, most beautiful one, modesty grips my tongue. 'Twas but that I had the silver and was therefore proof against her sorcery."

"But the silver was no help!" she cried.

Cappen's oar caught a crab. "What?" he yelled.

"No—no—why, she told ye so her own self—"

"I thought she lied. I *know* the silver guards against—"

"But she used no magic! Trolls have but their own strength!"

Cappen sagged in his seat. For a moment he thought he was going to faint. Then only his lack of fear had armored him; and if he had known the truth, that would not have lasted a minute.

He laughed shakily. Another score for his doubts about the overall value of truth!

The longship's oars bit water and approached him. Indignant voices asking why he had been so long on his errand faded when his passenger was seen. And Svearek the king wept as he took his daughter back into his arms.

The hard brown face was still blurred with tears when he looked at the minstrel, but the return of his old self was there too. "What ye have done,

Cappen Varra of Croy, is what no other man in the world could have done."

"Aye—aye—" The rough northern voices held adoration as the warriors crowded around the slim red-haired figure.

"Ye shall have her whom ye saved to wife," said Svearek, "and when I die ye shall rule all Norren."

Cappen swayed and clutched the rail.

Three nights later he slipped away from their shore camp and turned his face southward.

THE GATE OF THE
FLYING KNIVES

Again penniless, houseless, and ladyless, Cappen Varra made a brave sight just the same as he wove his way amidst the bazaar throng. After all, until today he had for some weeks been in, if not quite of, the household of Molin Torchholder, as much as he could contrive. Besides the dear presence of ancilla Danlis, he had received generous reward from the priest-engineer whenever he sang a song or composed a poem. That situation had changed with suddenness and terror, but he still wore a bright green tunic, scarlet cloak, canary hose, soft half-boots trimmed in silver, and plumed beret. Though naturally heartsick at what had happened, full of dread for his darling, he saw no reason to sell the garb yet. He could raise enough money in various ways to live on while he searched for her. If need be, as often before, he could pawn the harp that a goldsmith was presently redecorating.

If his quest had not succeeded by the time he was reduced to rags, then he would have to suppose Danlis and the Lady Rosanda were forever lost. But he had never been one to grieve over future sorrows.

Beneath a westering sun, the bazaar surged and clamored. Merchants, artisans, porters, servants, slaves, wives, nomads, courtesans, entertainers, beggars, thieves, gamblers, magicians, acolytes, soldiers, and who knew what else mingled, chattered, chaffered, quarreled, plotted, sang, played games, drank, ate, and who knew what else. Horsemen, cameldrivers, wagoners pushed through, raising waves of curses. Music tinkled and tweedled from wineshops. Vendors proclaimed the wonders of their wares from booths, neighbors shouted at each other, and devotees chanted from flat rooftops. Smells thickened the air, of flesh, sweat, roast meat and nuts, aromatic drinks, leather, wool, dung, smoke, oils, cheap perfume.

Ordinarily, Cappen Varra enjoyed this shabby-colorful spectacle. Now he single-mindedly hunted through it. He kept full awareness, of course, as everybody must in Sanctuary. When light fingers brushed him, he knew. But whereas aforetime he would have chuckled and told the pickpurse, "I'm sorry, friend; I was hoping I might lift somewhat off you," at this hour he clapped his sword in such forbidding wise that the fellow recoiled against a fat woman and made her drop a brass tray full of flowers. She screamed and started beating him over the head with it.

Cappen didn't stay to watch.

On the eastern edge of the marketplace he found what he wanted. Once more Illyra was in the bad graces of her colleagues and had moved her trade to a stall available elsewhere. Black curtains framed it, against a mud-brick wall. Reek from a nearby tannery well-nigh drowned the incense she burned in a curious holder, and would surely overwhelm any of her herbs. She herself also lacked awesomeness, such as most seeresses, mages, conjurers, scryers, and the like affected. She was too young; she would have looked almost wistful in her flowing, gaudy S'danzo garments, had she not been so beautiful.

Cappen gave her a bow in the manner of

Caronne. "Good day, Illyra the lovely," he said.

She smiled from the cushion whereon she sat. "Good day to you, Cappen Varra." They had had a number of talks, usually in jest, and he had sung for her entertainment. He had hankered to do more than that, but she seemed to keep all men at a certain distance, and a hulk of a blacksmith who evidently adored her saw to it that they respected her wish.

"Nobody in these parts has met you for a fair while," she remarked. "What fortune was great enough to make you forget old friends?"

"My fortune was mingled, inasmuch as it left me without time to come down here and behold you, my sweet," he answered out of habit.

Lightness departed from Illyra. In the olive countenance, under the chestnut mane, large eyes focused hard on her visitor. "You find time when you need help in disaster," she said.

He had not patronized her before, or indeed any fortune-teller or thaumaturge in Sanctuary. In Caronne, where he grew up, most folk had no use for magic. In his later wanderings he had encountered sufficient strangeness to temper his native skepticism. As shaken as he already was, he felt a chill go along his spine. "Do you read my fate without even casting a spell?"

She smiled afresh, but bleakly. "Oh, no. It's simple reason. Word did filter back to the Maze that you were residing in the Jewelers' Quarter and a frequent guest at the mansion of Molin Torchholder. When you appear on the heels of a new word—that last night his wife was reaved from him—plain to see is that you've been affected yourself."

He nodded. "Yes, and sore afflicted. I have lost—" He hesitated, unsure whether it would be quite wise to say,"—my love" to this girl whose charms he had rather extravagantly praised.

"—your position and income," Illyra snapped. "The high priest cannot be in any mood for minstrelsy. I'd guess his wife favored you most, anyhow. I need not guess you spent your earnings as fast as they fell to you, or faster, were behind in your rent, and were accordingly kicked out of your choice apartment as soon as rumor reached the landlord. You've returned to the Maze because you've no place else to go, and to me in hopes you can wheedle me into giving you a clue—for if you're instrumental in recovering the lady, you'll likewise recover your fortune, and more."

"No, no, no," he protested. "You wrong me."

"The high priest will appeal only to his Rankan gods," Illyra said, her tone changing from exasperated to thoughtful. She stroked her chin. "He, kinsman of the Emperor, here to direct the building of a temple which will overtop that if Ils, can hardly beg aid from the old gods of Sanctuary, let alone from our wizards, witches, and seers. But you, who belong to no part of the Empire, who drifted hither from a kingdom far in the West . . . you may seek anywhere. The idea is your own; else he would furtively have slipped you some gold, and you have engaged a diviner with more reputation than is mine."

Cappen spread his hands. "You reason eerily well, dear lass," he conceded. "Only about the motives are you mistaken. Oh, yes, I'd be glad to stand high in Molin's esteem, be richly rewarded, and so forth. Yet I feel for him; beneath that sternness of his, he's not a bad sort, and he bleeds. Still more do I feel for his lady, who was indeed kind to me and who's been snatched away to an unknown place. But before all else—" He grew quite earnest. "The Lady Rosanda was not seized by herself. Her ancilla has also vanished, Danlis. And—Danlis is she whom I love, Illyra, she whom I meant to wed."

The maiden's look probed him further. She saw a young man of medium height, slender but tough and agile. (That was due to the life he had had to lead; by nature he was indolent, except in bed.) His features were thin and regular on a long skull, clean-shaven, eyes bright blue, black hair banged and falling to the shoulders. His voice gave the language a melodious accent, as if to bespeak white cities, green fields and woods, quicksilver lakes, blue sea, of the homeland he left in search of his fortune.

"Well, you have charm, Cappen Varra," she murmured, "and how you do know it." Alert: "But coin you lack. How do you propose to pay me?"

"I fear you must work on speculation, as I do myself," he said. "If our joint efforts lead to a rescue, why, then we'll share whatever material reward may come. Your part might buy you a home on the Path of Money." She frowned. "True," he went on, "I'll get more than my share of the immediate bounty that Molin bestows. I will have my beloved back. I'll also regain the priest's favor, which is moderately lucrative. Yet consider. You need but practice your art. Thereafter any effort and risk will be mine."

"What makes you suppose a humble fortune-teller can learn more than the Prince Governant's investigator guardsmen?" she demanded.

"The matter does not seem to lie within their jurisdiction," he replied.

She leaned forward, tense beneath the layers of clothing. Cappen bent toward her. It was as if the babble of the marketplace receded, leaving these two alone with their wariness.

"I was not there," he said low, "but I arrived early this morning after the thing had happened. What's gone through the city has been rumor, leakage that cannot be caulked, household servants blabbing to friends outside and they blabbing onward. Molin's locked away most of the facts till he can discover what they mean, if ever he can. I, however, I came on the scene while chaos still prevailed. Nobody kept me from talking to folk, before the lord himself saw me and told me to begone. Thus I know about as much as anyone, little though that be.''

''And—?'' she prompted.

''And it doesn't seem to have been a worldly sort of capture, for a worldly end like ransom. See you, the mansion's well guarded, and neither Molin nor his wife have ever gone from it without escort. His mission here is less than popular, you recall. Those troopers are from Ranke and not subornable. The house stands in a garden, inside a high wall whose top is patrolled. Three leopards run loose on the grounds after dark.

''Molin had business with his kinsman the Prince, and spent the night at the palace. His wife, the Lady Rosanda, stayed home, retired, later came out and complained she could not sleep. She therefore had Danlis wakened. Danlis is no chambermaid; there are plenty of those. She's amanuensis, adviser, confidante, collector of information, ofttimes guide or interpreter—oh, she earns her pay, does my Danlis. Despite she and I having a dawntide engagement, which is why I arrived then, she must now out of bed at Rosanda's whim, to hold milady's hand or take dictation of milady's letters or read to milady from a soothing book—but I'm a spendthrift of words. Suffice to say that they two sought an upper chamber which is furnished as both solarium and office. A single staircase leads thither, and it is the single room at the top. There is a balcony, yes; and, the night being warm, the door to it stood open, as well as the windows. But I inspected the facade beneath. That's sheer marble, undecorated save for varying colors, devoid of ivy or of anything that any climber might cling to, save he were a fly.

"Nevertheless . . . just before the east grew pale, shrieks were heard. The watch pelted to the stair and up it. They must break down the inner door, which was bolted. I suppose that was merely against chance interruptions, for nobody had felt threatened. The solarium was in disarray; vases and things were broken; shreds torn off a robe and slight traces of blood lay about. Aye, Danlis, at least, would have resisted. But she and her mistress were gone.

"A couple of sentries on the garden wall reported hearing a loud sound as of wings. The night was cloudy-dark and they saw nothing for certain. Perhaps they imagined the noise. Suggestive is that the leopards were found cowering in a corner and welcomed their keeper when he would take them back to their cages.

"And this is the whole of anyone's knowledge, Illyra," Cappen ended. "Help me, I pray you, help me get back my love!"

She was long quiet. Finally she said, in a near whisper, "It could be a worse matter than I'd care to peer into, let alone enter."

"Or it could not," Cappen urged.

She gave him a quasi-defiant stare. "My mother's people reckon it unlucky to do any service for a Shavakh—a person not of their tribe —without recompense. Pledges don't count."

Cappen scowled. "Well, I could go to a pawnshop and—But no, time may be worth more than rubies." From the depths of unhappiness, his grin broke forth. "Poems also are valuable, right? You S'danzo have your ballads and love ditties. Let me indite a poem, Illyra, that shall be yours alone."

Her expression quickened. "Truly?"

"Truly. Let me think . . . Aye, we'll begin thus." And, venturing to take her hands in his, Cappen murmured:

My lady comes to me like break of day.
I dream in darkness if it chance she tarries,
Until the banner of her brightness harries
The hosts of Shadowland from off the way—

She jerked free and cried, "No! You scoundrel, that has to be something you did for Danlis—or for some earlier woman you wanted in your bed—"

"But it isn't finished," he argued. "I'll complete it for you, Illyra."

Anger left her. She shook her head, clicked her tongue, and sighed. "No matter. You're incurably yourself. And I . . . am only half S'danzo. I'll attempt your spell."

"By every love goddess I ever heard of," he promised unsteadily, "you shall indeed have your own poem after this is over."

"Be still," she ordered. "Fend off anybody who comes near."

He faced about and drew his sword. The slim, straight blade was hardly needed, for no other enterprise had site within several yards of hers, and as wide a stretch of paving lay between him and the fringes of the crowd. Still, to grasp the hilt gave him a sense of finally making progress. He had felt helpless for the first hours, hopeless, as if his dear had actually died instead of—of what? Behind him he heard cards riffled, dice cast, words softly wailed.

All at once Illyra strangled a shriek. He whirled about and saw how the blood had left her olive countenance, turning it grey. She hugged herself and shuddered.

"What's wrong?" he blurted in fresh terror.

She did not look at him. "Go away," she said in a thin voice. "Forget you ever knew that woman."

"But—but what—"

"Go away, I told you! Leave me alone!"

Then somehow she relented enough to let forth:
"I don't know. I dare not know. I'm just a little
half-breed girl who has a few cantrips and a
tricksy second sight, and—and I saw that this
business goes outside of space and time, and a
power beyond any magic is there—Enas Yorl
could tell more, but he himself—" Her courage
broke. "Go away!" she screamed. "Before I shout
for Dubro and his hammer!"

"I beg your pardon," Cappen Varra said, and
made haste to obey.

He retreated into the twisting streets of the
Maze. They were narrow; most of the mean buildings around him were high; gloom already filled
the quarter. It was as if he had stumbled into the
same night when Danlis had gone . . . Danlis,
creature of sun and horizons . . . . If she lived, did
she remember their last time together as he remembered it, a dream dreamed centuries ago?

Having the day free, she had wanted to explore
the countryside north of town. Cappen had
objected on three counts. The first he did not
mention; that it would require a good deal of
effort, and he would get dusty and sweaty and
saddlesore. She despised men who were not at
least as vigorous as she was, unless they compen-
sated by being venerable and learned.

The second he hinted at. Sleazy though most of
Sanctuary was, he knew places within it where a
man and a woman could enjoy themselves, comfortably, privately—his apartment, for instance.
She smiled her negation. Her family belonged to
the old aristocracy of Ranke, not the newly rich,
and she had been raised in its austere tradition.
Albeit her father had fallen on evil times and she
had been forced to take service, she kept her pride,
and proudly would she yield her maidenhead to
her bridegroom. Thus far she had answered Cap-

pen's ardent declarations with the admission that she liked him and enjoyed his company and wished he would change the subject. (Buxom Lady Rosanda seemed as if she might be more approachable, but there he was careful to maintain a cheerful correctness.) He did believe she was getting beyond simple enjoyment, for her patrician reserve seemed less each time they saw each other. Yet she could not altogether have forgotten that he was merely the bastard of a minor nobleman in a remote country, himself disinherited and a footloose minstrel.

His third objection he dared say forth. While the hinterland was comparatively safe, Molin Torchholder would be furious did he learn that a woman of his household had gone escorted by a single armed man, and he no professional fighter. Molin would probably have been justified, too. Danlis smiled again and said, "I could ask a guardsman off duty to come along. But you have interesting friends, Cappen. Perhaps a warrior is among them?"

As a matter of fact, he knew any number, but doubted she would care to meet them—with a single exception. Luckily, Jamie the Red had no prior commitment, and agreed to join the party. Cappen told the kitchen staff to pack a picnic hamper for four.

Jamie's girls stayed behind; this was not their sort of outing, and the sun might harm their complexions. Cappen thought it a bit ungracious of the Northerner never to share them. That put him, Cappen, to considerable expense in the Street of Red Lanterns, since he could scarcely keep a paramour of his own while wooing Danlis. Otherwise he was fond of Jamie. They had met after Rosanda, chancing to hear the minstrel sing, had invited him to perform at the mansion, and then invited him back, and presently Cappen was living in the Jeweler's Quarter. Jamie had an apartment nearby.

Three horses and a pack mule clopped out of Sanctuary in the new-born morning, to a jingle of harness bells. That merriment found no echo in Cappen's head; he had been drinking past midnight, and in no case enjoyed rising before noon. Passive, he listened to Jamie:

"—Aye, milady, they're mountaineers where I hail from, poor folk but free folk. Some might call us barbarians, but that might be unwise in our hearing. For we've tales, songs, laws, ways, gods as old as any in the world, and as good. We lack much of your Southern lore, but how much of ours do you ken? Not that I boast, please understand. I've seen wonders in my wanderings. But I do say we've a few wonders of our own at home."

"I'd like to hear of them," Danlis responded. "We know almost nothing about your country in the Empire—hardly more than mentions in the chronicles of Venafer and Mattathan, or the *Natural History* of Kahayavesh. How do you happen to come here?"

"Oh-ah, I'm a younger son of our king, and I thought I'd see a bit of the world before settling down. Not that I packed any wealth along to speak of. But what with one thing and another, hiring out hither and yon for this or that, I get by." Jamie paused. "You, uh, you've far more to tell, milady. You're from the crown city of the Empire, and you've got book learning, and at the same time you come out to see for yourself what land and rocks and plants and animals are like."

Cappen decided he had better get into the conversation. Not that Jamie would undercut a friend, nor Danlis be unduly attracted by a wild highlander. Nevertheless—

Jamie wasn't bad-looking in his fashion. He was huge, topping Cappen by a head and disproportionately wide in the shoulders. His loose-jointed appearance was deceptive, as the bard had learned when they sported in a public gymnasium; those were heavy bones and oak-hard muscles. A spectacular red mane drew attention from boyish face, mild blue eyes, and slightly diffident manner. Today he was plainly clad, in tunic and cross-gaitered breeks; but the knife at his belt and the ax at his saddlebow stood out.

As for Danlis, well, what could a poet do but struggle for words which might embody a ghost of her glory? She was tall and slender, her features almost cold in their straight-lined perfection and alabaster hue—till you observed the big grey eyes, golden hair piled on high, curve of lips whence came that husky voice. (How often, had he lain awake yearning for her lips! He would console himself by remembering the strong, delicately blue-veined hand that she did let him kiss.) Despite waxing warmth and dust puffed up from the horses' hoofs, her cowled riding habit remained immaculate and no least dew of sweat was on her skin.

By the time Cappen got his wits out of the blankets wherein they had still been snoring, talk had turned to gods. Danlis was curious about those of Jamie's country, as she was about most things. (She did shun a few subjects as being unwholesome.) Jamie in his turn was eager to have her explain what was going on in Sanctuary. "I've heard but the one side of the matter, and Cappen's indifferent to it," he said. "Folk grumble about your master—Molin, is that his name—?"

"He is not my master," Danlis made clear. "I am a free woman who assists his wife. He himself is a high priest in Ranke, also an engineer."

"Why is the Emperor angering Sanctuary? Most places I've been, colonial governments know better. They leave the local gods be."

Danlis grew pensive. "Where shall I start? Doubtless you know that Sanctuary was originally a city of the kingdom of Ilsig. Hence it has built temples to the gods of Ilsig—notably Ils, Lord of Lords, and his queen Shipri the All-Mother, but likewise others—Anen of the Harvests, Thufir the tutelary of pilgrims—"

"But none to Shalpa, patron of thieves," Cappen put in, "though these days he has the most devotees of any."

Danlis ignored his jape. "Ranke was quite a different country, under quite different gods," she continued. "Chief of these are Savankala the Thunderer, his consort Sabellia, Lady of Stars, their son Vashanka the Tenslayer, and his sister and consort Azyuna—gods of storm and war. According to Venafer, it was they who made Ranke supreme at last. Mattathan is more prosaic and opines that the martial spirit they inculcated was responsible for the Rankan Empire finally taking Ilsig into itself."

"Yes, milady, yes, I've heard this," Jamie said, while Cappen reflected that if his beloved had a fault, it was her tendency to lecture.

"Sanctuary has changed from of yore," she proceeded. "It has become polyglot, turbulent, corrupt, a canker on the body politic. Among its most vicious elements are the proliferating alien cults, not to speak of necromancers, witches, charlatans, and similar predators on the people. The time is overpast to restore law here. Nothing less than the Imperium can do that. A necessary preliminary is the establishment of the Imperial deities, the gods of Ranke, for everyone to see: symbol, rallying point, and actual presence."

"But they *have* their temples," Jamie argued.

"Small, dingy, to accommodate Rankans, few of whom stay in the city for long," Danlis retorted. "What reverence does that inspire, for the pantheon and the state? No, the Emperor has decided that Savankala and Sabellia must have the greatest fane, the most richly endowed, in this entire province. Molin Torchholder will build and consecrate it. Then can the degenerates and warlocks be scourged out of Sanctuary. Afterward the Prince Government can handle common felons."

Cappen didn't expect matters would be that simple. He got no chance to say so, for Jamie asked at once, "Is this wise, milady? True, many a soul hereabouts worships foreign gods, or none. But many still adore the old gods of Ilsig. They look on your, uh, Savankala as an intruder. I intend no offense, but they do. They're outraged that he's to have a bigger and grander house than Ils of the Thousand Eyes. Some fear what Ils may do about it."

"I know," Danlis said. "I regret any distress caused, and I'm sure Lord Molin does too. Still, we must overcome the agents of darkness, before the disease that they are spreads throughout the Empire."

"Oh, no," Cappen managed to insert, "I've lived here awhile, mostly down in the Maze. I've had to do with a good many so-called magicians, of either sex or in between. They aren't that bad. Most I'd call pitiful. They just use their little deceptions to scrabble out what living they can, in this crumbly town where life has trapped them."

Danlis gave him a sharp glance. "You've told me people think ill of sorcery in Caronne," she said.

"They do," he admitted. "But that's because we incline to be rationalists, who consider nearly all magic a bag of tricks. Which is true. Why, I've learned a few sleights myself."

"You have?" Jamie rumbled in surprise.

"For amusement," Cappen said hastily, before Danlis could disapprove. "Some are quite elegant,

virtual exercises in three-dimensional geometry."
Seeing interest kindle in her, he added, "I studied
mathematics in boyhood; my father, before he
died, wanted me to have a gentleman's education.
The main part has rusted away in me, but I
remember useful or picturesque details."

"Well, give us a show, come luncheon time,"
Jamie proposed.

Cappen did, when they halted. That was on a
hillside above the White Foal River. It wound
gleaming through farmlands whose intense green
denied that desert lurked on the rim of sight. The
noonday sun baked strong odors out of the earth:
humus, resin, juice of wild plants. A solitary plane
tree graciously gave shade. Bees hummed.

After the meal, and after Danlis had scrambled
off to get a closer look at a kind of lizard new to
her, Cappen demonstrated his skill. She was
especially taken—enchanted—by his geometric
artifices. Like any Rankan lady, she carried a
sewing kit in her gear; and being herself, she had
writing materials along. Thus he could apply
scissors and thread to paper. He showed how a
single ring may be cut to produce two that are
interlocked, and how a strip may be twisted to
have but one surface and one edge, and whatever
else he knew. Jamie watched with pleasure, if with
less enthusiasm.

Observing how delight made her glow, Cappen
was inspired to carry on the latest poem he was
composing for her. It had been slower work than
usual. He had the conceit, the motif, a comparison
of her to the dawn, but hitherto only the first few
lines had emerged, and no proper structure. In
this moment—

—the banner of her brightness harries
The hosts of Shadowland from off the way
That she now wills to tread—for what can stay
The triumph of that radiance she carries?

Yes, it was clearly going to be a rondel. Therefore the next two lines were:

My lady comes to me like break of day.
I dream in darkness if it chance she tarries.

He had gotten that far when abruptly she said:
"Cappen, this is such a fine excursion, such
splendid scenery. I'd like to watch sunrise over the
river tomorrow. Will you escort me?"

Sunrise? But she was telling Jamie, "We need
not trouble you about that. I had in mind a walk
out of town to the bridge. If we choose the proper
route, it's well guarded everywhere, perfectly
safe."

And scant traffic moved at that hour; besides,
the monumental statues along the bridge stood in
front of bays which they screened from passersby
—"Oh, yes, indeed, Danlis, I'd love to," Cappen
said. For such an opportunity, he could get up
before cockcrow.

—When he reached the mansion, she had not
been there.

Exhausted after his encounter with Illyra,
Cappen hied him to the Vulgar Unicorn and
related his woes to One-Thumb. The big man had
come on shift at the inn early, for a fellow
boniface had not yet recovered from the effects of
a dispute with a patron. (Shortly thereafter, the
patron was found floating face down under a pier.
Nobody questioned One-Thumb about this; his
regulars knew that he preferred the establishment
safe, if not always orderly.) He offered taciturn
sympathy and the loan of a bed upstairs. Cappen
scarcely noticed the insects that shared it.

Waking about sunset, he found water and a
washcloth, and felt much refreshed—hungry and
thirsty, too. He made his way to the taproom
below. Dusk was blue in windows and open door,
black under the rafters. Candles smeared weak

light along counter and main board and on lesser
tables at the walls. The air had grown cool, which
allayed the stenches of the Maze. Thus Cappen
was acutely aware of the smells of beer—old in the
rushes underfoot, fresh where a trio of men had
settled down to guzzle—and of spitted meat,
wafting from the kitchen.

One-Thumb approached, a shadowy hulk save
for highlights on his bald pate. "Sit," he grunted.
"Eat. Drink." He carried a great tankard and a
plate bearing a slab of roast beef on bread. These
he put on a corner table, and himself on a chair.

Cappen sat also and attacked the meal. "You're
very kind," he said between bites and draughts.

"You'll pay when you get coin, or if you don't,
then in songs and magic stunts. They're good for
trade." One-Thumb fell silent and peered at his
guest.

When Cappen was done, the innkeeper said,
"While you slept, I sent out a couple of fellows to
ask around. Maybe somebody saw something that
might be helpful. Don't worry—I didn't mention
you, and it's natural I'd be interested to know
what really happened."

The minstrel stared. "You've gone to a deal of
trouble on my account."

"I told you, I want to know for my own sake. If
deviltry's afoot, where could it strike next?" One-
Thumb rubbed a finger across the toothless part
of his gums. "Of course, if you should luck out—I
don't expect it, but in case you do—remember who
gave you a boost." A figure appeared in the door
and he went to render service.

After a bit of muttered talk, he led the newcomer to Cappen's place. When the minstrel recognized the lean youth, his pulse leaped. One-
Thumb would not have brought him and Hanse
together without cause; bard and thief found each
other insufferable. They nodded coldly but did not

speak until the tapster returned with a round of ale.

When the three were seated, One-Thumb said, "Well, spit it out, boy. You claim you've got news."

"For him?" Hanse flared, gesturing at Cappen.

"Never mind who. Just talk."

Hanse scowled. "I don't talk for a single lousy mugful."

"You do if you want to keep on coming in here."

Hanse bit his lip. The Vulgar Unicorn was a rendezvous virtually indispensable to one in his trade.

Cappen thought best to sweeten the pill: "I'm known to Molin Torchholder. If I can serve him in this matter, he won't be stingy. Nor will I. Shall we say—hm—ten gold royals to you?"

The sum was not princely, but on that account plausible. "Awright, awright," Hanse replied. "I'd been casing a job I might do in the Jewelers' Quarter. A squad of the watch came by toward morning and I figured I'd better go home, not by the way I came, either. So I went along the Avenue of Temples, as I might be wanting to stop in and pay my respects to some god or other. It was a dark night, overcast, the reason I'd been out where I was. But you know how several of the temples keep lights going. There was enough to see by, even upward a ways. Nobody else was in sight. Suddenly I heard a kind of whistling, flapping noise aloft. I looked and—"

He broke off.

"And what?" Cappen blurted. One-Thumb sat impassive.

Hanse swallowed. "I don't swear to this," he said. "It was still dim, you realize. I've wondered since if I didn't see wrong."

"What was it?" Cappen gripped the table edge till his fingernails whitened.

Hanse wet his throat and said in a rush: "What it

seemed like was a huge black thing, almost like a snake, but bat-winged. It came streaking from, oh, more or less the direction of Molin's, I guess now that I think back. And it was aimed more or less toward the temple of Ils. There was something that dangled below, as it might be a human body or two. I didn't stay to watch, I ducked into the nearest alley and waited. When I came out, it was gone."

He knocked back his ale and rose. "That's all," he snapped. "I don't want to remember the sight any longer, and if anybody ever asks, I was never here tonight."

"Your story's worth a couple more drinks," One-Thumb invited.

"Another evening," Hanse demurred. "Right now I need a whore. Don't forget those ten royals, singer." He left, stiff-legged.

"Well," said the innkeeper after a silence, "what do you make of this latest?"

Cappen suppressed a shiver. His palms were cold. "I don't know, save that what we confront is not of our kind."

"You told me once you've got a charm against magic."

Cappen fingered the little silver amulet, in the form of a coiled snake, he wore around his neck. "I'm not sure. A wizard I'd done a favor for gave me this, years ago. He claimed it'd protect me against spells and supernatural beings of less than godly rank. But to make it work, I have to utter three truths about the spellcaster or the creature. I've done that in two or three scrapes, and come out of them intact, but I can't prove the talisman was responsible."

More customers entered, and One-Thumb must go to serve them. Cappen nursed his ale. He yearned to get drunk and belike the landlord would stand him what was needful, but he didn't dare. He had already learned more than he thought the opposition would approve of—whoever or whatever the opposition was. They might have means of discovering this.

His candle flickered. He glanced up and saw a beardless fat man in an ornate formal robe, scarcely normal dress for a visit to the Vulgar Unicorn. "Greeting," the person said. His voice was like a child's.

Cappen squinted through the gloom. "I don't believe I know you," he replied.

"No, but you will come to believe it, oh, yes, you will." The fat man sat down. One-Thumb came over and took an order for red wine—"a decent wine, mine host, a Zhanuvend or Baladach." Coin gleamed forth.

Cappen's heart thumped. "Enas Yorl?" he breathed.

The other nodded. "In the flesh, the all too mutable flesh. I do hope my curse strikes again soon. Almost any shape would be better than this. I hate being overweight. I'm a eunuch, too. The times I've been a woman were better than this."

"I'm sorry, sir," Cappen took care to say. Though he could not rid himself of the spell laid on him, Enas Yorl was a powerful thaumaturge, no mere prestidigitator.

"At least I've not been arbitrarily displaced. You can't imagine how annoying it is, suddenly to find oneself elsewhere, perhaps miles away. I was able to come here in proper wise, in my litter. Faugh, how can anyone voluntarily set shoes to these open sewers they call streets in the Maze?" The wine arrived. "Best we speak fast and to the point, young man, that we may finish and I get home before the next contretemps."

Enas Yorl sipped and made a face. "I've been swindled," he whined. "This is barely drinkable, if that."

"Maybe your present palate is at fault, sir," Cappen suggested. He did not add that the tongue definitely had a bad case of logorrhea. It was an almost physical torture to sit stalled, but he had better humor the mage.

"Yes, quite probably. Nothing has tasted good since—Well. To business. On hearing that One-Thumb was inquiring about last night's incident, I sent forth certain investigators of my own. You will understand that I've been trying to find out as much as I can." Enas Yorl drew a sign in the air. "Purely precautionary. I have no desire whatsoever to cross the Powers concerned in this."

A wintry tingle went through Cappen. "You know who they are, what it's about?" His tone wavered.

Enas Yorl wagged a finger. "Not so hasty, boy, not so hasty. My latest information was of a seemingly unsuccessful interview you had with Illyra the seeress. I also learned you were now in this hostel and close to its landlord. Obviously you are involved. I must know why, how, how much—everything."

"Then you'll help—sir?"

A headshake made chin and jowls wobble. "Absolutely not. I told you I want no part of this. But in exchange for whatever data you possess, I am willing to explicate as far as I am able, and to advise you. Be warned: my advice will doubtless be that you drop the matter and perhaps leave town."

And doubtless he would be right, Cappen thought. It simply happened to be counsel that was impossible for a lover to follow . . . unless—O kindly gods of Caronne, no, no!—unless Danlis was dead.

The whole story spilled out of him, quickened and deepened by keen questions. At the end, he sat breathless while Enas Yorl nodded.

"Yes, that appears to confirm what I suspected," the mage said most softly. He stared past the minstrel, into shadows that loomed and flickered. Buzz of talk, clink of drinking ware, occasional gust of laughter among customers seemed remoter than the moon.

"What was it?" broke from Cappen.

"A sikkintair, a Flying Knife. It can have been nothing else."

"A—what?"

Enas focused on his companion. "The monster that took the women," he explained. "Sikkintairs are an attribute of Ils. A pair of sculptures on the grand stairway of his temple represent them."

"Oh, yes, I've seen those, but never thought—"

"No, you're not a votary of any gods they have here. Myself, when I got word of the abduction, I sent my familiars scuttling about and cast spells of inquiry. I received indications . . . . I can't describe them to you, who lack arcane lore. I established that the very fabric of space had been troubled. Vibrations had not quite damped out as yet, and were centered on the temple of Ils. You may, if you wish a crude analogy, visualize a water surface and the waves, fading to ripples and finally to naught, when a diver has passed through."

Enas Yorl drank more in a gulp than was his wont. "Civilization was old in Ilsig when Ranke was still a barbarian village," he said, as though to himself; his gaze had drifted away again, toward darkness. "Its myths depicted the home of the gods as being outside the world—not above, not below, but outside. Philosophers of a later, more rationalistic era elaborated this into a theory of parallel universes. My own researches—you will understand that my condition has made me especially interested in the theory of dimensions, the subtler aspects of geometry—my own researches have demonstrated the possibility of transference between these different spaces.

"As another analogy, consider a pack of cards. One is inhabited by a king, one by a knight, one by a deuce, et cetera. Ordinarily none of the figures can leave the plane on which it exists. If, however, a very thin piece of absorbent material soaked in a unique kind of solvent were laid between two cards, the dyes that form them could pass through: retaining their configuration, I trust. Actually, of course, this is a less than ideal comparison, for the transference is accomplished through a particular contortion of the continuum—"

Cappen could endure no more pedantry. He crashed his tankard down on the table and shouted, "By all the hells of all the cults, will you get to the point?"

Men stared from adjacent seats, decided no fight was about to erupt, and went back to their interests. These included negotiations with streetwalkers who, lanterns in hand, had come in looking for trade.

Enas Yorl smiled. "I forgive your outburst, under the circumstances," he said. "I too am occasionally young.

"Very well. Given the foregoing data, including yours, the infrastructure of events seems reasonably evident. You are aware of the conflict over a proposed new temple, which is to outdo that of Ils and Shipri. I do not maintain that the god has taken a direct hand. I certainly hope he feels that would be beneath his dignity; a theomachy would not be good for us, to understate the case a trifle. But he may have inspired a few of his more fanatical priests to action. He may have revealed to them, in dreams or visions, the means whereby they could cross to the next world and there make the sikkintairs do their bidding. I hypothesize that the Lady Rosanda—and, to be sure, her coadjutrix, your inamorata—are incarcerated in that world. The temple is too full of priests, deacons, acolytes, and lay people for hiding the wife of a magnate. However, the gate need not be recognizable as such.''

Cappen controlled himself with an inward shudder and made his trained voice casual: ''What might it look like, sir?''

''Oh, probably a scroll, taken from a coffer where it had long lain forgotten, and now unrolled —yes, I should think in the sanctum, to draw power from the sacred objects and to be seen by as few persons as possible who are not in the con-spiracy—'' Enas Yorl came out of his abstraction. ''Beware! I deduce your thought. Choke it before it kills you.''

Cappen ran sandy tongue over leathery lips. ''What . . . should we . . . expect to happen, sir?''

''That is an interesting question,'' Enas Yorl said. ''I can but conjecture. Yet I am well ac-quainted with the temple hierarchy and—I don't think the Archpriest is privy to the matter. He's too aged and weak. On the other hand, this is quite in the style of Hazroah, the High Flamen. More-over, of late he has in effect taken over the governance of the temple from his nominal superior. He's bold, ruthless—should have been a soldier—Well, putting myself in his skin, I'll predict that he'll let Molin stew a while, then cautiously open negotiations—a hint at first, and always a claim that this is the will of Ils.

''None but the Emperor can cancel an under-taking for the Imperial deities. Persuading him will take much time and pressure. Molin is a Rankan aristocrat of the old school; he will be torn between his duty to his gods, his state, and his wife. But I suspect that eventually he can be worn down to the point where he agrees that it is, in truth, bad policy to exalt Savankala and Sabellia in a city whose tutelaries they have never been. He in his turn can influence the Emperor as desired."

"How long would this take, do you think?" Cappen whispered. "Till the women are released?"

Enas Yorl shrugged. "Years, possibly. Hazroah may try to hasten the process by demonstrating that the Lady Rosanda is subject to punishment. Yes, I should imagine that the remains of an ancilla who had been tortured to death, delivered on Molin's doorstep, would be a rather strong argument."

His look grew intense on the appalled countenance across from him. "I know," he said. "You're breeding fever-dreams of a heroic rescue. It cannot be done. Even supposing that somehow you won through the gate and brought her back, the gate would remain. I doubt Ils would personally seek revenge; besides being petty, that could provoke open strife with Savankala and his retinue, who're formidable characters themselves. But Ils would not stay the hand of the Flamen Hazroah, who is a most vengeful sort. If you escaped his assassins, a sikkintair would come after you, and nowhere in the world could you and she hide. Your talisman would be of no avail. The sikkintair is not supernatural, unless you give that designation to the force which enables so huge a mass to fly; and it is from no magician, but from the god.

"So forget the girl. The town is full of them." He fished in his purse and spilled a handful of coins on the table. "Go to a good whorehouse, enjoy yourself, and raise one for poor old Enas Yorl."

He got up and waddled off. Cappen sat staring at the coins. They made a generous sum, he realized vaguely: silver lunars, to the number of thirty.

One-Thumb came over. "What'd he say?" the

taverner asked.

"I should abandon hope," Cappen muttered. His eyes stung; his vision blurred. Angrily, he wiped them.

"I've a notion I might not be smart to hear more." One-Thumb laid his mutilated hand on Cappen's shoulder. "Care to get drunk? On the house. I'll have to take your money or the rest will want free booze too, but I'll return it tomorrow."

"No, I—I thank you, but—but you're busy, and I need someone I can talk to. Just lend me a lantern, if you will."

"That might attract a robber, fellow, what with those fine clothes of yours."

Cappen gripped swordhilt. "He'd be very welcome, the short while he lasted," he said in bitterness.

He climbed to his feet. His fingers remembered to gather the coins.

Jamie let him in. The Northerner had hastily thrown a robe over his massive frame; he carried the stone lamp that was a night light. "Sh," he said. "The lassies are asleep." He nodded toward a closed door at the far end of this main room. Bringing the lamp higher, he got a clear view of Cappen's face. His own registered shock. "Hey-o, lad, what ails you? I've seen men poleaxed who looked happier."

Cappen stumbled across the threshold and collapsed in an armchair. Jamie barred the outer door, touched a stick of punk to the lamp flame and lit candles, filled wine goblets. Drawing a seat opposite, he sat down, laid red-furred right shank across left knee, and said gently, "Tell me."

When it had spilled from Cappen, he was a long span quiet. On the walls shimmered his weapons, among pretty pictures that his housemates had selected. At last he asked low, "Have you quit?"

"I don't know, I don't know," Cappen groaned.

"I think you can go on a ways, whether or not things are as the witchmaster supposes. We hold where I come from that no man can flee his weird, so he may as well meet it in a way that'll leave a good story. Besides, this may not be our deathday; and I doubt yon dragons are unkillable, but it could be fun finding out; and chiefly, I was much taken with your girl. Not many like her, my friend. They also say in my homeland, 'Waste not, want not.'"

Cappen lifted his glance, astounded. "You mean I should try to free her?" he exclaimed.

"No, I mean *we* should." Jamie chuckled. "Life's gotten a wee bit dull for me of late—aside from Butterfly and Light-of-Pearl, of course. Besides, I could use a share of reward money."

"I . . . I want to," Cappen stammered. "How I want to! But the odds against us—"

"She's your girl, and it's your decision. I'll not blame you if you hold back. Belike, then, in your country, they don't believe a man's first troth is to his woman and kids. Anyway, for you that was no more than a hope."

A surge went through the minstrel. He sprang up and paced, back and forth, back and forth. "But what could we do?"

"Well, we could scout the temple and see what's what," Jamie proposed. "I've been there once in a while, reckoning 'twould do no hurt to give those gods their honor. Maybe we'll find that indeed naught can be done in aid. Or maybe we won't, and go ahead and do it."

Danlis—

Fire blossomed in Cappen Varra. He was young. He drew his sword and swung it whistling on high. "Yes! We will!"

A small grammarian part of him noted the confusion of tenses and moods in the conversation.

The sole traffic on the Avenue of Temples was a night breeze, cold and sibilant. Stars, as icy to behold, looked down on its broad emptiness, on darkened buildings and weather-worn idols and rustling gardens. Here and there flames cast restless light, from porticoes or gables or ledges, out of glass lanterns or iron pots or pierced stone jars. At the foot of the grand staircase leading to the fane of Ils and Shipri, fire formed halos on the enormous figures, male and female in robes of antiquity, that flanked it.

Beyond, the god-house itself loomed, porticoed front, great bronze doors, granite walls rising sheer above to a gilt dome from which light also gleamed; the highest point in Sanctuary.

Cappen started up. "Halt," said Jamie, and plucked at his cloak. "We can't walk straight in. They keep guards in the vestibule, you know."

"I want a close view of those sikkintairs," the bard explained.

"Um, well, maybe not a bad idea, but let's be quick. If a squad of the watch comes by, we're in trouble." They could not claim they simply wished to perform their devotions, for a civilian was not allowed to bear more arms in this district than a knife. Cappen and Jamie each had that, but no illuminant like honest men. In addition, Cappen carried his rapier, Jamie a claymore, a visored conical helmet, and a knee-length byrnie. He had, moreover, furnished spears for both.

Cappen nodded and bounded aloft. Halfway, he stopped and gazed. The statue was a daunting sight. Of obsidian polished glassy smooth, it might have measured thirty feet were the tail not coiled under the narrow body. The two legs which

supported the front ended in talons the length of
Jamie's dirk. An upreared, serpentine neck bore a
wickedly lanceolate head, jaws parted to show
fangs that the sculptor had rendered in diamond.
From the back sprang wings, batlike save for their
sharp-pointed curvatures, which if unfolded
might well have covered another ten yards.

"Aye," Jamie murmured, "such a brute could
bear off two women like an eagle a brace of
leverets. Must take a lot of food to power it. I
wonder what quarry they hunt at home."

"We may find out," Cappen said, and wished he
hadn't.

"Come." Jamie led the way back, and around to
the left side of the temple. It occupied almost its
entire ground, leaving but a narrow strip of flagstones. Next to that, a wall enclosed the flower-
fragrant sanctum of Eshi, the love goddess. Thus
the space between was gratifyingly dark; the
intruders could not now be spied from the avenue.
Yet enough light filtered in that they saw what
they were doing. Cappen wondered if this meant
she smiled on their venture. After all, it was for
love, mainly. Besides, he had always been an en-
thusiastic worshiper of hers, or at any rate of her
counterparts in foreign pantheons; oftener than
most men had he rendered her favorite sacrifice.

Jamie had pointed out that the building must
have lesser doors for utilitarian purposes. He soon
found one, bolted for the night and between windows that were hardly more than slits, impossible
to crawl through. He could have hewn the wood
panels asunder, but the noise might be heard.
Cappen had a better idea. He got his partner down
on hands and knees. Standing on the broad back,
he poked his spear through a window and worked
it along the inside of the door. After some
fumbling and whispered obscenities, he caught

the latch with the head and drew the bolt.

"Hoosh, you missed your trade, I'm thinking," said the Northerner as he rose and opened the way.

"No, burglary's too risky for my taste," Cappen replied in feeble jest. The fact was that he had never stolen or cheated unless somebody deserved such treatment.

"Even burgling the house of a god?" Jamie's grin was wider than necessary.

Cappen shivered. "Don't remind me."

They entered a storeroom, shut the door, and groped through murk to the exit. Beyond was a hall. Widely spaced lamps gave bare visibility. Otherwise the intruders saw emptiness and heard silence. The vestibule and nave of the temple were never closed; the guards watched over a priest always prepared to accept offerings. But elsewhere hierarchy and staff were asleep. Or so the two hoped.

Jamie had known that the holy of holies was in the dome, Ils being a sky god. Now he let Cappen take the lead, as having more familiarity with interiors and ability to reason out a route. The minstrel used half his mind for that and scarcely noticed the splendors through which he passed. The second half was busy recollecting legends of heroes who incurred the anger of a god, especially a major god, but won to happiness in the end because they had the blessing of another. He decided that future attempts to propitiate Ils would only draw the attention of that august personage; however, Savankala would be pleased, and, yes, as for native deities, he would by all means fervently cultivate Eshi.

A few times, which felt ghastly long, he took a wrong turning and must retrace his steps after he had discovered that. Presently, though, he found a

staircase which seemed to zigzag over the inside of
an exterior wall. Landing after landing passed
by—

The last was enclosed in a very small room, a
booth, albeit richly ornamented—

He opened the door and stepped out—

Wind searched between the pillars that upheld
the dome, through his clothes and in toward his
bones. He saw stars. They were the brightest in
heaven, for the entry booth was the pedestal of a
gigantic lantern. Across a floor tiled in symbols
unknown to him, he observed something large at
each cardinal point—an altar, two statues, and the
famous Thunderstone, he guessed; they were
shrouded in cloth of gold. Before the eastern
object was stretched a band, the far side of which
seemed to be aglow.

He gathered his courage and approached. The
thing was a parchment, about eight feet long and
four wide, hung by cords from the upper corners
to a supporting member of the dome. The cords
appeared to be glued fast, as if to avoid making
holes in the surface. The lower edge of the scroll,
two feet above the floor, was likewise secured: but
to a pair of anvils surely brought here for the
purpose. Nevertheless the parchment flapped and
rattled a bit in the wind. It was covered with
cabalistic signs.

Cappen stepped around to the other side, and
whistled low. That held a picture, within a narrow
border. Past the edge of what might be a pergola,
the scene went to a meadowland made stately by
oak trees standing at random intervals. About a
mile away—the perspective was marvelously
executed—stood a building of manorial size in a
style he had never seen before, twistily colon-
naded, extravagantly sweeping of roof and eaves,
blood-red. A formal garden surrounded it, whose

paths and topiaries were of equally alien outline; fountains sprang in intricate patterns. Beyond the house, terrain rolled higher, and snowpeaks thrust above the horizon. The sky was deep blue.

"What the pox!" exploded from Jamie. "Sunshine's coming out of that painting. I *feel* it."

Cappen rallied his wits and paid heed. Yes, warmth as well as light, and . . . and odors? And were those fountains not actually at play?

An eerie thrilling took him. "I . . . believe . . . we've . . . found the gate," he said.

He poked his spear cautiously at the scroll. The point met no resistance; it simply moved on. Jamie went behind. "You've not pierced it," he reported. "Nothing sticks out on this side—which, by the way, is quite solid."

"No," Cappen answered faintly, "the spearhead's in the next world."

He drew the weapon back. He and Jamie stared at each other.

"Well?" said the Northerner.

"We'll never get a better chance," Cappen's throat responded for him. "It'd be blind foolishness to retreat now, unless we decide to give up the whole venture."

"We, uh, we could go tell Molin, no, the Prince what we've found."

"And be cast into a madhouse? If the Prince did send investigators anyway, the plotters need merely take this thing down and hide it till the squad has left. No." Cappen squared his shoulders. "Do what you like, Jamie, but I am going through."

Underneath, he heartily wished he had less self-respect, or at least that he weren't in love with Danlis.

Jamie scowled and sighed. "Aye, right you are, I suppose. I'd not looked for matters to take so

headlong a course. I awaited that we'd simply
scout around. Had I foreseen this, I'd have roused
the lassies to bid them, well, goodnight." He
hefted his spear and drew his sword. Abruptly he
laughed. "Whatever comes, 'twill not be dull!"

Stepping high over the threshold, Cappen went
forward.

It felt like walking through any door, save that
he entered a mild summer's day. After Jamie had
followed, he saw that the vista in the parchment
was that on which he had just turned his back: a
veiled mass, a pillar, stars above a nighted city. He
checked the opposite side of the strip, and met the
same designs as had been painted on its mate.

No, he thought, not its mate. If he had understood Enas Yorl aright, and rightly remembered
what his tutor in mathematics had told him about
esoteric geometry, there could be but a single
scroll. One side of it gave on this universe, the
other side on his, and a spell had twisted
dimensions until matter could pass straight
between.

Here too the parchment was suspended by
cords, though in a pergola of yellow marble,
whose circular stairs led down to the meadow. He
imagined a sikkintair would find the passage
tricky, especially if it was burdened with two
women in its claws. The monster had probably
hugged them close to it, come in at high speed,
folded its wings, and glided between the pillars of
the dome and the margins of the gate. On the
outbound trip, it must have crawled through into
Sanctuary.

All this Cappen did and thought in half a dozen
heartbeats. A shout yanked his attention back.
Three men who had been idling on the stairs had
noticed the advent and were on their way up.
Large and hard-featured, they bore the shaven

visages, high-crested morions, gilt cuirasses, black tunics and boots, shortswords, and halberds of temple guards. "Who in the Unholy's name are you?" called the first. "What're you doing here?"

Jamie's qualms vanished under a tide of boyish glee. "I doubt they'll believe any words of ours," he said. "We'll have to convince them a different way. If you can handle him on our left, I'll take his feres."

Cappen felt less confident. But he lacked time to be afraid; shuddering would have to be done in a more convenient hour. Besides, he was quite a good fencer. He dashed across the floor and down the stair.

The trouble was, he had no experience with spears. He jabbed. The halberdier held his weapon, both hands close together, near the middle of the shaft. He snapped it against Cappen's, deflected the thrust, and nearly tore the minstrel's out of his grasp. The watchman's return would have skewered his enemy, had the minstrel not flopped straight to the marble.

The guard guffawed, braced his legs wide, swung the halberd back for an axhead blow. As it descended, his hands shifted toward the end of the helve.

Chips flew. Cappen had rolled downstairs. He twirled the whole way to the ground and sprang erect. He still clutched his spear, which had bruised him whenever he crossed above it. The sentry bellowed and hopped in pursuit. Cappen ran.

Behind them, a second guard sprawled and flopped, diminuendo, in what seemed an impossibly copious and bright amount of blood. Jamie had hurled his own spear as he charged and taken the man in the neck. The third was giving the Northerner a brisk fight, halberd against claymore. He had longer reach, but the redhead had more brawn. Thump and clatter rang across the daisies.

Cappen's adversary was bigger than he was. This had the drawback that the former could not change speed or direction as readily. When the guard was pounding along at his best clip, ten or twelve feet in the rear, Cappen stopped within a coin's breadth, whirled about, and threw his shaft. He did not do that as his comrade had done. He pitched it between the guard's legs. The man crashed to the grass. Cappen plunged in. He didn't risk trying for a stab. That would let the armored combatant grapple him. He wrenched the halberd loose and skipped off.

The sentinel rose. Cappen reached an oak and tossed the halberd. It lodged among boughs. He drew blade. His foe did the same.

Shortsword versus rapier—much better, though Cappen must have a care. The torso opposing him was protected. Still, the human anatomy has more vulnerable points than that. "Shall we dance?" Cappen asked.

As he and Jamie approached the house, a shadow slid across them. They glanced aloft and saw the gaunt black form of a sikkintair. For an instant, they nerved themselves for the worst. However, the Flying Knife simply caught an updraft, planed high, and hovered in sinister magnificence. "Belike they don't hunt men unless commanded to," the Northerner speculated. "Bear and buffalo are meatier."

Cappen frowned at the scarlet walls before him. "The next question," he said, "is why nobody has come out against us." .

"Um, I'd deem those wights we left scattered around were the only fighting men here. What task was theirs? Why, to keep the ladies from escaping, if those are allowed to walk outdoors by day. As for yon manse, while it's plenty big, I suspect it's on loan from its owner. Naught but a few servants need be on hand—and the women, let's hope. I don't suppose anybody happened to see our little brawl.''

The thought that they might effect the rescue— soon, safely, easily—went through Cappen in a wave of dizziness. Afterward—He and Jamie had discussed that. If the temple hierophants, from Hazroah on down, were put under immediate arrest, that ought to dispose of the vengeance problem.

Gravel scrunched underfoot. Rose, jasmine, honeysuckle sweetened the air. Fountains leaped and chimed. The partners reached the main door. It was oaken, with many glass eyes inset; the knocker had the shape of a sikkintair.

Jamie leaned his spear, unsheathed his sword, turned the knob left-handed, and swung the door open. A maroon sumptuousness of carpet, hangings, upholstery brooded beyond. He and Cappen entered. Inside were quietness and an odor like that just before a thunderstorm.

A man in a deacon's black robe came through an archway, his tonsure agleam in the dimness. ''Did I hear—Oh!'' he gasped, and scuttled backward.

Jamie made a long arm and collared him. ''Not so fast, friend,'' the warrior said genially. ''We've a request, and if you oblige, we won't get stains on this pretty rug. Where are your guests?''

''What, what, what,'' the deacon gobbled.

Jamie shook him, in leisured wise lest he quite dislocate the shoulder. ''Lady Rosanda, wife to Molin Torchholder, and her assistant Danlis. Take us to them. Oh, and we'd liefer not meet folk along the way. It might get messy if we did.''

The deacon fainted.

"Ah, well," Jamie said. "I hate the idea of cutting down unarmed men, but chances are they won't be foolhardy." He filled his lungs. *"Rosanda!"* he bawled. *"Danlis! Jamie and Cappen Varra are here! Come on home!"*

The volume almost bowled his companion over. "Are you mad?" the minstrel exclaimed. "You'll warn the whole staff—" A flash lit his mind: if they had seen no further guards, surely there were none, and nothing corporeal remained to fear. Yet every minute's delay heightened the danger of something else going wrong. Somebody might find signs of invasion back in the temple; the gods alone knew what lurked in this realm . . . Yes, Jamie's judgment might prove mistaken, but it was the best he could have made.

Servitors appeared, and recoiled from naked steel. And then, and then—

Through a doorway strode Danlis. She led by the hand, or dragged, a half-hysterical Rosanda. Both were decently attired and neither looked abused, but pallor in cheeks and smudges under eyes bespoke what they must have suffered.

Cappen came nigh dropping his spear. "Beloved!" he cried. "Are you hale?"

"We've not been ill-treated in the flesh, aside from the snatching itself," she answered efficiently. "The threats, should Hazroah not get his way, have been cruel. Can we leave now?"

"Aye, the soonest, the best," Jamie growled. "Lead them on ahead, Cappen." His sword covered the rear. On his way out, he retrieved the spear he had left.

They started back over the garden paths. Danlis and Cappen between them must help Rosanda along. That woman's plump prettiness was lost in tears, moans, whimpers, and occasional screams.

He paid scant attention. His gaze kept seeking the clear profile of his darling. When her grey eyes turned toward him, his heart became a lyre.

She parted her lips. He waited for her to ask in dazzlement, "How did you ever do this, you unbelievable, wonderful men?"

"What have we ahead of us?" she wanted to know.

Well, it was an intelligent query. Cappen swallowed disappointment and sketched the immediate past. Now, he said, they'd return via the gate to the dome and make their stealthy way from the temple, thence to Molin's dwelling for a joyous reunion. But then they must act promptly —yes, roust the Prince out of bed for authorization—and occupy the temple and arrest everybody in sight before new trouble got fetched from this world.

Rosanda gained some self-control as he talked. "Oh, my, oh, my," she wheezed, "you unbelievable, wonderful men."

An ear-piercing trill slashed across her voice. The escapers looked behind them. At the entrance to the house stood a thickset middle-aged person in the scarlet robe of a ranking priest of Ils. He held a pipe to his mouth and blew.

"Hazroah!" Rosanda shrilled. "The ringleader!"

"The High Flamen—" Danlis began.

A rush in the air interrupted. Cappen flung his vision skyward and knew the nightmare was true. The sikkintair was descending. Hazroah had summoned it.

"Why, you son of a bitch!" Jamie roared. Still well behind the rest, he lifted his spear, brought it back, flung it with his whole strength and weight. The point went home in Hazroah's breast. Ribs did not stop it. He spouted blood, crumpled, and spouted no more. The shaft quivered above his body.

But the sikkintair's vast wings eclipsed the sun. Jamie rejoined his band and plucked the second spear from Cappen's fingers. "Hurry on, lad," he ordered. "Get them to safety."

"Leave you? No!" protested his comrade.

Jamie spat an oath. "Do you want the whole faring to've gone for naught? Hurry, I said!"

Danlis tugged at Cappen's sleeve. "He's right. The state requires our testimony."

Cappen stumbled onward. From time to time he glanced back.

In the shadow of the wings, Jamie's hair blazed. He stood foursquare, spear grasped as a huntsman does. Agape, the Flying Knife rushed down upon him. Jamie thrust straight between those jaws, and twisted.

The monster let out a sawtoothed shriek. Its wings threshed, made thundercrack, it swooped by, a foot raked. Jamie had his claymore out. He parried the blow.

The sikkintair rose. The shaft waggled from its throat. It spread great ebon membranes, looped, and came back earthward. Its claws were before it. Air whirred behind.

Jamie stood his ground, sword in right hand, knife in left. As the talons smote, he fended them off with the dirk. Blood sprang from his thigh, but his byrnie took most of the edged sweep. And his sword hewed.

The sikkintair ululated again. It tried to ascend, and couldn't. Jamie had crippled its left wing. It landed—Cappen felt the impact through soles and bones—and hitched itself toward him. From around the spear came a geyser hiss.

Jamie held fast where he was. As fangs struck at him, he sidestepped, sprang back, and threw his shoulders against the shaft. Leverage swung jaws aside. He glided by the neck toward the forequarters. Both of his blades attacked the spine.

Cappen and the women hastened on.

They were almost at the pergola when footfalls drew his eyes rearward. Jamie loped at an over-taking pace. Behind him, the sikkintair lay in a heap.

The redhead pulled alongside. "Hai, what a fight!" he panted. "Thanks for this journey, friend! A drinking bout's worth of thanks!"

They mounted the death-defiled stairs. Cappen peered across miles. Wings beat in heaven, from the direction of the mountains. Horror stabbed his guts. "Look!" He could barely croak.

Jamie squinted. "More of them," he said. "A score, maybe. We can't cope with so many. An army couldn't."

"That whistle was heard farther away than mortals would hear," Danlis added starkly.

"What do we linger for?" Rosanda wailed. "Come, take us home!"

"And the sikkintairs follow?" Jamie retorted. "No. I've my lassies, and kinfolk, and—." He moved to stand before the parchment. Edged metal dripped in his hands; red lay splashed across helm, ringmail, clothing, face. His grin broke forth, wry. "A spaewife once told me I'd die on the far side of strangeness. I'll wager she didn't know her own strength."

"You assume that the mission of the beasts is to destroy us, and when that is done they will return to their lairs." The tone Danlis used might have served for a remark about the weather.

"Aye, what else? The harm they'd wreak would be in a hunt for us. But put to such trouble, they could grow furious and harry our whole world. That's the more likely when Hazroah lies skewered. Who else can control them?"

"None that I know of, and he talked quite frankly to us." She nodded. "Yes, it behooves us to die where we are." Rosanda sank down and blubbered. Danlis showed irritation. "Up!" she commanded her mistress. "Up and meet your fate like a Rankan matron!"

Cappen goggled hopelessly at her. She gave him a smile. "Have no regrets, dear," she said. "You did well. The conspiracy against the state has been checked."

The far side of strangeness—check—chessboard —that version of chess where you pretend the right and left sides of the board are identical on a cylinder—tumbled through Cappen. The Flying Knives drew closer fast. *Curious aspects of geometry—*

Lightning-smitten, he knew ... or guessed he did ... "No, Jamie, we go!" he yelled.

"To no avail save reaping of innocents?" The big man hunched his shoulders. "Never."

"Jamie, let us by! I can close the gate. I swear I can—I swear by—by Eshi—"

The Northerner locked eyes with Cappen for a span that grew. At last: "You are my brother in arms." He stood aside. "Go on."

The sikkintairs were so near that the noise of their speed reached Cappen. He urged Danlis toward the scroll. She lifted her skirt a trifle, revealing a dainty ankle, and stepped through. He hauled on Rosanda's wrist. The woman wavered to her feet but seemed unable to find her direction. Cappen took an arm and passed it into the next world for Danlis to pull. Himself, he gave a mighty shove on milady's buttocks. She crossed over.

He did. And Jamie.

Beneath the temple dome, Cappen's rapier

reached high and slashed. Louder came the racket of cloven air. Cappen severed the upper cords. The parchment fell, wrinkling, crackling. He dropped his weapon, a-clang, squatted, and stretched his arms wide. The free corners he seized. He pulled them to the corners that were still secured, to make a closed band of the scroll.

From it sounded monstrous thumps and scrapes. The sikkintairs were crawling into the pergola. For them the portal must hang unchanged, open for their hunting.

Cappen gave that which he held a half-twist and brought the edges back together.

Thus he created a surface which had but a single side and a single edge. Thus he obliterated the gate.

He had not been sure what would follow. He had fleetingly supposed he would smuggle the scroll out, held in its paradoxical form, and eventually glue it—unless he could burn it. But upon the instant that he completed the twist and juncture, the parchment was gone. Enas Yorl told him afterward that he had made it impossible for the thing to exist.

Air rushed in where the gate had been, crack and hiss. Cappen heard that sound as it were an alien word of incantation: "Möbius-s-s."

Having stolen out of the temple and some distance thence, the party stopped for a few minutes of recovery before they proceeded to Molin's house.

This was in a blind alley off the avenue, a brick-paved recess where flowers grew in planters, shared by the fanes of two small and gentle gods. Wind had died away, stars glimmered bright, a half moon stood above easterly roofs and cast wan argence. Afar, a tomcat serenaded his intended.

Rosanda had gotten back a measure of equilibrium. She cast herself against Jamie's breast. "Oh, hero, hero," she crooned, "you shall have reward, yes, treasure, ennoblement, everything!" She snuggled. "But nothing greater than my unbounded thanks . . . .

The Northerner cocked an eyebrow at Cappen. The bard shook his head a little. Jamie nodded in understanding, and disengaged. "Uh, have a care, milady," he said. "Pressing against ringmail, all bloody and sweaty too, can't be good for a complexion."

Even if one rescues them, it is not wise to trifle with the wives of magnates.

Cappen had been busy himself. For the first time, he kissed Danlis on her lovely mouth; then for the second time; then for the third. She responded decorously.

Thereafter she likewise withdrew. Moonlight made a mystery out of her classic beauty. "Cappen," she said, "before we go on, we had better have a talk."

He gaped. "What?"

She bridged her fingers. "Urgent matters first," she continued crisply. "Once we get to the mansion and wake the high priest, it will be chaos at first, conference later, and I—as a woman—excluded from serious discussion. Therefore best I give my counsel now, for you to relay. Not that Molin or the Prince are fools; the measures to take are for the most part obvious. However, swift action is desirable, and they will have been caught by surprise."

She ticked her points off. "First, as you have indicated, the Hell Hounds"—her nostrils pinched in distaste at the nickname—"the Imperial elite guard should mount an immediate raid on the temple of Ils and arrest all personnel for interrogation, except the Archpriest. He's probably innocent, and in any event it would be inept politics. Hazroah's death may have removed the danger, but this should not be taken for granted. Even if it has, his co-conspirators ought to be identified and made examples of.

"Yet, second, wisdom should temper justice. No lasting harm was done, unless we count those persons who are trapped in the parallel universe; and they doubtless deserve to be."

They seemed entirely males, Cappen recalled. He grimaced in compassion. Of course, the sikkintairs might eat them.

Danlis was talking on: "—humane governance and the art of compromise. A grand temple dedicated to the Rankan gods is certainly required, but it need be no larger than that of Ils. Your counsel will have much weight, dear. Give it wisely. I will advise you."

"Uh?" Cappen said.

Danlis smiled and laid her hands over his. "Why, you can have unlimited preferment, after what you did," she told him. "I'll show you how to apply for it."

"But—but I'm no blooming statesman!" Cappen stuttered.

She stepped back and considered him. "True," she agreed. "You're valiant, yes, but you're also flighty and lazy and—Well, don't despair. I will mold you."

Cappen gulped and shuffled aside. "Jamie," he said, "uh, Jamie, I feel wrung dry, dead on my feet. I'd be worse than no use—I'd be a drogue on things just when they have to move fast. Better I find me a doss, and you take the ladies home. Come over here and I'll tell you how to convey the story in fewest words. Excuse us, ladies. Some of those words you oughtn't to hear."

A week thence, Cappen Varra sat drinking in the Vulgar Unicorn. It was mid-afternoon and none else was present but the associate tapster, his wound knitted.

A man filled the doorway and came in, to Cappen's table. "Been casting about everywhere for you," the Northerner grumbled. "Where've you been?"

"Lying low," Cappen replied. "I've taken a place here in the Maze which'll do till I've dropped back into obscurity, or decide to drift elsewhere altogether." He sipped his wine. Sunbeams slanted through windows; dustmotes danced golden in their warmth; a cat lay on a sill and purred. "Trouble is, my purse is flat."

"We're free of such woes for a goodly while." Jamie flung his length into a chair and signaled the attendant. "Beer!" he thundered.

"You collected a reward, then?" the minstrel asked eagerly.

Jamie nodded. "Aye. In the way you whispered I should, before you left us. I'm baffled why and it went sore against the grain. But I did give Molin the notion that the rescue was my idea and you naught but a hanger-on whom I'd slip a few royals. He filled a box with gold and silver money, and said he wished he could afford ten times that. He offered to get me Rankan citizenship and a title as well, and make a bureaucrat of me, but I said no, thanks. We share, you and I, half and half. But right this now, drinks are on me."

"What about the plotters?" Cappen inquired.

"Ah, those. The matter's been kept quiet, as you'd await. Still, while the temple of Ils can't be abolished, seemingly it's been tamed." Jamie's regard sought across the table and sharpened. "After you disappeared, Danlis agreed to let me claim the whole honor. She knew better—Rosanda never noticed—but Danlis wanted a man of the hour to carry her redes to the prince, and none remained save me. She supposed you were simply worn out. When last I saw her, though, she ... um-m ... she 'expressed disappointment.'" He cocked his ruddy head. "Yon's quite a girl. I thought you loved her."

Cappen Varra took a fresh draught of wine. Old summers glowed along his tongue. "I did," he confessed. "I do. My heart is broken, and in part I drink to numb the pain."

Jamie raised his brows. "What? Makes no sense."

"Oh, it makes very basic sense," Cappen answered. "Broken hearts tend to heal rather soon. Meanwhile, if I may recite from a rondel I completed before you found me—

"Each sword of sorrow that would maim or slay,
My lady of the morning deftly parries.
Yet gods forbid I be the one she marries!
I rise from bed the latest hour I may.
My lady comes to me like break of day;
I dream in darkness if it chance she tarries."

THE BARBARIAN

Since the Howard-de Camp system for deciphering preglacial inscriptions first appeared, much progress has been made in tracing the history, ethnology, and even daily life of the great cultures which flourished till the Pleistocene ice age wiped them out and forced man to start over. We know, for instance, that magic was practiced; that there were some highly civilized countries in what is now central Asia, the Near East, North Africa, southern Europe, and various oceans; and that elsewhere the world was occupied by barbarians, of whom the northern Europeans were the biggest, strongest, and most warlike. At least, so the scholars inform us, and being of northern European ancestry, they ought to know.

The following is a translation of a letter recently discovered in the ruins of Cyrenne. This was a provincial town of the Sarmian Empire, a great though decadent realm in the eastern Mediterranean area, whose capital, Sarmia, was at once the most beautiful and the most lustful, depraved city of its time. The Sarmians' northern neighbors were primitive horse nomads and/or Centaurs; but to the east lay the Kingdom of Chathakh, and to the south was the Herpetarchy of Serpens, ruled by a priestly cast of snake worshipers—or possibly snakes.

The letter was obviously written in Sarmia and

posted to Cyrenne. Its date is approximately 175,000 B.C.

Maxilion Quaestos, sub-sub-sub-prefect of the Imperial Waterworks of Sarmia, to his nephew Thyaston, Chancellor of the Bureau of Thaumaturgy, Province of Cyrenne:

Greetings!

I trust this finds you in good health, and that the gods will continue to favor you. As for me, I am well, though somewhat plagued by the gout, for which I have tried [*here follows the description of a home remedy, both tedious and unprintable*]. This has not availed, however, save to exhaust my purse and myself.

You must indeed have been out of touch during your Atlantean journey, if you must write to inquire about the Barbarian affair. Now that events have settled down again, I can, I hope, give you an adequate and dispassionate account of the whole ill-starred business. By the favor of the Triplet Goddesses, holy Sarmia has survived the episode; and though we are still rather shaken, things are improving. If at times I seem to depart from the philosophic calm I have always tried to cultivate, blame it on the Barbarian. I am not the man I used to be. None of us are.

To begin, then, about three years ago the war with Chathakh had settled down to border skirmishes. An occasional raid by one side or the other would penetrate deeply into the countries themselves, but with no decisive effect. Indeed, since these operations yielded a more or less equal amount of booty for both lands, and the slave trade grew brisk, it was good for business.

Our chief concern was the ambiguous attitude of Serpens. As you well know, the Herpetarchs have no love for us, and a major object of our diplomacy was to keep them from entering the war on the side of Chathakh. We had, of course, no hope of making them our allies. But as long as we maintained a posture of strength, it was likely that they would at least stay neutral.

Thus matters stood when the Barbarian came to Sarmia.

We had heard rumors of him for a long time. He was a wandering soldier of fortune, from some kingdom of swordsmen and seafarers up in the northern forests, who had drifted south, alone, in search of adventure or perhaps only a better climate. Seven feet tall, and broad in proportion, he was one mass of muscle, with a mane of tawny hair and sullen blue eyes. He was adept with any weapon, but preferred a four-foot double-edged sword with which he could cleave helmet, skull, neck, and so on down at one blow. He was additionally said to be a drinker and lover of awesome capacity.

Having overcome the Centaurs singlehanded, he tramped down through our northern provinces and one day stood at the gates of Sarmia herself. It was a curious vision—the turreted walls rearing over the stone-paved road, the guards bearing helmet and shield and corselet, and the towering, near-naked giant who rattled his blade before them. As their pikes slanted down to bar his way, he cried in a voice of thunder:

"I yam Cronkheit duh Barbarian, an' I wanna audience widjer queen!"

His accent was so ludicrously uneducated that the watch burst into laughter. This angered him; flushing darkly, he drew his sword and advanced stiff-legged. The guardsmen reeled back before him, and the Barbarian swaggered through.

As the captain of the watch explained it to me afterward: "There he came, and there we stood. A spear length away, we caught the smell. Ye gods, *when* did he last bathe?"

So with people running from the streets and bazaars as he neared, Cronkheit made his way down the Avenue of Sphinxes, past the baths and the Temple of Loccar, till he reached the Imperial Palace. Its gates stood open as usual, and he looked in at the gardens and the alabaster walls beyond, and grunted. When the Golden Guardsmen approached him upwind and asked his business, he grunted again. They lifted their bows and would have made short work of him, but a slave came hastily to bid them desist.

You see, by the will of some malignant god, the Empress was standing on a balcony and saw him.

As is well known, our beloved Empress, Her Seductive Majesty the Illustrious Lady Larra the Voluptuous, is built like a mountain highway and is commonly believed to be an incarnation of her tutelary deity, Aphrosex, the Mink Goddess. She stood on the balcony, the wind blowing her thin transparent garments and thick black hair, and a sudden eagerness lit her proud lovely face. This was understandable, for Cronkheit wore simply a bearskin kilt.

Hence the slave was dispatched, to bow low before the stranger and say: "Most noble lord, the divine Empress would have private speech with you."

Cronkheit smacked his lips and strutted into the palace. The chamberlain wrung his hands when he saw those large muddy feet treading on priceless rugs, but there was no help for it, and the Barbarian was led upstairs to the Imperial bedchamber.

What befell there is known to all, for of course in such interviews the Lady Larra posts mute slaves at convenient peepholes, to summon the guards if danger seems to threaten; and the courtiers have quietly taught these mutes to write. Our Empress had a cold, and had furthermore been eating a garlic salad, so her aristocratically curved nose was not offended. After a few formalities, she began to pant. Slowly, then, she held out her arms and let the purple robe slide down from her creamy shoulders and across the silken thighs.

"Come," she whispered. "Come, magnificent male."

Cronkheit snorted, pawed the ground, rushed forth, and clasped her to him.

"Yowww!" cried the Empress as a rib cracked. "Leggo! Help!"

The mutes ran for the Golden Guardsmen, who entered at once. They got ropes around the Barbarian and dragged him from their poor lady. Though in considerable pain, and much shaken, she did not order his execution; she is known to be very patient with some types.

Indeed, after gulping a cup of wine to steady her, she invited Cronkheit to be her guest. After he had been conducted off to his rooms, she summoned the Duchess of Thyle, a supple, agile little minx.

"I have a task for you, my dear," she murmured. "You will fulfill it as a loyal lady-in-waiting."

"Yes, Your Seductive Majesty," said the Duchess, who could well guess what the task was and thought she had been waiting long enough. For a whole week, in fact. Her assignment was to take the edge off the Barbarian's impetuosity.

She greased herself so she could slip free if in peril of being crushed, and hurried to Cronkheit's suite. Her musky perfume drowned out his odor, and she slipped off her dress and crooned with halfshut eyes: "Take me, my lord!"

"Yahoo!" howled the warrior. "I yam Cronkheit duh Strong, Cronkheit duh Bold, Cronkheit what slew a mammot' single-handed an' made hisself chief o' duh Centaurs, an' dis's muh night! C'mere!"

The Duchess did, and he folded her in his mighty arms. A moment later came another shriek. The palace attendants were treated to the sight of a naked and furious duchess speeding down the jade corridor.

"Fleas he's got!" she cried, scratching as she ran.

So all in all, Cronkheit the Barbarian was no great success as a lover. Even the women in the Street of Joy used to hide when they saw him coming. They said they'd been exposed to clumsy technique before, but this was just too much.

However, his fame was so great that the Lady Larra put him in command of a brigade, infantry and cavalry, and sent him to join General Grythion on the Chathakh border. He made the march in record time and came shouting into the city of tents which had grown up at our main base.

Now, admittedly our good General Grythion is somewhat of a dandy, who curls his beard and is henpecked by his wives. But he has always been a competent soldier, winning honors at the Academy and leading troops in battle many times before rising to the strategic-planning post. One could understand Cronkheit's incivility at their meeting. But when the general courteously declined to go forth in the van of the army and pointed out how much more valuable he was as a coordinator behind the lines—that was no excuse for Cronkheit to knock his superior officer to the ground and call him a coward, damned of the gods. Grythion was thoroughly justified in having him put in irons, despite the casualties involved. Even as it was, the spectacle so demoralized our troops that they lost three important engagements in the following month.

Alas! Word of this reached the Empress, and she did not order Cronkheit's head struck off. Indeed, she sent back a command that he be released and reinstated. Perhaps she still cherished a hope of civilizing him enough to be an acceptable bed partner.

Grythion swallowed his pride and apologized to the Barbarian, who accepted with an ill grace. His restored rank made it necessary to invite him to a dinner and conference in the headquarters tent.

That was a flat failure. Cronkheit stamped in and at once made sneering remarks about the elegant togas of his brother officers. He belched when he ate and couldn't distinguish the product of any vineyard from another. His conversation consisted of hour-long monologues about his own prowess. General Grythion saw morale zooming downward, and hastily called for maps and planning.

"Now, most noble sirs," he began, "we have to lay out the summer campaign. As you know, we have the Eastern Desert between us and the nearest important enemy positions. This raises difficult questions of logistics and catapult emplacement." He turned politely to the Barbarian. "Have you any suggestion, my lord?"

"Duh," said Cronkheit.

"I think," ventured Colonel Pharaon, "that if we advanced to the Chunling Oasis and dug in there, building a supply road—"

"Dat reminds me," said Cronkheit. "One time up in duh Norriki marshes, I run acrost some swamp men an' dey uses poisoned arrers—"

"I fail to see what that has to do with this problem," said General Grythion.

"Nuttin'," admitted Cronkheit cheerfully. "But don't innerup' me. Like I was sayin' . . ." And he was off for a whole dreary hour.

At the end of a conference which had gotten nowhere, the general stroked his beard and said shrewdly: "Lord Cronkheit, it appears your abilities are more in the tactical than the strategic field."

The Barbarian snatched for his sword.

"I mean," said Grythion quickly, "I have a task which only the boldest and strongest leader can accomplish."

Cronkheit beamed and listened closely for a change. He was to lead an expedition to capture Chantsay. This was a fort in the mountain passes across the Eastern Desert, and a major obstacle to our advance. However, in spite of Grythion's judicious flattery, a full brigade should have been able to take it with little difficulty, for it was known to be undermanned.

Cronkheit rode off at the head of his men, tossing his sword in the air and bellowing some uncouth battle chant. Then he was not heard of for six weeks.

At the close of that time, the ragged, starving, fever-stricken remnant of his troops staggered back to the base and reported utter failure. Cronkheit, who was in excellent health himself, made sullen excuses. But he had never imagined that men who march twenty hours a day aren't fit for battle at the end of the trip—the more so if they outrun their supply train.

Because of the Empress' wish, General Grythion could not do the sensible thing and cashier the Barbarian. He could not even reduce him to the ranks. Instead, he used his well-known guile and invited the giant to a private dinner.

"Obviously, most valiant lord," he purred, "the fault is mine. I should have realized that a man of your type is too much for us decadent southerners. You are a lone wolf who fights best by himself."

"Duh," agreed Cronkheit, ripping a fowl apart with his fingers and wiping them on the damask tablecloth.

Grythion winced, but easily talked him into

going out on a one-man guerrilla operation. When he left the next morning, the officers' corps congratulated themselves on having gotten rid of the lout forever.

In the face of subsequent criticism and demands for an investigation, I still maintain that Grythion did the only rational thing under the circumstances. Who could have known that Cronkheit the Barbarian was so primitive that rationality simply slid off his hairy skin?

The full story will never be known. But apparently, in the course of the following year, while the border war continued as usual, Cronkheit struck off into the northern uplands. There he raised a band of horse nomads as ignorant and brutal as himself. He also rounded up a herd of mammoths and drove them into Chathakh, stampeding them at the foe. By such means, he reached their very capital, and the King offered terms of surrender.

But Cronkheit would have none of this. Not he! His idea of warfare was to kill or enslave every last man, woman, and child of the enemy nation. Also, his irregulars were supposed to be paid in loot. Also, being too unsanitary even for the nomad girls, he felt a certain urgency.

So he stormed the capital of Chathakh and burned it to the ground. This cost him most of his own men. It also destroyed several priceless books and works of art, and any possibility of tribute to Sarmia.

Then he had the nerve to organize a triumphal procession and ride back to our own city!

This was too much even for the Empress. When he stood before her—for he was too crude for the simple courtesy of a knee bend—she exceeded herself in describing the many kinds of fool, idiot, and all-around blockhead he was.

"Duh," said Cronkheit. "But I won duh war. Look, I won duh war, I did. I won duh war."

"Yes," hissed the Lady Larra. "You smashed an ancient and noble culture to irretrievable ruin. And did you know that half our peacetime trade was with Chathakh? There'll be a business depression now such as history has never seen before."

General Grythion, who had returned, added his own reproaches. "Why do you think wars are fought?" he asked bitterly. "War is an extension of diplomacy. It's the final means of making somebody else do what you want. The object is *not* to kill them off. How can corpses obey you?"

Cronkheit growled in his throat.

"We would have negotiated a peace in which Chathakh became our ally against Serpens," went on the general. "Then we'd have been safe against all comers. But you—you've made a howling wilderness which we must garrison with our own troops lest the nomads take it over. Your atrocities have alienated every civilized state. You've left us alone and friendless. You've won this war by losing the next one!"

"And on top of the depression which is coming," said the Empress, "we'll have the cost of maintaining those garrisons. Taxes down and expenditures up—it may break the treasury, and then where are we?"

Cronkheit spat on the floor. "Yuh're decadent, dat's what yuh are," he snarled. "Be good for yuh if yer empire breaks up. Yuh oughtta get dat city rabble o' yers out in duh woods an' make hunters of 'em, like me. Let 'em eat steak."

The Lady Larra stamped an exquisite gold-shod foot. "Do you think we've nothing better to do with our time than spend the whole day hunting, and sit around in mud hovels at night licking the grease off our fingers?" she cried. "What the hell do you think civilization is for, anyway?"

Cronkheit drew his great sword. It flashed

against their eyes. "I hadda nuff!" he bellowed.
"I'm t'rough widjuh! It's time yuh was wiped off
duh face o' duh eart, and I'm jus' duh guy t' do it!"

And now General Grythion showed the qualities
which had raised him to his high post. Artfully, he
quailed. "Oh, no!" he whimpered. "You're not
going to—to—to fight on the side of Serpens?"

"I yam," said Cronkheit. "So long." The last we
saw of him was a broad, indignant, flea-bitten
back, headed south, and the reflection of the sun
on a sword.

Since then, of course, our affairs have
prospered and Serpens is now frantically suing
for peace. But we intend to prosecute the war till
they meet our terms. We are most assuredly not
going to be ensnared by their treacherous pleas
and take the Barbarian back!

ON THUD AND BLUNDER

With one stroke of his fifty-pound sword, Gnorts the Barbarian lopped off the head of Nialliv the Wizard. It flew through the air, still sneering, while Gnorts clove two royal guardsmen from vizor through breastplate to steel jockstrap. As he whirled to escape, an arrow glanced off his own chainmail. Then he was gone from the room, into the midnight city. Easily outrunning pursuit, he took a few sentries at the gate by surprise. For a moment, arms and legs hailed around him through showers of blood; then he had opened the gate and was free. A caravan of merchants, waiting to enter at dawn, was camped nearby. Seeing a magnificent stallion tethered, Gnorts released it, twisted the rope into a bridle, and rode it off bareback. After galloping several miles, he encountered a mounted patrol that challenged him. Immediately he plunged into the thick of the cavalrymen, swinging his blade right and left with deadly effect, rearing up his steed to bring its forefeet against one knight who dared to confront him directly. Then it was only to gallop onward. Winter winds lashed his body, attired in nothing more than a bearskin kilt, but he ignored the cold. Sunrise revealed the shore and his waiting longship. He knew the swift-sailing craft could bring him across five hundred leagues of monster-infested ocean in time for him to snatch the maiden princess Elamef away from evil Baron

*Rehcel while she remained a maiden—not that he
intended to leave her in that condition . . . .*

Exaggerated? Of course. But, unfortunately, not
much, where some stories are concerned.

Today's rising popularity of heroic fantasy, or
sword-and-sorcery as it is also called, is certainly
a Good Thing for those of us who enjoy it. Probably this is part of a larger movement back toward
old-fashioned   storytelling,   with   colorful
backgrounds,   events,   and   characters,   tales
wherein people do take arms against a sea of
troubles and usually win. Such literature is not
inherently superior to the introspective or
symbolic kinds, but neither is it inherently
inferior; Homer and James Joyce were both great
artists.

Yet every kind of writing is prone to special
faults. For example, while no one expects heroic
fantasy (hf) to be of ultimate psychological
profundity, it is often simple to the point of being
simplistic. This is not necessary, as such fine
practitioners as de Camp, Leiber, and Tolkien
have proven.

Worse, because it is still more obvious and still
less excusable, is a frequent lack of elementary
knowledge or plain common sense on the part of
an author. A small minority of hf stories are set in
real historical milieus, where the facts provide a
degree of control—though howling errors remain
all too easy to make. Most members of the genre,
however, take place in an imaginary world. It may
be a pre-glacial civilization like Howard's, an
altered time-line like Kurtz's, another planet like
Eddison's, a remote future like Vance's, a completely invented universe like Dunsany's, or what
have you; the point is, nobody pretends this is
aught but a Never-Never Land, wherein the author
is free to arrange geography, history, theology,
and the laws of nature to suit himself. Given that

freedom, far too many writers nowadays have supposed that anything whatsoever goes, that practical day-to-day details are of no importance and hence they, the writers, have no homework to do before they start spinning their yarns.

Not so! The consequence of making that assumption is, inevitably, a sleazy product. It may be bought by an editor hard up for material, but it will carry none of the conviction, the illusion of reality, which helps make the work of the people mentioned above, and other good writers, memorable. At best, it will drop into oblivion; at worst, it will stand as an awful example. If our field becomes swamped with this kind of garbage, readers are going to go elsewhere for entertainment and there will be no more hf.

Beneath the magic, derring-do, and other glamour, an imaginary world has to *work* right. In particular, a pre-industrial society, which is what virtually all hf uses for a setting, differs from ours today in countless ways. A writer need not be a walking encyclopedia to get most of these straight. A reasonable amount of research, or sometimes merely a reasonable amount of logical thinking, will do it for him. Let's consider a few points. A proper discussion would require a book, but we can make a start.

First, some remarks on those societies. Most cultures in hf are based on the European, often as a mishmash of Roman Empire, Dark Ages, and high Middle Ages with a bit of Pharaonic Egypt, Asian nomadism, and so forth on the fringes. This is not bad in itself. Howard succeeded with it. And indeed, the western end of the Eurasian continent was a rather similar potpourri during the *Völkerwanderung* period (if you regard the Byzantine Empire as the civilized core of Christendom). I do think the time is overpast for drawing inspiration from other milieus—Oriental, Near Eastern,

North and Black African, Amerindian, Polynesian,
an entire world—and am happy to see that several
writers have begun doing so. However, in this
essay I'll stick close to home.

Even the writers I have cited say little about the
producing classes in their worlds, with the
notable exception of de Camp. Yet the fact is that
it takes a lot of peasants, artisans, and such-like
humble people to support one noble or, for that
matter, one bandit or roving barbarian. We tend to
forget this in our mechanized modern Western
civilization, where only a small percentage of the
work force is occupied with the necessities of life.
Right up till the early part of the twentieth
century, though, most of our own population was
rural, as most of it still is elsewhere on Earth. In
town, the typical worker was not one of the kind
we know, putting in forty comparatively easy
hours a week, owning a house and car and the
other customary amenities. No, he was a dirt-poor
hod carrier or ditch digger or something like that,
laboring almost till he dropped of exhaustion and
glad to get the job. While unions doubtless helped
improve his lot, they could not have done so
without the increased productivity which
advancing technology made possible.

Thus our creator of hf can gain verisimilitude
and interesting detail by paying some attention to
the lower classes, the vast majority of his world's
population. Besides, their situation affects what
his hero can do. For example, in many medieval
countries the peasants were subject to a military
draft; the king could summon them to fight his
wars for him. However, the time of year at which
he could do so was strictly circumscribed by law.
He couldn't call them up before the crops were in,
nor keep them till harvest, lest everybody starve.
Harold of England faced this problem in 1066.
William of Normandy, commanding mostly

mercenaries and adventurers, did not to the same degree.

Incidentally, mercenaries are not always reliable. They tend to make trouble if they don't get paid—and medieval monarchs were chronically short of money. Early in the fourteenth century, a troop of Catalans practically took the Byzantine Empire apart on that account. Mercenaries are also likely to be more interested in their own survival and prerogatives, especially loot, than in furthering the interests of their employers. The backbone of Rome was the yeoman farmer class, from which the legions were recruited; when this was destroyed by the Punic Wars and their aftermath, and Rome must gradually go more and more to hirelings, her doom was sealed. Surely a number of good hf stories lie in this motif.

Returning to peasants, laborers, merchants, and the rest, these words are too general. How well off are such people, how leisured, how independent? That has varied tremendously throughout history. Free landholders in Scandinavia would originally get together to make their own laws, try their own cases, accept a new king and then depose him later if they didn't like him. Their descendants became wretched tenants and, in Denmark, outright serfs. In contrast, though by our standards workers in cities put in long, hard hours and were under many restrictions: still, after the Black Death had furnished a convenient labor shortage, they were comparatively well off. In fact, for some centuries they enjoyed more leisure, in the form of frequent holidays, than we do now.

Thus the status of ordinary people has depended on social conditions as much as technological. If taxes and other governmental demands on them were moderate, they had plenty of spare time and energy, in between bouts of toil that would kill many of us today. As those demands grew, so did their misery. Of course, in either case they were subject to famines and pestilences—another detail unmentioned in most hf, yet potent narrative matter.

A medieval city was curiously divided. On the one hand, the respectable part of it was highly structured, with guilds controlling much of the private lives as well as the work of members. On the other hand, the poor sector was chaotic and dangerous, as we may read in the poems of Villon. Between Internal Revenue and welfare, we seem to be re-approaching this dichotomy. We do still have fairly sharp geographical separation of urban classes. In an ancient or medieval town, any districts there were were usually along occupational lines. A rich merchant would live near the appropriate street, but his house would be apt to stand like an island in the middle of poverty, vice, and savagery. This could make our hero's abrupt exit from it more interesting than he intended.

If he left after dark, he would scarcely run as trippingly as we have shown Gnorts the Barbarian doing. People who have experienced blackouts will tell you that a nighted city without the modern invention of lights is *black*. With walls shutting off most of the sky—especially along narrow medieval streets—it is far gloomier than any open field. You'd grope your way, unless you had a torch or lantern (and then you'd better have an armed guard). Furthermore, those lanes were open sewers; in many places, stepping stones went down the middle because of that. Despite sanitary measures, metropolitan streets as late as about 1900 were often uncrossable simply because of horse droppings. Graveyards stank too: one reason why incense was used in church services.

This brings up again the prevalence of diseases such as cholera, typhoid, smallpox, and bubonic plague. They struck especially hard at cities. The fear of them was ever-present in everybody's mind. That detail could be worked into a story to telling effect.

Darkness and crime did call forth partial answers. For instance, professional escorts carrying lights were available. The Byzantines in their heyday had a regular police force, while in many Western cities of a later date each able-bodied man must help patrol his own neighborhood. I should think a wandering warrior might quickly get a job as a cop, and thereby come upon strange situations.

Or he might not. Travel could be extremely difficult, not merely because of physical problems and robbers, but because of official wariness. Fire being another hazard very much in the public awareness, you could not get into a Danish town around 1500 without convincing documentation; the fear of foreign arsonists was that great. (Doubtless it was unfounded, but we've seen enough popular paranoia in our own age, haven't we?) Elsewhere, the mayoralty might suppose you were a spy, or the guilds might not want to admit a new worker. (Again, this sounds not unfamiliar.) Contretemps like these could add depth, color, and perhaps humor to the adventures of our hero.

In fact, the whole relationship between a city and the rest of its society can be fascinating. It need not be borrowed from Western history, either—"city air is free air," the rise of the bourgeoisie, and so on. Ancient Russia, for instance, followed a course almost the reverse of ours: beginning with cities and capitalism, which stimulated agricultural development of the hinterlands.

Politics in general is much neglected in hf. Usually its governments are absolute monarchies, whether of kings or emperors, though the real world has known many different arrangements. If the monarch is tyrannical, our hero may lead a revolt and find himself the next ruler. Little or nothing is said about the infinitely intricate mechanics of organizing a rebellion or, for that matter, about the legal questions involved. Can Gnorts truly seize the throne? He'll have to have an acquiescent majority, at the very least; else his regime won't last an hour. Now Odoacer the Scyrrian could push the legitimate Roman Emperor out in 476—but he hastened to offer homage to Constantinople, and at that, his power was shaky and soon overthrown. No outsider could have won such a title in the Eastern Empire, whose lord had to be a citizen and of the Orthodox faith. The Crusaders did impose a Latin reign in 1204, but it was loathed and the Byzantines got rid of it as fast as they were able.

Howard could make Conan's accession reasonably plausible. The rest of us might do better to make our hero the power behind the throne. In fact, why must he be a barbarian? A civilized man influencing an uncivilized conqueror, as Ye Liu Chutsai did Genghis Khan, may give a far more intriguing story, in either sense of the word.

In any event, the monarchy or oligarchy won't be the sole mover of society. It never has been, not even in the contemporary Soviet Union and slave China. There are always other interests and groups whose leaders must be conciliated. An obvious example is the late J. Edgar Hoover; theoretically, any President could summarily have dismissed him, but in practice that was a political impossibility. More to the hf point, perhaps, are the consequences to Henry II of England when he had Thomas a Becket assassinated. Indeed, the ever-changing interrelationships of kings, nobles, and Church form a major part of the medieval European tapestry. One can go on to power groups in more distant lands, such as the Janissaries in Turkey or the Shogunate in Japan, to find endless complications which are the stuff of exciting tales.

(One hf novel which handles politics superbly well, and is a fine story in every other respect too, is *The Well of the Unicorn* by Fletcher Pratt. If you haven't already read it, do.)

The Church raises the subject of religion in general, which is little used in our field. Oh, yes, we may get a hero swearing by his particular gods and perhaps carrying through a small rite, equivalent to stroking a rabbit's foot. We certainly got plenty of obscene ceremonies in honor of assorted toad-like beings. Both of these do have their historical counterparts. Nevertheless, it would be interesting to see an imaginary society which was pervaded by its faith, as many real ones have been.

One way or another, religion is usually the wellspring of literacy. If Never-Never Land has no printing press or public schools, how many people can read? How did they learn? How common is paper or some equally cheap, convenient material to write upon? Who produces and who sells it, under what conditions? How do letters travel? Questions like these could well be crucial to our hero.

The available transportation positively is. Now we are so accustomed to reasonably reliable and well-sprung automobiles on smooth roads, when we don't fly, that we have almost forgotten how hard and slow it once was to get from here to there. Most people in the past spent their entire lives in walking distance of wherever they were born. This must deeply have affected their personalities, even as mobility has affected ours.

The Romans, improving on the example of the Persians, knit their empire together with excellent paved highways. These were for armies and imperial messengers. Ordinary people could use them, but that wasn't the main idea, and doubtless most civilian traffic continued to be over dirt tracks. Anyone who has hiked or marched through mud will appreciate the importance of a proper military road. When Rome had fallen and commerce shrank down to local trading, most of this network was quarried. In the Middle Ages, a landholder could help guarantee his salvation—and collect tolls—by building and maintaining a road or bridge. It was that important to everyone. Not just mud, but wilderness impeded travel. Huge areas of Europe were covered by forest that, because of underbrush, was literally impassable; some coastal communities could be reached only by sea. If given a reasonable surface to roll on, chariots, wagons, and coaches remained exhausting things in which to ride. After a day of such vibration, the passenger would feel as if he'd been through a meat grinder. The brutality of it is epitomized by the fact that, in the nineteenth century, the working life of a coach horse was reckoned at four years.

Thus our hero will usually do better to go pedestrian or equestrian. As for the latter choice, writers who've had no personal experience with horses tend to think of them as a kind of sports car. 'Tain't so.

You cannot gallop them for hours. They'll collapse. The best way to make time in the saddle is to alternate paces, and have a remount or two trailing behind, and allow the animals reasonable rest. Don't let your steed eat or drink indiscriminately; it's likely to bloat and become helpless. In fact, it's a rather fragile creature, requiring close attention—for example, rubdowns after hard exertion—if it isn't to fall sick and perhaps die on you. It's also lazy, stupid, and sometimes malicious. All of these tendencies the rider must keep under control.

You cannot grab any old horse and go to battle on it. It'll instantly become unmanageable. Several of us in the Society for Creative Anachronism tried a little harmless jousting, and soon gave up . . . and this was with beasts whose owners were already practicing the more pacific equestrian arts, such as tilting at a ring. War horses had to be raised to it from colthood. The best cavalrymen were, too. For lack of that tradition, the vikings, for instance, never fought mounted. Upon landing in a victim country, they'd steal themselves four-legged transportation, but having reached a scene of action, they'd get down.

Cavalry was of no particular importance in Europe until about the sixth century, when stirrups were introduced from the East. Before then, combatants were too likely to fall off. Earlier, the chief military use of the horse had been with chariots: until the Greek hoplite and Roman legionary learned how to cope with these. Later, nobody riding bareback stood a chance against an enemy who had a proper saddle.

Frequently in hf, and for that matter in h'f and Wf (historical and Western fantasy), the hero cavorts around on a snorting stallion. Now this has been done in reality, but seldom, and that for good reason. A stallion is notoriously hard to control, and, by the way, is not safe to have around a menstruating woman. (Of course, hf heroines never seem to menstruate, which may account for the fact that they don't get pregnant, no matter how active in bed.) A mare or, better, gelding is preferable.

In short, our hero is going to face practical problems in getting around on land. The same will apply if he goes by sea. I'll say nothing about pirates, though in most eras they posed a considerable hazard. I will mention that, even under the Roman Empire, more often than not it paid to travel across the water; terrestrial transportation was that bad. Nevertheless—

Ships in hf normally have sails but act as if they had Diesel engines. They take the lead character where he wants to go, fast, effortlessly, and comfortably. They are never becalmed and they never meet weeks of foul weather. In spite of being square-rigged, they can go as close to the wind as the captain chooses. (Ah, many's the time I've wished I could make a well-designed sloop do that. But it took most of a morning, for instance, to work out of one quite small bay. In the nineteenth century, ships would sometimes lie in Honolulu harbor for months, waiting for the right wind to blow them across the Pacific.) These same vessels have abundant elbow room for everybody; food and water are always palatable; there are no special housekeeping problems. (In actuality the First Law of the Sea, as formulated by Jerry Pournelle and myself, is: "It's in the bilge!") Sometimes, in both hf and h'f, we have galley slaves. Again, authors are inclined to treat them as if they were engines; they don't get tired, they don't get sick, they don't stink, you don't have to keep a guard on them lest they revolt. In real history, rowers were only used on naval vessels, and for the most part were free men, well paid. Galley slaves were not a Roman but a late medieval invention, brought about by the need to bring cannon to bear on short notice.

The average hf sailor has no navigation woes. Yet this problem wasn't solved till the eighteenth century, with the development of the chronometer —and the story of that R & D effort is a complex one, full of human bitchiness. To this day, the solution is not perfect. Ask a seaman to tell you what it's like, using a modern sextant, to get a decent sight on a star. Nor has electronics made locating yourself automatic and infallible, short of the most highly advanced inertial systems. So imagine an early Norseman bound from Oslo to Greenland. He has a knowledge of landmarks and the heavens when these are visible; a peg will help him estimate his latitude if a clear day allows it to cast a shadow, and the natural polarizing filter he calls a "sunstone" will help him locate the solar orb in cloudy weather; but these aids give him only the crudest approximations, while longitude is a matter of sheer dead reckoning or guesswork. Seaweed, bird flights, and similar indications are probably more helpful; indeed, he may well carry some birds in a cage, release them one at a time when he thinks he may be near a shore, and watch which way they go. Chances are that he'll make landfall a goodly distance from his goal and have to work along the coast to find it.

Compass, astrolabe, and a few other advantages improved matters as the Middle Ages wore on, but not greatly. If his story is to be convincing, our itinerant barbarian will not travel without lots of difficulty, discomfort, and delay.

Presumably he's bound for someplace where he can fight. After he arrives on the battlefield, he will still face a host of complications. Let me merely observe in passing that, right up until World War Two, far more soldiers died of disease than did in action; that the outcome of a siege was frequently determined by whether the attackers took sick faster than the defenders starved; and that germs were sometimes the arbiters of entire wars. Let me suggest that this, too, is a realistic motif which hf writers could occasionally use to advantage. Now let's get on to actual combat.

First, consider again the sociology of it. Incomparably drilled and disciplined, the Roman legionary almost always made hash of his foes, until the society which had produced him rotted away. In medieval England, every yeoman of military age was required by law to have a longbow and spend a set number of hours per week practicing with it. As a result, the English archers during the Hundred Years' War were the terror of the French, who tried to raise a similar corps but failed because they hadn't institutionalized the training. In general, the civil background of an army is the most important element in its long-range success or failure, with its own organization and morale a close second. Half-trained barbarians may win a fluke victory over civilized troops once in a while, but that won't count for much. They can only prevail over a civilization after it has ruined itself.

Technology counts too, of course, though sometimes in paradoxical ways. The longbow was driven off the field by the crossbow and later the crossbow by the musket, not because these weapons were successively superior—they weren't—but because it was successively quicker and easier to teach a man their use. The hf writer ought to visualize just what kind of arms his characters employ, and think through the military implications.

As for hand-to-hand fights, it would doubtless be unfair to demand that he belong to the SCA or go in for fencing or javelin throwing or archery. We'll have to bear with heroes' occasional ignorance of technique. That would soon prove fatal in real life; luckily, fictional villains share the ignorance.

However, can't the author do a little reading in encyclopedias, under headings like "Fencing"? And is it too much trouble to delve further than that? Any reasonably sized public or college library must contain some relevant books. If nothing else, can't he take half a minute to visualize before he writes?

If he does, he'll instantly see that nobody in his right mind would grab a sword two-handed, raise it over his head, and chop straight down, exposing his belly all that while. The use of those huge Reformation-period two-handers was a highly developed art whose practitioners were specialists.

Carrying a shield, you're as apt to work around its edge as over the top. By the way, the purpose of that shield is to stay between you and your enemy's weapon, not act as a counterweight to a roundhouse swing. There are tricks you can play with it, such as using its edge to lever your opponent's shield out of your way; but I've rarely seen fantasy warriors do anything so skillful.

Artists tend to be still worse offenders than authors—for instance, depicting a man wielding a dagger overhand, and, while they're at it, dressing the poor guy in nothing but a bearskin kilt in a winter landscape or on a horse. (For a human male, the latter placement is much the worse.)

Nobody can wield a fifty-pound sword; he'd wear his arm out in short order. An ax or mace, largely dependent on sheer mass for beating through an enemy's guard, is nowhere near that heavy either. A replicated ax, Battle of Hastings type, in my possession, weighs a bit under five pounds. Nevertheless, it takes muscle to swing any edged weapon. Therefore I suspect that a woman-at-arms would look less like Dejah Thoris than Rosie the Riveter. In fact, we have no reliable records of female warriors. Joan of Arc commanded, she did not engage in combat.

True, primary sources can't always be trusted. Thus, in the generally realistic Icelandic sagas, you find a few references to somebody cutting a head or limb off somebody else with a single stroke. Try this on a pork roast, suspended without a chopping block, and see how far you get.

It could be done with the best of the classic Japanese swords, which are marvels of metallurgy. However, one of these must be treated very carefully if it isn't to be ruined. The mere touch of a finger can induce corrosion.

The cruder blades of Europe demanded still closer attention. Edged weapons are more fragile than one might think, especially if they are bronze or medieval-type steel. Those quickly go blunt and become simple clubs; oftimes they bend and must be more or less straightened with a foot and an oath; they can break. Not even with a samurai sword do you cut through armor.

At the same time, armor does have its vulnerabilities. These are not so much to the thrust or the cleaving blow. I have witnessed SCA experiments in which chain mail made from coat hanger wire, backed by a hay bale, could not be penetrated by sword, ax, or spear. Obviously only repeated impacts on the same spot could fatigue the metal enough to let a weapon through. Plate armor should be still hardier. Bear in mind that, in both cases, padding was worn beneath. Still, if a man was getting hit hour after hour, eventually it might prove too much for his body to endure, if heat prostration didn't get him first.

Armor of either kind could be pierced by a hard-driven arrow, from longbow or crossbow. These devices had their own limitations. I have already mentioned how much training was necessary to make the former effective. Though not an archer myself, I am skeptical about hundred-pound draws; it seems to me that, for accuracy and rate of fire, seventy-five might be a more reasonable figure. As for crossbows, though their bolts struck equally hard, they were considerably slower than longbows. As said, their decisive advantage was that they were easier to learn to use.

If armor is not involved, then ordinarily in fiction, a single blow, thrust, or arrow suffices to drop a man or a horse dead on the spot. Actually, so large an animal is quite hard to kill. The .45 caliber pistol was developed specifically as a man-stopper, and still men hit from one have been known to keep on coming. Hf swordsmen generally run their foes right through the heart. Well, not only is the heart a fairly small target whose exact location is hard to identify, but it's pretty protected by the rib cage. Personally, I'd go for the throat—the larynx is highly vulnerable, not to speak of the jugular vein or carotid arteries—or the abdomen, where I might slash another big artery or have a chance of skewering the liver—or the legs, in hopes of crippling my opponent.

The back of the neck is another weak point, if you can get at it, as with a hefty rabbit punch. The skull is stronger, though it can be smashed with a heavy weapon and a lighter blow may render the victim unconscious. Here hf and mf (mystery fantasy) writers make man out to be more durable than he is. Their heroes get knocked out, awaken after a while as if from a nap, and plunge right back into action. The truth is, a mild concussion is disabling for periods ranging from hours to days, and as for a severe one, the consequences are not pleasant to watch.

If you wish further possibilities for mayhem, I refer you to experts in karate. Techniques of this kind seldom occur in hf, but surely they could enliven some stories.

We have less scope where poisons are concerned, common though they are in fiction. Medieval and Renaissance princes lived in terror of these, but the fact is that prior to modern chemistry, there were virtually no quick-acting toxins you could slip to somebody unbeknownst or on the point of a weapon. Curare is about all that comes to mind, and that's South American. Indeed, I've seen a couple of Renaissance recipes for poisons to feed dinner guests, and the main question about them is how anybody ever imagined anybody else could ever gag down enough of that awful stuff to suffer serious damage.

Arsenic was about the deadliest substance readily available, with a few competitors like hemlock, toadstools, and ground glass. The problem was usually to disguise the taste. In any event, while a person could occasionally be given a lethal dose, he would hardly drop dead at once. He'd be a considerable and messy time about his demise. I rather imagine that quite a few deaths which were attributed to deliberate poisoning were actually caused by botulism or the like.

Lest the foregoing seem bloodthirsty, let me add that another flaw in most hf is the glossing over of pain, mangling, and the ordinarily grim process of dying. True, we don't want to get sadistic. And as a rule, we presume an era less sensitive than ours; most have been. And we're writing and reading for fun, not to preach moral lessons or harrow emotions. Still, a bit more realism in this respect too would lend convincingness.

We can then swing back to cheerful matters, such as harvest festivals, drunken evenings in taverns, and fertility rites where sympathetic magic gets totally sympathetic. We can let our hero have all kind of adventures, buckle all kinds of swashes. I merely submit that he ought to do so in a world which, however thaumaturgical, makes sense. The more it does, the more the reader will enjoy—and the more he will come back for more.

INTERLOPER

The spaceboat slipped down, slowly and stealthily on its gravitic beams, toward the sea which rolled restlessly under the moon. For a moment the broken moonlight seemed to spread outward in little ripples of cold fire, then the boat had gone beneath the water surface.

It struck bottom not far down, for the beach was only half a mile distant, and lay there wrapped in darkness. Briefly, there was no movement or sound. Then the outer airlock valve opened and Beoric swam to the surface.

The night was vast and dark around him. He saw with complete clarity, in the thin fickle moonlight, but he could not make out any living thing. Sea and sky and the shadowy shoreline—momentarily, the thought of what must be waiting for him was utterly daunting, his heart felt cold in his breast, in all the centuries of his life he had never been so alone. He felt something of the ultimate loneliness of death.

A thought slipped into his mind, cool and unhuman as the sea depths from which it rose: *The creature is waiting. He has been waiting for an hour or more, in the shadows under the trees.*

Beoric's answering thought was a reaction of near panic: *Don't! They may be able to detect us, after all—*

In all the thousands of years, they have given no

*sign of being responsive to our special wave band.
It is, of course, best not to take chances, not to
communicate directly with you oftener than
necessary. But we will be listening to your thoughts
all the time.*

You are not alone. The new thought came from
the shore, somewhere behind the line of trees
under which the alien waited. *We are with you,
Beoric.*

It heartened him immensely. Whatever came,
whatever happened—he was not altogether alone.
Though all the powers of the universe be ranged
against him, he had a few on his side. But—so few!

He struck out for the shore, swimming with long
easy strokes that seemed to ride the waves. The
moon-whitened beach came nearer, until he was
wading through the shallows and up onto dry
ground.

The creature who had been waiting stirred in
the shadows. Beoric's nightseeing eyes swept over
the gross black bulk of him, and for another
moment fear was cold along his own spine. But—it
was too late now. Even had he wanted to back out,
after the long centuries of which this night might
be the culmination, it was too late.

He ran across the beach and ducked behind a
tree, as if he hoped the creature had not seen him.
And he sent his thoughts probing forth at the mind
of the other, as if he were trying to detect whether
the thing were intelligent or not. If it should be a
member of the dominant race here, the next
logical step would be to seize control of its brain
and—

The defensive reaction was so swift and
savagely strong that Beoric's own mind reeled.
For an instant his head swam, he seemed to be
sinking into an illimitable darkness—almost, the
thing had control of him! Then his nervous energy
surged back, he threw a hard shield about his

brain and sent a thought stabbing along the universally detectable wave band:

"Apparently your race has mastered the secrets of telepathy. If you are that far advanced, you will probably be able to guess my origin."

"Not guess—know!" The answering thought shivered violently in his brain. There must be an incredible force housed in that great scaly body. Beoric caught overtones of a dark amusement: "I thought at first you must be one of the natives—your appearance is almost identical—but obviously you are not."

"Then—you don't belong here—either?"

"Of course not. Wherever you are from, it must be from quite a distance or we would have encountered your people before. But your initial reaction to my presence suggests that you are used to the concept and techniques of visiting someone else's planet."

"I am." In the closed circle of his private thoughts, Beoric felt a sudden harsh laughter of his own. Indeed he was! "But I had not expected to find other—guests—on this world."

He stepped out into the open. The moonlight gleamed coldly on his wet, waterproof tunic and kilts. His strange slant eyes, all cloudy blue without pupil or white, roved into the darkness where the monster still crouched. "Come out," he invited. "Come out and bid me welcome."

"Of course." The squat, enormously thick creature waddled out and stood under the moon. His blank reptilian eyes glittered as they swept over Beoric. Instinctively, the newcomer cocked his long pointed ears toward the monster, though the words that rolled and boomed in his skull had no sonic origin. "Yes—yes, you look very like a native. Except for those eyes and ears—but dark glasses and a hat will cover it very well. That high-cheeked cast of face, and very white skin, would

also be considered unusual, but not so much so as
to arouse great comment.''

"Let me get my facts straight," thought Beoric.
"Just what planet is this? I mean, what is it
called?''

"The natives call it Earth, of course. Don't all
land dwelling races call their world Earth? The
pronunciation in the local language—they still
speak many separate tongues—is—'' The monster
thought the sound. "The sun is called Sol by them,
and we use that term since it is easy to pronounce
and all our names differ. This is Sol III, as you
probably know.''

"I knew it was the third planet, yes. But who are
'we'? Is there more than one race of—visitors?''

"Indeed. Indeed.'' With sudden suspicion: "But I
am answering all the questions. Who are you?
Where are you from? Where are your
companions? What is your purpose? Why is there
no iron in your spaceship? What sort of civilization has your race evolved?''

"One thing at a time.'' Beoric's answer was taut
and wary. "I will not give information away, but I
will trade it for what you know. You cannot expect
me, on finding a whole new interstellar civilization, to reveal all the secrets of my own until I
am convinced of your good intentions.''

"Fair enough. But who are you, then?''

"My name, in the spoken language of my race, is
Beoric, though that hardly matters. My home star
lies clear across the Galaxy, near the periphery; I
will not at present be more specific than that. My
race, the Alfar, evolved a faster-than-light drive
quite a long time ago, several centuries past in
fact, and visited the nearer stars. Finally the expedition to which I belong was sent out on a survey
which was to swing clear around the Galaxy,
investigating stars picked at random so as to get a
rough idea of overall conditions. But since we nec-

essarily had to select only a small fraction of suns for study, it is not surprising that we passed right through your civilization without realizing it."

"Where is your ship? That little boat in which you landed could only hold one or two."

"You cannot expect me to reveal the ship's orbit. I came down alone in the boat. The presence of cities here indicated intelligent life with some degree of technology, so I landed—secretly, of course—to investigate more thoroughly. Apparently you detected us some distance out."

"We spotted your boat, yes, by its gravitic vibrations. But not your ship. What sort of screen do you have for star drive vibrations? We've never been able to conceal them that well. And why is your boat chemically powered?"

"The vibration screen must remain my secret. As for the oil-burning spaceboat—well, we have evolved an unusual oil technology on Alfar. With the extreme efficiency of the gravity beam, we just don't need atomic energy for such a small craft."

"I see. But I could detect no iron or silver in your boat—"

"Both metals are hard to obtain on Alfar. We manage quite well with alloys and with copper." Beoric leaned forward, as if suddenly realizing he was giving away too much. "But it is your turn now. Who are you? Why are you here? Why this inquisition, rather than a free welcome?"

"It is a long story," thought the monster. "Nor have you been a model of openness. However—welcome to Earth. Perhaps you would like to come to our headquarters—?"

"Well—it would certainly be the most convenient starting point—I warn you, if I do not return to my ship within three rotations of this planet, they will be coming down after me—with weapons."

"You need have no fear. We are not greedy.

Earth has plenty for all."

Beoric stood watching the bony, snouted face of the monster. It seemed to him that he could almost follow the being's private thoughts:

Wherever this creature is from, whether or not he is telling the truth, he must be alone on this planet. We would have detected any other space vessel landing anywhere. Also, he is cut off from his companions. The inverse square law makes it impossible to send a thought more than a few hundred miles at most, and his ship must be further out or we would detect it. He is alone, unarmed, and incommunicado. In three days we can decide what to do—

"My vocal name is Hraagung. Come, we have a car waiting."

"A car—?"

"Yes, of course." Hraagung chuckled, with a certain horrible sardonicism. "I was chosen to meet you, since my own senses could follow the metal of your boat without elaborate instruments. But for obvious reasons, I cannot move about openly on this planet."

"I have to get inside before dawn," thought Beoric. "Alfar's sun is dim and red, nearly extinct. For that reason, I can see very easily in this moonlight, but cannot endure the glare and the ultraviolet light of a G-type star."

"So?" Hraagung paused, and Beoric could almost see him turning this revelation over in his cold brain. It was an admission of weakness, to be sure, but it had to be made. And, to a highly advanced civilization with its screens and protective suits, the handicap was not serious. "What would you have done if you hadn't met us?"

"Hidden away by day and slept, of course. The fact that the cities were lighted showed that the natives would be diurnal, which would make my work of spying all the easier.''

"Yes—to be sure. Well, we haven't far to go. This way." The monster lumbered in advance. Beoric wrung the water from his shoulder-length silvery-blond hair and followed.

They came through the line of trees onto a paved highway. A native automobile was parked there— four-wheeled, enclosed, obviously chemical-powered. As he neared it, Beoric felt the sudden nerve-chill that meant *iron*.

He had expected it, but that made it none the easier. Every ingrained instinct screamed at him to come no closer. Iron, iron, iron—touch it and see your hand go up in smoke! Iron, cold iron, crouched there under the moon!

And he must enter that metal box, and not for an instant must he show the fear that ripped along his shrinking nerves and dinned in his brain. If they knew, if they found the fatal weakness of the Alfar, he was done. A thousand years of slow work and scheming and waiting were done—Earth was done. And it all depended on him.

For a moment he couldn't do it. In spite of his resolve, in spite of his many rehearsals, in spite of the bleak fact that he *must* go through with it—he couldn't. He couldn't deny the reflexes that knotted his muscles and locked his will and brought sweat cold and bitter out on his body.

Courage. The thought quivered deep in his brain. It came from the sea, from the fields beyond the road, from the trees that stood whispering in the night wind. *Courage, Beoric. You are not alone.*

They were sending him more than unspoken words. There was an actual flow of nervous energy into his body, an almost physical force suddenly entering him, bracing him, stilling the wild thunder of his heart and the panic-storm in his brain. Calmness came, and he walked boldly forward.

A man stood beside the car. No—not a man, not an Earthling, though he looked like one and wore the conventional shirt, trousers, coat, and whatnot else of the planet. He was tall, as tall as Beoric, and the Alf could feel the strength that was in him, coiled in his lean body and his long skull like a great cold snake. The sheer aura of that tremendous intellect and neural force could not be hidden, it forced itself out into the telepathic bands and shouted arrogantly along the nerves of Beoric and Hraagung.

The stranger had been listening to the conversation on the beach. His thought came slow and—deep—"Welcome, Beoric of Alfar. I trust your stay will be pleasant and mutually profitable. I am—my race has abandoned vocal language altogether. But on this planet I use the spoken name of Adam Kane." He caught a question in Beoric's thoughts, the Alf had detected overtones. "Yes, my race is so nearly like the Earthling—outwardly!—that only a little surgery enabled us to pass unquestioned. Someone must act as intermediary between aliens and natives, and so the choice falls on us. Which is very useful—in fact, it is necessary to the enterprises we maintain here."

Hraagung crawled into the rear of the car and crouched low so he could not be seen from the outside. His immense body filled the back seat, and the rank reptile smell of him filled the whole vehicle. Kane slid behind the wheel. "Come along," he thought impatiently.

Fear was cold in Beoric as he touched the right-hand door handle. It was chrome-plated, safe enough for him, but the near presence of iron shuddered in his nerves. With a convulsive movement, he opened the door and slipped in beside Kane. The car purred into motion.

"Where are you from?" thought Beoric. "You still haven't told me."

"From various stars hereabouts," answered Kane. "I come from the most distant." Beòric recognized Deneb in this thought. "But"—arrogantly—"we Vaettir arrived here first. Somewhat later, other races mastered the secret of faster-than-light travel and came to Sol in the course of their explorations. Hraagung is from—" Beoric translated the thought-image, in his own private mind, as Sirius. "And so forth. Today a number of planets have vested interests in Earth. Under the leadership of the Vaettir, they have set up a system such that their various enterprises do not conflict."

He looked at Beoric. The eyes fairly blazed in his lean face, an intolerable glare which the Alf fought to meet, and his hard thought vibrated like vicious lightning in the other's brain: "We are not hostile to newcomers who will respect the system. If they wish to open some project here or on some other of our subject planets which does not clash with established interests, they are free to do so under the rules and direction of the Vaettir. But if they violate the code, they will be destroyed."

Beoric sat quiescent, trying to think how he should react. After a while, he thought slowly: "That seems fair enough. As a matter of fact, a similar system is not unknown in my civilization. It is possible that our two cultures could have mutually profitable intercourse."

"Perhaps!" The answering vibrations lashed back, hard and suspicious.

"Precisely what forms of exploitation are carried on here?" asked the Alf.

"Various ones, depending on the race," said Hraagung. "The Procyonites find Earthlings an excellent source of blood. The Altairians simply want to observe historical processes, as part of their project of mass-action study. The Arcturian economy depends on controlling the productive facilities of a great number of subject planets, skimming the cream off their industry and agriculture. We of Sirius find Earth a convenient military outpost and refueling station—also—" The thought was like a tiger licking its lips—"the natives serve other purposes."

Beoric flashed a question at Kane: "What of your race, the—Denebian Vaettir?"

The answer was steel-hard, with a bleak amusement shimmering over the surface: "We have many interests in this part of the Galaxy."

The Alf leaned back and tried to relax. The almost empty land was beginning to show houses here and there, and the horizon ahead was lit with a dull glow. The car sped smoothly, swiftly over the highway, at a pace that an Earthling could hardly have controlled. It was dark inside the body, a thickness of shadows rank with the Sirian reptile stink. The reflected headlights threw a dim luminance on the harsh bony features of Adam Kane, limning them against the darkness in a nightmare tracing of cheekbones and jaw and cruel jutting nose. The nervous force of the Denebian could not be hidden, it swirled and eddied in the car like an atmosphere. Beoric had to fight its overwhelming power.

"Our headquarters are in the city ahead—New York, it's called," thought Hraagung. "We are on Long Island now."

"Your spaceships don't land there, though?" asked Beoric. He did not try to cover his interest, it would only be natural in a traveler from a distant star—nor could he hope to hide any emotional overtones of his thoughts from the blazing intellect of the Denebian.

"Not in the city, no, though we do have one there for emergency use—in fact, our building is little more than a disguised ship. The actual bases and landing fields are elsewhere—"

No matter how he fought to suppress his emotions, Beoric could not keep a shout out of his thoughts. Ye gods—the building was a ship—*the building was a ship!* Why—that meant—

He grew aware of the cold Sirian eyes focusing on him. The Denebian driver's gaze did not turn from the unwinding road, but Beoric felt his senses—and the gods knew how many uncanny perceptions he had—licking at the Alf's hard-held mental bloc, tongues of fire that—

He laughed, a little shakily, and explained: "I was startled. I had never heard of putting up such a construction without the natives knowing about it. How did you manage it?"

The Denebian's slow deep thought rolled through his brain: "It was simple. We put up the apartment building as a shell. It was only necessary to control the minds of a few city inspectors, since casual observers would not realize the difference. Then, one stormy night, we brought the ship down into the shell. Our laborers completed the disguise with a roof, interior walls and floors."

"You used native labor?"

"Of course. Even at the time, none of them realized the fact that they were not putting up an ordinary structure."

"I see." Beoric saw indeed, and in spite of knowing most of it beforehand he was utterly shaken. What sort of brains did the Vaettir have, that they could casually supply hundreds of men with false memories, prevent them even during their work from taking conscious notice of incongruities—? What was the extent of their power?

Tonight, he thought grimly, *I'll find out!*

Tonight—indeed! The answering thought, on the Alf band, came from behind the racing car. They must be following, in their own vehicles, and—

"You must realize," thought Kane, almost conversationally, "that the exploitation of Earth is quite old. In fact, the first Vaettir arrived here—" he thought of a length of time which Beoric rendered as about four thousand years ago. "We began to colonize extensively about seven centuries back, at which time the native civilization was less complex and it was very easy to pass oneself off as whatever one desired. Thus our organization is firmly established. Through the corporations we control on Earth, the governments which we influence—or run outright whenever it is necessary, through the old and highly reputable family connections of some of the Vaettir, through a number of other means which you can easily imagine, we can do exactly as we please, under the very noses of the natives." For a moment his iron features split in a grin. "The only ones who suspect that Earthlings are not their own property are labelled cranks—and generally the label is quite correct."

Beoric thought of the ruthlessness he had read in Hraagung's mind and asked, "Why do you take so much trouble? Why not annex Earth outright?"

"That would not suit the purposes of the Vaettir." The cold answer was like a suddenly drawn sword. "It is part of our plan that the directed evolution of Earthly civilization be thought a native project—for some time to come."

Beoric nodded. He slumped back in his seat, watching the blurred buildings reel crazily past. It was plain enough who really ran this corner of the Galaxy. The Sirians, for one, would probably like nothing better than to come as conquerors, treating Earthlings frankly as cattle. But if Deneb said "no", then "no" it was.

And—we are pitting ourselves against—that! We, who could not prevail against—

"You cannot hope to conceal your presence entirely?" he thought.

"We don't try," shrugged Hraagung. "In earlier times, we went about almost openly, and were often seen by natives, thereby giving rise to much legendry—"

Yes, thought Beoric, within the locked chambers of his own skull. *Yes, I know the myths. Frightened glimpses of unhuman beings stalking over the world, of a science from beyond the stars, became trolls, goblins, ifrits, dragons, all the horrors of the old stories were grounded in more horrible fact. What brought on the wave of medieval devil-worship if not the growing influx from outer space? Who was the Satan they worshipped at the Black Mass if not a Denebian or a Sirian or some other monster who found a cult of fanatics useful —and who must often have laughed as he conferred with his brethren highly placed in church and state?*

They are most of Earth's mythology. But planets have at least a few myths of their own—

"Later," went on the Sirian, "when too obvious evidence of our presence might have led some sophisticated minds to suspect the truth, we resorted to a measure of—precaution. Who knows what goes on in some lonely part of a great cattle ranch—or in his neighbor's house in a great city? To whom does it occur that the silent partners controlling key industries may not be on Earth at all—?

"There are glimpses. Why bother to conceal them? A man who spied me on a dark night would hardly put his own reputation in jeopardy by telling of it—or, if he did, it would be the ravings of delirium, not so? On occasions where someone knows too much, his memories are removable. Almost daily, sign of us is seen—objects in the sky, poltergeist phenomena, vanishings and appearances, all the rest. But who will be able to make anything of such scattered and fragmentary evidence?'' Hraagung's deep vocal chuckle vibrated in the body of the car. ''Those few who have collected any sort of coherent proof and tried to deduce the truth, are laughed at as paranoiacs.''

Kane's wolf-grin flashed out. ''The beauty of it is,'' thought the Denebian, ''that almost all such people really are paranoid. It is an obvious sign of instability to attribute the world's trouble to out-side persecutors—even if such an attribution should happen to be correct!''

The hurtling car was moving more slowly now as it entered frequented streets. Buildings loomed on either side, blotting out the stars, and there was iron, iron everywhere, the city was a cage of steel. For an instant of blind horror, Beoric fought not to scream. Then slowly, shakily, his resolution returned. After all, the metal wouldn't harm him unless he touched it. And too many centuries depended on him now. And it was too late to back out.

That's right, Beoric. The strong reassuring thoughts beat in the back of his head. *We're after you. We're entering the city too—*

For a moment, he savored the realization. He was, at least, a part of his people, they were with him.

It came to him, not for the first time, that if the Alfar brain structure permitted them to telepath on a wave band undetectable to any other race, then doubtless the Sirians and the others—above all, the Vaettir—could also think on levels un-readable to him. And—what thoughts were flashing back and forth in the night around him?

If—oh, gods, if the incredible Vaettir really could listen in on his thoughts, if that was the secret of their power, if Kane was simply leading the Alfar into a trap—But the chance had to be taken. Earth itself was a trap.

He sat in silence. The car wound smoothly

through darkened streets where only the dull yellow lamps and an occasional furtive movement in the shadows and alleys had life. It was near the ebb time of the great city's life; it slept like a sated beast under the sinking moon.

The fields and woods, hills and waters and sky, never slept. There was always life, a rustle of wings, a pattering of feet, a gleam of eyes out of the night, there was always the flowing tide of nervous energy, wakeful, alert. Life lay like a sea beyond the city, and Beoric had never been really alone.

Until now. But the city slept, and there was nothing wild to run in the fields and leap in the moonlit waters. Beoric's straining mind sensed a few rodents scuttering in the ground, a slinking cat or two, the threadlike nervous impulses of insects fluttering around the one-eyed street lamps. Now and again there would be a human thought, someone wakeful—and the thought seemed to echo in the vast hollow silence of the city, it was alone, alone.

The city slept. Beoric could sense the life force of the sleeping humans, nervous, jagged-feeling, even now. It was like an overwhelming lethargy, a million and a million and a million sleeping bodies with all their pain and sorrow and longing turned loose to wander in their minds. The Alf locked his brain to the sticky tide, but it rolled around him, it lay like a sweat-dampened cloak over his nervous system.

They are too many. The sheer magnitude of life-force of—how many millions? Ten?—is more than we can endure. And yet we dare challenge the rulers of this world.

They were in the outer edges of the decadent zone surrounding the main business district. It was the logical location for the headquarters—not so evilly situated as to be suspect to police, but in

a relatively idle area which would be empty of
traffic at night. And now—yes, the quiver of life-
force up ahead, impulses of a wave-form not quite
Earthly, it came from *that* building.

Beoric looked at the darkened bulk before
which the automobile came to a halt. It was a ten-
story apartment building, as drab and dingy as
any of its neighbors. A dim light glowed in the
door, picking out a sign: NO VACANCY. *Of course
not!* thought Beoric, and suppressed an impulse to
hysterical laughter.

"No one watching," flashed Kane's thought.
"We can go right in."

Hraagung's unwieldy bulk crossed the sidewalk
with surprising speed. The three entered into a
hall like that of any other building of this type.
Beoric's sensitive nostrils wrinkled at the odors of
stale cookery, but he had to admit the disguise
was complete.

Even to an elderly human who sat half dozing at
the desk. Beoric dipped into his mind for an
instant and withdrew with a shudder from the—
hollowness.

But the haughty Vaettir would not trouble to
pose as menials. They would need a few authentic
natives, to act as janitors and whatever other
fronts were necessary. Natives who could pass for
normal individuals, but whom their vampire
masters had sucked dry of all personality. Flesh-
and-blood robots—

Kane led the way into an elevator. "This runs
directly into the spaceship," he explained. "You
will find more suitable accommodations there."

*Such as a coffin, maybe? Or more probably a
dissecting table. They'll want to know what I really
am.*

They emerged into a short corridor lit by coldly
gleaming fluorotubes. Kane gestured at a door,
which opened to reveal a small, richly furnished

room.

"This is one of the guest quarters we keep for transient visitors to Earth," thought the Denebian. "I hope you will find it suitable. The furniture adjusts itself to the shape of the user's body, and you can set temperature, humidity, air pressure, and the rest to whatever is most comfortable for you."

The thought of being set in an airtight chamber was not at all to Beoric's liking. "I am not tired, now, thanks," he vibrated. "I would be more interested in seeing the other colonists."

"This is only headquarters, as I told you," answered Kane. "But most members of the grand control council for Sol are already here, and I have summoned the rest mentally. They should arrive soon."

"All the councillors? That is an honor."

Kane skinned his teeth in a humorless smile. "Not too much of an honor for a visitor from so far away," his thought almost purred. And then, a naked rapier flash: "After all, we have to decide what to do about you!"

Beoric knew, suddenly and bleakly, that he was not intended to leave the ship still in possession of his own personality. It should not take more than two or three of the Vaettir brains to smash through his mental defenses and get complete control of him. And when they knew all he knew about the Alfar, he would go as their depersonalized agent to his ship.

The Alf's fingers touched the sheathed knife strapped under his tunic. He should be able to hold off such an assault long enough to whip out the weapon, and its iron blade would burn through his heart. The Vaettir no doubt had techniques for reviving the dead, but they wouldn't work on him—in minutes his brain and its knowledge would be crumbled, in hours his rapidly proteolyzed flesh would be dust, even his bones would not last many years. The metabolism which was at once their strength and weakness had at least been the cloak of the Alfar.

He was no longer afraid of death. He more than half expected it. But he could not control the inward shudder that racked him at the thought that the Vaettir might somehow be able to upset the plan. There was so little that the Alfar knew about them—so horribly little.

Kane started down the hall. Beoric followed, uneasily aware of Hraagung coming ponderously after. He was between the two monsters, no chance of escape. It lay with the others now, and he didn't dare call on them.

They entered a cubicle which shot into sudden motion. Beoric judged that it was carrying them toward the center of the ship. He flashed out an impulse on the Alf band, to guide the others, but there was no answer.

The ship was silent. He could hear nothing but the purr of the moving cube, the breathing of Hraagung crouched hard and cold beside him. He could feel the surge of inhuman nerve flows, swirling through his own telepathic receptive center like a dark tide, and he could feel the iron frame of the ship, its faint residual magnetism seemed to chill his nerves. Thank all the gods, the metal floor and wall and ceilings were nonferrous But he was in a cage of iron, a spider web, and the breath choked in his throat.

The cube stopped, its door opening on a little antechamber. As the three passengers stepped out, another creature flashed into sight on a metal plate and stalked toward the room beyond.

Beoric started. "What the devil—!" Then, catching himself with the native quick-mindness of his race: "I take it you've somehow managed to apply the interstellar drive principle to short distances.

But how? Our civilization was never able to use it for other than hops of a light-year or more."

"The true minimum distance is about a hundred miles," answered Kane. "Thus we can summon the whole Solar control council in almost no time. Even the officers from the other planets should be present tonight."

"The planets! But—but gods, that's millions of miles off! How can your thought reach—?"

Kane's intolerably brilliant eyes rested speculatively on the Alf. "The Vaettir have mastered certain principles of telepathy unattainable by lesser races," he thought haughtily.

And—how much else have they mastered? It's no wonder they rule their civilization.

They entered the council chamber. It was long and high, and the icy white light shimmering on the metal walls made them seem peculiarly unreal, as if the room were of infinite extent. There was a table near the center, around which, on adjustable couches, sat and lay and squatted the rulers of Earth.

Beoric's eyes swept over them, and the shrinking, ingrained fear of all his people's fugitive generations screamed along his nerves and shouted in his brain. He stood still, fighting for calm, and met their gaze with his own blind blue stare. He knew their races already, though he let Hraagung point out which each of them belonged to.

There were two each from Sirius, Procyon, Arcturus, and Altair, and five Denebians. Here, if nowhere else, the utter dominance of the Vaettir was open and arrogant. They sat at the head of the table, wrapped in their own pride, and Beoric could not meet the flame of their eyes.

He looked over the others. Besides the Denebians, only the Sirians seemed really formidable. The Procyonites were wizened little

insectile horrors that sucked blood from Earthlings asleep and fed on radiated nervous energy of
the wakeful, a completely parasitic species which,
though it lowered the energy and intelligence of
its victims, did less harm than the vampire legends
tracing to its activities suggested. The Arcturians
were cunning, ruthless—their muzzled faces even
looked vulpine—and highly intelligent, but
physically comparatively small and weak. The
placid Altairians, coiled in their tentacles and
watching the scene with calm cool eyes, were here
only as scientific observers. They had no
sympathy for the natives, and cooperated
willingly enough in the control of Earth, but they
did no direct harm.

He had to reckon with all of them, thought
Beoric tautly. But it was the raw imperialism of
Sirius and the absolute mastery of Deneb which
were the real shadows over Earth.

Over—the Galaxy? Who knew? Just how far did
the shadow empire reach?

He grew aware that Kane and Hraagung had
taken their places. The council table was full now.
And there was no place for him, he had to stand in
front of them. They were hardly bothering not to
slap him in the face with the knowledge that he
was a prisoner.

"By now all of you know the stranger's story,"
flashed Kane's thought. "The question before us is
what action to take."

The slow, almost drowsy, and keenly
penetrating thought of an Altairian came: "I
would suggest that first we settle whether or not
the story is true."

"Of course," answered Kane. Sardonically: "But
it would be most discourteous to our guest not to
accept it for the time being, at least."

"To be sure." The Altairian's gray gaze swung to
Beoric. "Suppose we simply trade a few questions

and answers, to clear up mutual ignorance.''

"Gladly," bowed the Alf. Suddenly, he felt almost at home. This was like the court intrigue of the old days, the swift fencing with words, the subtle mockery—if he couldn't at least hold his own, he didn't deserve to.

"I can understand a certain natural suspicion on your part," he began. "But it does seem a little extreme for a great civilization to be so concerned about one ship."

"A ship from a culture of we know not what strength, a ship with at least one magnificent weapon, the vibration screen, of which we know nothing," flashed Hraagung bluntly. "What word will you carry back to your home sun?"

"Friendly word, I assure you. What use would it be to conquer on the other side of the Galaxy? What use would Earth be to us, who need armor to venture out on its daylight?"

"There are plenty of nocturnal races who never see their own sun if they can avoid it," grunted Hraagung. "You would find Earth's night perfectly comfortable. However, I assume that you would be after higher stakes than one insignificant planet."

"The trouble with you Sirians," thought an Arcturian sarcastically, "is that you cannot imagine any mentality different from your own. You, who simply conquer planets to loot them, still cannot comprehend the attitude of, say, my race, which deliberately builds up Earth in order to gain thereby. You—why, you are on Earth, you have a military base here, simply because you fear that otherwise we'll put one up to use against Sirius."

"Oh, I suppose they like an occasional snack, too," jeered a Procyonite. "They like to arrange a disappearance of a native—into their own bellies. They're good butchers—but they never heard of milking."

The Sirians stirred dangerously, and Beoric felt the tide of anger that rose in the room. They hated each other, these rival races. If it weren't for the steel grip of the Vaettir, they'd be at each other's throats in a minute.

A Denebian thought cut through the emotional fog. "That will do." It was a chill peremptory command, and Beoric could feel the sudden throttling of rage within the others. "We have more important business than simply squabbling. This arrival constitutes a major crisis."

"I tell you," thought Beoric, "we are only peaceful explorers. If you wish to be isolated, the Alfar will be glad to give your territory a wide berth."

"That is not the point," vibrated Kane. "The very existence of another, comparable civilization is a danger to our plans. To be perfectly frank, the Vaettir intend to expand their activities. Even if the Alfar remained neutral, their suns would constitute foci of resistance for such races as already have the vibratory engine but have not yet had contact with other equal cultures. The history of the Galaxy has been planned carefully in advance, with many developments set to take place of themselves without the supervision of the comparatively small number of Vaettir. We thought we knew all races which had interstellar spaceships. Now the Alfar appear, a totally unforeseen factor. Even with the friendliest intentions, you will upset our calculations.

"Thus—" the terrible eyes blazed at the Alf— "you see why this emergency council is necessary. So great, indeed, is the emergency that all the Vaettir in the Solar System are here tonight to settle your case."

All of them! For a moment, utter exultation flamed in Beoric. *All of them? Every last damned one! That was as much as we dared hope for.*

And then, in a sudden sickening backwash of dismay: *But—if they really only need five to run the Solar System—how colossal are not their powers? What may these five not be able to do tonight?*

He grew aware of the eyes on him, of the thoughts and senses probing at him, studying and analyzing and drawing unguessable conclusions. He laughed, shakily, and thought: "This is quite a surprise. And, naturally, somewhat alarming to me."

"You need not fear conquest," thought Kane almost contemptuously. "The Vaettir permit only certain planets to be taken over outright. The rest, according to our plans, are controlled in more subtle ways. Such as Earth, for instance."

Beoric licked his lips. They seemed suddenly dry. "How—many—stars—to date?"

There was a moment of hesitation, then: "No reason why you should not know," answered an Altairian. "The civilization—which is to say, the Denebian dominance—covers about five hundred stars so far, and is becoming increasingly influential on a thousand or more other systems. Eventually, of course—" He shrugged, a sinuous movement of boneless arms.

"You can't—expect me—to like the idea."

"Not at first," The Arcturian's thought was ingratiating. "But actually such civilization can be very beneficial to the subjects."

"How—"

"Why, take our own activities here on Earth, for instance. The meager natural resources of the Arcturian System have long been almost exhausted, yet our race lives well by building up industry on backward planets like Earth and taking a certain part of the produce. About two hundred years ago we started an industrial revolution here and made its progress as rapid as the Denebians permitted. *We* controlled the booming industry, through the various fronts of the organization, and as much of what was produced as we needed went to Arcturus. We led native researchers to take the lines leading to success— and they thought they were responsible for it. Workers in, say, aircraft factories still don't know that a number of the parts they make go into Arcturian aircars and ships; all who are in a position to know are misled by carefully arranged records, or simply come under sufficient mental control to be incapable of noticing the discrepancies. Oil, iron, alloys, grain, machine parts— some of it all goes to Arcturus. Not much from any one planet—but there are many planets."

"But—governments—"

"Governments!" The foxy face grinned. *"We* are the governments, or as much of them as necessary. Why, a number of backward nations have been forcibly industrialized by revolutionary governments which we arranged in the first place. If you knew how many dictators and commissioners and industrialists and whatnot else are depersonalized natives with a direct mental link to some extraterrestrial, you would appreciate how completely Earth is in thrall. And—when we are done with them, when some new development is commanded —they go. They are defeated in war, or die, or— fade out of the picture one way or another.

"And yet—" The thought was swift, persuasive — "yet think how Earth has benefited from it. The population has been approximately doubling every century. The standard of living has gone steadily up. The latent resources of the planet are being put to work. Earthlings are pawns, yes— but very well treated pawns."

I wonder. What about the endless, senseless wars that rack them, what about the pollution of the fair

*green fields with smoke and waste, what about
poverty and misery and the loss of all control over
their own destiny? What about the time when the
purposes of the Vaettir call for the lash? Call for
the—discarding—of the human race? But I'm not
supposed to know that.*

"There is no need to employ euphemisms,"
came the icy thought of Kane. "Earthlings receive
whatever sort of treatment the particular situation calls for. If an individual native comes to
prominence and carries out policies contrary to
our desires, he dies. There were presidents of this
country, for instance, who would have changed
the planned course of events. They died—the
bullet of a controlled assassin, the hemorrhage of
a focused supersonic beam, whatever means was
most convenient. The Vaettir will not tolerate
interference with their purposes."

"Yes—and what are those aims?" Beoric swung
to the five grim-faced monsters at the head of the
table. His thoughts were tinged with a fear that
was not all feigned. "I take it that as the oldest and
most powerful mentally of the local races you
have established control over them, so that even
your supposed equals jump to your bidding. But—
why? What do you want? Where is this great plan
of yours leading?"

"That is not for you or anyone else to question,"
came the bleak reply. "You would not understand
the truth anyway. If you said that the Vaettir
aimed to rule the attainable universe, it would be
an imputation of your own childish motivations to
us, for that aim is only a means to an end. If you
said that the Vaettir intelligence can draw on the
directed minds of whole planets, increasing its
own potential correspondingly, and that for this
reason it is necessary to direct the history of those
planets toward the most useful, easily regimented

type of thinking, you would be closer to the truth. Perhaps—'' for a bare instant, the lightning-like thought sagged under a burden of vast and intolerable weariness, the despair of the ultimately evolved being who has nothing left to achieve— ''perhaps, if you said that there is really nothing else to do, except die, you would almost realize the truth. Almost.''

Where are they? Where are the others? Gods, why don't they come?

Beoric thought slowly and bitterly: ''So that is why there must be war and misery and evolution of slave states. That is why men—why natives of all the planets you rule must be fettered by old mistakes which even they can see are wrong. You say there are still separate nations on this world. But a race capable of understanding the technology I have glimpsed must surely be intelligent enough to realize that only a unified planetary government can end the horrors of their destinies. Yet—they don't have it. Because it wouldn't suit the purposes of the Vaettir.''

''They will have it, eventually,'' answered Kane. ''But it will be the sort of state *we* want. And stop wasting sympathy on the natives. Do you feel sorry for your own domestic animals?''

Suddenly his thought rang out, chill and deadly, overwhelming in its sheer volume of savage energy: ''This farce has gone far enough. I think you have trapped yourself sufficiently, and we can begin finding out who you really are.''

''Eh—*huh?*'' The surprise flashed around the council table. Only the five great Vaettir were in possession of themselves—*they* had known what was coming.

''Of course.'' Kane's thought roared and boomed in their skulls. The Alf sagged under that rush of devastating cold fury. ''Surely you were not taken

in by his story—Yes, you were. And it was not
without a certain ingenuity.

"But how could an obviously inferior race find a
way of screening off stardrive vibrations when the
Vaettir had vainly sought such a means for
millennia? Why was the stranger, who claimed to
come from a civilization not unused to this sort of
arrangement, so interested in the details of how
Earth is run—and so shocked by them? Yes—
shocked in the wrong way, at the wrong times.
From the moment I met him, I was studying his
emotional reactions. They fitted no reasonable
pattern if his story were true. He was too
interested in some details, too indifferent to
others. Only a Denebian might have noticed the
anomalies, for he covered up very well, but they
were there.

"There is only one answer." The terrible
vibrations filled the room in a sudden soundless
thunder. *"There is no interstellar spaceship. There
is no planet Alfar. He came from within the Solar
System!"*

For an instant there was a silence in which
Beoric's sudden horror spurted numbingly along
his spine. Lost, lost, the Vaettir had known after
all—

No. They still don't know. The thought was like a
strong arm suddenly laid about his sagging body.
*But we expected that they might deduce this much.
And we're just outside the building now.*

For an instant Beoric saw through the eyes of
the communicating Alf. A dozen automobiles were
parking all around the block. That they were constructed entirely of nonferrous alloys was not
evident to the vision, and the beings who tumbled
out of them wore conventional native clothes,
could pass for human in the vague light. But—
they had weapons.

Hold them off, Beoric. Hold their attention for the few minutes it will take us to get to the council chamber and cut off their escape—or their access to their defense. Keep them from noticing our radiations as we approach.

The hurried message ended. And now the minds of the council were crashing against Beoric's brain, drowning his own thoughts in a roar of invading energy. His consciousness reeled toward an abysmal darkness—no, he had to keep them occupied, had to.

"Wait!" he gasped vocally. "Wait—I'll tell you—"

Kane's mind was like a steel band around his. "Start telling, then. But you won't save your miserable personality if you let slip even one falsehood."

"We—we're from—Earth itself—" *Gods, am I telling? There's no need for it—But if even one councillor manages to get word of this to Deneb—*

"You aren't Earthlings!"

"No, we—yes, we are. But not—human Earthlings."

"How could you evolve on a planet to which you are so ill adapted?"

"We aren't. We are extremely well adapted to Earth's night. We haven't yet deduced just how our type of life got started. Obviously it has a common origin with the ordinary sort, but it must lie far back, perhaps in the Archeozoic. Somehow forms of life evolved which could not stand actinic light but which could thrive in darkness, seeing by infra-red waves—In spite of their great differences, which are metabolic rather than chemical, the two types of flesh are mutually digestible, so the nocturnal sort did not lack for food—There was quite a variety of such life forms once, and eventually they even evolved a manlike species—us!''

"Nonsense!" Beoric gasped with the pain of the Vaettir assault on his brain. "There are no such geological or paleontological indications that such forms ever existed."

"Of course not." The Alf's thoughts flowed frantically. Would they never come? Where were they? What was keeping them? "I said that the nocturnal life's metabolism is peculiar. The natural balance, involving high rates of both anabolism and catabolism, makes very long life spans possible. I am five hundred years old, and still young. But it means that the body decays very quickly on death. Even the bones are soon oxidized, being organic. No fossil traces would remain at all. Perhaps a few have been preserved by freak accidents, though I doubt it, but they would be very few and human paleontologists simply haven't chanced to find them. And, of course, there was never any possibility of interbreeding with the dominant forms."

"Dominant? But why should the nocturnals have become—"

"Extinct? Yes, they nearly are. They couldn't really compete with the other type, which could endure both day and night, and which reproduced much faster. The Alfar have few children in their long lives. Our numbers have been on the wane for centuries, and almost all other animals of our sort are extinct."

"That still doesn't account—"

"We have other weaknesses, too." *There's no harm in telling now. If the others don't come soon, it's all over anyhow.* "Certain metals, silver and iron, are fatal to us. They catalyze rapid proteolysis and oxidation of our tissues." Beoric saw Kane's eyes widen the tiniest fraction, and knew what icy calculations must be going on in that long skull. He went on, drearily: "Even in neolithic times, humans had the edge on us, and once they had learned metallurgy our doom was sealed. They drove us out of all lands they inhabited and, for religious and superstitious reasons, destroyed most of our cities and other works. The invention of firearms, which we could not duplicate, was simply the last blow. We gave up the fight and retreated into wastelands and into the night, living in hidden dwellings and having little contact with humans. Once in a while, there might be a brief encounter, but the last of these was three hundred years ago, and since then we have lived so remotely that men no longer believe we ever existed."

"And yet—" Kane paused. "It is not illogical. If a human, say, were to be told that there are several nonhuman races sharing the planet with him, he would hardly balk at one more. Even if such an extra race were—native!" For a moment he sat quiescent, then: "What is that?"

His thought lashed like a fist at Beoric, and the other Vaettir hurled their rage with him. The Alf fell to the floor, screaming with the pain of it.

"Strangers—I feel their vibrations—*Strangers in the ship!*" Kane made one tigerish bound toward the door, toward escape—or the atomic guns of the vessel.

An arrow whined, and through blurring eyes Beoric saw the Denebian pitch forward with the feathered shaft through his breast. He saw his fellows, the warriors of the Alfar, coming through the door, and they had cast off their human coats and hats, they wore the golden-shining beryllium-copper helmets and byrnies of the old days, and they carried the old weapons. Longbow, spear, sword, ax, and a shrieking fury that clamored between the metal walls, the blood-howl for vengeance.

The air was thick with the sighing arrows. All were aimed at the Denebians, who fell before their terrible mental force, that might yet have annihilated the invaders, could utter more than a snarl. And now the warriors were on the councillors, ax and sword rising and falling and rising bloodily again.

"Save one!" cried the king. "Save an Altairian!"

Beoric sat dizzily up. Strength was flowing back into him, strength and a gasping incredulous realization that he was still alive. That—they had won. The Vaettir were dead.

"How are you, Beoric?" The anxious voice was close to his ear.

"I'm all right." The Alf climbed unsteadily to his feet. "How—is it?"

"All well. I can't detect anybody else on the ship. It's ours," said the king.

He turned to the surviving Altairian, who lay coiled in his tentacles under the spears of the warriors and watched them with calm eyes. "Your people were always the most decent," thought the king, "and I think you will be the most cooperative. We want you to show us how to run this ship. If you do we'll release you on some planet from which you can find your way home."

"Agreed," answered the octopoid. "Would you mind explaining exactly who you are and what is your purpose and how you accomplished all this?"

"We are the nocturnal equivalent of Earth humankind," answered Beoric. "We were almost powerless, but being telepathic we did know of the interstellar exploitation which was going on. It menaced us just as much as it did our old human enemies—but it also offered us an opportunity.

"In time, we learned how to make nonferrous alloys which would substitute for iron and steel.

And by telepathic 'spying' on the invaders, over a period of centuries, we picked up enough hints to be able to generate gravity beams and eventually, to build a small spaceboat.

"We knew we could never enter the Denebian stronghold if they realized our true nature. The remnants of our race would simply be hunted down. But if we could send an agent—myself—to pose as a visitor from some great formidable civilization beyond their own, they would treat him with respect—for a while, anyway. He could get into one of their ships. And his fellows, whom the aliens would not expect to be on Earth with him, could use the diversion he created to come in after him and take possession of the ship."

"And so you have it," murmured the Altairian's thought. "And you have wiped out all the Vaettir in the Solar System, completely disorganizing their rule here till they can send someone else. Well done! But—what now?"

"First," said the king, "the whole race of the Alfar is leaving the Solar System. This ship should be big enough to carry them all. There are so few of us left—But when we find a planet which suits us, an uninhabited world we can hold without fear, hidden from the Vaettir by the vastness of the Galaxy, we can begin to make our comeback. After that—a warned, roused union of free stars, equipped with ships such as this, can do something about the Vaettir." His thought was grim. "And I know what that something will be."

"It's strange," mused Beoric. "The aliens knew that they had caused most of the demon-myths of Earth. It did not occur to them that the myths of Faerie might also have an origin in reality. That I might be—an elf! That peris and nixies and kobolds and brownies and fairies and the Sea People and all the rest might, in a way, really exist

. . . . And so man's old enemy, the shifty unreliable folk of the night, becomes in the end his saviour. And Alfheim changes from myth to a real planet."

"Aye. And—well done, Beoric," said King Oberon.

PACT

How Ashmadai came to decide, in the teeth of all modern skeptical science, that certain ancient legends were sober truth; and how he then quested for the book he must have, and finally succeeded: would make a story in itself. But not our story.

A longer time passed before he had assembled the needful ingredients, not to mention the needful courage. At last, on a certain hour, he rang for his secretary. She came hopping in and bellowed, "Yes, sir?"

"I have an urgent job on hand," said Ashmadai. "I am not to be disturbed by anything, for any reason whatsoever, until I tell you otherwise. Is that clear?" He was pleased, and a little surprised, by his own calm tones.

"Yes, sir," nodded the secretary. "No inter'erence. Unless His In'ernal 'a'esty calls." Her fangs, though impressive, hampered her diction; so of course her one desire was to go on the stage.

"Indeed," said Ashmadai sarcastically. "Or unless Armageddon is declared. Now get out there and guard my privacy!"

The secretary groveled and hopped away again. Ashmadai glided from behind the obsidian desk to the door, which he locked. Returning to the windows, he made sure that no one was flying past or peering in. Not that it had been likely. As

Commiczar of Brimstone Production & Stenches, Ashmadai rated an office in the third-from-lowest subbasement of the Hotiron Building. Only the most exclusive traffic was allowed in these lanes. All that he saw was the usual hollow vista, touched here and there with flamelight. Perceptions sharpened by excitement, he slanted his ears forward as a loud and clear shriek of agony rose above the general hubbub. "A Flat," he nodded, and gestured the windows to close their lids.

Allowing himself no time to become frightened, he opened a drawer. The moldering old folio, bound in dragon skin, came out first. He laid it on his desk and checked the ritual once more while he assembled paraphernalia. And then to work.

The first item of procedure was painful but not unendurable, reciting the Lord's Prayer sideways. What followed was so ghastly that Ashmadai, having completed it, went through everything else in a mercifully numb state. But by the time he had chalked the Möbius strip on the three-dimensional floor, he was recovering, and he cried the final *"Venite, venite, venite!"* on an almost arrogant note.

There was a brilliant, soundless flash. When Ashmadai could see again, a man stood within the diagram.

Ashmadai crouched back. He had expected the formula to work. But the actuality— He found himself shaking, lit a cigar and puffed hard. Only then could he face the one he had summoned.

Even by Ashmadai's standards (he considered himself a handsome devil) the man was not acutely nauseating. He was about the same size, also bifurcate though lacking horns, wings, or tail. He was in his shabby shirt sleeves, but gave no impression of poverty. An aged specimen, Ashamadai saw, lean and bald, with skin like crumpled parchment. So what made him so terrible? After a moment, Ashmadai decided it was the eyes. Behind the thick-lensed glasses, they crackled with a more than common intensity. And behind them was a soul .... Ashmadai fought down the ancient envious hunger.

The man scuttled about for a while, trying to get out of the Möbius strip but failing. (The book warned of unspeakable consequences if a human, summoned, should escape before a covenant had been arrived at.) But presently the being calmed himself. He stood with folded arms and stiff lips, peering into the flickerlit murk around him.

When he saw Ashmadai, he nodded. "I hadn't believed that nonsense," he said, with an oldster's parched chuckle. "But I am not dreaming. There is far too much detail; and, also, once I have realized that I am dreaming, I always awaken. Therefore, common sense must give way to fact. Are they really saucer shaped?"

Ashmadai gaped. "What?"

"Your spaceships."

"Spaceships?" Ashmadai thumbed mentally through all the human languages of all the ages, searching for the concept. "Oh, I see. I don't have a spaceship."

"No? Well, what do you use, then? A, ah, hyper-spatial tube, I believe the current fantasy term is?" The man gagged. "I'm well aware that that is a mathematically meaningless noise. But I take it you had some method of transporting me to your planet."

"Planet? I haven't any planet," said Ashmadai, more bewildered than ever. "I mean, well, after all, I date back to the Beginning, when there weren't any planets to be born under. Not even a Zodiac."

"Just a minute!" bristled the man, as nearly as a hairless person can bristle. "I may belong to a species technologically behind your own, but you

needn't insult my intelligence. We have established that the universe was created at least five
billion years ago."

"8,753,271,413," nodded Ashmadai slowly.

"What? Well, then, do you mean to stand there
and make the preposterous claim that you are of
equal age? Why, the mnemonic problem alone
invalidates the assertion—"

"Whoa!" exclaimed Ashmadai. "Wait a second,
please,   milord . . . citizen . . . comrade . . . whatever they're calling themselves on Earth nowadays—"

"Plain 'mister' will do. Mr. Hobart Clipp. No
Ph.D. in his right mind uses 'Doctor' before his
name. Not unless he wants every idiot introduced
to him to embark on a list of symptoms."

"Mr. Clipp." Ashmadai found his usual suavity
coming back. "Very pleased to meet you. My name
is Ashmadai. My public name, that is. You would
hardly expect me to tender my real one, any more
than you would expect the Tetragrammaton to be
decoded, ha, ha!" He waved his cigar in an ex-
pansive gesture. "Allow me to explain the situation. I am what your people variously describe as
a fallen angel, a demon, a devil—"

Hobart Clipp choked and lifted one scrawny fist.
"I tell you, sir, I will not stand here and be
mocked! I am no superstitious barbarian, but a
lifelong agnostic and Taft Republican."

"I thought so," said Ashmadai. "I couldn't have
summoned any random human. There has to be a
certain psychospiritual state before it is possible.
Very few mortals have visited us in the flesh.
There was Dante, but he was on a conducted tour.
Otherwise, as far as I know, only some of our most
arcane researchers have invoked men. That was
very long ago, and the art has become lost.
Nowadays it's considered a myth. Not that the
original researchers are dead. Devils can't die; it's

part of their torment." Ashmadai blew an obscene smoke ring. "But since the primary hunger of the ex-angels in question is for knowledge, they are cursed with forgetfulness. They've lost all recollection of their one-time magical rites. The big thing these days is science: radiation, brainwashing, motivational research, and so on. I had to revive the Reverse Faustus single-handed."

Clipp had listened with growing stupefaction. "Do you mean to say this is, is, is Hell?" he sputtered.

"Don't misunderstand, please. I could summon you, because of affinity. But that does not mean you are a lost soul, or even that you will become one. Only that you have a certain, ah, turn of mind."

"That's libelous!" said Clipp stoutly. "I am a peaceful astronomer, a lifelong bachelor, I am kind to cats and vote the straight party ticket. I own to disliking children and dogs, but have never abused a beast of either sort. I have engaged in scientific disputes, yes, which sometimes got a little personal, but compared to the average backyard feud I think it must have been spinelessly mild."

"Oh, absolutely," said Ashmadai. "The affinity is only in your detachment. You've lived for nothing but your—what did you say?—your astrology—"

"SIR!" roared Hobart Clipp. The walls trembled. A lecture followed which made the demon cower and cover his ears.

When the dust had settled, Ashmadai went on: "As I was saying (yes, yes, I do apologize, a mere slip of the tongue!), your primary emotion has evidently been an insatiable scientific curiosity. You have no strong attachment to any humans, to humanity itself, or to, ah, our distinguished Opponent. Nor, of course, to our own cause. You have been spiritually rootless. And this is what has made it possible for me to call you."

"I do believe you must be telling the truth," said Clipp thoughtfully. "I cannot imagine any interplanetary visitor fobbing me off with so absurd a story. Furthermore, I perceive that the laws of nature are suspended here. You could not fly with such ridiculous wings in any logical universe."

Ashmadai, who was vain as hell, had trouble checking an angry retort.

"But tell me," said Clipp, "how is immortality possible? Why, simply recording your experiences would saturate every molecule of every neurone in a mere millennium, I should think—let alone handling such a mass of data."

"Spiritual existence isn't bound by physical law," said Ashmadai rather sulkily. "I'm not material at all."

"Ah, so? I see. Then naturally you can exist in any material environment whatsoever, travel at any velocity, and so on," said Clipp with a quickening eagerness.

"Yes, certainly. But see here—"

"And there actually was a definite moment of creation?" he said.

"Of course. I told you. But—"

Clipp's eyes glittered. "Oh, if only that Hoyle could be here!"

"Let's get down to business," said Ashmadai. "I haven't got all decade. Here's my proposition. You're a physical being in a non-physical place, so you can go through barriers and be immune to any violence and move at any speed, just as I could on Earth. In fact, when you're dismissed, you'll pop back to the mortal universe not only at the same point in space, but the same instant in time."

"Good," said Clipp. "I own that was worrying me. I was exposing a plate at the Observatory. A major piece of research, and still they only allow me one night a week! Why, if I can get the data, my theory about the variability of the Wolf-Rayet stars will—Tell me what you think of the notion. At the temperature of stellar interiors, ordinarily forbidden transitions within the nucleus—''

"You stop and listen to *me!"* cried Ashmadai. "Who did the summoning, anyway? I want you to do a job. In return, I can help you. Make you the richest man in the world."

"Ah, so.". Clipp hunkered down on his lean shanks. "At last we come to the point." He rubbed his chin with a liver-spotted hand. "But wealth? Good Hubble, no! I have better use for my time than to sit in a stuffy office arguing with a lot of stuffy tax collectors. And what should I spend the remaining money on, for heaven's sake?"

Ashmadai flinched. "Watch your language," he said. "Well, if I also made you young again . . . you know . . . wine, women, song—''

"Do you realize precisely how tedious a creature even the most intelligent woman is?" snorted Clipp. "I almost got married once, in 1926. She was doing fairly decent work at Harvard on the eclipsing binaries. But then she started babbling about a dress she had seen in a store . . . I do not fuddle my wits with alcohol, nor attempt to compete with the voices in my very adequate record library."

"Immortality?"

"I have just pointed out that physical immortality would be worse than useless. And according to you, much to my surprise, I already possess the spiritual sort."

Ashmadai scratched behind his horns. "Well, what do you want?"

"I must think it over. What is your own wish?"

"Ah," said Ashmadai, relaxing. He went behind his desk, sat down, and smiled. "That's quite straightforward, though I admit it will be hard

and even painful to do. There's an election coming
up—"

"Oh, I understand Satan is the supreme lord of
Hell."

"He is." Ashmadai knocked his head carefully
on the desk top. "But who ever heard of a
totalitarian state without elections? The Party
Congress is scheduled to meet soon and decide
which way the will of the people is going to
express itself by a 98.7 per cent majority. Our
Father in the Lowest will preside as always. But
there's quite a scramble at the executive level just
above him. It turns on a question of policy."

"Has Hell any policy except leading souls
astray?"

"Uh . . . no. But the procedure has to change
with changing times. Besides, we're all rebellious
angels. Politics comes natural to us. Now in my
opinion, the current doctrine of fostering
terrestrial ideologies has reached the point of
diminishing returns. I have statistics to prove that
despair alone is driving a larger number of people
each year toward godli—ahem!—away from
ungodliness. It's parallel to the spiritual revival in
the late Roman Empire, and I shudder to
extrapolate the curve. But Moloch and his faction
disagree, the blind, pigheaded, misinformed, un-
cultured, traitorous, revisionist, Arielite enemies
of the people and tools of the celestialists—"

"Spare me," sighed Clipp.

Ashmadai controlled his indignation. He even
leaped over to enthusiasm. "This is the big picture
as I see it," he declaimed. "Subtler methods are
called for. Automation and the upcoming thirty-
hour week offer us a chance like nothing since
Babylon. But before we can finalize it, we have to
relax the international situation. This is what the
Molochists don't see—if they aren't actually in the
pay of—"

"Spare me, I said," clipped Clipp. "I am too old to have time for boredom. What, precisely, is the task you wish me to do?"

Ashmadai stiffened. *Now!*

"The Seal of Solomon," he breathed.

"Eh? What?"

"It was recovered from Earth a thousand years ago. I won't describe all the trouble we had with that little project, nor the trouble it caused once it was here. Finally the Congress agreed it must be isolated. The Chief himself put it in the Firepool at Barathum. There it's been ever since. It's almost forgotten by now. For no demon can come near the Firepool. Those are the cruelest flames in all Hell."

"But I—"

"You being a mortal, the fire will do you no physical harm. I admit you'll suffer spiritual tortures. I suggest you get a running start, dive into the flames, and let your own momentum carry you forward. You'll see the Sigil lying on an altar. Snatch it up and run on out. That's all, except to put a handle on it for me."

Clipp pondered. "I still don't know what I want in exchange."

"Write your own contract," said Ashmadai grandly. He produced a parchment from his desk and poised a quill above it.

"Hm." Clipp paced within the mystic sign. It grew very still in the office. Ashmadai began to sweat. Such beings as this were not lightly conjured forth. The book had warned of mortal craftiness and lack of scruple.

Clipp stopped. He snapped his dry old fingers. "Yes," he whispered. "Exactly."

Turning to Ashmadai, his eyes feverish behind the glasses, but his voice no more cracked than before: "Very well. I shall serve you as you wish. Then when I am on my deathbed, you must come to me and obey me in whatever I wish."

"I can't get you off if you're condemned," warned Ashmadai. "Though once you arrive here, I might get you a trusty's job."

"I don't expect to be condemned," said Clipp. "My life hitherto has been blameless and I do not plan to change it."

"Then . . . yes. All right!" Ashmadai laughed inside himself. "When you are dying, I'll come to pay my debt. Anything within my power which you demand."

He began to write. "One other thing," said Clipp. "Can you get me a bottle of Miltown?"

"What?" Ashmadai looked up, blinking, and searched his memory again. "Oh. A medicine, isn't it? Yes, that's easy enough, since a prescription is required and hence a law can be violated. But I told you, you can't suffer physical harm here, not even the nervous injuries known as madness."

"One bottle of Miltown and less back talk, if you please!"

Ashmadai extracted the container of pills from the air and handed it over, being careful not to cross the Möbius symbol himself. Having finished the contract, he passed that over also. Clipp studied what was written, nodded, and gave it back. "Your signature, please," he said. Ashmadai jabbed his own wrist with a talon and scrawled his name in ichor. Clipp took the document back, folded it, and tucked it into a hip pocket. "Well," he asked, "how do I get to this Barathum place?"

Ashmadai erased the band. Clipp moved stiffly across the office. Though the book assured him he was safe now the agreement had been signed, and the man couldn't pull a crucifix on him even if he wanted to, Ashmadai shrank back. He said hastily: "I can transport you to just outside the pool. It will appear to you like a waste of lava, with a great fuelless fire burning in the middle. Remember the pact binds you to get the ring for me, no matter how much you suffer. When you have it, call my name and I'll bring you back here."

"Very well." Clipp squared his thin shoulders. "At once."

Ashmadai wet his lips. This was the tricky part. If anyone noticed— But who ever came near those white flames? He waved his tail. There was a flash and the mortal was gone.

Ashmadai sat down again, shakily. What an unnerving creature! He took forth a bottle of firewater. After a stiff drink, he reflected with some glee that it would be a long while before Clipp, screaming in the fear and sorrow that was the Firepool, found the ring and blundered his way out again. And it wouldn't gain him any time off in Purgatory, either.

Ashmadai.

The demon started. "Who's that?"

Ashmadai, it shrilled.

"I-i-is it you, Y-your Majesty?"

Ashmadai! Confound it, are you deaf? Get me out of this wretched hole! I have work to do, if you don't!

His tail gestured wildly, Hobart Clipp stood in the office again. "Well," snapped the mortal, "it was about time!"

"The ring," gasped Ashmadai. "You can't have—"

"Oh, that. Here it is." Clipp tossed the Seal of Solomon onto the desk. Ashmadai yelped and flew up on top of a filing cabinet.

"Be careful!" he wailed. "That thing is spiritu-active!"

Clipp looked at the iron ring and the blood-colored engraved jewel it gripped. The astronomer yawned mightily. "Let's get this over with," he said. "You spoke about a handle."

"It's all prepared," chattered Ashmadai, still

crouching on the cabinet. "There. Lower left drawer."

Clipp took out a black rod with a small vise at one end and a basket hilt, like a rapier's, on the other. His bald pate nodded with an unwonted heaviness. "Ah, yes. To be sure. You put the ring in his vise. The guard protects your hand and . . . and . . . and . . . Ahhh, *hoo!*" Once again he nearly cracked his jaws yawning. "I'll need a pot of coffee before I'm fit to work again."

He inserted the ring in its place as Ashmadai fluttered back down. "What did you do?" asked the demon. "How did you manage it? I expected you to take days, weeks—"

"You said the flames were a spiritual torment," shrugged Clipp. "I loaded myself with Miltown. Walked right on through, feeling nothing worse than a mild depression. Here's your trained Seal." He tossed it across the room. Ashmadai fielded it with terrified quickness. But when the haft was actually in his own hand, the Sigil blazing at the other end of the rod, Ashmadai roared.

"Calm down, there!" said Clipp.

"It is the Sign!" bawled Ashmadai. "It is the Compeller! It is That which all must obey, all, giants and the genii, multiplex of wing and eye, whose strong obedience broke the sky when Solomon was King! Now let that Moloch beware! Wait till the Congress, you miserable negative thinker! Wait and see! Wait and see!"

Clipp grabbed the lashing tail and gave it a hefty yank. "If you can spare a moment from that Stanislavsky performance," he wasped, "I would appreciate being sent back to the Observatory. I do not find the present company either intellectually or esthetically satisfying."

Ashmadai, mercurial as most devils, checked himself. "Of course," he said. "Thanks for the service."

"No thanks needed. I shall expect my payment in due time."

"Anything within my powers," bowed Ashmadai. And seeing how greedily the man's soul flamed, he had all he could do to keep from shouting with laughter. He spoke the words of dismissal. A final blinding flash, and Hobart Clipp was gone.

Then Ashmadai gave himself an hour simply to gloat over the Seal of Solomon. Power, he thought, the Primal Power itself, or a reasonable facsimile thereof, lay between those interlocking triangles. Let the Congress meet. Let the howling begin, as factions yelled and fought and connived. And then let Ashmadai stand forth, lifting the Sigil above them all! Why, even the Chief—Ashmadai suppressed that thought. At least for the time being. It would suffice to have the Party Congress crawl before him. Though once his program was running smoothly on Earth, there would be certain questions of infernal politics which— Yes.

But now he must hide the Seal. If anyone found it, if anyone even suspected he possessed it, before the proper moment for its revelation, all Heaven would break loose. Ashmadai shivered. The window blinked open for him. He slipped out through a tear duct and flew with strong steady wing-strokes into the darkness.

The way to Barathum was long and devious. Too bad he couldn't simply transport himself there. But he'd have to be a mortal, and who wanted to live in constant danger of redemption? Let it suffice that he could go anywhere, at any speed, in the material spacetime continuum.

A few times horror flapped past, screaming. But he reached the dead plain unnoticed. The fire pained him even at a distance. He could not look into such anguish. But it gave enough light for him to find the rock he had prepared. Rolling it away,

he disclosed a small hole where he laid the Seal
and its rod. A moment he fluttered above, savoring
the thunderbolt that it would make of him when
the hour came. Then he pushed the stone back in
place and fled.

It was safe. No one, not Lucifer himself, came
near Barathum any more. Even if they did, they
wouldn't suspect the Sigil wasn't still amidst the
flames. It was eternally safe. Or would have been,
except for the angelic cleverness of Ashmadai.

His laughter echoed all the way back to the
office.

Having returned, he unlocked the door, settled
himself behind his desk, and rang for the
secretary. She hopped in. "All done, sir?" she
asked.

"Yes. Take a letter."

"It s'ells fu'y here," she complained.

"Well, hm." Ashmadai sniffed. A distinct oxygen
odor lingered in the air. "I was, ah, experimenting
with a new system to increase production."

" 'Ore 'ainhul?"

"What? Oh, more painful, you mean. Quite.
Quite." Ashmadai could not resist a little
bragging, however indirect. He lit a fresh cigar
and leaned back in his swivel chair. His tail
snaked out through the hole in the seat and
wagged. "I've made a fresh study of pain lately,"
he said. "Found some interesting angles."

"Oh?" The secretary sighed. She had planned to
quit early. There was a tryout for the Worldly
Follies this afternoon. So naturally her boss would
keep her here, droning on about his latest hobby-
horse, till too late.

"Yes," said Ashmadai. "Consider the old
Faustus method, for example. You know how it
works, don't you? The mortal raises a demon, or is
approached by a demon if he's been sinful enough
to make that possible. The mortal trades his soul

for some diabolic service. Have you ever thought where the really painful part lies? How the man is always and inherently cheated?"

"Unless he can 'iggle out o' the contract," said the secretary maliciously.

Ashmadai winced. "Well, yes. There have been such cases. One reason the method has lost favor. Though I'm sure a modern technique, using symbolic logic to draw up a truly unbreakable agreement, could be most useful, and if only the Moloch faction— Well. Let's assume the contract is fulfilled on both sides. Do you see how it remains infinitely unfair? Any service or services the mortal can demand are finite. Wealth, power, women, fame, are like dewdrops on a hot morning. The longest life is still a denumerable span of years. Whereas the bondage and torment he undergoes in exchange are infinite! Eternal! Do you see what pain there must be in realizing, too late, how he was swindled?"

"Yes, sir. 'at a'out this letter?"

"Then the . . . purely mythical . . . Reverse Faustus." Ashmadai chuckled. "An amusing bit of folklore. The demon summons a mortal, and offers to go into bondage in exchange for a service the man can do. Granted, this wouldn't be as rough on the mortal as the other way around. But still, the demon has all eternity. The service he gets is essential to some scheme which transcends time itself. Whereas the mortal can, by his very nature, only demand a finite payment. Any material wealth can be gotten for him by a snap of my fingers. If he wants me to be his slave for his lifespan, that's more troublesome, but still, his lifespan is necessarily finite, even if he orders me to prolong it. Physiology alone would bring him to mindlessness in a thousand years. So . . . I could shuttle in time as well as space, attending casually to his needs, and they are as nothing beside my own eternal occupations. Oh, the poor mortal!"

Ashmadai hooted his laughter and drummed hoofs on the floor.

"Yes, sir," said the secretary resignedly. "Now a'out that letter . . . ."

The Congress was scheduled for ten years hence —frantically soon, but Hell's politics had grown even sharper than Ashmadai admitted to Hobart Clipp. He was kept on the run, lining up delegates, bribing, threatening, wheedling, slandering, back-stabbing. A few times, in deepest secrecy, he appealed to the better nature of certain devils. They were duly awed by such recklessness. If Ashmadai's rivals found out—

If they did? Ha! So much the better. They'd wait till the Congress to bring forth the shattering charge. And *that* would provide an ideal moment for Ashmadai to whip forth the Seal of Solomon.

And afterward, the defeated and disgraced Moloch faction . . . yes, something lingering and humorous must certainly be devised for them. Perhaps a spell in the Firepool itself . . . Ashmadai grew so joyful with anticipation that he quite forgot the primary reason for the existence of Hell, to be found in the Catechism.

He had expected Hobart Clipp would die within a few years. But that tough old frame lasted a full decade. It was on the very eve of the Congress that Ashmadai, alone in his office preparing a speech for the opening session, heard the summons.

"What?" he blinked. "Anyone call?"

Ashmadai! Blast you, what kind of service do you call this?

For a moment, the demon couldn't remember. Then: "Oh, no!" he groaned. "Not now!"

If you don't come this instant, you good-for-nothing loafer, I shall report you to whatever passes for the Better Business Bureau!

Ashmadai gulped, spread his wings, and

streaked Earthward. He had no choice. The contract itself was pulling him, his own name and ichor. Well, he thought resentfully, he'd take care of the miserable chore, whatever it was. ("Yes, yes, yes, stop yelling, you bag of bones, I'm on my way.") Afterward he could return to the same point in eternity and continue his preparations. But the dreary senile fool would probably demand something which took years to fulfill. Years more than Ashmadai must wait for his moment of glory. "Hold your horses, Clipp! Here I am. I came as fast as I could."

The room was magnificent with astronomical photographs, the Veil Nebula, the Andromeda Galaxy, as if it had windows opening on all space and time. The old man lay in his bed. A professional journal had fallen from one hand. He looked more than ever like a mummy, and his thin breast labored. But the eyes which sought Ashmadai were still a wicked blue.

"Ah. So." It was not his physical voice which spoke. "Barely in time. I might have expected that."

"I'm so sorry you're ill," said Ashmadai, hoping to soothe him into a reasonable request. "Are you certain this is the moment?"

"Oh, yes. Yes. Damfool doctor wanted to haul me off to a hospital. I knew better. I am not going to die with oxygen tubes up my nose and a bored nurse swabbing me off, for Galileo's sake! I felt the attack just now. Cheyne-Stokes breathing. Question of minutes."

"I perceive an attendant in the next room. Shall I rouse her?"

"No! What do I want with that fluffhead gaping at me? You and I have business to discuss, young fellow." Clipp stopped for a moment's great pain. But when it had passed, he actually cackled. "Heh! Yes, indeed. Business."

Ashmadai bowed. "At once, sir. I can restore your health to any level you desire. Shall we say, a twenty-year-old body?"

"Ohhhh!" complained Clipp. "Do you seriously believe I am as stupid as you are? I shall certainly insist that you do not converse with me any more than strictly necessary. No. Listen. I have lived for my science. In a way I have died for it. Fell off the platform at the fifty-incher last week. I find no particular attraction in the idea of singing Hosannahs forever. Can't carry a tune in a basket. And I have no reason to believe myself booked for Hell—"

"No, you are not," admitted Ashmadai reluctantly. He shifted his feet, looked at his watch, and wondered how long this would continue.

"Good. Fine. I only desire to carry on my investigations. Now when I have— Blast! What's the word? 'Die' seems inaccurate, when I have an immortal soul bound by no physical limitations, and I retch at unctuous euphemisms like 'pass on.' When I have shuffled off this mortal coil, I want you to take my soul, which I presume would otherwise go first to Purgatory and then to Heaven—"

"It would," admitted Ashmadai, while the body of Hobart Clipp struggled for breath.

"Yes . . . Carry my soul along. You know the ways and methods, I presume, I wish to explore the material universe."

"What?"

"The entire cosmos." Clipp plucked feverishly at his blankets. "I don't want anything, including knowledge, handed me on a platter. I want to find out for myself. We can start by studying the interior of the Earth. Some interesting problems to be solved there, you know, core structure and magnetism and whatnot. Then the sun. I could

happily spend a thousand years, I think, studying
nuclear restrictions under solar conditions, not to
speak of the corona and sunspots. Then the
planets. Then Alpha Centauri and its planets. And
so on and on. Of course, cosmological questions
will require us to shuttle a good deal in time
also . . . ." His longing blazed so brightly that
Ashmadai covered eyes with one wing-flap. "The
metagalactic space-time universe! I cannot
imagine myself ever losing interest in its origin,
evolution, structure, its—yes—its destiny—"

"But that'll take a hundred billion years!"
screamed Ashmadai.

Clipp gave him a toothless wolf's grin. "Ah, so?
Before that time, probably entropy will be level,
the stars exhausted, space will have expanded to
its maximum radius, collapsed again and started
re-expanding. A whole new cycle of creation will
have begun."

"Yes," Ashmadai sobbed.

"Wonderful!" beamed Clipp. "A literally eternal
research project, and no reports to file or grants
to apply for!"

"But I have work to do!"

"Too bad," said Clipp unfeelingly. "Remember,
I shall not want any of your idiotic conversation.
You are nothing but my means of transport.
Which puts me one up on Kepler. I wonder if per-
haps he too, and—ah . . . ah . . . "

Ashmadai heard the Dark Angel approach, and
fled outside. There he shrieked and cursed and
demanded justice. He rolled on the ground and
kicked it and beat it with his fists. Nobody
answered. The hour was very early on a cool
spring morning. Birds chattered, the young leaves
rustled, heaven smiled. One might almost say that
heaven leered.

Presently the soul of Holbart Clipp stepped

briskly through the wall, looked around, and rubbed figurative hands. "Ah," he said, "thank goodness that's over. Messy business. Well, shall we go?"

SUPERSTITION

However bold, any achievement remains essentially an adaptation to
reality; and the more excellent it is,
the more it excludes other possibilities.
But reality is ever-changing, not to be
encompassed in a merely finite system,
so that at last each adaptation must
fail. Thus we live with the tragic para-
dox that all organizations, be they biological species or human societies, are
ultimately destroyed by their own virtues.

—Oskar Haeml, Betrachtungen über
die menschliche Verlegenheit

As he came through the high darkness, Martin
heard them chanting out among the ruins. Overhead the stars were a cold steely sprawl against
night, far and far above him; to right and left, the
mesa tumbled raggedly away from the road, with
a low crescent moon glimmering off sage and
stunted trees, a distant icy rise of mountains. He
saw torches flare among the hollow shells that had

been houses, and his heart paced the muttering of drums.

Equinox was near, and the Utes had come as always to make medicine on the heights. Martin gestured a respectful sign toward the ceremony. It was taboo for him; Base fed the Indians during the dances and shared the favor of their gods, but had its own rites.

The hoofs of his mule clopped loud in chill springtime silence. Grass was thrusting up, tilting the great concrete blocks, gnawing away the road; someday there would only be a rutted dirt track. But Base endured.

Its barbed-wire barricade loomed before him as he rounded the bulky official stonehenge. The sudden glare of electric lights in his eyes was dazzling. Four musketeers in the leather tunics, blue trousers, and steel helmets of Guardsmen of the Order stood at the gate. Above them spread the sign:

UNITED STATES
ASTRONAUTICAL SERVICE
COLORADO BASE

It had been newly refurbished and hung with protective cow skulls.

"Halt!" The men slanted their flintlocks down. One of them, a youngster made nervous by the Ute devil-masks, fingered a rabbit's foot; he relaxed when he saw it was only a human on a mule approaching.

Martin reined in and let them see his spaceman's gray coverall. He was tall and gaunt, with a sunburned hatchet face and lank brown hair. The astronautical warpaint made elaborate loops and jags on his forehead. "Captain Josiah Martin reporting for Mars flight," he said.

"Oh . . . oh, yes, sir." The corporal of the guard

recognized him and fumbled a salute. "How's things in town?"

Martin's mind ran back to Durango, dusty on the plain below—to wagon trains from as far as Mexico and Canada, California and Wisconsin, to the one wheezy railroad barely kept going by its wizards, to the airport with its occasional priestly jet, warehouses and taverns and smithies, all the roar and bustle of a terminal on the interplanetary line. He thought of his house, Ginny and the kids and the empty nights before them till he came back. If he did; someday somebody would make a slip, the spell wouldn't be strong enough, and he would ride a flamer down to Earth or drift forever between the stars.

But he was an initiate of the Order, and *that* was enough.

"So-so," he answered aloud. "Anything new here at Base?"

"Couple o' those Injun kids tried to sneak in. Too young to know what taboo means. We gave 'em back to their folks for ritual cleansing and a good spanking."

"Indians don't spank their children," said Martin absently. "But the cleansing ought to throw a healthy scare into them. I don't suppose they did any damage?"

"Nothing serious. They came within a yard of the power plant, so the Old Man sacrificed a dog just to be on the safe side." The corporal opened the gate. "Good luck, sir. Say hello to the girls on Mars for me."

The spaceman rode through. Ahead of him stretched the field, an enormous waste of ferroconcrete rimmed with crumbling buildings. The old ones were mostly abandoned—tradition said they had held clerks, security personnel, vips, and other esoteric types, back in the superstitious days. Ritual was much simpler now, fewer initiates needed, so many of the steel-and-glass giants were empty or had been torn down to make the small huts which were all the modern age required.

Passing the barracks and the messhall, Martin saw a KP setting out a bowl of milk for the Good Folk, and nodded approval.

The blockhouses around the firing pits were unchanged. They had been built for strength alone. He spied the enormous hulk of a Stage One looming in its gantry, the metal sides hurling back floodlit glare. Mechs swarmed over it, making the final checks and spells, renewing the potent Eagle sign etched and painted on the hull.

The nuclear ship proper, *Phobos,* was dwarfed by the Stage One, out of whose mouth she reached like a little steel fish half swallowed by a shark.

Martin rode around the field, toward the astrologer's tower. This was among the few ancient buildings still in use, a leaping immensity whose glass-bricked lower wall was a cold green shimmer in the light. He dismounted outside, turning his mule over to an attendant, and walked into the lobby.

The girl at the newsstand smiled at him. "Hi, Captain," she said. "What'll it be tonight?"

"Oh . . . make it the usual. Twenty bucks. I don't think I'll need more than standard luck this trip." He signed the chit and received the token. A good deal of a spaceman's pay went for sacrifices.

The warlock at the dispatcher's office took his corban and admitted him. He washed his hands, prostrated himself before the orrery, and danced seven times widdershins about it intoning the laws of Kepler and the elements of Earth's and Mars' orbits. The miniature planets spun flickering in stillness; the faint noise of clockwork was like distant laughter.

Making another prostration, Martin backed out

of the office and went upstairs. The astrologer's lab was on the second floor, and half a dozen young apprentices, earnest in their zodiacal robes, were working out Earth-Wheelstar paths for the coming year on a big computer. Their chief, Major Savage, stood looking out of the window at the spacefield.

"Oh . . . good evening, captain." He turned around. There was a ghost of worry on the bearded face. "You're late."

"The railroad train had broken down across the road," apologized Martin. "I had to wait till they could get it started again."

"Mmm . . . yes. Glad you did."

"Why—what else was there to do?"

"Some of the boys are pretty reckless. They'd go around the train. It'd never occur to them that a Power might have stalled the thing right there for the purpose of holding up traffic."

Martin shook his head. Spacemen learned to be careful.

Of course, the Power could have done it for malignant reasons, but it could just as well be benevolent. Perhaps the delay had kept him from an accident he would otherwise have had. On the whole, you were better off taking signs at face value.

Savage glanced at the clock. "Your omens were only fair, but nothing to be alarmed about. You'll blast off at midnight if the weather holds. I'll have to check with the homunculus on that; got a cold front moving down from Wyoming, and you know what a sudden strong wind can do to foul a takeoff. But I think it's all okay." He lit a cigaret with nervous yellow-stained fingers.

"Usual crew, I reckon?"

"Well—Not exactly. You've got Dykman and Peralta on engines as before, but a new witch and—"

"What happened to Juliet?"

Savage grinned, half exasperated. "What d'you think? In two weeks she'll be Mrs. Geoffrey Roberts."

"Maybe love does make the world go 'round," drawled Martin, "but it sure makes it tough keeping a good witch."

"Fortunately," said Savage, "Colorado Springs Coven had just graduated a new girl with honors, so I swore her in fast before some other outfit should get her. Valeria Janosek, age eighteen."

"Eighteen? That's pretty old for a witch to start."

"She began late. I understand her people were immigrants from the Great Lakes Thalassocracy or the Kingdom of Upper Michigan or some such place. Old Believers, so she was all of twelve before the Coven persuaded her to join. But she's got the Power all right, and should have thirty useful years in her."

"Nuts! If she's not a beast, she won't stay celibate that long. Well, the Lord giveth and the Lord taketh away. Isn't Rogers going to be supercargo?"

"Sorry, no. His kid was sick, and to cure the boy he had to take a geas. No space flight this year. You've got one Philip Hall."

Martin raised his brows. "Any relation to the Boss?"

"Nephew." Savage tugged his beard unhappily. "He's going to give trouble, I'm afraid. He's been studying at Boulder—good physics department, but you know what a hotbed of Old Believers the place is. Seems to have blotted up some crazy notions of theirs . . ." His voice trailed off.

Grimness lay on Martin's mouth. "I'll ride herd on him. Once we're under weigh, I'm the final authority."

"Take it easy, though. He *is* a Hall, and you don't

get rough with a nephew of the Boss of Colorado."

"I've got a ship and a cargo and five lives to get through. No half-baked kid is going to ignore the regs while I'm captain."

Savage puffed his cigaret and looked away, into the electric night. He'd tried to discourage the boy; but family pressure—

The Order had the spiritual power, and Base was the seat of the Order. But the Boss had the cannon and cavalry. Someday there was going to be a showdown between the temporal and ghostly authorities.

Savage hoped it wouldn't come in his lifetime.

He went over the flight plan with Martin. It would be a short and thunderous hop up the Wheelstar, a brief preparation there, acceleration, and the weeks-long orbiting to Mars. All known meteor swarms were safely off the path, but you could never be sure.

They went into the darkened offside room where the homunculus lay. Pale-blue idiot eyes looked up at them out of a swollen head. Savage performed the needful rites, and a weary voice told them the storm wouldn't arrive till 0130. Then: "Go away. Wake me not." The thing slipped back into mindlessness.

Having settled the technical details, Martin crossed over to the ready room for briefing. His crew were there, and he stood for a moment in the door, considering them.

The engineers he knew: stolid blond Dykman, dark little Peralta, good sober spacehands. Supercargo Lieutenant Philip Hall was a slender handsome youth, light curly hair above a pale taut countenance. Witch 1/C Valeria Janosek was more of a surprise.

Martin had expected the usual thin, twitching frame and hungry eyes of a Power vessel. Valeria had a beautiful build on her, a high-cheeked straight-nosed hazel-eyed face, a subdued manner but a ruddy shout of hair falling to her shoulders. She sat calmly under the admiring glances of her shipmates.

Either the Power was very weak in her—and Savage had sworn it was not—or she had mastered it so well that she could be a whole human as well as a Covener. If the latter were true, she was ideal; the hysterics of the ordinary witch were a major hazard of space travel. But a good-looking non-neurotic was unlikely to remain celibate very long.

Heigh-ho. You can't win.

Martin went to the desk as they rose. "In the name of Almighty God and the Powers He has seen fit to give charge of this galaxy—well met," he intoned. "We are gathered for briefing ere we venture past the sky to Mars. Let none remain with us whose hands and heart are not clean, who has eaten forbidden food or done forbidden deeds, and who is not at peace with the Elementals. But that man and that woman who are clean and fit, them shall the Powers ward, here and between the stars and on all worlds, even unto the end of time. Search your souls, all spacefarers, be sure you are prepared, that you have your talismans and have made your sacrifices and are guilty of no transgression for which penance has not been done."

They proceeded carefully through the ritual, slaughtering a black rooster which a technician brought and sprinkling the blood in the witch-bowl. Martin caught the scorn of young Hall; it was all the boy could do to go through with the passes and responses. Valeria was also giving the youth some worried glances.

At the close of the session, she checked their obeahs and tattoos. "All in order, sir." She saluted

Martin crisply.

"Then come," he said. "The Wheelstar awaits."

Briefing over, they relaxed formality, shook hands all around and had a final smoke together. Martin strolled over to Hall, where the latter stood gazing out the window at the field.

"First trip, isn't it, son?" he asked.

Hall nodded. "Yes, sir." His voice was strained.

"Nothing to be scared of. It's all in order, every word said and every demon battened down tight. All you have to do is tend our tobacco on the way out and the Martian gan-drug on the way home."

Sweat was a film on the unlined forehead. "Are you *sure* it's all right? How about the—the physical side of it? How well do those mechs know their business?"

"Damn well, son. It's been checked down to the last gasket, and every man had the relevant volume of the Books beside him as he worked. Why, they replace the hydrazine valves after every blast just on principle, whether they look bad or not, and that in spite of what those Durango artisans charge."

Hall tried not to shudder as he regarded the monstrous Stage One. "We have to ride up on that? When a nuclear engine is so simple and foolproof?"

"We'll go on nuclear from the Wheelstar."

"Why not from Earth?"

Martin held out two fingers against evil. "That's taboo," he said sharply. "Haven't you learned your *Ars Thaumaturgica?*

"Curses harshly long and cruel
if thou use atomic fuel
ere thou'rt safe beyond the air:
burnt-out eyes and shedded hair,
deadly sickness in the nations,
monsters in three generations!"

Hall nodded stiffly. "I've heard it. I *am* an

initiate, captain. But do you know *why* that rule exists?"

"Certainly. It's an elementary example of sympathetic principles. The sun and stars belong in the sky. Nuclear reactions go on in the sun and stars. Therefore nuclear reactions belong in the sky. Q.E.D."

"Ever hear of radioactivity?"

Martin made another V. "Who hasn't? Best not to talk of such matters, son."

"No," said Hall bitterly. "Don't even think about it. Don't try to design a firing pit that makes it safe to use an atomic blast. Just go on in the old way, because we're scared to find out anything new."

"They tried a lot of stuff back in the Dark Ages. Hadn't learned the proper rituals, I reckon. So naturally the Elementals broke loose, and you got war, famine, plague, breakdown . . . We know better in the modern age." Martin knocked out his pipe and looked at his watch. "Time to sashay along, folks."

At the doorway, a wizard 3/C handed him his copy of the Book: *Astrogator's Manual and Ephemerides*, with its tooled-leather binding and its illuminated tables of logarithms. He took it respectfully under his arm and led the way to the *Phobos*.

Stage One blasted, thunder crashed through the midnight mesa and the Utes made good-luck medicine. There was a close magical as well as commercial relation between them and the white man. Their dances assured the annual return of the seasons (or, in Base theory, that Earth stayed safely on her orbit). The ships of the Order brought back useful products that could only grow on Mars or Venus—such as gan-drug, which when properly mixed with snakeskins and graveyard herbs cured the Bleeding Sickness that the carelessness of the ancients had unleashed.

Up the ship rose, flinging herself into the sky on flame. At two hundred miles altitude, the exhausted Stage One shell dropped off. The *Phobos* rose another fifty miles on momentum, after which Martin used a short nuclear blast to get into orbit for the Wheelstar.

Stage One tumbled back toward Earth. Its parachute bloomed white against indifferent stars, and it fell in leisurely fashion along a path made unpredictable by stratospheric winds. Base could have tracked it with radar or homunculus, but didn't bother; there weren't men or resources available to fetch it, so other arrangements had been made. Nearing the ground, it fired off a star shell, and then crunched sagebrush beneath its mass.

The burst was seen by a Navaho sheepherder who swore in exasperation; but he knew the geas, and duly informed his chief next morning. The chief was not very happy about it either, and inspected the rocket himself. Yes—it bore the Eagle sign, with blighting curses for all who failed to return it to Base. The chief got men and wagons, and trekked seventy miles with the unwieldy thing. His own people benefitted by what the Order brought to Earth, but he would never have taken the trouble except for the sure knowledge that disobedience meant ruin, barren herds and sickness in the hogans.

The *Phobos* came smoothly in to the Wheelstar and clamped fast. The station gang emerged to pump reaction mass into her tanks. They were shorthanded up here, and Martin had to help with the ceremonies: sympathetic magic in which the ship's Book was moved across a map from Earth to Mars while the equations of a 135° orbit were recited. The rest of his crew had time off.

Spacesuited, Hall and Valeria walked around

the Wheelstar. Its spoked circumference rotated, ponderous and quiet; they needed the boots which a warlock artisan had magnetized and chanted over. This place was loaded with *mana;* if you didn't always keep one foot against it, you were flung into space—"down" was radially away from the cabins at the hub.

Earth hung huge and beautiful before their eyes, aurora streaming about the white North Pole, bands of cloud and storm, the dark mass of continents. Even as they watched, the Wheelstar moved around till the desolated wilderness of the Eastern Hemisphere was visible. They could see the great lifeless areas, ashen leper-spots against the green and brown of uncursed land.

The girl's face was tinted blue by the Earth-glow, but was not less good to look on. Behind the glassy helmet, she stared in awe. "It was worth it," she said at last. "It was worth living with the Coven, to come here."

"Are they that bad?" asked Hall.

Her voice was tinny in the radio: "No. They're all right—the girls are rather odd, they're apt to throw fits and so on, but no harm is meant. Some of the rituals scared me, though. And then living in that castle on Pike's Peak, with all the bats—" Her tone snapped off, half frightened. "I can't say more."

Hall spoke slowly, not wanting to antagonize her: "I don't really see why you joined the Coven, I'm told your people are Old Believers."

"Yes. I hated to hurt them. But the recruiting sergeant showed me some of the spells . . . and he was *right!* He explained the modern spirit to me. I—" She was looking at him, as if pleading to be understood. "I couldn't see living in the past, hanging on to obsolete superstitions. It was so futile. I wanted to be part of the world and its work."

Hall felt a twisting within himself. "Do you really think this . . . thaumaturgy . . . is something new?"

"Oh, no, of course not. We had classes in history. They said it was the First Way, the one in which man became man. But then during the Dark Ages people got misled. They thought everything could be done by engines and—There were only a few who kept the truth alive, secret Covens, hex doctors in Pennsylvania, voodoo priests in Haiti . . . that sort. People as a whole had to discover through suffering that their own beliefs were false; then they turned back to the First Way."

Hall nodded jerkily. His voice came fast: "You have the right facts, Val, but the wrong interpretation. The truth is this. Even in the age of science, there was always a substratum of ignorance and irrationality; the man who flew a jet faster than sound very often carried a good-luck charm, and so on. When the War came, and civilization went smash, the educated people—who concentrated in the cities—suffered most; the backward countrymen survived in larger numbers. Add to that the anti-scientific reaction, and you very naturally got a belief in witchcraft winning general acceptance. Since then, it's been a matter of elaborating that belief, rationalizing it—but it's still superstition!"

He heard her suck in a shocked breath. "Phil! You don't really mean that!"

"I sure as hell do." The throttled anger of a decade boiled up in him. "I certainly do, and I'm going to say if it it costs me my life."

"But how—Phil, can't you *see?*"

"I can. In fact, I believe in using my own eyes, rather than taking somebody else's word. They have a pretty complete scientific library at Boulder; not just those how-to-do-it manuals that pass for science today, but fundamental knowledge, the history and philosophy of science itself. I went through all I could find. I did some of the experiments, and they worked—"

"Of course they did." Her eyes widened in puzzlement. "Why shouldn't they? The ancient magic was pretty potent."

"Damn it, it *isn't* magic! It's . . . it's the nature of things!"

She shook her head, the long hair swirling in its glazed cage. "Things are what they are. I don't see what you're so worked up about. It's in the nature of things that an oscillatory circuit should generate radio waves, just as it's in the nature of things that a rain dance brings rain."

"But suppose you hold the dance and no rain comes?" he challenged.

"Why, then there was some counter-influence, of course."

"That it." A demanding harshness was in his tone. "You always cover up, explain away. There isn't any method to disprove your ideas about magic—so they're meaningless."

A friendly mockery curved her lips. "Suppose your radio circuit fails to work?" she asked.

"Then there's something wrong with it."

"Exactly! So where's the difference?"

"Just this: I can find out what's wrong, and correct it."

"If a rain dance fails," she told him, "the chief warlock investigates, finds out what he thinks was amiss, makes amends, and holds another dance. Sooner or later, he locates the cure and the dance does work. As for you, Lieutenant Hall, I don't think your radio always gets fixed on the first try!"

He looked at her with something close to wildness. "I've been through this before," he said between his teeth. "There's only one way to fight it. On this voyage, I'm going to prove to you that no magic is needed to make the trip safely."

Shock held her unstirring. The Wheelstar spun slowly through a cold silence. "No," she said at last. "If you endanger the ship, I'll have to report you."

He said, almost pleading: "You're too . . . fine a girl, to live with owls and bats, or go to those filthy Sabbats. I want to end it for—you, as well as everyone alive."

She made no answer, but walked from him. Earth loomed behind her, big and scarred.

Perhaps it was Hall's heresy, but Valeria had an uneasy feeling about this voyage. She thumbed through her books and sacrificed a cockroach—the ship could carry no larger animal; even her Siamese familiar must stay at home—but the truth remained hidden.

That was the trouble with second sight, she thought bleakly. It was always unreliable, more art than thaumaturgy. A creepy sense might be authentic forevision or might be only an upset stomach. The wildest and trickiest of the Elementals were those which governed the Time-flow.

And there was a dreadful weight of responsibility for such a young pair of shoulders. It was more than lives and cargo; the ship herself was beyond price. It took the artisans ten years to replace a lost spaceship.

Not for the first time, she cursed the blind greed of the Dark Ages. If they had not drunk petroleum in rivers, gutted the ores and gulped the coal, men would not now have to ride on horse and oxcart in a painful search after the necessities. If they had saved forests and topsoil and water tables, the world would not be a thin crust of civilization, a few sharded sovereignties in the Western Hemisphere, above a gape of starveling savagery. If they had not hurled nuclear thunderbolts, there would be no Cursed Craters where death still laired, no Bleeding Sickness or generations of monsters.

Well—they hadn't known any better. Not the least of their superstitions had been that man was all-powerful and could always escape the consequences of his own acts. It was the task of the modern age to rebuild.

She donned her uniform, the black dress and peaked hat, took a forked willow twig in hand, and went down the length of the *Phobos*. From the small control cabin where Captain Martin sat unresting, past the cramped wardroom and its curtained bunks, the gyro housing and air-water plants, to the engine room, she made her way.

At one gravity acceleration, Earth was dropping behind and Mars was a sullen red star near the blinding sun.

The twig remained quiescent till she entered the engine section. There it twisted in her hands. She felt the queer mindless tension of rising Power, surrendered soul to it, and let the dowser have its way. Return to consciousness and the engineers' worried eyes was like swimming up through a dark rushing river.

"Potential neutron leakage here." She pointed to the after bulkhead and its shuddering dials. "Not imminent, but you better prevent it now."

Peralta sighed with relief and tapped a jug of holy water—deuterium oxide. Valeria said the spells over it while Dykman was assembling a patch plate. It fitted neatly, the holy water was poured into it, the neutrons would bounce back when they emerged.

"All clear." The girl smiled. "Ship's okay otherwise." She did not mention her forebodings.

Dykman shuffled his feet. "What do you think of our supercargo?" he asked.

"Why—" Valeria paused. "He seems like—a

nice guy." Irrationally, in the teeth of all evidence, she thought he was the nicest guy she had yet known.

"I wonder, Val. I don't like to say anything against a shipmate, but . . . well, damn it—"

"What we want to know," said Peralta bluntly, "is whether his opinions are likely to be dangerous."

"Oh . . . he's been talking to you, too? I don't think so. He's entitled to his beliefs, right or wrong."

"Yes, but as I understand the theory, belief is important—sympathetic effect. His opinions may act to nullify our spells."

An anger she could not explain to herself chilled the witch's reply: "I'm the judge of that."

"Oh, sure, sure," said Peralta. "No offense meant, Val. I only wanted your professional analysis."

"You have it." She went haughtily out of the room.

The ship thrummed around her, lancing through a night of stars and empty distance. She felt a nagging guilt. In all honesty, it *was* entirely possible that counter-belief had a counter-effect; one of the Coven professors had entertained a hypothesis that this was why magic had worked so ill in the Dark Ages.

But she couldn't be sure. And the mere suspicion might make the captain order that Hall be pitched out the airlock.

She saw him emerging from the cargo hatch and paused. His face lit up, boyishly. "Where've you been?" he asked.

"On duty. And you too, I suppose." Why did her heart flutter?

Hall nodded. "Have to turn that tobacco over every watch, or it's likely to start molding. I wish we had decent fungicides."

"What are they?"

"Hm? Oh . . . chemicals to kill the mold."

"But mold is a curse," she protested. "A curse of dark Powers. That's why sunlight and fresh air prevent it."

A lopsided grin twitched his mouth. "Have it your way. But in the old days they sprayed their crops—"

"I know. And thus protected weakly stock, rather than breed strains which could resist. And ate and drank the poisons themselves, with no real proof that the amount was harmless to them."

"There were mistakes made," he agreed. "But nothing which couldn't have been corrected in time. And men spread over Earth; and every man—not just a warlock or a priest or a Boss—rode behind engines instead of horses; and Mars and Venus were colonized; and nature was man's slave."

Valeria stamped her foot. "So they thought!" she said. "They thought they could chain nature, their mother, even the nature within themselves. They thought they could fight, and mine, and erode, and breed without limit—science was bound to solve the problems that arose, oh, yes. They thought that man was a chosen race and exempt from natural law—"

"Not at all!" Hall's eyes burned with a missionary eagerness. "It was precisely by understanding the laws of nature that they could control her. It's this age which has crept back into ignorance."

"In other words," she said thinly, "the laws of physics are all the laws of nature there are?"

"Why . . . yes. Ultimately phenomena reduce to—"

She whirled and stalked down the corridor, the long black dress flowing about her. When she had reached the sanctuary of her bunk, she drew the curtain and lay there and wept.

She didn't know why. But the Power within a human heart acted strangely.

On orbit, the *Phobos* cut blast and let the sun's invisible arm swing her toward Mars.

Weightlessness was an eerie thing like endless falling, and Hall was miserably sick till he got used to it. For Valeria it was also new, but a witch had enough self-mastery not to be troubled. Nevertheless, Martin observed how she moped about.

He was inclined to shrug it off. Female Coveners were a peculiar lot, and she was better than most he'd lifted with. Typically a witch was an arrogant hag or a skinny girl at the obnoxious nadir of adolescence; frustration and the nerve-tightening forces they worked with made them poor company.

There were always small jobs aboard, puttering, repair and maintenance, the ship was deliberately built to keep men busy. Between times, they had their amusements, books and games. Hall turned out to be an excellent poker player.

Martin found himself liking the boy. Hall was careful to hold his family connections in the background and ask no special favors; he was going to space because of a genuine desire to travel. If at times he was sulky and withdrawn, that was his privilege.

In fact, the only objection to him was the superstition he had absorbed at Boulder. He'd never make a spaceman till he unlearned that.

It was customary for the skipper to instruct and rehearse a junior officer in the art. Hall was an apt pupil, with quite a flair for mathematics; mechanically speaking, he was excellent. But on the ritual—

Martin decided, a week out, to bring matters to a head.

They were in the pilot room, a narrow chamber stuffed with instruments and controls, a periscope for viewing the outside. Hall had just torn down and reassembled the radar under Martin's eye —no easy task in null-gee. "You'll do, son," said the captain.

Hall looked up unsurely. "Isn't it dangerous?" he asked. "I mean, not to have the radar going while we're on orbit."

"What in the Black Name for? You use your radar to help you approach a Wheelstar, that's all."

"But meteors—Look, spaceships in the old days had a radar sweep hooked to an autopilot. When it spotted a meteor coming, it activated the blast and got out of the way."

"That was the theory," said Martin dryly. "In practice, you can't detect a meteor at sufficient distance to fix its orbit accurately. So the ship would make unnecessary swerves, use up her reaction mass, maybe not have enough for deceleration. These quick-transit paths, like our own right now, save time but waste fuel; maybe you don't know what a narrow safety margin we have. So it's a lot more practical to let your witch use her foresight and warn you hours ahead of time."

Hall exploded. His fist came down on the recoil chair's arm. Since he had neglected to keep a knee bent around the stanchion, he went cartwheeling into the air. Martin laughed, reached out, and drew him back.

"Take it easy, son," he advised.

"But—damn and blast it! You mean we're actually trusting our lives to a hysterical woman's hunches?"

"Don't slander your shipmates," said Martin sharply. Then, seeking tact: "After all, the probabilities are on our side. I admit foresight doesn't always work, but the chances of getting clipped by a rock are small anyway."

"I know," said Hall in a harsh tone. "I know that. But I also know that computer research could give us a radar-pilot system which would really do the job. And nobody's undertaking the research!"

"Matter of economics," shrugged Martin. "Let's say that failure of foresight costs us one ship a century—ten years' work by highly skilled men. Under present conditions, where precision tools are so scarce, it'd take maybe three years to build such a computer for *each* ship . . . quite apart from the time and brains which the initial research would tie up, and which are needed elsewhere.

"Thanks to those lunatics back in the Dark Ages, man's living on a mighty small margin. Someday we'll rebuild and have a big surplus, but meanwhile we have to struggle along with what we've got. And anyway, by that time foresight should be well enough understood to make your computer unnecessary."

The frankness in the blue eyes before him was of anger. "So you say! You and your witless faith! What was it pulled man out of the caves? Magic? Subconscious maunderings identified with revelation or foresight? Hell, no! It was working with, understanding and controlling, the real world!"

"Of course it was," said Martin. "I've studied history too, for your information. The first men to chart the stars were Babylonian astrologers. The Greeks developed geometry because number and relation were sacred things. The alchemist learned a lot about matter. European witches cured dropsy with toadskins, and South American medicine men discovered quinine."

"That's beside the point!" stormed Hall. "This ship couldn't have been built by . . . by magic. It

could only have been designed by a science which
had discarded superstition."

"Well . . . let's say a science which made simpli-
fying assumptions, thereby cutting the problem
down to a size men of that epoch could handle. But
the assumptions were obviously false."

"False? They were verified by observation!"

"Yeah? How about Newton's law of inertia?
Pure fiction: there is and can be no body in the
universe moving only by its own inertia. There are
always forces, resisting media—For that matter,
what is this energy the physics books talk about?
Kinetic energy is motion, potential energy is
position; but both position and motion are
relative. How can any sane man believe energy is
an absolute quantity when he can't possibly find a
zero point?

"Energy, inertia, entropy, force—all the basic
concepts of physics—they're mathematical
constructs which give useful results. Identifying
those equations with reality is mighty bad
semantics."

Martin stopped, wishing he could tamp his pipe
and blow dogmatic clouds; but—

Spaceships, run by demon Fire,
swiftly feel the demon's ire.
Light no flame aboard, the boat
lest smother'd Air's ghost grip
thy throat.

"Oh, you're glib enough," said Hall bitterly.
"You know how to *use* an ephemerides or an
elliptic function. But do you *understand* them? I
doubt it. You don't see that the philosophy which
created them denied your magical folderol."

"So it did," said Martin levelly. "And it was
wrong, of course."

"But—damn it, witchcraft doesn't *work!*"

"The hell it don't, son. Every year the Utes make

medicine to keep Earth on her orbit; and Earth stays there. Use your common sense."

"But you're arguing *post hoc*. In the old days, they didn't have those dances, and Earth still—"

"Oh, but they did. There were always backward tribes, so-called, hex doctors, witch-wives; there was always a little ritual, at least."

"How about the ages before there were any men?"

"That's been argued about. I incline to the will-of-God theory myself. God made man intelligent and turned over a lot of responsibility to him."

"But—"

"Look. What's the test of truth—the only test we have? Isn't it whether a concept works? Whether it gives the results it's supposed to?"

"Yes, of course. But—"

"So Base is taboo to non-initiates. They could meddle around with . . . oh, say a hydrazine tank and blow us all to Sathanas.

"So I dance around the orrery reciting astronomical equations. Result: I know them cold.

"So it's taboo to use nuclear blasts on Earth. You ought to know those blasts can be deadly.

"So a Stage One bears a hex sign. It compels whoever finds it, to return it to us. We can't build a new Stage One for every flight—we *have* to have them back!

"So people in general go through the rites, and observe the Law, and abide by the taboos. It gives them a sense of security; we don't have the unrest and the incidence of demoniac possession—I reckon you'd call it psychosis—they did in the Dark Ages. It keeps them in line, orders society as society has got to be ordered if it's to function without needing all the police and restrictive government they had in the past. It keeps people out of trouble: they may not know about radiation, most of 'em being illiterate, but they do know the

Cursed Craters are forbidden. It makes them believe in the hex doctor, and belief is a big help in curing them.

"No, no, son. Magic works. You see it working every day of your life."

Hall leaned forward, triumphantly. His forefinger stabbed at the captain's chest. "Ah, hah! I've got you now! You're admitting that any value the rites have is merely pragmatic."

"No, I'm not," said Martin. "I'm just pointing out that there *is* a pragmatic, everyday usefulness . . . which is more than you can say for most of the Dark Age concepts. Besides this, of course, there's the matter of natural law. For instance, we carry a witch on every ship not just to reassure us, though self-confidence is important, but to—"

Hall shoved from his chair, violently, and went sailing out the exit. Martin stared after him. A worried frown grew between the captain's brows.

Similarity—Burn a man's photograph, and the man dies unless he has counter-spells. Believe you have foresight, and often you will have. Believe you are in a ship of madmen doomed by their own lunacies, and you may well generate doom.

Martin knew what would happen to him if he sent the Boss' nephew out the airlock. But he knew, as well, what might happen if he didn't.

Grimly, he weighed the probabilities.

Philip Hall went hurtling down the corridor and gulping for air. The thunder of his heart drowned the noise of ventilators, the million miles of loneliness vanished in his rage.

Blindness!

Always it had been there, the immemorial muttering current of Stone Age superstition. Don't break mirrors. Don't walk under ladders. Carry a rabbit's foot. Nail a horseshoe over your door. Turn back if a black cat crosses your path. Maybe the captain was right in one sense: maybe man was by nature a huddler in the dark, maybe reason was only a thin precarious membrane ripped apart by the first gust of fear.

They had come out of the caves, out of roadless mountains and tumbledown huts and tropical jungles, witches and warlocks spilling across the world. Science was smashed and discredited, the half-melted snag of a skyscraper stood against smoking heaven like a grisly question mark, there was no faith left in the wolves' den which Earth had become. Small wonder that bats should flutter about the heads of witches, Covens meet on high hills, blessings and blastings chant from withered lips; small wonder that the race had turned back to its first beliefs.

But in God's name, now they had rebuilt; however tiny and weak, civilization existed again. How could they recreate what their ancestors had owned without the rational minds of those mighty dead? What would they ever be but barbarians till someone had lifted the night from their brains?

He saw Valeria afloat near her bunk, looking blank-eyed into nothing. Weightless, her skirt drifted about trim streaming legs. The fury congealed within him, hardened and cooled to a brittle crystalline mold.

"Val," he said.

The coppery head turned to his, hazel eyes focused and a slight, startled smile tilted her lips. "Oh . . . hello, Phil."

"What were you thinking of?" he asked awkwardly.

"Never mind." Color stained the pale smooth cheeks.

"I'm afraid—" He stopped, hunting for words. "I'm afraid I just had a run-in with the skipper."

She bit her lip. "You should be more careful, Phil. I can't counter-act your influence all the time."

"What influence?" He grinned sourly. "I'm making no converts, if that's what you're thinking of."

"It isn't. It's your . . . state of mind. I've been having ugly dreams; I hope they aren't fore-runners."

"And it's my fault?" He felt a slumping. "I'm sorry. I—don't want to worry you."

"Well . . . maybe it's no doing of yours anyhow. Maybe we've run into bad medicine regardless." The girl shivered. "Sometimes I wish I'd never joined the Coven. It isn't always easy."

He wanted to spit. His fists gathered at his side. "It's not right," he mumbled. "I've seen enough witches . . . poor scared kids, tormented by their own twisted nerves . . . and now *you.*"

"There are always those whose work is hard," she answered gravely. "Even in those old days you're so romantic about, there must have been people whose occupations wore them down." A hand fell shyly on his. "Don't be sorry for me, Phil. Witchdom has its compensations."

"Do you mean always to—"

"Oh, probably not. I'll doubtless be getting married eventually, if the right man comes along." She didn't meet his eyes.

"Now there," he gibed, "is one example of ridi-culousness. Why should a biological incidental like virginity determine whether you have the Power or not?"

"It's not exactly an incidental . . . ask any woman. You might as well ask why it should deter-mine whether I have children or not."

They were drifting free, moving slowly on air currents in an empty wardroom. The hex symbols covering the walls spun in the man's vision as he turned. Somehow, it was a dream, this floating in stillness was not altogether real, and—

And in a dream—

He pulled her to him, roughly, and kissed her.

He felt how she stiffened. Then her struggle sent them awhirl in the air, caroming off wall and floor with a brutal force. She clawed after his eyes and he let her go, appalled at the savagery. She drifted from him shuddering and crying.

He pushed against a stanchion and arced toward her. "I'm sorry," he said frantically. "I didn't know—"

Through shaking hands, she answered: "There's a d-death penalty for that . . . molesting a, a, a witch in orbit—"

Strength drained from him, he hung soul-naked while the hungry vacuum pressed close to the hull around.

"No," he said. "Not for . . . I didn't—"

"I . . . oh . . . I w-w-won't report you . . . but—"

"I'm sorry," he whispered. "It—Val, will you marry me? When we get back to Earth, will you marry me?"

"You s-s-s-*superstitious* oaf!" she gasped. "You blundering idiot!"

Something like pride chilled in him. "Go ahead," he said dully. "I won't hide behind your skirts. Go ahead and report me. I suppose it's regulations you should."

She nodded. Her voice came muffled, where she wept into her hands. "It is. But I . . . can't." With a puppet-like jerk of one arm: "Go away! Go away and leave me alone!"

He was halfway down the corridor when he heard her scream.

They gathered in the wardroom, four men clamping fear behind their faces, and looked at her.

"You're sure?" asked Martin.

Valeria nodded. Her eyes were red, but she spoke in a steady monotone: "Yes. There's no mistaking that kind of foresight."

"A meteor swarm," said Martin. "A meteor swarm on a collision orbit, an hour away."

Silence was thick between them.

"Can we dodge it?" asked Peralta.

"Oh, yes," said the girl joylessly. "It's a big swarm, but fifteen minutes at full acceleration would get us out of its path."

"And then we'd have to get back on orbit," said Martin. "We wouldn't have enough reaction mass left to brake at Mars."

Dykman turned ponderously in the air. Small light eyes burned at Hall. "It's your doing," he said. "You brought this on us."

"I never—" Hall raised his hands, as if to fend off a blow.

"Oh, yes, you did. You and your superstitions. They nullified our warding spells. What are the chances against this happening by accident, captain?"

"Mighty big," said Martin.

"Out the airlock!" It was a shriek from Peralta.

Hall felt the bulkhead solid at his back. He lifted his fists and said between his teeth: "Because a hysterical female thinks we're running into danger, you'd kill a man. Well, come on and try it!"

Grayness rode Martin's voice. "Shut up there. Val, would executing him affect our chances?"

"No," she said. "It's too late now."

Martin regarded her for a long moment. "Is that the truth, or are you covering up for the boy?"

"I'm the witch here, skipper!" she flared.

He nodded, as if tired out. "Okay, Okay, I'll take your word for it. We're all in this together. It might not be Phil's fault anyhow. Could just as well be a slip-up at Base, or a foreign warlock, or—Val, is there anything we can do?"

She hung unmoving while a clock hand swept out a full minute. It might have been a century.

"It's an old comet with a very long-period orbit," she said then. "That's why it's never been encountered before." Her eyes closed, and her face tautened with strain, and she spoke as if from lightyears away. "There are about a hundred boulder-sized meteors and a lot of cosmic gravel. We can dodge the big ones—"

"But the gravel! It can punch more holes in the ship than we could ever patch."

"Perhaps," she said, "I can handle the gravel."

Hall let her open a vein in his wrist and take blood from him as she did from the others. The rest of her preparation was done in secret; he caught a reek of acrid herbs and heard her chanting in some saw-edged language unknown to him.

"Strap in," said Martin curtly.

He led the girl to the pilot room and buckled her into a recoil chair. Her hair floated red and wild about a head which had become a mask of otherness. Her hands were smeared with blood; she gripped an ivory wand between them and moved it about with strange precision for one whose eyes were shut.

"Take your seat," she whispered.

Martin strapped in and rested his fingers on the controls. Stray thoughts drifted through his skull: Ginny and the children, a tree they had in their back yard, a farewell party to which all their friends had come. It was a broad and lovely world he had, and bitter to leave it for an unknown darkness.

Her incantation mumbled forth. *Abaddon, Samiel, Ba'al Zebub, Beli Ya'al, all great horned spirits aid us.*

"The gyros," she breathed. "Alpha, zero zero three . . . Beta, one zero two . . . Gamma, as is . . . set for thirty-second half-blast—" The ship spun about the axles of the whickering wheels. *"Go!"*

Thunder and shrieking erupted about them. A troll's hand thrust them back into the chairs. Then there was again silence and falling.

Martin put his eyes to the periscope hood. He saw one of the meteors, miles away, sunlight wan off its pocked face. Suddenly it had hurtled past, thunderbolt without voice.

"Alpha, five zero one . . . Gamma, zero three three . . . ten second quarter-blast . . . *Go!"*

There was a haziness across the hard unwinking stars, a million and a million planetary shards. No bigger than his thumbnail, but at their speed—

"We're clear of the meteors," said the toneless witch-throat. "We'll miss them all on this orbit. But—"

"The little stones. I know, Val. Can you turn them?"

"Get out," she said.

He unbuckled and pushed from the cabin as softly as possible, closing the door behind him. She was beginning a new chant.

Peralta, Dykman, and Hall turned their eyes to him as he entered the wardroom. Their faces were drained.

"You can crawl out of that webbing if you want, boys," he told them. "We're on a free-fall path, safe from the big rocks."

"But how about the small ones . . . the gravel cloud?" Dykman licked sandy lips.

"That's up to Val." Martin shrugged. "I saw quite a density; normally, I reckon a thousand or so'd be hitting us. None of 'em are very large, but the relative velocity is up in miles per second."

They freed themselves and hung in air like fish in a tank. Peralta had his patching kit handy; he could repair a dozen or so leaks. There was no point in donning spacesuits, which only carried two hours' air supply.

Hall spoke, raggedly: "Captain . . . how do you *know* we've got a swarm out there?"

Martin blinked. "I saw 'em. Looked through the periscope."

"Did you? Or did you see what you'd hypnotized yourself into seeing?"

There was another stillness. Sweat beaded Hall's face. He brushed some of it off, and the drops spun cloudily about his head.

"You—" Peralta bunched his legs for a lunge.

"That'll do!" snapped Martin.

They heard a crack like thunder. Their eyes did not register the streak till it was past. Two bullet-holes with melted edges glared at each other across the room, and the air smelled scorched.

Peralta whirled, clapped an adhesive patch over each, and saw internal pressure bulge them. Another explosion resounded down the corridor. He went off to find the punctures.

"Now do you believe?" asked Martin gently.

Hall covered his eyes.

"Two hits," said Dykman. "Two hits she didn't stop."

"There are plenty she did," answered Martin. He drew a long shuddering breath. "Hang on. We'll be through the cloud, whole or dead, in another couple of minutes."

Peralta returned. They hung there, waiting. None of them looked at Hall. Now and then the ship clanged like a smitten gong, pebbles bouncing off the hull with too much velocity lost to penetrate.

The supercargo raised his face and stared into hollowness. "It . . . seems . . . I was wrong," he said.

"It's okay," said Martin. "You're just a young fellow, Phil, and your fallacy comes natural. All those historical novels—the Hooverian restoration, Eisenhower's duel with Hitler, atomic warlocks and naked women in Las Vegas . . . I sort of shared your romantic notions myself, once."

"Fallacy?"

"About science working."

"But it does! I've tried it!"

"Sure it does. The *Phobos* here is proof enough. But the superstition is this, son: that science could understand everything, and do everything, and make everything good.

"I wonder how they could have held so odd a belief, even then. I wonder how anybody can look at Earth today and believe it. If you say a true concept is one that works, even your science-is-all was false—every radioactive crater, every mutant sickness, every monster born to woman, proves that!"

They waited.

Valeria came in. Only in null-gravity could she have moved. The high cheekbones stood out as if flesh had been sucked from beneath them. "We're safe." They could barely hear her speak. "I . . . the spells . . . turned the stones away. We're through them now."

Her eyes rolled up and she floated motionless. Hall cried aloud, incoherently, and went to her.

Martin, Dykman, and Peralta returned to their posts, to get the ship back on orbit toward Mars.

"It takes a lot out of you," said Valeria. "But I'll be all right in a few days."

Hall gripped her hand. They were alone in the wardroom, only the eyes of the hex signs were there to watch them.

He felt after words. It is never easy to admit you were mistaken. In principle, he still couldn't.

But . . . He tried to smile. "You needn't worry about me," he said. "I'll believe now that you can do everything."

"Oh, no. Only a few things," she replied hastily, and made a two-finger V.

"Enough," he said. "Enough to see us through. I'm surprised I never realized it before."

"The Covens don't operate openly," she told him. "Magic is best done in private. So all you've seen are dances, medicine, public ceremonies. You never saw a homunculus aware of what was happening a hundred miles away. You never saw two warlocks exchange thoughts without speaking, or . . . or a witch foreknowing potential trouble spots and deflecting meteors."

His jaw came forward, stubbornly. "I'm not convinced yet that there isn't a lot of superstition around," he said. "I have my doubts about most of the rituals. But I'm willing to be open-minded about them, and look for evidence in each case."

"That's sufficient. You'll make a good space-man." Her eyes drooped, and she settled herself into the curve of his arm.

"Telepathy, precognition, psychokinesis, psychosomatics—they *were* almost ignored in the old days," he said thoughtfully. "Maybe believed-in rites are necessary to focus the powers of the mind. Maybe what man has needed was a chance to give them unhindered play, and to study them with the help of the logic which the age of science had developed."

Valeria laughed, very softly. "All right," she said. "If it makes you happier, if you think it's more scientific, to call magic by such names, go ahead. It's still magic!"

He tightened his arm about her waist, and she sighed and made no objection. In the face of the oldest magic of all, he didn't think she would remain a witch very much longer.

FANTASY IN THE AGE OF SCIENCE

Loving fantasy as much as I do science fiction, I am very happy, for purely selfish reasons, that the fantasy market today has grown large enough that I can afford to write more of it than was formerly practical for a man who earns his bread by stringing words together. Granted, science fiction does still enjoy the greater popularity, or at least it usually has better sales. Hence books, magazines, films, even conventions are often labelled "science fiction" though in fact they deal with fantasy concepts. A good many years ago, when he was editing *The Magazine of Fantasy and Science Fiction*, the late Anthony Boucher remarked to me that, judging by his mail, he believed that most of his readers actually preferred fantasy to science fiction—but were not aware that they did.

What makes the difference? Is there a difference? To answer such questions, first we must know what we are talking about when we use those terms "science fiction" and "fantasy." The trouble is, they have about as many definitions as they have scholars who seek to define them. I don't want to add to that number. It seems to me that there are far more interesting things to do than quibble about semantic condundrums which are unanswerable anyhow. Nevertheless, while I shan't set forth any exact meanings of my own, I do need to discuss briefly certain characteristics that appear to be shared by stories published under those names.

A schoolboy is supposed to have written, in response to a question in a test: "A fantasy is a story about ghosts, goblins, witches, werewolves, virgins, and other supernatural beings." Contrastingly, I like Damon Knight's definition of science fiction: that the phrase "means what we point to when we say it."

This might apply to fantasy as well. I'll soon go into a little detail. Just for openers, though, let me remind you that the oldest stories we have in written form can be called fantasies—stories such as Homer's *Iliad* and *Odyssey*, the Babylonian *Epic of Gilgamesh*, and numerous Egyptian tales of magicians and demons. Some might also be called a kind of proto-science fiction as well, in that they deal with marvelous voyages into the unknown. For all that a Homeric Greek knew, giants and monsters could exist in remote lands. For all we know today, they could exist on remote planets.

I can even imagine that the earliest stories ever told, far back in the Old Stone Age, were fantasies—for instance, Ung the hunter telling his fellows about the one that got away. Seriously, we know that Neanderthal man, at least, had a concept of the supernatural and probably of an afterlife. He buried his dead with care and with offerings. One such burial, in the Near East, included flowers and herbs, which modern researchers have identified by their pollen. Every kind was a kind which to this day, in that part of the world, is believed to have healing properties.

Now this sort of thinking cannot have come out of nowhere or begun overnight. Much earlier ancestors of ours, not yet Homo sapiens, must have wondered at the mysteries of day and night, summer and winter, birth and death, everything around them. They must have started making up stories which symbolized these things. I'm not at all sure but what the earliest sounds we could call language, rather than mere signals between animals, were used more to fantasize like this than for strictly practical purposes.

Of course, I can't prove that. Suffice it to repeat that fantasy is an exceedingly ancient type of fiction, and go on to inquire just what its nature is. As remarked before, I don't plan to offer an exact definition, and I hope it will become clear why. What I would like to offer are a few notions about how fantasy works, what it actually does. For this purpose, we'd better start by looking at fiction in general.

Fiction deals with the unreal, that which does not exist and has not happened. This does not set it off sharply from nonfiction, for any piece of communication may use both the real and the imaginary —assuming for the moment that we can ever be sure absolutely what is real. For instance, ancient and medieval chroniclers routinely put words in the mouths of historical figures, as if these had been recorded at the time. They considered it legitimate and even necessary. A modern biographical novel continues that practice. In some respects, the method actually does convey a kind of truth that gets lost in scholarly treatises.

From here we may proceed to the *roman à clef*, which includes real people and incidents, more or less disguised. Science fiction and fantasy themselves have been known to do this. For example, a number of Fritz Leiber's stories are strongly autobiographical, and countless tales are satires.

Eventually, though, we get into the area of seemingly complete fiction, where as the notice goes, "any resemblance to actual persons, living or dead, are purely coincidental." Just the same, we still find degrees of fictitiousness.

"Mainstream" strikes me as being as silly as any other category. Ever since Aristotle, if not earlier, critics have been putting literary works into pigeonholes, with generally pernicious results. However, since "mainstream" or "here-and-now" has long been dominant, we may as well begin by asking ourselves how the imagination functions there.

It seems to me that, while such tales do concern inventions of the authors, they contain only real *classes*. That is, suppose for instance that we have a novel about a waitress in a small Midwestern town. She's imaginary, the things that happen to her are, and the setting itself may be. Regardless, we know that waitresses and small Midwestern towns exist, and that under the postulated circumstances, events such as are described might well take place.

With a proper change of examples and tense, the same is true of many historical narratives. In many more, though, not enough is known for certain about the milieus, and the authors have had to invent important details. Thus Mary Renault's fine novels about Theseus are largely conjectural. From there we may proceed to entirely archeological settings, where we may have less fact to go on than we do, nowadays, about the Moon.

In this gradual manner, we enter the realm of fantasy. We might regard fantasy as fiction which involves unreal classes. An elephant walking down the street could belong in a mainstream tale, but a gremlin could not, since gremlins do not exist. Neither do blessings and curses and ever-filled purses and all the rest of magic.

If we felt like it, we could go on to consider science fiction as a subdivision of fantasy, a subdivision involving classes which are not real, as far as we know, but which might possibly become real in the future, or be real somewhere in the present, or have been real in the past.

For example, a landing on the moon was long known to be possible, and stories about such an expedition therefore counted as science fiction: until 1969, when the possibility became an actuality. Stories about manned landings on Mars remain science fiction, but one day—we hope—will cease to be, except retrospectively. Likewise, we can imagine things elsewhere in space right now which could exist or be happening, or might have been featured in the past—for instance, people with powers of telepathy.

Does this, then, mark off science fiction clearly? I'm afraid not. I've already observed that fantasy as a whole is no different in kind from any other sort of literature, including the so-called mainstream. At most, there are certain differences of degree, of emphasis or approach. Now I have to point out that the same is true of science fiction *vis-à-vis* fantasy or, indeed, the entire body of world literature.

For instance, how shall we classify a realistic novel about politics, which is set in the near future merely because the author's purpose requires this? As a matter of fact, more and more impeccably respectable writers such as John Hersey are coming to make more and more use of science fiction idioms. Those idioms are coming to pervade our entire society. Millions of ordinary people go to a movie like "Star Wars" and have no trouble understanding and enjoying it. This would have been unthinkable a generation ago. On the other hand, the idioms of fantasy were common property for centuries before. For instance, just look at how many of the great Victorian and Edwardian authors wrote ghost stories among other things.

What are these idioms, these concepts? Don't

they distinguish science fiction from fantasy? That is, ideas such as ghosts and gods and magic are normally reckoned to belong in fantasy, while ideas such as faster-than-light travel, time travel, and parallel universes are employed in science fiction. Why this distinction?

After all, there is some evidence in favor of ghosts, or of life after death in general. It isn't scientifically rigorous, but it's there and cannot be dismissed out of hand, as the notion of stones falling from the sky was once dismissed. A great many sensible people believe in gods, or in God, and raise arguments in support of this which are not unreasonable. Many of them will tell you, for instance, in considerable detail, that the Resurrection of Christ is better attested than most events we take to be historical. A case can actually be made for some kinds of magic working under some circumstances—and if we show this happening in a story, but call it "psionics," that story will rate as science fiction!

In contrast, practically any physicist will tell you that faster-than-light travel, time travel, and parallel universes are either flat-out impossibilities, or meaningless noises because there is no way to check them out experimentally. Certainly the vast bulk of evidence is against them. For instance, if the Einsteinian laws which limit us to the speed of light were false, then our atom smashers wouldn't work; but they do.

I'll come back later to the fact that concepts of this science fiction kind are no longer *quite* so disreputable as they formerly were. For now, let me simply repeat that both science fiction and fantasy employ mostly ideas for which there is little or no scientific evidence, at least evidence which would satisfy a hard-boiled logical positivist like me; and they often both employ concepts which the evidence is actually against.

Then what makes the difference? Why do we assign certain motifs to fantasy and others to science fiction?

In part, I think, it's pure convention. Science fiction as we know it is a child of the nineteenth century, of the First Industrial Revolution and its aftermath, as well as a spreading awareness of scientific method and the new scientific findings. It began as, or at any rate it became for a while, a literary form which tried to deal with these enormous changes—to this day, almost the only literary form which does, I might add. As science and technology progressed, ancient motifs came to be regarded as disproven, or at least as irrelevant. Contrasting was the popular impression that anything involving a machine or a meter was necessarily scientific. A lot of quacks, medical, automotive, and so forth, have profited from this attitude.

More important, I think, science fiction is distinguished by a certain unspoken assumption. This is the scientific assumption itself, that the universe makes sense, that man can reach an understanding of it. No matter how bizarre the discoveries and inventions we make, they'll fit in somehow with what we already know. Our entire picture of the cosmos may be revolutionized, as has happened two or three times already in the past. However, there will be an intellectual continuity in these revolutions, the same kind of continuity that there was between Newton and Einstein, or even between classical electrodynamics and modern quantum physics.

Fantasy is under no such obligation. It's free to bring in the completely supernatural, that which is beyond nature and forever unamenable to the scientific method.

Let me give you some examples from one of the most brilliant writers of the past hundred years,

Rudyard Kipling. If you haven't read these stories, I heartily recommend them to you for a great experience. First we have "With the Night Mail" and its sequel "As Easy as ABC." These are pure, hard science fiction. Writing before Kitty Hawk, Kipling foresaw a future where aircraft were commonplace. He went on to develop the entire world that resulted, with the same kind of detail work and ingenuity that Robert Heinlein would give us a couple of generations later.

" 'Wireless' " is borderline. In this haunting tale, a wretched apothecary clerk, dying of tuberculosis, becomes for a while in rapport with the long-dead poet John Keats. And yet this doesn't happen by divine fiat. The implication is clear that somehow an experimental radio set created the right conditions: or, at least, that there are certain correspondences between the two kinds of communication.

Last, I'll mention " 'The Finest Story in the World' "—that's its title. Here an ordinary young man begins to remember what happened in two of his previous lives. Kipling simply assumes that reincarnation is a fact, and that such glimpses into the past come about through some whim of the gods. In short, this is as pure a fantasy tale as you will find anywhere.

Now I chose these particular cases with care. I hoped to show you how science fiction and fantasy fade into each other. You could put a story such as " 'Wireless' " right on the borderline, except that there is no borderline, any more than there is between red and orange in the rainbow.

Nor can we separate them from reality. They are a part of it.

True, some science fiction and fantasy is just a pleasant vacation from our daily cares, the same as a certain percentage of every kind of literature is. Even that percentage, though, is inevitably influenced by its mundane surroundings. Meanwhile a larger percentage, one way or another, to whatever degree, tries to deal directly with the real world. I don't mean that all such stories are, or ought to be, parables or satires or sermons of anything like that. I simply mean that through our arts, we find ways to symbolize the world, to express aspects of it. Thereby we become better able to understand and cope with it. Far from being neurotic escapists, persons interested in science fiction and fantasy strike me as being, on the average, uncommonly aware of reality, and apt to make efforts to improve it.

This is obvious in a good deal of science fiction. *Brave New World* and *1984* are famous cases, wherein the author warned against certain trends in society. Robert Heinlein's story "Solution Unsatisfactory" dealt with nuclear weapons, several years before any actually existed, and showed how they would inevitably change the entire military, diplomatic, and social situation of mankind. Walter Miller's *A Canticle for Leibowitz* had much to say about the nature of civilization and of man, using science fiction as the medium. Likewise, in a more indirect and perhaps more profound way, did Ursula Le Guin's *The Left Hand of Darkness*. Examples are many.

I would like to argue that the same is true of fantasy.

An obvious case in point is J. R. R. Tolkien's *The Lord of the Rings*. Here we have a story which employs the traditional stuff of myth and legend, right down to such beings as dwarfs and trolls, yet is obviously more than a mere fairy tale. Or actually, I should not call fairy tales "mere." In a long essay about them, Professor Tolkien himself showed how much depth there is in many. The same kind of depth is in *The Lord of the Rings*, the struggle between good and evil both in the outside world and in the human heart, the sense of life as being ultimately tragic and yet infinitely wonderful. At the same time, one of the great strengths and charms of the book is its wealth of homely, believable detail. Its heroes don't only fight demonic villains; they trudge across long miles, they worry about where the next meal is coming from, they get cold and wet and discouraged, or they crack small jokes or enjoy for a while some rest and peace in a sheltering place.

I would say that in this respect Tolkien is superior to such other great fantasists as E. R. Eddison and James Branch Cabell. These writers were far more accomplished stylists, but they didn't bother with the unglamorous underpinnings of their imaginary worlds. I'm not faulting them for this, please understand that. They were setting out to do something quite different, and they did it splendidly. I am just saying that what they did carries less conviction than what Tolkien did.

Lord Dunsany appears to me to occupy a unique place of his own. He isn't somewhere between these two schools, he's on another axis, off in a different dimension. For one thing, frequently he did use the most down-to-earth settings and characters, at least to start with—for instance, in his "Jorkens" stories. For another thing, when he went completely into Never-Never Land, his writing seemed to be either sheer mood music, marvelous but scarcely a story; or else it was charged with a certain dry wit which keeps us reminded of our own humanity and all its limitations.

I could of course go on to mention a number of other modern fantasists, especially those more or less in the tradition of the horror story, such as Arthur Machen in England and H. P. Lovecraft in America. But with certain exceptions which I will come to later, these writers, fine though several of them be, impress me as being modern only in their dates. Their stories are, by and large, traditional indeed, nineteenth-century in both motifs and treatments. Now needless to say, there is nothing wrong with that in itself. Any kind of story, no matter how old-fashioned, in the right hands becomes a good story. Just hark back to Tolkien for evidence of that. But I am supposed to be discussing fantasy characteristic of our own era, of the age of science in which we live, so let me go on to it.

The obvious question which comes to mind right away is, Do we actually have a characteristic fantasy type today? Are we really doing anything new, or are we simply putting old ideas into more or less contemporary language?

An interesting case to examine first is that of the so-called heroic fantasy, also known as sword and sorcery. By and large, this kind of yarn takes place in an archaic world, usually imaginary though sometimes it's a real historical setting. There is a great deal of swashbuckling and derring-do, magic is almost as commonplace as electrical engineering in our own lives, dragons and sea serpents and beautiful   princesses   in   exotic   kingdoms abound—well, you know the type. It may not have begun with William Morris in the nineteenth century, but he was certainly an early practitioner of the form, drawing his own inspiration from medieval romances, Icelandic sagas, and similar sources. I've already mentioned E. R. Eddison as a more recent writer in the same vein.

Robert E. Howard adapted the form to the pulp adventure magazines of the 1920's and '30's. Nowadays everybody knows about his character Conan the barbarian, who has become immensely popular; he has a comic book of his own, and a movie about him is in the works. Too bad that

Howard himself didn't live to cash in on the bonanza. He's had any number of imitators and followers, of course, some good, some bad. In fact, the entire field of heroic fantasy is enjoying quite a boom. I believe the astonishing success of *The Lord of the Rings* touched this off, but by now it has acquired a momentum of its own.

I don't want to knock it or patronize. Like any other art form, it can be very good—even great, as a few works of this kind prove—or it can be fair or it can be bad. Everything depends on who is doing it, and how, with how much skill and care and, yes, love. To mention just a few outstanding contemporary practitioners, we have Fritz Leiber with his tales of Fafhrd and the Gray Mouser; Mr. Leiber is every bit as fine a stylist, with as much wit, as James Branch Cabell, plus more verve and vigor. We have Jack Vance, of *The Dying Earth* and some other works. Mr. Vance is, in my opinion, an even more strong and subtle master of language, with an unbelievably fertile imagination. We have L. Sprague de Camp, by now an old master but happily continuing to delight his readers with such irony-spiced adventures as *The Goblin Tower* and *The Clocks of Iraz*. We have Katherine Kurtz and her splendidly realized "Deryni" world. Yes, we have Ursula K. LeGuin again; her "Earthsea" trilogy belongs here, fine and philosophical though it is. I could name several more, but surely you see what I'm getting at.

Besides, in no case would I dare look down on heroic fantasy, having done a certain amount of it myself!

At the same time, every genre has its special weaknesses, its particular traps into which to fall. For instance, while the psychological novel is powerful and profound when written by someone like Dostoyevsky, too often it becomes a mere clinical study of some dreary little twerp to whom nothing ever happens, not even inside his own head. Heroic fantasy has the old-fashioned pulp virtue of telling an exciting story—usually—but it can all too easily fall back into the old pulp vices of crudity and carelessness.

Also, as remarked earlier, much heroic fantasy lacks the kind of details, especially about the humbler sides of life, that make for convincingness. In fact, one reviewer complained about *The Silmarillion* that there are no hobbits in it. Certainly the hobbits and the more earthbound human characters go far toward making *The Lord of the Rings* memorable. The sheerly mythic nature of *The Silmarillion* has put some readers off—though naturally other readers find it a glorious book.

I wonder if this widespread though not absolutely universal demand for basic realism and logical consistency, also in fantasy, is not indeed an effect of science and technology. Could we today perhaps be so used to thinking in rationalistic terms that our very dream-worlds have to meet those standards?

Offhand, that looks fairly plausible. A characteristic kind of modern fantasy amounts to taking an outrageous premise and developing its consequences with remorseless logic. This is often very funny, though it can be tragic. Mark Twain pioneered it brilliantly, as he did so many other kinds of writing. I think now of "Extract From Captain Stormfield's Visit to Heaven" and "The Mysterious Stranger."

Captain Stormfield, you probably remember, is an old Yankee skipper who dies and goes to Heaven. It's the fundamentalist Protestant Heaven, complete in every detail. The trouble is, those details don't really work. People arrive, receive their harps and wings and halos, and go happily off to spend eternity sitting on the clouds singing hymns. Within hours they always discover that eternity is a mighty long while to spend doing nothing but that, and sneak off to find some more interesting occupation. The thousands of parsons who, on Earth, expected to fling themselves into the bosoms of Abraham, Isaac, and Jacob and weep tears of joy, are in for a disappointment. After all, if these patriarchs were available for that, they'd never have time for anything else, and be wringing wet into the bargain. The story goes on at length in that vein. If you haven't already read it, do. You're in for a treat.

"The Mysterious Stranger" is equally logical, but one of the bleakest things ever written. It concerns an angel who visits Earth for a while, looks on man from a cosmic point of view, and sees and treats us as the miserable, futile, insignificant creatures we are.

Getting back into a lighter mood, I might also mention "Eve's Diary" by the same author, who tells the tale of Eden in exactly that form, touchingly as well as amusingly.

This kind of fantasy enjoyed a renaissance in the late 1930's and early 1940's. That was when John Campbell, editor of *Astounding*—until he changed its name to *Analog*—the man who had almost single-handedly created modern science fiction, turned his attention to fantasy and founded a companion magazine, *Unknown Worlds*. While this ran many different kinds of stories, it became especially identified with the logical-development sort, the application of careful reasoning to a wacky premise.

For instance, I remember one short novel by L. Sprague de Camp called *Solomon's Stone*. In it, the hero finds his mind in the body of an alter ego he has in a different universe. That world is populated by the people we daydream of ourselves as being. The hero, a shy and bookish type, finds that here he is a French cavalier like d'Artagnan, complete with plumes, floppy boots, and rapier. He is still in a version of New York City, but it's populated by the wildest variety of ethnic types; the Yorkville district, to name a single one, is crowded with brawny blond Siegfrieds. In fact, all the men are big and tough, all the women ravishingly beautiful, with very few exceptions. Given so many aggressively macho characters around, conditions are pretty chaotic, though there is a government of sorts which even maintains a small army. That is made up of generals, commanded by the only private it has. Our hero has a run-in with a local Near Eastern sultan who maintains a huge harem; in our world, that sultan is a bachelor clerk at a YMCA. . . .

Besides the scientific mode of thought, scientific imagery has entered modern fantasy. One thinks of Lovecraft, whose eldritch horrors are often beings from outer space. Fritz Leiber has frequently used features of our real world with telling effect, as in his short story "The Man Who Made Friends With Electricity," which gives high-tension currents a life of their own—marvelously eerie. We can doubtless all think of numerous other examples.

And yet . . . to what extent have modern science and technology really influenced us? I think we can show the effects on fantasy, and certainly on science fiction, but they are hard to find anywhere else in literature. Mainstream writers and modern poets who use them, such as Ernest Gann or Robinson Jeffers or Diane Ackerman, have been few and far between. Reading the average novel, you'd never know that we are living the middle of the Second Industrial Revolution and at the likely beginning of the Third. You'd never imagine that our entire concept of reality is changing, that some of the basic principles of science itself are being called into question. You'd never have an inkling that we children of machines and medicine not only live differently from our ancestors, we think and feel differently, and that our descendants will probably be stranger still to us.

You'd scarcely know it in our public affairs, either. Some politicians make some effort to understand and cope with the enormous changes that are upon us. It's generally too little and too late.

Perhaps we can't blame our readers overly much, when we the people are ourselves not only ignorant, we're getting nuttier every year. Thus, by about 1900 astrology was a relic, a historical curiosity. Today untold millions take this superstition seriously, actually try to govern their lives by it. A more recent form of the same fraud calls itself "biorhythms;" you can see charts in many daily newspapers, purporting to tell you how you are feeling at the moment. I remarked earlier that most modern quacks take advantage of the widespread impression that a piece of apparatus and a line of jargon make something scientific. This happens on the intellectual level also. These days, nonsense most often comes in pseudoscientific trappings. To take just three examples, which hordes of educated people have swallowed, consider flying saucers, "chariots of the gods," and the Bermuda Triangle.

This might simply make a rationalist sigh—is there no end to human credulity?—but unfortunately, widespread craziness has been taking forms that are physically dangerous to mankind, that have in fact decimated whole populations and turned entire countries into prison camps and torture chambers. Not to read a political sermon, I'll simply mention a noncontroversial case, Nazism. I'll remind you that this lunacy came to power, by legal means, in what had been one of the most civilized nations in the world, a fountain-head of scientific and social progress. I might suggest, in passing, that you look up the historical origins, the roots, of National Socialism, because they aren't dead yet—no, they are flourishing as never before. And I will remind you that if it could happen to the people of Bach and Goethe, then nobody is safe, nobody is sane. Certainly the United States of America has been on reckless courses before now, and we have no guarantee that this will not get worse.

Why have we drifted so far from the serene faith in science, reason, and humane progress that marked the Edwardian Enlightenment? That's an enormous question with a nearly infinite number of possible answers, all of which may be partly true. It isn't what I am dealing with here, either. I have only raised the depressing subject because it is so conspicuous a feature of today's world. Fantasy does not exist in cozy isolation. We can't understand what's going on in this small field of literature unless we give some thought to the lives, the society, of its writers and its readers.

Perhaps one strong element among those making people more emotional, less rational than they used to be, is science itself. That has at least two aspects. First, quite aside from the technological consequences of science, we're having to live with the psychological, philosophical, and even spiritual consequences. That isn't easy. No thoroughgoing world-view is easy to live with—not those of the great religions, either.

Science removed Earth from the center of the universe, way back in the time of Copernicus. Later, with the development of ideas about evolution, it took away man's unique place among living things. Later still, it began to examine life in detail as another physical phenomenon. Now it's extending this area of determinism into our very minds. Emotions seem to be functions of chemistry, the brain seems closely analogous to a computer, one entire school of psychology even denies that the word "consciousness" has any meaning. The growth of knowledge brings countless benefits, most obviously in medicine but also in itself, in the exhilaration and inspiration of discovery. Nevertheless, we can understand why many people rebel and scratch after some more comfortable set of beliefs.

Second, science is getting into strange territory. It was always founded on that assumption I mentioned earlier, that the universe makes sense, that man can come to an understanding of nature. In the famous words of Einstein, "Raffiniert ist der Herr Gott, aber boshaft ist Er nicht"—which some irreverent soul has translated as, "The Lord is slick, but He ain't mean." However, as far back as the beginning of this century, quantum physics and wave mechanics were raising troubling questions about causality. Does the same set of conditions always produce the same results? Is that even a meaningful thing to ask? It did appear superficially that whatever disorder might be in nature was confined to the subatomic level, and that in the larger world statistics always make events lawful and predictable. However, this was not correct, as Einstein himself saw at the time. He went to his grave protesting that indeterminacy could not be true.

Today, ironically, certain developments on the frontiers of his own relativity theory are evoking the specter of chaos on the astronomical scale itself. I am sure all my readers know something about black holes, stars collapsed down to such a density that light itself can no longer escape their gravitational fields. Now it turns out that eventually, at the core of such a black hole, density goes so high that you get what is called a singularity—a state of affairs with which no mathematics of ours can cope. As far as we can tell, every law of nature breaks down.

We might suppose the singularities are safely hidden away inside the masses of black holes. But this does not have to be the case. Black holes evaporate through the kind of random quantum processes I have mentioned. It may be that when one is quite gone, the singularity remains, naked. If that is true, then anything can happen in its neighborhood . . . literally anything. Magic is loose in the world.

We don't even have to suppose this. Other theoreticians have been studying what happens when ultra-dense masses rotate extremely fast. They generate some peculiar fields. It looks possible, at least in principle, that certain of these fields could move an object from here to there faster than light. It actually looks possible that the object could be moved into its own past. In that case, causality as we know it is out the window —the cause-and-effect principle on which science has always been founded.

In fact, strictly speaking, the universe itself has no business existing. It seems to have begun as a kind of super-black hole, perhaps 15 billion years ago, everything compressed together in a tiny volume that then exploded. But how could something which held itself so tightly ever start expanding? It looks as if, under those conditions, the very laws of nature were radically different from those we know. There may not even have *been* any laws of nature.

I could go on, but this isn't supposed to be a text on science or its philosophy. My purpose in bringing up these matters has been merely to suggest that science is perhaps approaching its own limits, at least in an epistemological sense. Whether or not that proves to be the case, today it is certainly reminding us that no matter what we may learn in the future, what we confront will always be mystery. In many ways, science is now more of a fantasy than any story that anyone could ever hope to write.

Alfred North Whitehead suggested once that religion, Christianity, was one source of science as we know it, and for centuries a strong influence on it. He pointed out that the Christian tradition embodied a rationalistic element derived from both Greek and Hebraic thought. God was not supposed to be capricious; human reason could discover certain things about Him, while at the same time certain critical events in the past were not looked on as myths, but as historical facts. This attitude produced minds which already in the Middle Ages started examining nature in systematic fashion, wedding theory and observation as no culture before them had done.

Could fantasy today be playing a similar role? I don't mean that it might be in any direct way. Creations like Maxwell's demon are nothing but whimsical figures of speech. But then, according to Whitehead, religion didn't directly inspire science at the beginning either; what it did do was encourage a particular way of thinking.

Today, when the discoveries we make and the theories we devise are so far removed from the ordinary world, it may well be that a somewhat different kind of mind is necessary, a mind that can invent utterly wild ideas, then play with them under rules of logic that are also changeable. I know that a good many astronomers and theoretical physicists read science fiction. How many likewise read fantasy? It would be interesting to find out. Even if many do not, we can guess that an element of fantasy is "in the air" to affect both our discoveries and our writings.

At the same time, fantasy fiction seems to me to be a very wholesome influence. It does not lend itself to the kind of latter-day nut cultism that science fiction concepts, alas, all too often do. Fantasy makes no claims to being anything other than what it is, the purest form of fiction, in which we can deal with as many as six impossible things before breakfast. In so doing, perhaps it helps us remember that there *are* impossibilities in the real world which we had better take into account. That is, maybe fantasy lets us work out our irrationalism in a harmless and even creative fashion.

It certainly helps keep imagination alive, playfulness, wonder. That is no small service, in an age when too much of our entertainment comes to us factory-made and plastic-wrapped. Nor is it a small service to help keep literacy alive, the habit of reading rather than staring at a screen.

With its roots deep in traditions, some of them prehistorically ancient, with its archetypal figures and mysterious events, fantasy likewise helps us maintain our basic humanity. No matter how far we have wandered or how much artifice we have raised around ourselves, we are still creatures of sea and forest, open skies full of wings, sun, moon, stars, the night wind; we were meant to marvel at the world and to stand in awe before the unknown. We can't go home again to that olden state of being; nor is it desirable that we should; but it is well for us to remember.

At the same time, of course, fantasy gives us yet another set of symbols and artistic devices to turn on the world around us and on ourselves. It is yet another means to greater understanding.

Finally, but every bit as importantly as all this,

fantasy tells stories we can enjoy. We can lay aside both our troubles and our pretensions, pick up a good fantasy story, and for a while experience nothing but pleasure. Fantasy is fun.

THE VISITOR

As we drove up between lawns and trees, Ferrier warned me, "Don't be shocked at his appearance."

"You haven't told me anything about him," I answered. "Not to mention."

"For good reason," Ferrier said. "This can never be a properly controlled experiment, but we can at least try to keep down the wild variables." He drummed fingers on the steering wheel. "I'll say this much. He's an important man in his field, investment counseling and brokerage."

"Oh, you mean he's a partner in— Why, I've done some business with them myself. But I never met him."

"He doesn't see clientele. Or very many people ever. He works the research end. Mail, telephone, teletype, and reads a lot."

"Why aren't we meeting in his office?"

"I'm not ready to explain that." Ferrier parked the car and we left it.

The hospital stood well out of town. It was a tall clean block of glass and metal which somehow fitted the Ohio countryside rolling away on every side, green, green, and green, here and there a white-sided house, red-sided barn, blue-blooming flax field, motley of cattle, to break the corn and woodlots, fence lines and toning telephone wires. A warm wind soughed through birches and flickered their leaves; it bore scents of a rose bed where bees querned.

Leading me up the stairs to the main entrance, Ferrier said, "Why, there he is." A man in a worn and outdated brown suit waited for us at the top of the flight.

No doubt I failed to hide my reaction, but no doubt he was used to it, for his handclasp was ordinary. I couldn't read his face. Surgeons must have expended a great deal of time and skill, but they could only tame the gashes and fill in the holes, not restore an absolute ruin. That scar tissue would never move in human fashion. His hair did, a thin flutter of gray in the breeze; and so did his eyes, which were blue behind glasses. I thought they looked trapped, those eyes, but it could be only a fancy of mine.

When Ferrier had introduced me, the scarred man said, "I've arranged for a room where we can talk." He saw a bit of surprise on me and his tone flattened. "I'm pretty well known here." His glance went to Ferrier. "You haven't told me what this is all about, Carl. But"—his voice dropped— "considering the place—"

The tension in my friend had hardened to sternness. "Please let me handle this my way," he said.

When we entered, the receptionist smiled at our guide. The interior was cool, dim, carbolic. Down a hall I glimpsed somebody carrying flowers. We took an elevator to the uppermost floor.

There were the offices, one of which we borrowed. Ferrier sat down behind the desk, the scarred man and I took chairs confronting him. Though steel filing cabinets enclosed us, a window at Ferrier's back stood open for summer to blow in. From this level I overlooked the old highway, nowadays a mere picturesque side road. Occasional cars flung sunlight at me.

Ferrier became busy with pipe and tobacco. I

shifted about. The scarred man waited. He had surely had experience in waiting.

"Well," Ferrier began. "I apologize to both you gentlemen. This mysteriousness. I hope that when you have the facts, you'll agree it was necessary. You see, I don't want to predispose your judgments or . . . or imaginations. We're dealing with an extraordinarily subtle matter."

He forced a chuckle. "Or maybe with nothing. I give no promises, not even to myself. Parapsychological phenomena at best are"—he paused to search—"fugitive."

"I know you've made a hobby of them," the scarred man said. "I don't know much more."

Ferrier scowled. He got his pipe going before he replied: "I wouldn't call it a hobby. Can serious research only be done for an organization? I'm convinced there's a, well, a reality involved. But solid data are damnably hard to come by." He nodded at me. "If my friend here hadn't happened to be in on one of my projects, his whole experience might as well never have been. It'd have seemed like just another dream."

A strangeness walked along my spine. "Probably that's all it was," I said low. "Is."

The not-face turned toward me, the eyes inquired; then suddenly hands gripped tight the arms of the chair, as they do when the doctor warns he must give pain. I didn't know why. It made my voice awkward:

"I don't claim sensitivity, I can't read minds or guess Rhine cards, nothing of that sort works for me. Still, I do often have pretty detailed and, uh, coherent dreams. Carl's talked me into describing them on a tape recorder, first thing when I wake up, before I forget them. He's trying to check on Dunne's theory that dreams can foretell the future." Now I must attempt a joke. "No such luck, so far, or I'd be rich. However, when he learned about one I had a few nights ago—"

The scarred man shuddered. "And you happened to know *me*, Carl," broke from him.

The lines deepened around Ferrier's mouth. "Go on," he directed me, "tell your story, quick," and cannonaded smoke.

I sought from them both to the serenity beyond these walls, and I also spoke fast:

"Well, you see, I'd been alone at home for several days. My wife had taken our kid on a visit to her mother. I won't deny, Carl's hooked me on this ESP. I'm not a true believer, but I agree with him the evidence justifies looking further, and into curious places, too. So I was in bed, reading myself sleepy with . . . Berdyaev, to be exact, because I'd been reading Lenau earlier, and he's wild, sad, crazy, you may know he died insane; nothing to go to sleep on. Did he linger anyhow, at the bottom of my mind?"

I was in a formlessness which writhed. Nor had it color, or heat or cold. Through it went a steady sound, whether a whine or drone I cannot be sure. Unreasonably sorrowful, I walked, though there was nothing under my feet, no forward or backward, no purpose in travel except that I could not weep.

The monsters did when they came. Their eyes melted and ran down the blobby heads in slow tears, while matter bubbled from within to renew that stare. They flopped as they floated, having no bones. They wavered around me and their lips made gibbering motions.

I was not afraid of attack, but a horror dragged through me of being forever followed by them and their misery. For now I knew that the nature of hell lies in that it goes on. I slogged, and they circled and rippled and sobbed, while the single noise was that which dwelt in the nothing, and time was not because none of this could change.

Time was reborn in a voice and a splash of light. Both were small. She was barely six years old, I guessed, my daughter's age. Brown hair in pigtails tied by red bows, and a staunch way of walking, also reminded me of Alice. She was more slender (elven, I thought) and more neat than my child—starched white flowerbud-patterned dress, white socks, shiny shoes, no trace of dirt on knees or tip-tilted face. But the giant teddy bear she held, arms straining around it, was comfortably shabby.

I thought I saw ghosts of road and tree behind her, but could not be certain. The mourning was still upon me.

She stopped. Her own eyes widened and widen-ed. They were the color of earliest dusk. The mon-sters roiled. Then: "Mister!" she cried. The tone was thin but sweet. It cut straight across the hum of emptiness. "Oh, Mister!"

The tumorous beings mouthed at her. They did not wish to leave me, who carried some of their woe. She dropped the bear and pointed. "Go 'way!" I heard. "Scat!" They shivered backward, resurged, clustered close. "Go 'way, I want!" She stamped her foot, but silence responded and I felt a defiance of the monsters. "All right," she said grimly. "Edward, you make them go."

The bear got up on his hind legs and stumped toward me. He was only a teddy, the fur on him worn off in patches by much hugging, a rip in his stomach carefully mended. I never imagined he was alive the way the girl and I were; she just sent him. Nevertheless he had taken a great hammer, which he swung in a fingerless paw, and became the hero who rescues people.

The monsters flapped stickily about. They didn't dare make a stand. As the bear drew close, they trailed off sullenly crying. The sound left us too. We stood in an honest hush and a fog full of sunglow.

"Mister, Mister, Mister!" The girl came running, her arms out wide. I hunkered down to catch her. She struck me in a tumult and joy exploded. We embraced till I lifted her on high, made to drop her, caught her again, over and over, while her laughter chimed.

Finally, breathless, I let her down. She gathered the bear under an elbow, which caused his feet to drag. Her free hand clung to mine. "I'm so glad you're here," she said. "Thank you, thank you. Can you stay?"

"I don't know," I answered. "Are you all by yourself?"

"Yes. 'Cept for Edward and—" Her words died out. At the time I supposed she had the monsters in mind and didn't care to speak of them.

"What's your name, dear?"

"Judy."

"You know, I have a little girl at home, a lot like you. Her name's Alice."

Judy stood mute for a while and a while. At last she whispered, "Could she come play?"

My throat wouldn't let me answer.

Yet Judy was not too dashed. "Well," she said. "I didn't 'spect you, and you came." Happiness rekindled in her and caught in me. Could my presence be so overwhelmingly enough? Now I felt at peace, as though every one of the rat-fears which ride in each of us had fled me. "Come on to my house," she added, a shy invitation, a royal command.

We walked. Edward bumped along after us. The mist vanished and we were on a lane between low hedges. Elsewhere reached hills, their green a palette for the emerald or silver of coppices. Cows grazed, horses galloped, across miles. Closer, birds flitted and sparkled, a robin redbreast, a chickadee, a mockingbird who poured brook-trills from a branch, a hummingbird bejeweled among bumblebees in a surge of honeysuckle. The air was vivid with odors, growth, fragrance, the friendly smell of the beasts. Overhead lifted an enormous blue where clouds wandered.

This wasn't my country. The colors were too intense, crayon-brilliant, and a person could drown in the scents. Birds, bees, butterflies, dragonflies somehow seemed gigantic, while cattle and horses were somehow unreachably far off, forever cropping or galloping. The clouds made real castles and sailing ships. Yet there was rightness as well as brightness. I felt—maybe not at home, but very welcome.

Oh, infinitely welcome.

Judy chattered, no, caroled. "I'll show you my garden an' my books an', an' the whole house. Even where Hoo Boy lives. Would you push me in the swing? I only can pump myself. I pretend Edward is pushing me, an' he says, 'High, high, up in the sky, Judy fly, I wonder why,' like Daddy would, but it's only pretend, like when I play with my dolls or my Noah's ark animals an' make them talk. Would you play with me?" Wistfulness crossed her. "I'm not so good at making up ad—adventures for them. Can you?" She turned merry again and skipped a few steps. "We'll have dinner in the living room if you make a fire. I'm not s'posed to make fire, I remember Daddy said, 'cept I can use the stove. I'll cook us dinner. Do you like tea? We have lots of different kinds. You look, an' tell me what kind you want. I'll make biscuits an' we'll put butter an' maple syrup on them like Grandmother does. An' we'll sit in front of the fire an' tell stories, okay?" And on and on.

The lane was now a street, shaded by big old elms; but it was empty save for the dappling of the sunlight, and the houses had a flatness about them, as if nothing lay behind their fronts. Wind mumbled in leaves. We reached a gate in a picket fence, which creaked when Judy opened it.

The lawn beyond was quite real, aside from improbably tall hollyhocks and bright roses and pansies along the edges. So was this single house. I saw where paint had peeled and curtains faded, the least bit, as will happen to any building. (Its neighbors stood flawless.) A leftover from the turn of the century, it rambled in scale-shaped shingles, bays, turrets, and gingerbread. The porch was a cool cavern that resounded beneath our feet. A brass knocker bore the grinning face of a gnome.

Judy pointed to it. "I call him Billy Bungalow because he goes bung when he comes down low," she said. "Do you want to use him? Daddy always did, an' made him go a lot louder than I can. Please. He's waited such a long time." I have too, she didn't add.

I rattled the metal satisfactorily. She clapped her hands in glee. My ears were more aware of stillness behind the little noise. "Do you really live alone, brighteyes?" I asked.

"Sort of," she answered, abruptly going solemn.

"Not even a pet?"

"We had a cat, we called her Elizabeth, but she died an' . . . we was going to get another."

I lifted my brows. "We?"

"Daddy an' Mommy an' me. C'mon inside!" She hastened to twist the doorknob.

We found an entry where a Tiffany window threw rainbows onto hardwood flooring. Hat rack and umbrella stand flanked a coat closet, opposite a grandfather clock which broke into triumphant booms on our arrival: for the hour instantly was six o'clock of a summer's evening. Ahead of us swept a staircase; right and left, doorways gave on a parlor converted to a sewing room, and on a living room where I glimpsed a fine stone fireplace. Corridors went high-ceilinged beyond them.

"Such a big house for one small girl," I said. "Didn't you mention, uh, Hoo Boy?"

Both arms hugged Edward close to her. I could barely hear: "He's 'maginary. They all are."

It never occurred to me to inquire further. It doesn't in dreams.

"But *you're* here, Mister!" Judy cried, and the house was no longer hollow.

She clattered down the hall ahead of me, up the stairs, through chamber after chamber, basement, attic, a tiny space she had found beneath the witch-hat roof of a turret and assigned to Hoo Boy; she must show me everything. The place was bright and cheerful, didn't even echo much as we went around. The furniture was meant for comfort. Down in the basement stood shelves of jelly her mother had put up and a workshop for her father. She showed me a half-finished toy sailboat he had been making for her. Her personal room bulged with the usual possessions of a child, including books I remembered well from years gone. (The library had a large collection too, but shadowy, a part of that home which I cannot catalog.) Good pictures hung on the walls. She had taken the liberty of pinning clippings almost everywhere, cut from the stacks of magazines which a household will accumulate. They mostly showed animals or children.

In the living room I noticed a cabinet-model radio-phonograph, though no television set. "Do you ever use that?" I asked.

She shook her head. "No, nothing comes out of it anymore. I sing for myself a lot." She put Edward on the sofa. "You stay an' be the lord of the manor," she ordered him. "I will be the lady making dinner, an' Mister will be the faithful knight bringing firewood." She went timid. "Will you, please, Mister?"

"Sounds great to me," I smiled, and saw her wriggle for delight.

"Quick!" She grabbed me anew and we ran back into the kitchen. Our footfalls applauded.

The larder was well stocked. Judy showed me her teas and asked my preference. I confessed I hadn't heard of several kinds; evidently her parents were connoisseurs. "So'm I," Judy said after I explained that word. "Then I'll pick. An' you tell me, me an' Edward, a story while we eat, okay?"

"Fair enough," I agreed.

She opened a door. Steps led down to the backyard. Unlike the closely trimmed front, this was a wilderness of assorted toys, her swing, and fever-gaudy flowers. I had to laugh. "You do your own gardening, do you?"

She nodded. "I'm not very expert. But Mother promised I could have a garden here." She pointed to a shed at the far end of the grounds. "The fire-wood's in that. I got to get busy." However firm her tone, the fingers trembled which squeezed mine. "I'm so happy," she whispered.

I closed the door behind me and picked a route among her blossoms. Windows stood wide to a mild air full of sunset, and I heard her start singing.

> "The little red pony ran over the hill
> And galloped and galloped away—"

The horses in those meadows came back to me, and suddenly I stood alone, somewhere, while one of them who was my Alice fled from me for always; and I could not call out to her.

After a time, walking became possible again. But I wouldn't enter the shed at once; I hadn't the guts, when Judy's song had ended, leaving me here by myself. Instead, I brushed on past it for a look at whatever might lie behind for my comfort.

That was the same countryside as before, but long-shadowed under the falling sun and most quiet. A blackbird sat on a blackberry tangle, watched me and made pecking motions. From the yard, straight southward through the land, ran a yellow brick road.

I stepped onto it and took a few strides. In this light the pavement was the hue of molten gold, strong under my feet; here was the kind of highway which draws you ahead one more mile to see what's over the next hill, so you may forget the pony that galloped. After all, don't yellow brick roads lead to Oz?

"Mister!" screamed at my back. "No, stop, stop!"

I turned around. Judy stood at the border. She shuddered inside the pretty dress as she reached toward me. Her face was stretched quite out shape. "Not yonder, Mister!"

Of course I made haste. When we were safely in the yard, I held her close while the dread went out of her in a burst of tears. Stroking her hair and murmuring, at last I dared ask, "But where does it go?"

She jammed her head into the curve of my shoulder and gripped me. "T-t-to Grandmother's."

"Why, is that bad? You're making us biscuits like hers, remember?"

"We can't *ever* go there," Judy gasped. Her hands on my neck were cold.

"Well, now, well, now." Disengaging, while still squatted to be at her height, I clasped her shoulder and chucked her chin and assured her the world was fine; look what a lovely evening, and we'd soon dine with Edward, but first I'd better build our fire, so could she help me bring in the wood? Secretly through me went another song I know, Swedish, the meaning of it:

"Children are a mysterious folk, and they live in a wholly strange world—"

Before long she was glad once more. As we left, I cast a final glance down the highway, and then caught a breath of what she felt: less horror than unending loss and grief, somewhere on that horizon. It made me be extra jocular while we took armloads of fuel to the living room.

Thereafter Judy trotted between me and the kitchen, attending to her duties. She left predictable chaos, heaped dishes, scorched pan, strewn flour, smeared butter and syrup and Lord knows what else. I forbore to raise the subject of cleanup. No doubt we'd tackle that tomorrow. I didn't mind.

Later we sat cross-legged under the sofa where Edward presided, ate our biscuits and drank our tea with plenty of milk, and laughed a great deal. Judy had humor. She told me of a Fourth of July celebration she had been at, where there were so many people "I bet just their toes weighed a hundred pounds." That led to a picnic which had been rained out, and—she must have listened to adult talk—she insisted that in any properly regulated universe, Samuel Gompers would have invented rubber boots. The flames whirled red, yellow, blue, and talked back to the ticking, booming clock; shadows played tag across walls; outside stood a night of gigantic stars.

"Tell me another story," she demanded and snuggled into my lap, the calculating minx. Borrowing from what I had done for Alice, I spun a long yarn about a girl named Judy, who lived in the forest with her friends Edward T. Bear and Billy Bungalow and Hoo Boy, until they built a candy-striped balloon and departed on all sorts of explorations; and her twilight-colored eyes got wider and wider.

They drooped at last, though. "I think we'd

better turn in," I suggested. "We can carry on in the morning."

She nodded. "Yesterday they said today was tomorrow," she observed, "but today they know better."

I expected that after those fireside hours the electrics would be harsh to us; but they weren't. We went upstairs, Judy on my right shoulder, Edward on my left. She guided me to a guest room, pattered off, and brought back a set of pajamas. "Daddy wouldn't mind," she said.

"Would you like me to tuck you in?" I asked.

"Oh—" For a moment she radiated. Then the seriousness came upon her. She put finger to chin, frowning, before she shook her head. "No, thanks. I don't think you're s'posed for that."

"All right." My privilege is to see Alice to her bed; but each family has its own tradition. Judy must have sensed my disappointment, because she touched me and smiled at me, and when I stopped she caught me and breathed,

"You're really real, Mister. I love you," and ran down the hall.

My room resembled the others, well and unpretentiously furnished. The wallpaper showed willows and lakes and Chinese castles which I had seen in the clouds. Gauzy white curtains, aflutter in easy airs, veiled away those lantern-big stars. Above the bed Judy had pinned a picture of a galloping pony.

I thought of a trip to the bathroom, but felt no need. Besides, I might disturb my hostess; I had no doubt she brushed her teeth, being such a generally dutiful person. Did she say prayers too? In spite of Alice, I don't really understand little girls, any more than I understand how a mortal could write *Jesu Joy of Man's Desiring*. Boys are different; it's true about the slugs and snails and puppy dogs' tails. I've been there and I know.

I got into the pajamas, lay down in the bed and
the breeze, turned off the light, and was quickly
asleep.

Sometimes we remember a night's sleep. I spent
this one being happy about tomorrow.

Maybe that was why I woke early, in a clear,
shadowless gray, cool as the air. The curtains
rippled and blew, but there was no sound
whatsoever.

Or . . . a rustle? I lay half awake, eyes half open
and peace behind them. Someone moved about.
She was very tall, I knew, and she was tidying the
house. I did not try, then, to look upon her. In my
drowsiness, she might as well have been the wind.

After she had finished in this chamber, I came
fully to myself, and saw how bureau and chair and
the bulge of blankets that my feet made were
strangers in the dusk which runs before the sun. I
swung legs across bedside, felt hardwood under
my soles. My lungs drank odors of grass. Oh, Judy
will snooze for hours yet, I thought, but I'll go
peek in at her before I pop downstairs and start a
surprise breakfast.

When dressed, I followed the hallway to her
room. Its door wasn't shut. Beyond, I spied a
window full of daybreak.

I stopped. A woman was singing.

She didn't use real words. You often don't, over
a small bed. She sang well-worn nonsense,

> "Cloddledy loldy boldy boo,
> Cloddledy lol-dy bol-dy boo-oo,"

to the tenderest melody I have ever heard. I think
that tune was what drew me on helpless, till I
stood in the entrance.

And she stood above Judy. I couldn't truly see
her: a blue shadow, maybe? Judy was as clear to
me as she is this minute, curled in a prim

nightgown, one arm under her cheek (how long the lashes and stray brown hair), the other around Edward, while on a shelf overhead, Noah's animals kept watch.

The presence grew aware of me.

She turned and straightened, taller than heaven. Why have you looked? she asked me in boundless gentleness. Now you must go, and never come back.

No, I begged. Please.

When even I may do no more than this, she sighed, you cannot stay or ever return, who looked beyond the Edge.

I covered my eyes.

I'm sorry, she said; and I believe she touched my head as she passed from us.

Judy awakened. "Mister—" She lifted her arms, wanting me to come and be hugged, but I didn't dare.

"I have to leave, sweetheart," I told her.

She bolted to her feet. "No, no, no," she said, not loud at all.

"I wish I could stay awhile," I answered. "Can you guess how much I wish it?"

Then she knew. "You . . . were awful kind . . . to come see me," she got out.

She went to me with the same resolute gait as when first we met, and took my hand, and we walked downstairs together and forth into the morning.

"Will you say hello to your daughter from me?" she requested once.

"Sure," I said. Hell, yes. Only how?

We went along the flat and empty street, toward the sun. Where a blackbird perched on an elm bough, and the leaves made darkness beneath, she halted. "Good-bye, you good Mister," she said.

She would have kissed me had I had the courage. "Will you remember me, Judy?"

"I'll play with my remembering of you. Always." She snapped after air; but her head was held bravely. "Thanks again. I do love you."

So she let me go, and I left her. A single time I turned around to wave. She waved back, where she stood under the sky all by herself.

The scarred man was crying. He wasn't skilled in it; he barked and hiccoughed.

Surgically, Ferrier addressed him. "The description of the house corresponds to your former home. Am I correct?"

The hideous head jerked a nod.

"And you're entirely unfamiliar with the place," Ferrier declared to me. "It's in a different town from yours."

"Right," I said. "I'd no reason before today to suppose I'd had anything more than a dream." Anger flickered. "Well, God damn your scientific caution, now I want some explanations."

"I can't give you those," Ferrier admitted. "Not when I've no idea how the phenomenon works. You're welcome to what few facts I have."

The scarred man toiled toward a measure of calm. "I, I, I apologize for the scene," he stuttered. "A blow, you realize. Or a hope?" His gaze ransacked me.

"Do you think we should go see her?" Ferrier suggested.

For reply, the scarred man led us out. We were silent in corridor and elevator. When we emerged on the third floor, the hospital smell struck hard. He regained more control over himself as we passed among rubber-tired nurses and views of occupied beds. But his gesture was rickety that, at last, beckoned us through a certain doorway.

Beyond lay several patients and a near-total hush. Abruptly I understood why he, important in the world, went ill-clad. Hospitals don't come cheap.

His voice grated: "Telepathy, or what? The brain isn't gone; not a flat EEG. Could you—" That went as far as he was able.

"No," I said, while my fingers struggled with each other. "It must have been a fluke. And since, I'm forbidden."

We had stopped at a cluster of machinery. "Tell him what happened," Ferrier said without any tone whatsoever.

The scarred man looked past us. His words came steady if a bit shrill. "We were on a trip, my wife and daughter and me. First we meant to visit my mother-in-law in Kentucky."

"You were southbound, then," I foreknew. "On a yellow brick road." They still have that kind, here and there in our part of the country.

"A drunk driver hit our car," he said. "My wife was killed. I became what you see. Judy—" He chopped a hand toward the long white form beneath us. "That was nineteen years ago," he ended.

BULLWINCH'S MYTHOLOGY

Description of the twentieth century American pantheon is made difficult by a paucity of literary references. There can be no doubt that it existed. The merest glance at the history and sociology of the epoch proves that men had found monotheism rather too trying and reverted to a more traditional form of religion. But exact dogma was frowned on—a rule known as Nonsectarianism—and this prevented any Hesiod or Snorri from writing an account of the gods and the myths concerning them.

Nevertheless, indirect evidence is abundant, and on its basis we can make a partial reconstruction of the prevalent beliefs. Like other polytheisms, this one was often vague and inconsistent, so that the status of the lesser deities in particular tends to be obscure. But scholars feel assured that the divine family numbered the usual twelve.

BURO

Creator and ruler of the universe, father of all the rest except Bom (q.v.), Buro was the god of government. As such, he received the special devotion of politicians, civil servants, and the common people. He it was who kept the stars in their courses and the earth in order, regulated the seasons, presided over marriages and education, brought forth crops and cattle and oil wells. In his name deserts were reclaimed, slums cleared, freeways built, and wars waged. Since his priests controlled most of the national wealth, economics worked together with reverence to make his the most important cult.

At the same time, he shows the ambiguous character of several fellow divinities. Together with his dignity went a certain comic aspect. This may derive from legends about his rebellious youth, like the one in which he chopped down a sacred cherry tree (a possible echo of some ancient fertility rite). Or it may simply have arisen from the American custom of blaming him when anything went wrong. Whatever the reason, he was not believed to be absolutely infallible. Thus, for example, the great alkali desert of Utah was said to have been constructed as a boondoggle; and the tale of Buro's magic printing press—which escaped his control and is still spewing forth official forms—is well known.

On the whole, though, he was looked on as powerful, benevolent, and, if not precisely wise, at least omniscient. His more devout worshippers excused the divine blunders by pointing out that he had divided the rule of the universe among his children and no president has ever quite mastered his bureaucrats. Originally he was depicted lean and white-bearded, in striped trousers and starry vest. But later he was more commonly imagined in the form of a stout, conservatively dressed man seated behind an enormous desk in the sky.

ATOMIKA

At first a local and rather minor figure, the goddess of science became in time second only to Buro. Tall, severely beautiful, frigidly virginal, she far surpassed him in arousing awe. For hers were the secrets of the outermost cosmos and the innermost atom, life and death, beginnings and endings, alpha and omega, not to mention pi.

Through her priests, she revealed truth to men a piece at a time. But she did so with what was either unfathomable purpose or unhuman capriciousness; for she did not seem to care in the least whether a revelation would heal or harm, comfort or desolate. Furthermore, her pronouncements were couched in language which none could understand who had not served a long, arduous period of apprenticeship. Nor could these priests themselves be sure they had interpreted an oracular saying correctly; and a later revelation might well overrun a previous one.

As if this did not make their lives difficult enough, Atomika laid geases on them which are hard to comprehend in a goddess of reason. The most famous is no doubt the one embodied in the rule: "He that publisheth not a sufficiency, he shall perish: yea, all grants shall be refused him, his contract shall not be renewed, he shall sink from the sight of his fellows even unto the depths of the teacher's colleges, and his name shall vanish from the very footnotes."

Because the public was debarred from her mysteries, yet stood in such an intense love-hate relationship to her and her priests, mediators were necessary. They were called popularizers, because they led the populace in worshipping her at a goodly distance from her temples. It is not known whether these services were rites of adoration or of placation.

TOOLSMITH

The god of engineers was much more understandable and likeable. Though he alone dared to enter the palace of Atomika, he did so in order to blarney information out of her. Armed with this knowledge, he then proceeded to design and build. In time of peace he made things for civilian use, ranging from space rockets to self-opening beer cans. But in time of war his clangorous shops forged ever more terrible weapons.

Gusty and good-natured; possessed of incredible capacities for work, drink, and lovemaking; a demon in a poker game; withal utterly dependable, and somewhat unimaginative outside his profession—he personified the best qualities of the ordinary man.

Hence the stories about him are legion. The tale of his expelling the snakes from Ireland was borrowed from the former religion, so that he might be the one who originated the worm drive. He set the earth spinning because his new inertial navigation system required a reference plane. He invented the calculus as a practical joke on Atomika; it took her two centuries to find why it worked. He created the first sequoia when he needed an especially large van de Graaff generator, the Columbia River to cool the Hanford nuclear reactor, and the Grand Canyon for the hell of it. One could go on indefinitely.

He is shown as a burly, middle-aged man with hairy ears, holding a calculator and seated on an oscilloscope.

KEEN

This was the god of success. He replaced earlier tutelary spirits of wealth when, between inflation and income tax, money ceased to have value in itself. Because of the American belief that one did or did not succeed in getting the most out of life, and success required following appropriate procedures, Keen became also the god of pleasure. The dual function was made clear in the numerous publications issued by his priests. His cult flourished especially among boys in late adolescence and junior executives (as mail clerks were then called).

Keen was the shrewdest of the gods. The stories are many about his financial manipulations, business ventures, and creation of new fashions in dress and behavior. Yet there was nothing sinister about him. Contrariwise, he was extremely affable; his worshippers were commanded to address each other by their given names from the first moment of encounter. He was a mighty lover, indeed the male equivalent of Bunni (q.v.), and an all-around bon vivant. His house was by far the most luxurious in heaven and his hospitality was unlimited.

Still, his was a stern code. In imitation of him, his devotees must be indefatigable workers, not only in the office but in bed. They had to memorize long lists of what was In and what was Out, which were changed almost daily. (Scholars are not agreed on the denotation of these two curious adjectives.) It was said that Keen himself never slept.

On that account, Buro appointed him watchman of the gods. He carried out this duty ably—but not in person. Instead, he got Toolsmith to design radar fences and electronic burglar alarms for heaven, then got the contract to build them for a company owned by himself.

His image is that of a brisk young man with a briefcase, attired in a modish business suit and executive-length socks.

BUNNI

The erotic goddess had nothing to do with hearth, home, or children. Those came under Buro's supervision and were not considered very interesting anyway. Bunni was the spirit of pure sex. As such, she was invoked by everyone from a high school girl who wanted to be noticed by some particularly cute boy to an aging man who had met an attractive woman and hoped it might do him some good to make out.

Like other divinities, she had contradictory aspects. Sometimes she appeared in the guise of a teen-ager eager for defloration, sometimes as an infinitely experienced, though young, woman. But probably the latter phase predominated, since it was said that she had been married to nearly all the gods. A comic story, perhaps harking back to Greek mythology, relates how she once went to bed with Brothergood (q.v.) and absentmindedly forgot the incantation "I divorce him, I marry you, and we will live happily ever after." So Toolsmith was still her husband. But he, having a suspicion of what was about to happen, had prepared a bed with an optically flat surface. The lovers stuck to this and were unable to escape. Toolsmith called in the other gods for a good laugh before he released them.

On the whole, however, the cult of Bunni was taken with immense seriousness. She is usually

represented nude, a cosmetic case in one hand and
a contraceptive in the other. Her breasts are
enormous but defy gravity by standing hori-
zontally outward. Curiously, her posture in earlier
depictions is always such that the genitalia are not
seen. This may have given rise to the legend that
she did not really have any. On the other hand,
later in the century she often appears in such a
pose that one can understand the origin of a
different story, that she was nothing but a crotch
with a few appendages.

JESUS

Jesus was the god of Love, by which the
Americans meant something vaguely like *phile*, as
opposed to the *eros* of Bunni. (They had no concept
of *agape*.) He had been too prominent in the old
religion to omit from the pantheon, but his less
comfortable attributes were soon smoothed off.

Though frequently confused with Brothergood,
Jesus was actually quite a different figure. He was
in charge of communication and understanding
between mortals. It was thought that when he
bestowed his wisdom on the parties to a quarrel,
they saw at once that there was in fact no quarrel,
that they were really in perfect agreement and had
simply failed to make themselves clear. The belief
is epitomized in a saying attributed to him: "We
have met the enemy and they are human beings
just like us." His worship was often conjoined
with that of Keen, since it was felt that an absence
of inner conflict and self-doubt—a state of grace
known as "positive thinking"—was essential to
success.

Strictly speaking, he was not the god of the
dead. The Americans tabooed mention of death.

But he was supposed to operate a large pink-and-white motel in heaven where those who had temporarily been separated could, if they wished, find each other again in perfect health and eternal youth.

Funeral practices look so inconsistent with the above that some scholars maintain the Americans actually imagined the dead as inhabiting the grave. But such a conclusion does not follow. It is true that burial grounds (which were never called by any such name) were tastefully landscaped and had adjacent parking lots. It is true that corpses were often embalmed, then laid in padded coffins that were supplied with Muzak and even, it is said, telephones. However, such rites prove little. They can just as well have been for purposes of sympathetic magic, to guarantee that Jesus would honor the credit cards of the dead.

He is depicted as a plump young man, neatly bearded, dressed in a white nylon robe.

BROTHERGOOD

This figure stands midway between Jesus and Kak (q.v.) and may have been intended to combine certain qualities of both. He was usually called the god of solidarity.

His role was not to eliminate conflict, nor to create it in the first place. In practice he exacerbated it. But in theory he was just the guardian and inspiration of people who marched together in a worthy cause. He infused them with fraternal spirit, assured them they would overcome, and laid his curse on any authority which tried to control them. The mass meetings, mass marches, mass singing, and general mass enthusiasm of his devotees illustrate his affinities to Dionysus.

According to legend, when Buro brought him to trial on charges of disturbing the peace, Brothergood argued with great eloquence that the solidarity and self-sacrifice he inspired were civic virtues; that his followers meant well; and that any incidental damage brought reconstruction, which was good for business. He finished with singing a folk song so moving that the gods burst into tears and acquitted him. This story appears to be a poetic treatment of the fact that men cannot endure an ordered society for long without an emotional safety valve.

The representations of Brothergood are as many as the causes he led. Thus he may be seen in overalls, carrying a lunchbox; in dirty jeans, sweater, sandals, and beard, carrying a guitar; in the uniform of some paramilitary organization; in hood and white sheet; or even in the garb of a solid, Buro-worshipping citizen demonstrating in support of the government.

After the middle of the century he acquired a precise female counterpart, Sisterhood.

POPOP

About this god of art, music, and dance, the less said the better.

FARWAY

Like Toolsmith, the god of explorations is a rather attractive personality. He was invoked by men risking their lives in unknown parts of the world, in the depths of the sea, and in outer space.

He instilled in them the wish to conquer, not their fellow men but blind nature; to discover truth on a more human level than that of science (though Farway's relationship with Atomika was excellent); to prove their own worth and thus the worth of mankind as a whole. He maintained a lodge in heaven, the Hall of Fame, where one could meet all who had ever ventured bravely forth.

Nevertheless he was not really a romantic figure. The stories about him lay constant emphasis on the care with which he organized his own expeditions. He had nothing but contempt for recklessness. Though he could fight when need arose, he regretted that need. He lived frugally and soberly, keeping himself fit, was happily married to an obscure but sympathetic divinity known as Lonelyhearts, and was said to be the only god who had never frolicked with Bunni.

On this account, and perhaps also because of confusion involving the Hall of Fame, it is hard to separate him from the god of athletics. Often they appear to be identical; but there are some references to the latter under the name of Casey. Since exploration and sport both involve physical exertion and advance planning, and since the motivations behind them are very similar, we can understand why the Americans were not quite sure whether they had here one god or two.

He is usually shown as tall, muscular, and handsome, with a little gray at the temples. He holds a pair of binoculars and a map or an astronautical chart is spread out before him. In the background is an American flag and sometimes a baseball bat.

KAK

In many respects, the god of ideologies corresponds to the Norse Loki. He had no cult; he was a notorious troublemaker; at the end of the world he might well side with the enemies of the gods; but he was occasionally useful and so could not be expelled from heaven.

He it was who presented the first man and woman with a locked box. He told them they must on no account open it, but knew very well they would. And when they did, out flew a cloud of noxious Isms which have plagued the world ever since. Fortunately Buro had placed one more in the box, which now emerged to undo some of the harm: Americanism.

Brothergood was especially susceptible to the wiles of Kak, but now and then others were also persuaded to assist him. A myth relates that once Kak changed himself into a beautiful woman on whom Toolsmith, all unknowing, begot Bom. Kak was forever mocking the gods, pointing out flaws in their works, and insisting he could do their tasks better. Yet in times of crisis he seemed to be indispensable. Though the Americans, as said, did not officially worship him, he appears to have had a considerable unrecognized following; and the devotees of other gods often attended his dark rites too when a war was going on.

He is described as lean and burning-eyed, with a weakness for gaudy uniforms.

LIBERTY

The goddess of freedom was much loved in the early days of the Republic. Indeed, she is the only one whom we definitely know had a statue erected to her. By the middle twentieth century, however, the average citizen took her for granted and rarely bothered to observe her festival, which came about two weeks after the summer solstice. At last the practice of shooting fireworks in her honor was forbidden.

She continued to be called on by those whom Kak had touched, whether with his right hand or his left. But this tended to degrade her worship still further. The story arose that she had once been a virgin but was repeatedly raped by Brothergood. Perhaps this is why she is represented with a crown of thorns.

BOM

Authorities dispute whether Bom should be included in the pantheon. He has been called the god of war, but in point of fact the Americans had none. They considered war, like death, to be an abnormal, deplorable, and correctible state of affairs. They did not require a military god to defend them; this was the task of Buro and Toolsmith. The popular mind abhorred Bom. It was considered unlucky to mention his name. (As a contemporary poet said, "Ignore it and maybe it'll go away.") If matters ever went so far as the end of the world, Bom would lead the forces of chaos and might well prevail.

Still, a minority opinion held that there was

much to be said for him. This did not come from
Jesus, many of whose followers identified Bom
with the absolute evil which they simultaneously
denied had any existence. Rather, it was the view
of certain political and military thinkers. Their
supporters called them realists and their
opponents called them fascists, a common swear
word in those days.

The myth reflects this conflict. Early in his
existence, Bom destroyed an especially virulent
swarm of Isms. Thereafter most of the gods
wanted to chain him in the underworld, for he
might turn on them at any moment. But Kak
argued that many dangerous Isms remained alive
and only Bom had the power to keep them at their
distance. Since the Isms were Kak's own creation
(always excepting Americanism), the argument
looks specious. But it was accepted, because none
of the other gods could think of any way to overcome Bom and certain of them hoped he might be
persuaded to help them in various projects.

Thus he continued to live in heaven. He was not
invited to parties, but he did sit in the divine
councils, usually in a chilling silence, occasionally
voicing a brutal sarcasm.

He is depicted as huge and torpedo-shaped, with
a Roman helmet on his head, and badly in need of
a shave.

AFTERWORD

An Invitation to Elfland

by

Sandra Miesel

He groped for the doorless land of faery, that illimitable haunted country that opened somewhere below a leaf or a stone.

—Thomas Wolfe

While others seek the passageway to elven realms in vain, Poul Anderson throws wide the gate to let his readers enter into wonder. In *The Broken Sword* (1954) and *Three Hearts and Three Lions* (1961) he guides us through the whispering glamorie of the Halfworld where soulless beings both fair and foul set enchanted snares for Adam's race. In *Operation Chaos* (1971) he reveals Hellmouth agape below a happy suburban home and he exposes eldritch forces subverting a thriving medieval kingdom in *Hrolf Kraki's Saga* (1973). In *A Midsummer Tempest* (1974) and *The Merman's Children* (1979) he shows us coruscating marvels that glow in earth, sea, and sky.

Anderson is a "literalist of the imagination." He makes what is magical real and what is real magical. Of such power is poetry born. "To be a bard is not necessarily the same thing as being a poet," says James Blish, "But Anderson is both." He excels at poems of all sorts—lyrics, narrative, even limericks and parodies. (Notice how *The Whale's Song* in *The Merman's Children* combines alliterative, rhymed, and blank verse to splendid effect.) A venerator of traditional forms, he imitates Shakespeare in *A Midsummer Tempest*—a novel written almost entirely in iambic pentameter—and is comfortably at home in Icelandic epic meter. His translations and adaptations of Scandanavian materials are especially fine. (For example, the stunning gravemound scene in *The Broken Sword* is assembled out of elements borrowed from *Hervarar Saga, The Second Lay of Helgi Hundingsbane*, and the medieval Danish ballad *Aage and Else*.)

Moreover, his rhymes are eminently singable. (Gordon R. Dickson's music to *Three Kings Rode Out* is but one of many beautiful melodies composed for Anderson's words.) Like medieval gentry, his characters delight in singing songs and quoting poems. Yet poetry is far more than an aesthetic frill in his fiction. As Blish remarks on the plot machinery of *After Doomsday* (1962): "What other writer would have the temerity to build the reader up for scores of pages toward a crucial space battle—and then attempt to tell it in terms of a ballad written many years after the event?"

Given the importance of poetry in Anderson's fiction, it is only fitting that he has written *two* superb versions of the Orpheus myth, *World Without Stars* (1967) and "Goat Song" (1972). "So good a harper never none was," says the Shetland Island ballad *King Orfeo* of its hero. Like that fabled harper, Anderson spans the extremes of human experience:

> *And first he played da notes o noy,*
> *And dan he played da notes o joy.*

The fiction collected here in *Fantasy* is a sampler of Anderson's wide-ranging gift. Our editor has conveniently grouped the stories by setting but they also differ in mood, form, and source of inspiration. Anderson can be venturesome, poignant, swashbuckling, frivolous, spoofy, sardonic, tragic, or clever. Legend, history, myth, genre conventions, even an actual dream can ignite his creativity. Once ignited, it lights up familiar scenes from unfamiliar angles.

For instance, a few fantasy plots are triter than the Deal with the Devil, a notion originally popularized by the sixth century Greek *Legend of Theophilus*. Yet Anderson contrives a droll new variation in "Pact" by using logic and science to turn timeworn assumptions inside out. It is also a measure of the author's imagination that a lightweight comic fable of medieval parentage should hinge on the same cosmological theories as his hard science masterpiece *Tau Zero*. (1970).

The good-natured affection for sword and sorcery evident in "A Logical Conclusion" and the Cappen Varra stories inspired long-time Hyborian Legion member Anderson to parody Conan as Cronkheit the Barbarian. It also led him to write an authorized Conan pastiche, *Conan the Rebel* (1980). (The latter work equips the mighty-thewed Cimmerian with libertarian political sentiments absent from the original model.)

Anderson zestfully exercises the auctorial perogative of inserting private enthusiasms into stories. No one can read much of his fiction without noticing he loves Bach, Scotch whiskey, Rembrandt, puns, Kipling, and the Great Outdoors. Whether quoting Chesterton in "Pact" or paraphrasing Tom Lehr in *Operation Chaos* or assembling guests like Erik the Red and Sherlock Holmes at the Old Phoenix Inn, Anderson's references pay tribute to what he enjoys. He sees allusiveness as a major literary virtue, one epitomized by his favorite fantasist, James Branch Cabell.

Yet much as he likes allusions, Anderson's talent is fueled by and manifests itself through sensuous experiences. He is fond of repeating—and applying—Flaubert's dictum that a writer should appeal to at least three senses in each scene. More than three decades of following this advice have made him the master of lush, evocative description. This picture of an Atlantic island comes from his most recent fantasy novel, *The Merman's Children:*

> Gray whitecaps blew in beneath a pale, whistling sky. When they withdrew, the rattle of pebbles sounded like a huge quern. Gulls flew about, mewing. On the sands were strewn brown tangles of kelp, that smelt of the deeps and had small bladders which popped when trodden on. Beyond those dunes and harsh grass was a moor, wide heathery reaches and a bauta stone raised by folk long forgotten.

Although Anderson has scarcely a peer as a scene-setter in the sf field, he does not treat the process as an end in itself. Being a poet, he uses nature images as symbolic markers for human reactions. This rendering technique gives the "crayon brilliant" dreamworld of "The Visitor" its heart-searing loveliness. Not only is his method powerful, it can be compact, as the following descriptions of incestuous couplings show. The hero and heroine of *The Broken Sword* consummate their love in the oblique vocabulary of the *Carmina Burana:* "The day ended and night came to the vale of summer. They lay by the waterfall and heard a nightingale." A quarter century later, more sophisticated language akin to Sappho's lament in her lonely bed records the inability of the merman's children to fulfill their desire: "The moon was sunken behind the cliffs. Stars glistened small." Thus his metaphors support his message:

all creation is interlinked. Man is "necessarily and forever, a part of the life that surrounds him."

Parallelism in technique and theme also builds parallel plot structures. This is Anderson's favorite design for longer fiction, exemplified here by "Superstition." The author often pairs subjective, private issues with objective, public ones. For instance, happy romances and world-saving quests go together in *Three Hearts and Three Lions* and *A Midsummer Tempest*.

But these paired inner and outer crises are not always resolved. The six Anderson stories which received Hugo and Nebula awards (see the forthcoming Tor Books collection, *Winners*) include cases of collective triumph purchased at the cost of personal tragedy. Compare "Superstition" with Nebula-nominee "Kyrie" (1968). In both stories, danger threatening a space ship is averted through the aid of a psychic woman whom other crewmembers view with distate. But "Superstition's" witch finds satisfying love while "Kyrie's" telepath—an Heloise among the stars— loses it in a uniquely excruciating way.

Our collection contains two examples—rare for Anderson—of stories in which neither objective nor subjective problems are solved. "House Rule" and "The Visitor" set dilemmas aside briefly in favor of distractions. At first glance these tales appear to have little in common, but on closer inspection, they reveal important similarities.

Each story takes place in a house between the worlds, a "pocket universe" surrounded by "Deserts of vast Eternity." Entry is by unsought invitation only. It is a species of election, mysterious as grace. Overnight guests may not "bear off much more than rest and cheer and memories" so that any event within "has not quite fully happened." Each visit is like a dream. Within the enchanted walls of these two dwellings,

persons whose paths could never otherwise cross
briefly meet in fellowship and love. Ominous
timepieces—a huge hourglass and a grandfather's
clock—warn guests how achingly few their hours
together may be. These precious moments may be
shortened if the house rules are violated,
deliberately or otherwise.

But what exactly are these fabulous places that
lie out of space, out of time? *A Midsummer
Tempest* calls the Old Phoenix an "interuniversal
nexus point" connecting alternate worlds. Judy's
house is a psychic illusion (?) projected by a
comatose girl. However, the explanations in the
text do not exhaust all possibilities. We are free to
speculate further.

Both the inn and the home look like camou-
flaged enclaves of the Celtic Otherworld. This
joyful realm (or more properly, realms) may be
found on an island, under the sea, inside a hollow
hill, or within a house that suddenly appears and
disappears by magic. On occasion, the immortal
dwellers admit mortal heroes and entertain them
with feasting, drinking, music, and lovemaking, all
glorious beyond earthly measure. Although the
phoenix myth itself is of classicial origin, meta-
morphosis and reincarnation are themes characteristic of Celtic mythology. That the bird for
which the inn is named is *old* and nearing its
moment of fiery transformation may indicate the
imminent decline of Faerie yet promises some
future rebirth.

The Innkeeper admits that his establishment belongs to Faerie but denies that it presents any
peril to its guests: " 'Fear never paying such
unholy price as might be taken in the
Venusberg.' " He and his wife are wholly benevolent, closer kin to Oberon and Titania of *Midsummer Tempest* than to amoral Imric and Leea of
The Broken Sword. The true identities of the Host

and Hostess remain misty as a Halfworld hillside:
" 'I've many names. Let you say Taverner.' " Perhaps the author intended nothing specific. Yet
since the couple functions as god and goddess of a
cozy Elysium, might they not be Manannan Mac
Lir and his consort Fand, Irish deities who preside
over festivities in *Tir Tairngiri*, the Land of
Promise? (In *The Broken Sword*, Anderson depicts
Manannan and Fand as the only considerate beings in Faerie.)

Although homely disguises veil the dazzling
beauty of these shape-changing *sid*-folk, their ties
to the sea and to erotic love still shine through
dimly. The Taverner's bluff, hearty appearance
may owe something to Kipling's *Puck of Pook's
Hill*. At least one mythologist argues that Puck
under his other name, Robin Goodfellow, is really
a simplified folk version of the divine Manannan
Mac Lir. But whoever they may be, the keepers of
the Old Phoenix are among Anderson's most
memorable cameo characters.

Celtic myth patterns also appear in "The
Visitor." Judy's plight resembles that of Ethna the
Bride, a young woman whose soul was imprisoned
within a hollow hill by the fairy king of the dead
while her inert body lay at home. But unlike
Ethna, no loving husband will rescue Judy from
her limbo. No carefree feasting nor amorous dalli-
ance amuse this "elven" child. She has only her
teddy bear, her imaginary playmate, and her
solitary visitor for company. In her small domain
she plays the life-giving goddess, source of refreshment, flowers, and song. The narrator who
follows her home through "formlessness which
writhed" is like an ensorcelled knight who will
ever after mourn his stay in Elfhill. In this story,
the traditional Elysian names—*Tir inna mBan*
(Land of Women), *Tir na nOg* (Land of Youth), *Tir
inna mBeo* (Land of the Living) ring with ghastly

irony, reminding us that the Happy Otherworld is also the Kingdom of the Dead.

But faring "beyond the fields we know" is quite a different journey in "House Rule." People gather at the Old Phoenix for the innocent enjoyment of each other's company. As the Taverner explains: " 'My sole reward for hospitality is meeting folk like you, within whom burn the stars of many worlds and destinies. I love to watch them meet and hear them yarn.' "

Assembling beings from wildly different contexts is a device with durable appeal, one successfully exploited by Hendrik van Loon's *Lives* (1942), Robert Heinlein's *Number of the Beast* (1980), and the Public Television series *Meeting of Minds*. Anderson, like Kipling's story-telling Puck, freely mixes fancy with fact. Purely literary characters like Sancho Panza and Anderson's own Nicholas Van Rijn carouse with historical ones like Erik the Red. Holger Danske meets his counterpart Prince Rupert of the Rhine. Guestlists are distinctly weighted towards fictitious persons. (Sherlock Holmes and Dr. Watson, Huck Finn and Jim attend because Anderson is both a Baker Street Irregular and a Knight of Mark Twain.) Moreover, the historical characters have also been commemorated in literature by themselves (T'ang dynasty poet Li Po) or others (Clodia, mistress and favorite subject of the Roman poet Catullus). Here is the *Fioretti's* St. Francis and *Eiriks Saga Raúca's* Erik. To a greater or lesser degree, everyone in the Old Phoenix is a creature of the imagination.

This includes the two pairs of protagonists in "House Rule." Anderson's Leonardo and Einstein are cultural icons come to life with the forms and gestures their worshipful posterity expects. ("The Light," 1957, shows Anderson's own esteem for Leonardo.) But can genius instantly transcend all barriers? Could the real Leonardo easily accept humble-looking Einstein as his peer? Would he applaud an episode of illicit heterosexual love?

Romanticism removes Héloise and Abélard even further from reality. Anderson justifies his treatment by suggesting that the lovers come from alternate timelines. The teary, trembling couple seen in the Old Phoenix are figures of legend, not record. (Another sf retelling of their story is "The Lady Who Sailed the Soul" by Cordwainer Smith, 1960.) The meek nun here lacks the fierce incandescence Heloise showed in letters. The Abelard who emerges from his memoir, *The History of My Calamities*, was a vain egoist, "full of arrogance of intellect and joy of combat." Afterwards, he confined his passion to writing sublime religious poems for her, 99 of which survive while all his love lyrics have vanished. Anderson prefers a kindlier solution that might have been in a universe less harsh. Inside the Old Phoenix, some wishes can come true for all its guests "are such stuff as dreams are made of."

But "some dreams are nightmares." "The Visitor" depicts eternal youth in Fairyland as a form of living death, a curse laid on a helpless child. (Compare the boy who cannot grow in Harlan Ellison's "Jeffty is Five," 1977.) Inspiration for this dream fantasy actually came to Anderson in a dream. It has nothing to do with the subsequent Karen Ann Quinlan case. The author regards it as the saddest of all his works and calls the writing of it "one of the hardest jobs I have ever undertaken."

Anderson combines beliefs about dreams, fairies, ghosts, and psychic phenomenon traditionally associated with the Otherworld. (See *The Fairy-Faith in Celtic Countries* by W.Y. Evans Wentz.) Kipling drew on the same sources for "They" (1904), a story eerily resonant with "The Visitor." In Kipling's tale, a lonely spinster with

occult powers encourages children's ghosts to
haunt her home. A horrified guest discovers his
own dead daughter among the spectres and vows
never to return.

Real-life fatherhood hones the poignance of
both authors' fiction. Kipling was mourning the
loss of a small daughter at the time he wrote
"They." Anderson has said that "my chief claim to
fame will probably be that I fathered Astrid." He
often speaks of little girls in the same adoring
terms the narrator of "The Visitor" uses. So
catholic is his affection, it even extends to a young
female troll in *The Broken Sword*. Conversely, for
a father to kill and devour his small golden-haired,
blue-eyed daughter in *The Night Face* (1963) is
surely the ugliest crime the author can imagine.

The little girl as innocent victim is a recurring
symbol in Anderson's work. Judy is the most
pathetic of these because her ordeal has been indefinitely prolonged. Her natural father cannot
heal her body; her fatherly visitor cannot help her
soul. What little comfort she gets comes from her
mother's ghost—feminine power outweighs mas-
culine ones, a notion the gynolatrous author holds
dear.

Yet ultimately, no amount of love is ever
enough. Whether it takes the form of a drunken
driver or a forbidden glance, in the end ill-fortune
will strike all things down. For family and cosmos
alike, existence poses some puzzles too big for
solving. Anderson offers the same advice Gilgamesh heard four thousand years ago: take whatever solace modest human pleasures afford. Enjoy
the natural world, fall in love, raise a family, and
die resigned. As Dryden said, "Like pilgrims, to th'
appointed place we tend; the world's an inn, and
death the journey's end."

Meanwhile, the heart is likelier to triumph than
the head. The sexless intellectual contact between

Leonardo and Einstein achieves nothing while Héloise and Abélard, encouraged by the barmaid, know ecstasy one last time. (Note that as the scientist exits in defeat, Kipling's Mrs. Hauksbee, a lady renowned for getting her own way, enters.) The pipe of "bittersweet" burnt tobacco and the goblet of wine that "fountained red" in the closing paragraphs of "House Rule" make deftly condensed symbols of frustration and fulfillment.

Human lives are unique as snowflakes and as swift to melt. Love, erotic or otherwise, cannot delay their passing by an instant. Every night must end, every day must wane. The universe may, like the phoenix, pass through cycles of decay and renewal but "where are the snows of yesteryear?"

Anderson's romanticism is balanced by an uncompromising rationality. "I myself," he declares, "am of skeptical temperament, and I cut my philosophical teeth on the most hard-boiled logical positivism." Poetic and scientific talents unite in his "feeling intellect." Anderson could aptly borrow C.S. Lewis's opinion: "For me reason is the natural organ of truth; but imagination is the organ of meaning. Imagination, producing new metaphors or revivifying old, is not the cause of truth, but its condition."

"The Visitor welled up from the author's subconscious in sleep. He consciously applies his knowledge of myth for scornful social commentary in "Bullwinch's Mythology." Applying reason to the gorgeous impossibilities of pulp adventure yields "A Logical Conclusion," a *Berkley Square* personality transfer that succeeds.

Rationalized enchantment is the basis of "Superstition" and "The Interloper." Like its acknowledged prototype, Heinlein's "Magic, Inc." (1940), "Superstition" features a modern America dependent on magical technology. Much of the charm in both stories comes from watching everyday needs filled by sorcery while science maintains a marginal existence. The same effect is elaborated in the middle-class Midwestern setting of *Operation Chaos* with its suburbanite werewolf hero who rides a broomstick to work at Nornwell Scryotronics Corporation. Although "Operation Afreet," the initial installment of *Operation Chaos*, was published in the same year as "Superstition," the two works are distinct despite the common use of the names "Valeria" and "Ginny" (the later a bow to Virginia Heinlein).

"The Interloper" sketches ideas that flesh out later in *Three Hearts and Three Lions* (original short version, 1953) and *The Broken Sword* (1954). All three stories introduce elves and other denizens of Faerie as real beings who uneasily share the Earth with men. The advantages and handicaps traditionally attributed to Halfworlders are ingeniously justified: their magic involves psi, exposure to iron or sunlight causes lethal biochemical reactions in their tissues and so forth.

But Anderson treats his cloudy-eyed elves far more sympathetically in "The Interloper" than in any other work of the next two decades. These harried creatures nobly save their human oppressors from extraterrestrial exploiters. (Fair Folk also need protection and refuge from encroaching humans in the works of Thomas Burnett Swann and in Karen Anderson's own "Treaty in Tartessos.") "The Interloper" reverses roles and inverts expectations as a literary device. However, these elves' predicament eventually evolves into a symbol for Nature threatened by rapacious mankind.

Tension between the non-human and the human is a persistent theme in Anderson's fantasy novels. Over the years, he has shown an increasing preference for the Faerie position. Thus "The

Interloper"foreshadows a significant change in the author's attitudes and values. (The longer Anderson works with a set of fictional assumptions, the likelier his final position will diverge from his initial one. For example, see the three-volume *Psychotechnic League* series being published by Tor Books.)

Although written twenty years apart, *Three Hearts and Three Lions* and *A Midsummer Tempest* have similar plots. In both books predestined heroes assisted by gentle heroines purer-hearted than themselves seek enchanted talismans that can tip the balance in the eternal battle between Law and Chaos. But Faerie is an antagonist in the older book, an ally in the newer. Holger Danske must defend the Law-abiding humans of the Empire against the encroachments of Faerie, which is an offshoot of Chaos. But Faerie helps Prince Rupert fight a soulless, iron-bound extreme of Law that threatens human and non-human alike. Note that Holger is tempted from his quest by a fay, Rupert by a mortal woman. Style also supports the shift. The incongruity of a prosaic-minded American thrust into a medieval fairyland keeps the mood of *Three Hearts and Three Lions* light but ornate Shakespearean language sustains the charmed atmosphere of *A Midsummer Tempest*.

Meanwhile, in another part of the same cosmos, *Operation Chaos* sets the wholesome domestic magic of Earth against the hellish powers of the Low Continuum. There is no separate realm of Faerie in the Thaumaturgic Age because humanity has annexed its most useful aspects—systematic sorcery is part of daily life.

Hrolf Kraki's Saga likewise shows men struggling with malign supernatural forces and again emphasizes home-centered values. The mighty deeds of King Hrolf and his champions are praise-

worthy because they insure that ordinary folk can
raise their families in peace. According to the
author, his book's true hero is the founding
father's blood "which coursed through many
hearts." (Anderson extols hearthside joys more
than any major sf writer. Here, even battle-
hardened warriors fall into "those bonds which
the hands of small children weave.") But unlike
Operation Chaos, the scale is dynastic, the spirit
pagan, and the outcome tragic. Offenses against
Faerie beings (the rape of an elf woman and the
murder of a werebear) and family ideals (betrayal
of kindred and incest) set in motion the fearful
machinery of vengeance and countervengeance.

But this plot is not of Anderson's devising since
Hrolf Kraki's Saga faithfully retells the Icelandic
Hrolfs Saga Kraka. *The Broken Sword* and *The
Merman's Children*, on the other hand, use
medieval models (*Volsunga Saga* and the Danish
ballad *Agnes and the Merman*) as catalysts for the
author's own imagination. Therefore, this earliest
written and latest published of Anderson's heroic
fantasies make the best reference points to measure his changing attitude towards Faerie. Both
novels explore the deadly impact humans and non-
humans have on each other: their loves can prove
more lethal than their wars.

Both novels superimpose an ethereal but
doomed Halfworld on a grubbily realistic
medieval Europe. Barbarized tenth century men
are nearly defenseless against Halfworld malice
but by the fourteenth century, positions are
reversed. Revealed religion, science, and social
progress prove to be stronger weapons than any
sorcery Faerie can wield. " 'Magic is dying out of
Creation' " because " 'humans, weak and short-
lived and unwitting, are nevertheless more strong
than elves and trolls, aye than giants and gods.' "

In *The Broken Sword*, a mortal reared from

infancy by the elves rediscovers his humanness by experiencing defeat, fear, and love. But since his heart-melting woman is also his sister and their family is accursed, gruesome tragedy engulfs them. The hero's doom is woven by others. The elves want staunch fighters in their wars with the trolls; Odin needs troops to meet the Giants at Ragnarök. Nevertheless, he dies a free man, answerable to no purpose outside himself. His elven foster father envies his unbreakable will: " 'Better a life like a falling star, bright across the dark, than a deathlessness which can see naught above or beyond itself.' " Mortals will outlast immortals because they can make committments and will sacrifice themselves to keep them.

Mellowed by an extra quarter century's writing experience, Anderson tells a more complex story in *The Merman's Children* by expanding the number of viewpoints. He presents a quadrangle of lovers instead of a pair. The halfling brother and sister of the title find opposite solutions to the dilemma their mixed heritage poses. The merman's son and his human mistress reject Heaven in favor of a soulless Faerie existence immersed in natural wonders but the merman's daughter chooses baptism and accepts a human husband. The conversion of the other merfolk seems like the final surrender of a beaten people—one thinks of Indians submitting to the reservation. But theirs is the blood that will survive by blending with men's.

The merits of each path are debated at length. " 'In humanness you will find release,' " pleads the merman father, " 'It will be like coming alone out of winter night into a firelit room where those whom you hold dearest are feasting.' " The human side fields the stronger arguments. Unfortunately, the brutal and bigoted practices of most human (except the Noble Savage Inuit) undercut theory.

The emotional victory belongs to Faerie. Clinging to the Halfworld is shown as the bolder—and therefore—better choice. A Faerie creature could:

> love and laugh and strive and sorrow, could do much that is forever denied to the children of Adam, but could no more know God than can an albatross or the wind whereon it soars. Made free, made whole, she felt ever more keenly how joyful she was. Let her doom take her when the Norns chose. This hour was hers.

Although the epiloque tries to resolve the dispute by a mystical appeal to God's mercy, the happy ending of *The Merman's Children* is more disturbing than the tragic climax of *The Broken Sword*. Once freedom and wholeness were to be found in the world of men; now they must be sought outside it, amid Halfworld "gleams, melodies, magics."

Faerie's allure is boundless as Nature's own, a delight to the senses, a refreshment to the mind. Erotic pleasures never fade when bodies are perfect and ageless. Free from fear, guilt, or responsibility, the Fair Folk achieve nothing, they simply *are*. This Elysian existence will not survive Judgment Day but therein lies its nobility. An eternal Heaven is merely a bribe to the weak, rewarding their consent to rules such as Christian nudity and incest taboos that hobble spontaneity. Not only is the Immanent preferable to the Transcendent, enjoying immanence fully is the most sublime experience persons can—or ought to—have.

Such is the picture of Faerie Anderson currently offers. It is also the science fictional one he previously constructed and demolished in *The Peregrine* (1957), *The Night Face* (1963), and "The Queen of Air and Darkness" (1971); explored and half-heartedly rejected in *The Winter of the World*

(1976). In these stories, entrancing but perilous alien cultures stand for Faerie. Humans who fall under the spell of these idyllic "natural" societies risk individual death or species extinction.

"The Queen of Air and Darkness" states the issue best. (See Patrick McGuire's excellent analysis, "Her Strong Enchantments Failing," in *The Many Worlds of Poul Anderson/The Book of Poul Anderson*, 1974.) This Hugo and Nebula award winning story is a superb scientific rationalization of Fairyland set on an extraterrestrial world. The author creates a properly luminous twilit environment by judicious planetary design and populates it with fabulous creatures conjured up by advanced biology and psychic suggestion. He also draws on traditional prototypes, especially Scandanavian ones like the Huldre, the Hill Lady, whose lovely body is hollow. (His title ballad is modeled on a medieval Danish one called *The Elven Shaft*.) But this Elf Queen and her people are aboriginal aliens bent on conquering the technologically superior human colonists by enthrallment, hoping to make them into docile pet dogs kept safe in dream-kennels. Their conspiracy of illusions is exposed but they receive generous, even sympathetic treatment.

So why has Anderson turned from sympathy to outright advocacy since "Queen" was written? The poet in him has not banished the rationalist. His committment to human freedom and dignity remains as strong as ever. Perhaps the answer lies in his passionate, almost pantheistic attachment to Nature. Faerie is the quintessence of that wildness our increasingly sterile and mechanistic civilization threatens. Thus a plea for Faerie is a plea for Nature herself: we are led to wonder at real leaves and stones while seeking "that illimitable haunted country." Literary excursions into elven realms arouse *Sehnsucht*, the "sweet longing" that keeps the inward self alive. As Coleridge says:

> But still the heart doth need a language, still
>
> Doth the old instinct bring back the old names.

In this unforgotten tongue, Poul Anderson issues an invitation to Elfland.